Spinning My Wheels

WES SNOWDEN

Published by CORVENT CREATIVE, 2021.

This is a work of fiction. Similarities to real people, places, or events are entirely coincidental.

SPINNING MY WHEELS

First edition. July 1, 2021.

Copyright © 2021 WES SNOWDEN.

ISBN: 9798744586546(paperback)

Written by WES SNOWDEN.

TABLE OF CONTENTS

Foreword	v
Eyes of the Heart	1
King of the Seas	38
Snowfall in Venice	82
Once upon a Green	175
Never in Time	213
Yesterday's Giant	245
Dolphins at Sunset	272
Fortesque	327
A Word from the Author	365
About the Author	367

FOREWORD

During the great plague of 2020 and 2021, like many of my fellow sufferers, I found myself suffering from 'lockdown fatigue,' a debilitating condition well known to many of us.

In my desperate search for a 'boredom killer,' I decided to reach far into the past and revisit some of my earlier literary works. Having just published my sixth novel, 'On Distant Shores,' I didn't relish the challenge of taking on another full-length book without taking a breather.

Unfortunately, as many others have learned to their chagrin, sometimes it's not that easy to go back. When examined from a more seasoned eye, my eight earlier short stories all demanded a substantial time-consuming rewrite. With the able assistance of my good friend and erstwhile copy editor, David Hughes, the eight stories have been updated into a new collection called 'Spinning my Wheels.'

Every story in the book is totally unique. For the most part, they were designed to be relatively short, enjoyable 'feel good' reads. The exception might be 'Snowfall in Venice," which is a longer and a more serious story.

Whether you're looking for romance on a Windjammer, an escape into a golf fantasy, or a thrilling voyage on a whaler out of Nantucket in 1768, you're bound to find it between the covers of 'Spinning my Wheels.'

I hope you enjoy reading the stories as much as I did in writing them.

Keep safe. Better days are coming!

Wes Snowden
July 1st, 2021

EYES OF THE HEART

"What you see is what you get."
"You can't judge a book by its cover."
"Appearances can be deceiving."

I'll admit these are all hackneyed old sayings. Still, there must be a ring of truth about them, even if it's only because they've been repeated so many times, by so many people, over the years.

Take me, for example. If I asked a hundred people in the local coffee shop to guess what I do for a living, I'd be willing to take a bet not a single person would get it right.

Do you know why I think that? Because every one of the people who attempted would likely base their guess solely on my external appearance. Believe me, I know from bitter personal experience this approach can be dead wrong.

After taking one look at my stocky build, large hands, stubby fingers, and broken nose, they would jump to an instant conclusion. He's a prison guard. No, he's a bulldozer operator. How about a long-distance truck driver? Or perhaps an ex-boxer or army drill sergeant.

In some ways, I couldn't blame them. It's always been the same. Your eyes see something, then your brain spits out a conclusion. That conclusion is usually influenced by a lifetime of biases. That's why I'm confident I would win the bet.

Despite my gruff exterior, my job is of an exceedingly delicate nature. I've spent my entire career arranging eye-catching colorful floral arrangements.

I'm a florist and damned proud of it.

• • • •

I inherited the Hunter & Son flower shop after my father, Duncan Hunter, passed away five years ago. My dad had started the business in downtown Red Deer, Alberta, way back in 1952. I worked there part-time when I was still in school, and I guess I just never escaped after he died.

Now, at thirty-five, I'm still single. Not that I want to be. So far, I just haven't met a girl who can get past the unfortunate initial impression of my appearance. I'm not a wealthy man, which would probably help my love life, but I manage to keep the flower shop doors open due to a lack of business competition. Most weeks, I even have enough money left over for a night on the town.

My favorite spot for an evening out is the Red Deer Café and Pub. I'm a creature of habit, so I always order the homemade lasagna with extra cheese. Being Friday now, I closed the shop for the day and headed down Main Street, nodding hello to many folks in passing. As soon as I entered the café, the weekly bantering ritual started. I always looked forward to trading barbs with Molly.

"Hi there, handsome, looking for a good time?" the beefy waitress behind the counter said with an exaggerated wink.

I laughed. "If I were looking for a good time, Molly, I sure as hell wouldn't come to this horrible dump."

We laughed together, then Molly proceeded to serve my usual plate of lasagna with extra cheese. I liked Molly. She was close to sixty and a little on the chubby side but with a heart as warm as you would ever find.

"Don't you ever get tired of eating the same old thing, Morgan?"

I reflected for a moment. "I guess I never really thought about it too much. Maybe it's okay to live a life with no surprises."

I finished up my dinner and proceeded with the second part of my ritual, the weekly purchase of a Super Powerball Lottery ticket for ten dollars in cash.

"You should stop blowing your money on those useless lotteries," the waitress said. "You've been buying those damned things for as long as I can remember and still never seen a penny in return."

"Wait until you see me driving down Main Street in my new Aston Martin convertible, then you won't be laughing. You'll be begging me for a ride."

I bid Molly goodnight and headed back to my one-bedroom flat above the shop. As I entered the darkened premises, I had a thought.

Maybe I should get myself a cat. I might not be so lonesome.

● ● ● ●

LOSING SIGHT:

My vision problems started slowly. At first, I thought I was being sent some old flower inventory from Winnipeg's central flower warehouse. All of the colors of my favorite flowers seemed faded and lifeless. Even the red roses that usually give me a lift appeared drab.

Then one day, when I tried to sort fresh daffodils, I had trouble determining the white from the pale yellow. Despite my reluctance, I decided that I might be approaching the age when glasses would be needed, so I made an appointment with the only optometrist in town.

When Doctor Amos Gregory completed my eye examination, he appeared troubled. "When did you say you first noticed the problem, Morgan?"

I thought for a moment. "I'm not sure, Doc. It seems to have come on gradually."

The doctor went into the back room and returned with a small booklet. He opened the book to show two pages completely covered with random colored dots.

"Take a look at these pages and tell me if you can identify any numbers in the dots."

I stared intently at the pages but couldn't discern any pattern among the dots. "Sorry, Doc, all I can see are a whole bunch of dots. They all look like the same color to me."

The doctor shook his head. "I'm very sorry, Morgan, but this test confirms it. You're in the final stages of becoming totally color blind."

"Colorblind? Can you fix it with glasses?"

"No, the condition is not treatable, I'm afraid."

I walked back to the shop, thinking in stunned silence. *Colorblind. How the hell will I manage to run the flower shop if I can't see the colors of the flowers?*

I knew I could identify the floral species by their distinct shape and smell. Still, the blending of colors into appropriate bouquets was almost an art form. I stopped in at the Red Deer Café and told Molly the bad news.

"Oh, dear, I'm so sorry to hear that. What are you going to do?"

"Molly, I haven't got a clue." I stayed for coffee then, feeling dejected, I went back to work.

• • • •

The following Friday morning, I received a rush order for a floral arrangement for delivery to the Red Deer General Hospital. I assembled a bouquet of assorted flowers, judging the floral arrangement almost entirely on the individual blossoms' shape. I hoped it looked okay.

I headed to the north end of town in my beaten-up old delivery van, deep in thought about my sight problem. My musing was rudely interrupted by the high piercing sound of a siren directly behind me. The flashing lights of the patrol car indicated that I should pull over to the side of the road. I quickly braked the van to a stop.

A heavyset highway patrol officer knocked on the window. "Do you know why I pulled you over, sir?"

"I don't have any idea, but I don't think I was speeding, Officer."

"I stopped you because you just ran a red light without even making the slightest attempt to slow down."

I apologized to the officer and meekly accepted my traffic ticket. There was no way I was going to admit that I thought the light was green.

From that day on, things only got worse. In addition to my color blindness, my normal vision was deteriorating as well. I was having problems matching up the written cards with the correct bouquets.

Spinning My Wheels

The flowers I sent to Mason's Funeral Emporium for old Ned Foreman's funeral read: *"Congratulations on your new home."* Mrs. Edna Green, who had just given birth to a rather homely baby girl, received her flowers with a card that said: *"Our condolences on your unfortunate accident."*

The situation got so bad that people stopped ordering flowers from the Hunter & Son Flower Shop.

I was at my wit's end. Unpaid bills kept piling up at a faster and faster rate. It finally got to the point that I was afraid to answer the phone. It all came to a head when the Red Deer Savings & Loan Corporation sent a personal delegation to confront me at my shop.

"Morgan, I'm very sorry," the assistant manager said. "The bank has been lenient with you, but your mortgage is now over one-hundred-twenty days in arrears. You have to make a payment within the next fourteen days, or the bank will have to repossess your shop."

I knew the bankers personally, and I realized they were just doing their job. I promised them I would do my best to make a payment before escorting them to the door.

Totally dejected, I ambled over to the Red Deer Café and Pub. I took a seat at the counter with my head down.

Molly could tell I was upset. "This one's on me, kiddo," she said as she placed a steaming plate of my favorite lasagna, with extra cheese, in front of me.

"Many thanks, Molly. You're a real friend. I appreciate everything you do for me."

Molly turned away so I wouldn't see the tears running down her face. She didn't turn fast enough.

"On the bright side, since you paid for my meal, I can spend my last ten bucks on this week's extra special Powerball Lottery."

"Whatever happens, you'll never change," Molly scolded. "That's for sure."

Despite her scowling disproval, I bought my ticket. There was no damned way I was going to miss the upcoming special Powerball Lottery. With no winner for almost six months, the jackpot now had reached an astronomical amount of two-hundred and fifty-million, tax-free dollars.

The draw was taking place at the White House by the new president of the USA. This Powerball was going to be unique because, for the first time, the president had granted the Powerball Lottery a pardon for any taxes that would usually be due.

For the next several days, I tried everything I could think of to raise enough money to pay my mortgage. Nothing worked. There was no way to avoid eviction from my business and my home. I'm not a quitter, but I was becoming overwhelmed by my situation.

Colorblind, losing my remaining sight, alone and broke, I took the bottle of champagne I had been saving for a special occasion. I slowly walked up the worn stairs to my bedroom. After donning my best suit, I took a bottle of prescription sleeping pills and the champagne then lay down on my bed.

I drank the entire bottle of champagne, still intently staring at the tablets. My circumstances seemed dire, but something deep inside me rebelled.

"No, damn it, I won't give up," I said out loud.

As I flushed the pill bottle's entire contents down the toilet, I pledged to find a better solution to my worries.

I fell asleep on the bed but was soon startled out of my deep slumber by a loud banging on the front door. Still groggy from the champagne, I stumbled down the stairs then opened the front door to a chaotic scene.

Molly, grinning from ear to ear, stood there crying her eyes out. Dozens of neighbors dancing in the street were all loudly screaming at the same time. The garbled message that finally penetrated my sleep-deprived brain sounded like an insult. I was bewildered.

"Why are these people calling me a filthy bitch?" I asked Molly.

"No, Morgan, they're saying you're filthy rich. You just won the biggest Powerball lottery in history!"

◆ ◆ ◆ ◆

FILTHY RICH!

What a difference a tax-free, two-hundred and fifty-million bucks makes. I ordered a custom-decorated Aston Martin Viper for myself, paid off the Red Deer Savings & Loan mortgage debt, and even bought the Red Deer Café and Pub for Molly.

My biggest problem was fending off all the people who now wanted to become my new best friend. A deluge of loan requests, special deals, and once-in-a-lifetime investment opportunities stacked up on my doorstep.

I also couldn't help but notice that more than a few young ladies in the town were paying more attention to me than they had in the past. After a few futile dates, I concluded that the girls were much more interested in my wallet than my wisdom.

Much of my time was spent trying to avoid the various newspapers and magazines that wanted to do feature articles about my rise from "rags to riches." Fortune Magazine ran a four-page spread describing my life before the lottery, with a particular focus on my color blindness and other vision problems. The publicity brought on a whole new wave of special offers to cure my condition. I threw them all in the garbage.

One afternoon, I sat at the café complaining to Molly. "You know something, life was a lot simpler for me before I won this damned lottery."

Molly laughed. "If all that loot is a big problem for you, buddy, I think I can help you get rid of most of it." We both laughed and agreed that I could take care of the money problem without her assistance.

"What are you going to do with the flower shop, Morgan?"

"I've decided to keep the shop as a hobby. I hired two local girls to run it for me, and so far, they're doing a good job."

Other than that, I didn't have a clue what my future might hold.

● ● ● ●

One afternoon, I was in the shop watching Mary Maxwell and Joan Hartford, my new assistants, make up floral bouquets. They were pretty busy. New orders flooded in because of all the publicity the shop had been receiving. As I watched the girls at work, I felt a little sad. I missed the joy of colors. I was also aware that my diminishing eyesight meant my Aston Martin driving days would soon end.

Joan called over. "Morgan, oh sorry, I meant to say, Mr. Hunter. The mailman dropped off a special delivery, registered envelope for you. Mary had to sign for it. I hope that's okay?"

"Yes, Joan, that's fine. And in the future, it's okay for you to call me Morgan." I took the envelope over to my desk to study it, curious about the contents.

At first glance, I was intrigued. The envelope was of the highest quality stock. My name and address were beautifully written in stylish calligraphy. It had arrived via special delivery and registered mail. I opened the letter then read the handwritten note. As far as I could tell, the letter and its contents seemed genuine, but I couldn't be sure.

Since winning the lottery, I have been subjected to numerous authentic-looking special offers. I almost threw the letter in the wastebasket, but on impulse, I decided to reread it.

Institute de la Vision,
1244 Rue des Barres,
Paris, France

Mon Cher Monsieur Hunter,

Please allow me to introduce myself. My name is Marcel Chambeau. I am the Director of the Institute de la Vision in Paris, France. Our English-speaking clients usually refer to us just as the "Vision Institute."

We read about your situation in a recent issue of Fortune

Magazine, and, after careful consideration, we decided to approach you. We have a brilliant ocular surgeon on the Institute staff who has pioneered a new and radical procedure for your type of condition. His name is Doctor Henri Batiste. He feels there is a high probability this new procedure could provide a total cure for you.

We realize that you have probably been approached by many people and are likely to be highly skeptical. We fully understand this, and that is why our Medical Board is prepared to make the following proposition.

If you decide to come to Paris, Doctor Batiste will examine you. If appropriate, he will perform the new procedure on you at no cost to you of any kind. However, if the operation is successful and you are entirely pleased with the results, we would expect a donation of five million dollars to our research fund.

We await your response,

Marcel Chambeau

I slowly reread the letter while seated at my desk. *Probably bullshit, but what have I got to lose? This procedure might work. If it does, I could have my total sight restored.*

I rushed over to the Red Deer Café to show the letter to Molly.

"What are you waiting for, you big goof?" she said. "An operation could be the answer to all your prayers."

I smiled as I thought about the possibilities. I had never been outside of Alberta, and the idea of going to Paris was quite stimulating. I got up and headed for the exit.

"Where are you going, buddy? You haven't finished your lasagna."

I laughed. "Well, Molly, I'm off to see my travel agent. I have to pack my bag because I'm off to Paris!"

● ● ● ●

ADVENTURE IN PARIS

Paris was overwhelming.

I arrived in the city a full two days ahead of my scheduled appointment at the Vision Institute. I was already in full tourist mode. So far, I had wandered the beautiful cobblestone streets visiting the Louvre, the Eiffel Tower, and even enjoyed a boat trip down the River Seine. The tour guide told me that Paris had been a famous city for over two thousand years. He also mentioned the river was almost five hundred miles long before merging into the English Channel after passing under the thirty-seven bridges of Paris.

After all the touring, I was famished. I spotted a neighborhood bistro with an outdoor eating area, took a seat, and waited until a thin waiter reluctantly approached me. The man looked down his nose as if I were a piece of dog shit scraped off the sidewalk.

"Bonjour Monsieur. Que voulez-vous manger?"

I stared at the man until the exasperated waiter grumbled in heavily accented English, "What do you want to eat?"

When I said I wanted a beer and a plate of lasagna with extra cheese, the waiter looked insulted.

He sneered. "At La Regelade Saint Honore, we do not serve zee lasagna!"

Two local medical students passing by took pity on me. "Monsieur, could we suggest you try the Plat de Jour. It is usually good here."

I ordered the daily special then asked the students to join me. The waiter eventually arrived with a steaming plate of confit de canard with a side dish of heavily salted, thinly cut Pommes frites.

I was stunned. I had no idea that food could taste this good.

I ordered extra beers for my new friends and spent an enjoyable afternoon listening to tales of Paris. The boys told me they had heard of Doctor Henri Batiste. As far as they knew, both the doctor and the Vision Institute were first-class and reputable.

• • • •

THE VISION INSTITUTE

After a full day of tests, Doctor Henri Batiste finished my examination. He was now studying the numerous photographs and ultrasounds of my eyes while I anxiously waited in his reception room.

Batiste turned to the director of the Vision Institute. "Marcel, this man's condition has quite deteriorated, but I do believe he is a candidate for the new procedure. If we are going to do something, I think we should proceed without delay."

The director agreed. He asked the nurse to bring me into the conference room. He shook my hand and asked me to take a seat.

"Monsieur Hunter, from our side, we are prepared to go ahead with the operation. If you wish to proceed, would you please confirm that you are willing to make the five-million-dollar donation to our research fund? Providing, of course, that you are pleased with the results."

I signed the commitment document and waited to hear more details about the procedure.

Doctor Batiste had set up a whiteboard with representations of the human eye taken from various angles. He pointed to the board. "Normally, the optic nerve in your eye sends signals that are directly interpreted by your brain. In your case, Morgan, the optic nerves have become frayed. They are sending intermittent signals that the brain cannot decipher. We need to create a situation that will allow these optic nerves to heal themselves."

I nodded my understanding then asked, "How can you possibly do that, Doctor Batiste?"

The doctor smiled. "Our new procedure is quite radical. It is designed to create a period for the healing to take place. In simple terms, what we do is re-route your optical signals away from your brain, through a different organ in your body."

"I'm not sure I understand," I said. "What organ?"

Henri Batiste met my gaze. "I know it sounds strange, but for exactly one year, Morgan, you will see the world through your heart instead of through your brain."

"Surely, this can't be possible," I scoffed.

"It is difficult, but not impossible. We call the revolutionary new procedure Les Yeux du Coeur, or, in English, Eyes of the Heart. For twelve months, you will only see what your heart, not your brain, wants you to see."

I hesitated. I wanted to believe in the possibility of success. Still, I wasn't sure what the impact of the operation would be on my life. On the other hand, I knew I was now facing a slow descent into blindness. Worst case, if the operation failed, I wouldn't be any worse off.

I decided to take the plunge and proceed with the operation. Doctor Batiste gave me the consent forms to sign. I have to admit my hands were trembling when I signed.

● ● ● ●

The next day, I lay on an operating table with my head held immobile by surgical straps. A tremor of fear coursed through my body when a gowned figure in a surgical mask approached.

I recognized Batiste by his accent. He spoke in a low, reassuring voice, but his message was anything but comforting.

"I am sorry we have to do this procedure under a local anesthetic," Batiste said softly. "We need you to be awake to guide us through the operation. Hopefully, the tranquilizers will smooth things over."

"Are you kidding?" I moaned. "I'm not going to stay awake while you cut me up. Get me to hell out of here."

Batiste laughed. "First of all, we will not be 'cutting you up' as you so delicately phrased it. Our procedure is done with micro-precision through certain arteries. I guarantee you won't feel a thing."

"Well, I'm here. Better start now, before I change my mind," I warned.

When the precision, laser-guided, operating robot started to simultaneously insert chromium-tipped needles deep into the pupils of both of my eyes, a thought flashed into my brain.

It's my birthday today. How the hell did I ever get myself into this?

The powerful tranquilizers left me hazy enough to barely remember the operation. However, I did recall responding to numerous instructions during the procedure.

After the operation, I remained in a darkened room for ten days, wide bandages covering my eyes completely. I think I must have been sedated because I did little but sleep. Doctor Batiste checked on me every day, murmuring his satisfaction after completing his examinations.

On the morning of the ninth day, Batiste quietly entered my room. My enhanced sense of smell told me he was carrying a basket of fresh fruit.

"Morgan, tomorrow, we will remove your bandages," he said confidently. "Let me tell you a little about what you can expect."

I waited expectantly while Batiste continued. "You must prepare yourself for some confusion at the beginning."

I laughed. "I'm always confused. So, what's the difference?"

"Quite a bit of difference, mon ami," the surgeon said gravely. "Starting to see the world with your heart instead of your mind will require a significant adjustment in your attitude."

"What kind of adjustment?"

Batiste hesitated. "Some of our earlier patients had great difficulty at first. It seems if you are a pessimist at heart, the world will be a dark place. If you are an optimist, on the other hand, it will be like seeing the world through rose-colored glasses."

"Are there any other side effects?"

"Some patients reported seeing a faint aura when they looked directly at another person. A few patients became convinced that a greenish aura projects from the good people in their lives and a red aura projects from any of the bad individuals they encounter."

"Do you believe this is really possible?"

"We have no way of confirming these reports, of course. Perhaps, if you see any unusual manifestations, you could let us know immediately. Now, are you ready for the big unveiling?"

I started to sweat. Doctor Batiste was finally removing the bandages. In a few moments, I would know the results.

● ● ● ●

Batiste continued talking as he slowly removed one layer of bandages at a time. I tried to concentrate on his words, but it was difficult because of my apprehension.

"I must remind you again," Batiste said. "It is important you understand that this is an extremely precise procedure from a timing standpoint."

"Refresh me," I said. "I'm not sure I knew this before."

"It was all spelled out in the pre-op material we gave you. I hope you read it," Batiste scolded. "It's important because, on your next birthday, your optic nerves will automatically be re-routed from your heart, back to your brain."

"Will I receive any warning?"

"I'm afraid not, mon ami. The timing can't be adjusted."

"Will my vision be normal again?" I asked.

Batiste nodded. "But you must be aware this changeover from the heart to brain signals could be a shattering experience. So please make sure you are in the company of friends or family on the date the transition takes place."

I nodded my understanding. *Not much I can do now but ride it out for a year and see what happens,* I thought.

With the last bandage removed, I experienced a sudden bout of dizziness. Batiste assisted me to the bedside, then flushed my eyes with a solution. I saw blurred flashes of light before my vision gradually started to clear.

It may have been my imagination, but I thought I felt my heart give a strange tremor at the same time.

"Go ahead, Morgan. Take a look in the mirror," Batiste said softly.

"I'm afraid to," I whispered.

"Take a chance, mon ami," Batiste encouraged. "See the world through your heart for the first time."

When the doctor extended his arm to support me, I tentatively took it. He guided me in the direction of a full-length mirror hanging on the door. I kept my eyes closed tightly. When we stopped moving, he dropped my arm then told me to open my eyes. I counted to ten to draw on my courage then I did as he instructed.

• • • •

I was stunned!

The figure in the mirror, staring back at me, had clean, sharp facial features, no waxy complexion or nasal hairs. It was me, but a much more handsome version than I remembered stared back.

Batiste laughed at my expression. "You are seeing yourself now as your heart sees you, Morgan, not as your brain did. This way is truly how the *Eyes of the Heart* procedure is meant to be."

"Wow," I said. "I can't quite believe it."

"Over the coming year, you will be amazed at the positive changes in your life. As you probably know, the brain and heartfelt emotions are often at odds. The brain evaluates in a certain logical way, while our heart processes events quite differently."

I nodded. "I'm anxious now to go home. What do you think?"

"We want you to stay close for a few days so we can monitor your progress," Batiste cautioned. "Feel free to leave the hospital for short trips but don't overdo it."

I took Batiste as his word. Over the next three days, I went shopping for a whole new wardrobe, ate lunch in sidewalk cafes, and munched baguettes on the banks of the Seine. On my last morning, I strolled through a local fresh market. The brilliant colors of the multitude of fruits and produce almost brought tears to my eyes.

If you want to experience the treat of a lifetime, go to Paris in the springtime—and see it through your heart.

Finally, I received my release from the Institute's care, with a strong reminder from the director to be sure to send in progress reports. After thanking Batiste, I returned to the hotel, packed, and departed for the airport.

I left my check for five million for the research fund behind. So far, I considered the donation to be a tremendous bargain.

• • • •

UP IN THE CLOUDS

Soon I was up in the clouds, both mentally and physically. I reclined in my first-class deluxe slumber seat aboard a gleaming new Air France Boeing 777, enroute to Vancouver from Paris, France. I sipped on a glass of chilled Dom Perignon champagne, then reflected on all that had happened to me in such a short time.

I could hardly wait to see Molly to tell her all about my Paris experience. My full vision had returned completely. The colors of the rainbow were now back in all their vibrant hues. I looked out the cabin window soaking up the brilliance of the blue, blue sky and puffy clouds in various shades of white and gray.

I noticed that some, not all, individuals seemed to emit a faint aura of color. I recalled Doctor Batiste telling me some patients had reported seeing a green aura around good people and a red aura around the bad ones.

I looked around the first-class cabin. Sure enough, the young couple with a newborn baby reflected shades of light green. On the other hand, the inebriated executive leering at the beautiful cabin flight attendant's shapely backside was definitely in the red zone.

I fell asleep after a gourmet meal, then didn't wake up until the plane touched down, feather-soft, on the tarmac at Vancouver International Airport.

I caught a connecting flight to Calgary, where I had left my car. I drove to Red Deer but didn't go home. I went straight to the café.

"Bonjour, Madame Molly. Vous allez bien?" I said in my newly acquired French accent.

Molly roared with laughter. "That's the worst fake accent I've ever heard. Now sit your ass down, eat your lasagna and tell me all about your trip."

"Oui, Madame, but frankly I now prefer confit du canard avec frites."

We both cracked up then continued chuckling as I told her all about my adventures in France. She was amazed when I described the operation in detail, especially about how my optic nerves were re-routed.

"However, I don't want anyone to know about my procedure," I cautioned. "This is a strict secret between us."

"What's it like?" Molly asked. "You know, seeing through your heart."

"It's hard to explain. Everything seems so fresh and new. One thing I know for sure is that now that I see through my heart instead of my brain, I'm a much happier guy."

I said goodbye to Molly, then headed home to unpack. I was anxious to catch up on some sleep then head off for a new look at life.

● ● ● ●

Even though I was no longer color blind, I kept my two assistants on at the flower shop to do all the routine jobs. If the store got extra busy, I would pitch in and help the customers. One busy Friday in early autumn, I looked up as a new customer entered the shop. My mouth fell open. I felt like an idiot.

I never believed in 'love at first sight' until it happened to me. I literally felt like I had been run over by a cement truck. Our new customer was a woman, but not just any member of the fairer sex. She was about my age, tall and willowy with long blond hair, highlighted with streaks of silver. And that's just the beginning.

It was difficult not to gape since this beautiful stranger emitted a brilliant green aura, brighter than any I had encountered since the operation on my eyes. It finally dawned on me she was talking in my direction.

"I'm sorry," I stammered. "I missed that."

"I asked if I could place a standing order for two dozen red and white carnations for delivery every Friday afternoon?"

Despite being terribly tongue-tied, I managed to say, "Could I please have your name and address for the delivery?"

She unleashed a lovely smile. "The address is 26 Parkview Place, and my name is Aimee Blanchard."

I screwed up my courage. "I know most people in town, but I don't think I've seen you before."

"Probably not," she answered in a pleasing, velvety, slightly accented voice. "I moved here from Montreal only last month."

"Well, it's nice to meet you, Mrs. Blanchard," I said with a smile. "I'm Morgan Hunter. Welcome to Red Deer. Not the most exciting place on Earth to spend a winter, but at least the people are friendly."

"They certainly are," she replied. "I've already had several invitations for dinner. And, by the way, it's Ms. Blanchard or Aimee. I'm not married."

She grinned, waved goodbye, then headed for the parking lot. My eyes continued to be glued on her until her lovely figure disappeared around the corner. As I stood, transfixed, I became vaguely aware of my two assistants giggling behind the counter.

"Are you okay, Morgan?" Joan asked. "You have a funny look on your face."

"Yeah, I'm fine," I lied. "I'm just going over to the café for a coffee. The shop is in your capable hands."

I rushed across Main Street. The café was almost empty since it was still an hour before the lunch crowd would arrive. The noise of pots and pans banging in the kitchen gave away Molly's location.

"Molly," I yelled. "Customer waiting out here. I desperately need a coffee. No, make that a draft beer instead."

The café owner stuck her head out the swinging doors. "Did you say beer? I've never known you to drink alcohol during the day. What the hell's going on?"

"It's finally happened to me, Molly. It was love at first sight."

"You wouldn't know love at first sight if it bit you in the behind," Molly hooted as she poured me a mug of coffee."

"I'm not kidding. I'm smitten."

"Okay, Romeo. Who is this enchantress?"

"She's new in town. Her name is Aimee Blanchard, and she's tall, slim, and gorgeous."

When Molly put her hands on her hips, I knew she was about to become belligerent. I waited for the caustic barrage.

"Just like a man," Molly scoffed. "You meet a new woman, and all you can see is her damned figure."

"I'm hurt," I protested. "You didn't even give me a chance to tell you the real 'turn-on' for me."

"Okay, go ahead."

"Remember I told you a few people emit an aura?"

"Yeah, that 'Eyes of the Heart' thing," Molly responded.

"Well, Aimee gives off a beautiful emerald green aura. I've never seen anything quite like it. Her aura actually sparkles."

"So, what are you going to do about this green goddess?"

"She ordered flowers for this Friday. I'm going to deliver them myself and then see what happens."

"Good luck," Molly grinned. "And Morgan…"

"What?"

"Don't bugger it up!"

● ● ● ●

THE DELIVERY MAN COMETH

When Friday finally arrived, it found me smiling behind the wheel of my new Aston Martin Viper. I smiled as the Viper roared down Main Street with twin exhausts emitting a throaty growl in the afternoon air. Two dozen of my best red and white carnations sat on the front seat beside me. I felt my excitement level rising as I drew closer to seeing Aimee again.

I pulled into the driveway at 26 Parkview Place, then took a good look around. A gleaming new Chrysler Imperial sat in front of a manicured, recently painted bungalow. It appeared like Aimee was doing well financially.

I didn't care a hoot about her wealth. I was just happy to know that if all went well and she was attracted to me, it wouldn't be simply for my Powerball money.

When Aimee answered the door after the first knock, she seemed surprised to see me. Then she flashed me that beautiful smile I remembered.

"Oh, it's you, Mr. Hunter. I didn't realize you were the delivery man. My, what beautiful flowers. Thank you so much for delivering them."

Instead of coming back with a witty response, I stood there gaping with a dumb look on my face. I couldn't help myself. Aimee's sparkling emerald aura did make her look like a 'green goddess,' as Molly had said.

"Are you okay, Mr. Hunter? You look a little dazed. Would you like some cold water?" Aimee seemed worried.

"Thank you," I stumbled. "It must be the heat that's affecting me."

Another stupid response on my part since the temperature, if anything, was running a little below average for this time of the year.

I recovered somewhat after she invited me in. Once inside her beautifully decorated living room, she motioned for me to take a seat by the window. She moved gracefully to the kitchen then returned moments later with a pitcher of ice-cold lemonade.

"You might prefer this to water, sir. I made it myself from fresh lemons."

"Please call me Morgan. I feel old when people call me sir."

"Okay, but only if you call me Aimee in return," she laughed. Her gentle laugh had a lovely tinkling sound.

"It's a deal," I said, as I fumbled for an excuse to explain my weird behavior. "I have to apologize for seeming out of it. Since I returned from Paris, I've never quite shaken off my jet lag."

"I love Paris," Aimee said softly. "You can probably tell from my name that I have a French background."

I smiled. "Aimee is such a pretty name. What does it mean?"

"Aimee is an old French and Latin name. It means, Beloved." Aimee blushed a little as she explained her name.

"May I ask how you happened to be in Red Deer? It seems a long way from the magical sights of Paris."

Aimee's face saddened for a moment. "I'm here to sell the house. My father died recently, and I inherited his estate. I'm not in a hurry, though. I'm ready for a change of scenery. It helps that I'm an artist. I can work anywhere."

I nodded, not quite sure what to say next. Aimee refilled my glass, and we chatted for another hour or so. Then Aimee looked at her watch and became alarmed.

"Oh, I'm so sorry, Morgan," she apologized. "My babbling is keeping you from your deliveries. You better get back to work before you get fired."

I grinned. "I think I'm safe. My boss is a great guy. One of the best. He's a generous, kind, adorable person. In fact, I wish I was just like him."

My 'over-the-top' answer clued Aimee in. She started to laugh with that musical tinkling sound again. It was music to my ears.

"You're the boss, right?"

"Yes, you got me. I've owned the place for years."

"Does that mean you can stay for another glass of lemonade?"

I took Aimee up on her offer, then we chatted more. I didn't get back to the shop until almost closing time. My two assistants nudged each other when they spotted the massive grin on my face.

"That took a long time for a simple delivery, boss," Mary said with a grin.

"Maybe he couldn't find the right address," Joan added.

"Look at the grin on his face, Joan. There's no question about it.

He found the right address for sure. I guess we can call off the search party now."

I just let their words bounce off my thick hide. I didn't care. The girls could make all the wisecracks they wanted. Nothing would dampen my mood.

I was one happy camper, and I wasn't afraid to show it.

• • • •

As time flew by, Aimee and I began a whirlwind romance. Every Friday, without fail, became our special date night. I always delivered her flowers in the afternoon. Then, with the top down on the Viper, we would go for a drive in the country. I loved taking sideways glances at Aimee as she sat with her golden hair flowing in the wind.

Sometimes Aimee would set up her easel and paint while I sat at her side reading. Her paintings seemed remarkable to my untrained eye. I wasn't her only fan, though, because she always had a waiting list of buyers.

One of our favorite spots was located just outside the town border. A grove of weeping willow trees provided a sheltered picnic spot on the banks of a meandering stream. When the mood struck us, we often danced on the soft grass to the music from my portable radio.

One Friday, while we were dancing to a slow romantic song, Aimee whispered that she needed to tell me something important. I led her back to the picnic blanket, then poured us two chilled glasses of Chablis.

"What's on your mind?" I asked gently.

Aimee looked pensive. "I don't know if this is good news or bad. I've received an unsolicited offer for the house. It's a terrific offer with no conditions."

I sat stunned for a moment. I had forgotten Aimee's original reason for coming to Red Deer was to dispose of her father's house. The reality that she might be leaving town hit me hard. I struggled for something to say.

"When do you have to answer?"

"They've given me until next Friday. The buyer wants to close the deal at the end of the month but take possession January 15th."

"Wow. A big decision," I said. "What are you going to do?"

"I honestly don't know. I still have a week to decide, so I'll sleep on it for a few days."

We packed up our gear, then we headed for Aimee's place. We were both deep in silent thought as we drove. I dropped her off and headed home. As I passed the Red Deer Café, I noticed Molly getting ready to close for the evening. I parked out front, then banged on the door.

"We're closed," Molly hollered from the back.

"Hey, Molly, it's me. Morgan"

"We're still closed."

"C'mon, Molly. I need to talk to you," I said, then I threw out the bait I knew she couldn't resist. "Actually, I need your advice."

Molly bit hard. She waddled to the entrance door, unlocked it then motioned for me to take a seat at the counter.

"Coffee or beer?"

"Beer," I replied.

Molly cracked the tops off two cold Banff Springs Ale bottles, poured the brew, then planted her ample backside on the seat alongside me.

"Okay, shoot."

"Aimee has an offer on her house. She might be leaving town."

"You want my advice?"

"Yep."

"Marry her without delay."

"That's it?"

"Yes. Now finish your beer and go. My favorite show starts in half an hour."

"C'mon, Molly, I'm serious. Marriage is a big deal for a lifelong bachelor like me. I haven't known Aimee for a long time. What if I make a mistake?"

"Do you want her to stay?"

"Absolutely."

"Okay, tell me what you like about her."

I thought for a moment, then said, "As a starter, we're well matched. We have fun together. Aimee's sense of humor makes me laugh, and she is very easy to talk to. Do you want more?"

"Keep talking."

"Okay, she's a gifted artist, a great cook, intelligent and kind. Aimee wants to help in setting up the charitable foundation for sight-impaired people. She's also a very warm and loving person. In fact, our sex…"

"Stop," Molly interrupted. "I've heard enough. Besides, I know Aimee well enough to know she's the real thing. Now, tell me what you don't like about her."

I sat there for a few minutes, searching my brain for something I didn't like about Aimee. Molly could tell by my face that I had drawn a blank.

"I rest my case, Morgan. Marry the woman if she'll take you. You've been living on your own far too long. And do it now before she leaves town or some other guy moves in on you."

I nodded, then hugged Molly and departed for home. I had a lot to think about.

The following morning, after a long night of tossing and turning, I decided to phone Aimee. Her musical voice brought a smile to my face. She knew it was a call from me because she had arranged for a unique ringtone.

"Bonjour, Morgan, mon ami."

"And bonjour to you, Aimee. I've been thinking about the offer for your house."

"Yes?"

"Could you delay your answer until we have a chance to talk? I have to go to Calgary for a meeting on Monday, but I could take you for dinner Wednesday night."

"I'll be ready and waiting at the door for you. Have a safe trip."

"See you soon," I said, then started packing for my trip.

◆ ◆ ◆ ◆

Although I did have a legitimate business reason for going to Calgary, my main goal was to find an engagement ring for Aimee. One of the advantages of being filthy rich is the ability to make things happen. With a team of the most expensive jewelers at work, I was able to head for home with an absolute gem of a ring.

Tuesday, as I traveled back by train, I had a chance to reflect on something that troubled me a little. Although my vision was still excellent, I rarely saw anyone emitting an aura. After my 'Eyes of the Heart' operation, I usually spotted a few people showing either a red or green aura almost every day.

But in a crowded city like Calgary, I hadn't seen a single person with an aura in over two days. In fact, now that I gave it some thought, even Aimee's aura lately had become only faintly visible. I made a mental note to write to Doctor Batiste to see if the change was significant.

Although it was late when I arrived back in Red Deer, I knew the café would still be open. I dropped my bag off then headed across Main Street for a late dinner. Molly rushed to the counter when she spotted me. She poured a coffee and gave me the third degree at the same time.

"What did she say?"

"Who?"

"Aimee, you dummy. What did she say when you popped the big question?"

"I haven't had a chance yet."

"You're stalling, Morgan."

'No, I'm not," I protested, then I brought out the ring. "Does this look like I'm stalling?"

Molly's jaw dropped when she took a close look at the large, flawless solitary diamond, beautifully set in white gold. The stone sparkled under the overhead lights.

"Holy crap," Molly exclaimed. "If I had known there was a rock like this to be had, I would have married you myself."

"Too late," I laughed. "I'm proposing to Aimee tomorrow night. It's a special day for me."

"What's so special about tomorrow?"

"It's my birthday."

"Congratulations, bub. Your dinner is on me tonight. What will you have?"

"Oh, I don't know. How about lasagna with extra cheese?"

Molly sighed. "I feel sorry for Aimee if she becomes your wife."

"Why?"

"She'll die of boredom," Molly said over her shoulder as she headed for the kitchen to get my meal.

• • • •

The following morning, I woke up with a raging headache and slightly blurred vision. My heartbeat felt erratic as well. As I lay there, I remembered it was my birthday. The day my vision was programmed to revert to normal. After seeing life through my heart for an entire year, it became second nature for me, so I rarely gave it a thought anymore.

I vaguely recalled Doctor Batiste had mentioned the possibility of some readjustment problems. I took some aspirins, returned to my bed, and decided to stay there for the day. Hopefully, a day off would fix me up in time to meet Aimee for our special dinner.

It was nearly dark when I woke up. My head still hurt but not nearly as bad as it had earlier. After a quick shower, I dressed, made sure I had the ring, then headed for the Viper. Halfway to the car, I remembered the flowers. I nipped back into the shop and quickly made up a lovely bouquet of red and white carnations.

I drove fast through the cool night air with the top down to help clear my brain fog. But when I pulled into Aimee's driveway, something seemed wrong. I was puzzled because her gleaming Chrysler Imperial wasn't there in its usual spot. An old model Ford Taurus sat in its place. Nothing seemed quite like I remembered.

Maybe she has a visitor, I thought.

I grabbed the carnations then headed to the front door. I wasn't sure if it was the fading light, but the house seemed smaller and looked like it needed a paint job. I checked the address to see if I had turned into the wrong place. The street number was correct.

I tried to clear my thoughts before knocking on the door. Even though my head was pounding again, I could hardly wait to show Aimee the ring. I knocked and waited for my green goddess to answer.

When the door opened, my heart plunged. I was stunned—almost frightened at what I was seeing. It was my Aimee standing there, but it wasn't the woman I knew so well.

Aimee's golden, silver-streaked hair was now a dull mousy brown. The tall and willowy figure I knew and loved was also much shorter and squarer. Even her beautiful smile seemed a little tired and worn. Her soft voice was still the same, but everything else was so different.

"What's wrong, Morgan? You look like you just saw a ghost."

I tried to comprehend what was happening. Then it hit me. For the first time, I realized I was seeing Aimee as she really was and not as my 'Eyes of the Heart' had wanted me to see her.

In my confusion, I dropped the flowers. My head was pounding. I had to get away to try and come to grips with reality.

"This is all a giant mistake," I blurted. "You're not the woman I wanted. I need to go. Just forget we ever met."

I turned and stumbled down the driveway, vaguely aware of the loud, painful sobs coming from the doorway behind me.

I returned home, heartbroken, and retreated to my bed for days. When my headache finally subsided, I staggered to the washroom for a shower. As I passed the full-length mirror, I gasped. This was the first time I had looked carefully at myself since my vision had reverted to normal.

Gone was the sharp-featured, handsome man that my heart had seen. Now staring back at me was the image of a stocky, pudgy, nasal-haired guy with a waxy complexion.

I was looking at reality.

Then, it hit me hard. The truth was that Aimee had fallen in love with me, just the way I was with all my physical faults. Still, I had cruelly abandoned her for not being the vision of beauty I conjured up from my heart.

I stumbled over to the café to tell Molly what had happened.

• • • •

"God, you're a fool," Molly said scathingly. "That woman was far more than you deserve. You should be ashamed of yourself."

"I am," I moaned with my head down.

But Molly wasn't finished. "Think about it. When I asked you what you liked about Aimee, you said she was a kind, warm, loving woman and a whole lot more. Everything you mentioned was about her character. You didn't say one single word about her physical attributes."

"I know. I feel like a total shit. If I'd been blind, Aimee would still have been the same woman I fell for."

"So, what are you going to do about it?"

"I'm going out there right now to beg her to forgive me. I'll tell her about the operation on my eyes. Hopefully, she'll understand."

I pushed the Viper to the limit, but when I pulled into Aimee's driveway, her car wasn't there, and neither was she. For several days, I tried to find her every way I could think of, to no avail. I finally decided to hire a private investigator to help with the search.

I gave them as much information as I could about Aimee, then told them not to spare the expense. Just find her. It took several weeks before I got a call from Conrad Jackson, the investigator.

"Good news, Mr. Hunter. We tried every trace technique we know of, then we got a hit using a database of new rental applications. It looks like Aimee Blanchard is hiding out in a little town out west. It's called Bend, Oregon."

"Great. Send me your bill right now. I need her new address."

Jackson gave me the address over the phone. I wrote it down then started planning for what I hoped would be a rescue mission. I really missed Aimee, and I wanted her back at any cost.

• • • •

HEARTBREAK

I parked my rented Hyundai Sonata at the top of the long tree-lined driveway and waited. The muddy drive's unpaved surface led down to a small log cabin, perched on a hillside, overlooking the little town of Bend, Oregon. Rays from the early morning sun reflected off the freshly deposited dew, glistening like a blanket on the small green lawn in front.

I used the cover of the trees to mask my approach to the building. As I drew closer to the house, I felt my heart hammering in my chest. I knew that this time it had to be perfect—no second chances. I tightened my grip on the beautiful bouquet of red and white carnations I was carrying.

When I reached the building, I froze, physically afraid to knock on the front door. My whole future was at stake. To calm myself, I decided to peek through the side window before going any further. My heart soared when I spotted Aimee sitting at a freshly set breakfast table, hair done up in curlers, wearing a fuzzy white bathrobe. She looked happy as she sat sipping on a steaming cup of coffee.

The lace curtains partially obstructed my view of the room, so I moved slowly to the other side of the window for a better look. As I peered through the streaked glass, I felt an intense pain hit me below the belt.

Aimee wasn't alone.

A handsome, athletic-looking young man, also wearing a bathrobe, sat opposite Aimee. Judging from the smiles and hand gestures, they were engaged in an animated conversation. My despair deepened when Aimee moved to the man's side, ruffled his hair, then planted a loving kiss on the guy's cheek.

I felt like a peeping tom. I was embarrassed, nervous, angry, resentful, jealous, and upset all at the same time. As I turned to leave, a neighbor's dog must have sensed my presence. Although I was doing my best to be silent, the animal started to bark loudly.

I have to get out of here, I thought.

Using the trees as cover, I zig-zagged my way back up the lane. In my haste, I didn't see a patch of wet grass ahead. I slipped, fell to my knees, and sent the flowers flying. I tried to retrieve the carnations, but I abandoned the chase when I heard the front door opening.

Back in the car, I sat numb, filled with regrets, trying to hold back the moisture from my eyes. I had waited too long, and I had hurt Aimee too much. I should have located her sooner before she had a chance to find someone else. I slowly turned the car to the north and headed for home.

During the long trip back, I had ample time to reflect on my stupidity. How could I have been such a fool? When I first met Aimee, my eyes showed me a vision of loveliness that my heart wanted me to see. When my regular sight returned, I saw her physically as she really was. The shock had caused me to react badly.

I realized now that Molly was correct. The many things I loved about Aimee were not visual at all.

Her thoughtfulness, compassion, easy-going personality, and much more were the attributes that counted. The ones that made up her inner beauty. I should have recognized the beautiful green aura around Aimee resulted from her essential goodness, not her external appearance.

On my return to Red Deer, I tried to resume everyday life. I had great difficulties because my thoughts kept drifting back to the good times I had spent with Aimee. In desperation, I started to date a local, recently divorced woman. She turned out to a scheming nag who made no bones about her plan to become the future Mrs. Morgan Hunter.

After several months I broke off the relationship. Even without my 'Eyes of the Heart,' I could sense a red aura radiating intensely from the woman's internal bitterness. I wanted no part of a life with her.

Molly did everything she could to cheer me up, but I remained despondent and lonely. I had tons of money, a brand-new Viper, and my newly purchased mansion. I had everything a man could want, but I didn't have Aimee.

It got so bad I even lost my taste for lasagna with extra cheese.

I finally went out and bought myself a cat so I wouldn't be alone for the upcoming Christmas season.

The cat was a pain in the ass. And a cold fish to boot. Now, I wished I had gone for the puppy instead.

● ● ● ●

FINAL CHAPTER

Christmas Eve at the Red Deer Café & Pub. The weather outside had turned bitterly cold, with the driving snow taking on a tinge of ice as it fell. A decent crowd of locals had taken refuge from the storm. Molly, God love her, was doing her best to liven things up a little by adding some overproof rum to the Christmas punch. This was her annual attempt at a Christmas party.

When Molly donned a red Santa hat and started singing *Rudolph the Red-Nosed Reindeer* at the top of her lungs, I reached my limit.

"You're a hell of a lot better at making lasagna than you are as a singer," I groused. "I'm leaving. I'd rather spend the rest of the evening listening to that damned cat."

Molly appeared upset. "You can't go."

I laughed. "Why on earth not?"

"I forbid it," Molly said, fumbling for an excuse.

"What?"

Molly sighed. "I didn't want to get your hopes up, but on my way to work, I noticed some lights on at Aimee's house. I knocked on the door. No one answered, so I dropped an invitation for tonight's party through the mail slot."

"Nice try," I said sadly. "The house is sold. The light you saw was from the new owners."

"I don't think so. I'm sure the new owners don't take possession until January 15th…"

Molly stopped talking abruptly when the café door opened, allowing a blast of arctic air to enter the room. The festive chatter halted as a woman entered the room, covered in a blanket of fresh snowflakes. She had a plaid scarf wrapped around her face, but I recognized her from her walk.

It was Aimee Blanchard. The woman I had mistreated so badly.

Several patrons rushed over to welcome her back. Aimee had always been a favorite of the local folks. Because we lived in a small town, almost everyone knew why Aimee had left Red Deer. The sad story of my despicable behavior toward her had fueled the gossip mill for weeks.

Unless her escort was still parking the car, it appeared that Aimee was on her own. I had no idea what to say or how to approach her, so I remained rooted on my stool at the counter.

When the fuss over her arrival quietened down, Aimee looked around the room. When she spotted me, she turned and started to head for the exit. For a moment, I thought she was going to walk out on me. The café went dead silent when she turned back to slowly move in my direction.

I stood up, beamed a smile, then opened my arms for a welcoming hug. My smile turned out to be highly premature. Aimee brushed my arms aside, then slapped me hard, once forward, then backward in the classic French style.

"You bastard," she moaned before fleeing in tears to the sanctuary of an empty booth at the far side of the café.

I rubbed my face then looked at Molly for guidance. She motioned for me to remain where I was.

"Let me talk to her, Morgan. No guarantees. Still, I'll see if she'll at least give you a chance to explain."

Molly ambled over to the booth. She talked for a minute or two then took a seat. In my desperation to set things right, I took that as a good omen. It took another ten minutes before Molly raised her bulk and moved back to my side.

"She's angry, and she's hurt, but she said she'll talk," Molly advised. "Take this bottle of champagne and go and give it your best shot."

"Thanks," I mumbled. "You're a real friend in need."

"But Morgan…"

"Yes?"

"Don't put your foot in your mouth this time. This is your last chance, buster."

• • • •

Neither Aimee nor I said a word until after I uncorked the champagne. I poured two glasses then I took the first step.

"Aimee, I was a total shit," I confessed. "Let me have a chance to explain, then you can either hit me over the head with the bottle or forgive me."

"I'm listening."

I told Aimee the whole story. How I went color blind. My close call with suicide when I thought I would lose my home and business. Winning the Powerball draw and my trip to Paris for the experimental operation.

After listening in silence, Aimee posed a question. "I don't understand how a person could see through their heart. How does that happen?"

"It's hard to explain. As close as I can describe it, you see people and things as your heart wants you to see them. After a year, your vision goes back to being processed by your brain."

"Am I so ugly that you were repelled when you saw the real me?"

"No, not at all," I protested. "The day I came to your house was the first day of the adjustment. I had a splitting headache, but I wanted to see you for a special reason. I wasn't mentally ready for the shift. Hell, when I first looked at myself, I was shocked too. I had conned myself into believing I was one of the world's most handsome eligible bachelors."

Aimee smiled for the first time. "Believe me, you really were kidding yourself. I was attracted to you for many reasons, but a pin-up poster you're not."

I reached across and took Aimee's hand. "I know that, and I'm smart enough now to know I fell in love with you just because of the warm, loving person you are. When I realized what a mistake I made, I tried everything to find you."

"I know," she whispered.

"What?"

"When I saw the carnations lying in the driveway, I knew you must have been there. I waited and waited, hoping you would show up. Why didn't you come back? I just assumed you changed your mind again."

"I went to Oregon to find you to apologize for the fool I am. When I looked through your window and saw how happy you looked with your new man, I knew I was too late."

"You really are a fool, Morgan. The man in the house was my brother, Johnny. He was on extended leave from Iraq. He came to visit me before going back."

"Oh crap," I said. I was upset that I hadn't stayed but also ecstatic that Aimee hadn't found a new man.

"You said you came to my house on your birthday for a special reason," Aimee said. "May I ask what the special reason was?"

I looked at Aimee through unclouded eyes. There was no doubt in my mind. This was the down-to-earth woman I wanted to be with for the rest of my life. A real woman, not some mystical goddess conjured up by my Eyes of the Heart.

Faint heart never won fair maiden, I said to myself.

● ● ● ●

I decided to take a chance. I fumbled in my pocket for the engagement ring I was still carrying. I don't know why I kept it. Probably as a daily reminder of how much I had lost. I dropped to my knees in front of everyone in the crowded café. Aimee gasped when I opened the lid.

"This was my special reason, Aimee. It should have been on your finger that same night. Will you forgive me and be my wife? I'll never mistreat you again."

The café fell silent. After a prolonged delay, Aimee stood up. She stared down at me, holding the ring.

"No, I don't want your damned ring," she said coldly as she grabbed her coat then rushed from the room.

Molly hurried over and gave me a hand to get up off my knee. I felt like a total fool. After a moment of embarrassed silence, the patrons began talking again as if nothing had happened.

I hobbled over to the counter, then sat back on my usual stool. Molly quickly poured me a glass of the Christmas punch. After adding an extra shot of overproof rum, she placed it in front of me.

"You look like you could use this, my friend."

"You're not kidding. I feel like a deflated balloon. What an ass I've been."

I finished my rum punch, then put on my coat. I didn't want to spend another minute trying to pretend nothing happened.

Molly hugged me. "Merry Christmas, you big bum. Don't worry. Next year will be much better than this one."

I could see tears forming in Molly's brown eyes, so I hugged her in return then departed with my head down. Heavy snow made trudging across Main Street difficult. By the time I reached home, I was frozen. I headed upstairs and took a hot shower to warm up before hopping into my lonely bed.

● ● ● ●

As children worldwide know well, strange things have been known to happen at that mystical moment when Christmas Eve transforms into the magic of Christmas Day. Well, something unusual happened to me that night. Something I'll never forget.

I had drifted off into a troubled sleep when I felt a smooth, warm body press against my bare back. I couldn't see what was happening because of the darkness. But unless he had been taking hormone shots, the silky soft, nicely rounded, nocturnal visitor who slipped into bed beside me certainly wasn't Santa Claus.

"Aimee," I gasped. "How the hell did you get in?"

"You never asked for your key back when you dumped me," she

whispered as she increased the pressure of her warm body against my back.

"Does this mean I'm forgiven?"

"Yes, you fool," she giggled. "I know my treatment in the café was cruel, but I wanted you to get a taste of how it feels to be rejected."

"Lesson learned, believe me."

Aimee started nuzzling the back of my neck. I could feel goosebumps erupting over my entire body.

"Turn over," she whispered. "I want to give you your Christmas present."

I love presents. That night I loved Aimee's gift in particular. In fact, I loved all three of them.

After I gave Aimee her gift in return, I held her in my arms. She snuggled in real close, then we began to talk.

"Could I be so presumptuous as to assume your recent amorous activity means you wish to accept my modest proposal of marriage?"

"Let me think about it," she said with a smile.

"Nope. Immediate answer required, or I'm giving the ring to Molly."

"Okay, I thought about it."

"And your answer is?"

"Go ahead and give it to Molly."

I smothered Aimee with kisses until she finally relented. When she stopped giggling, she gave me the answer I longed to hear.

"Yes! Yes! A thousand times yes."

"How would you like to go to Paris for our honeymoon?" I asked Aimee after we regained our breath.

"I'd love to. It's my favorite place on Earth."

"I want to introduce you to Doctor Batiste. I also want to talk to him about the procedure he pioneered. The guy has invented a miracle procedure that keeps a person from going blind, but it has some serious flaws."

"Sure. Look what happened to you."

"I know. That's why they need to insist that a patient has to be accompanied by a psychologist or other trained professional on the day their vision switches back to normal. I'm sure Batiste will understand when we tell him about our experience. Especially when he hears I would be interested in backing a branch of the Vision Institute in Montreal."

"I'm tired now," Aimee whispered. "Hold me tight until I fall asleep. I'm going to dream about you kissing me at the top of the Eiffel Tower."

● ● ● ●

Later, as I lay in the darkness with Aimee curled up beside me, I recalled that my dear old mother always had a saying for almost every occasion. If I tore a hole in my pants playing baseball, she would say, "A stitch in time saves nine." When I would moan about some minor complaint, she would always retort, "When life gives you a lemon, make lemonade."

Mom wasn't always right, but she was always a wise woman. I kissed Aimee softly on the forehead as she slept. Then, as I started to drift off to sleep, the words to one of my mother's favorite sayings drifted back into my mind. It was a message I'll never forget a second time.

"Beauty lies in the eye of the beholder, son," she would say, nodding her graying head.

No truer words were ever spoken, was the last thought I remember before snuggling close to Aimee and falling asleep.

KING OF THE SEAS

LONDON, ENGLAND APRIL 7ᵀᴴ, 1768

I'm sure everyone has at least one relative they dislike with a passion. I know I certainly do. In my family, it's detestable Uncle Rolland Crabb. As big a money-grubbing, backstabbing, all-round bitter bastard as was ever born.

Rolland is the managing partner of Halton, Barney & Crabb, one of England's largest importers of general merchandise. Exotic products flowed into the company's vast array of warehouses from all parts of the world.

The business is obscenely profitable because our leader rules the company with an iron hand. The Crabb, as we refer to him, is always on the lookout for the next penny to squeeze.

If I had a choice, I'd stay as far away from this irritating little man as possible. However, circumstances didn't leave me with much of an alternative. Unfortunately, my late father, William Whitehall the Third, had proved to be as inept at gambling as he was in running the family estate. On my father's death, instead of inheriting an estate of some substance, I found myself surrounded by hordes of unhappy creditors, all demanding to be paid immediately. The alternative was the debtor's prison.

This sad state of affairs caused me to be placed under the wing of Rolland, my mother's older brother. My uncle is the type of man who doesn't take kindly to fools or needy relatives. In his lofty opinion, I appear to fit into both those categories.

I suppose, in the spirit of fairness, there is a tiny grain of truth behind his negative opinion of me. At the age of twenty-four, I've been living a rather good life in London up until now. After being born and bred on our estate in Wiltshire, England, I considered working to be an affront to my position as a gentleman. I also think it highly unfair that Rolland insists I show up for work as his special assistant.

Despite my protests that my position at Halton, Barney & Crabb was only a temporary situation, my friends at the Mayfair Club take great delight in referring to me as 'the shopkeeper.' In fact, I was enjoying a mid-afternoon refreshment with these same friends at the club when my uncle's man, Grumbles, rudely interrupted to summon me to his master's presence.

"Sorry to interrupt yer pleasures, sir," Grumbles whined. "Mister Crabb insists you attend him in his office without delay."

I looked at the little man with distaste. As far as I was concerned, Grumbles was a self-serving lackey who would climb over your still twitching corpse if it helped him shine in the Crabb's eyes.

I turned to my friends, "Sorry to scoot before the bill arrives, chaps. Duty calls, and I must obey. Look after my share, will you?"

A litany of outrageous comments about my financial status followed our departure from the club. I took it in stride.

After all, what are friends for?

"I say, Grumbles, do you know what the Crabb wants?" I asked as our hackney cab rumbled over the cobblestone streets.

"No, sir. But he's right fit to be tied," Grumbles chortled.

I knew Rolland's man took great delight in seeing me humbled in front of his boss. I had a feeling from Grumble's sly smile that I was in for another tirade. Unfortunately for me, my instincts proved correct when, a short while later, I found myself standing like an errant schoolboy in front of Rolland's massive desk.

"Where the bloody hell have you been, Jeremy?" Uncle Crabb demanded as he laid his quill pen aside.

I looked at the shriveled, dried-up carcass on the other side of the ink-stained desk. I tried to keep my face from showing my true inner feelings. It was difficult because Rolland was eating and shouting at me at the same time. As usual, today's lunch was beef drippings on black bread. As uncle ranted, tiny bits of beef fat sprayed out in my direction.

"Sorry, uncle. I was unexpectedly called away by an important matter," I muttered as I wiped a gob of suet from my lapel.

Crabb snorted. "Horse-feathers. You're busy doing nothing as usual. This wasting your life on drink, gambling, and vulgar women has got to stop. It's time for you to start performing, or else."

I had an uneasy feeling I was about to find out first hand what the Crabb's message of what "or else" meant. I was hoping whatever upcoming odious task he had in mind wouldn't take too long to accomplish. My overriding ambition at the moment was to finish the job and get back to the delights of London as soon as I could.

"Candles," the Crabb grunted. "What do you know about them?"

"I don't know much," I said, trying to suppress a grin. "But I'm sure you will enlighten me on the subject."

"Don't be an ass," the Crabb snapped. "Candles are the biggest profit maker we have. Or at least they were."

"What's happened?"

"If you paid a penny's worth of attention, you would be well aware that those thieving upstarts in the colonies are bleeding us dry."

Despite my lack of interest in the subject, I listened with half an ear while the Crabb droned on. At the end of his diatribe, I learned that the cost of high-quality candles had been climbing steeply. My uncle's fury was fueled even further by news of a price increase from our Yankee suppliers that would soon effectively double the current price.

"If those traitorous scum think they have me over a barrel, they have another think coming," the Crabb fumed.

"Can't we simply buy our supply somewhere else?" I ventured.

"No, you dolt. The best candles in the world are made from high-quality whale oil. Those twats in New England control the entire supply of the raw materials. They weren't happy with the obscene profits from trading oil, so they started their own manufacturing capability."

I tried to smother my yawn. "This is all very educational, sir, but what does it have to do with me?"

When the Crabb turned his ferocious gaze in my direction, I tried to shrink back in the old horsehair stuffed chair waiting behind me. I had a sinking feeling that I was about to find out that what he had in mind for me would be disastrous.

As it turned out, I was right on the money.

"Against my better judgment," the Crabb scowled, "I'm going to send you to the colonies on a mission of great importance to this company."

"I'm sorry," I gasped. "Where did you say I was going?"

"The colonies. To the island of Nantucket, to be precise. It's the main location for the den of thieves who are trying to hold us for ransom. I've decided it's past time for us to control our own source of supply."

"But, Uncle," I protested. "Wouldn't it be easier just to pay the Yankee's exorbitant price increase and then gouge our loyal customers as you've always done before?"

"Don't be impudent," Rolland snapped. "We need a long-term strategy to keep these vampires from draining us dry. We're going to end this now, once and for all."

"Even If I were to make a dangerous trek to the wilds of America, what am I expected to do?"

"After you arrive in Nantucket, you're to get inside one of their blasted candle factories. I don't care how. Once inside, you have to uncover any specialized manufacturing secrets they might have. Also, you need to be on the lookout for any of the suppliers who may be vulnerable so we can buy them out cheaply."

Knowing the way Uncle Crabb's devious mind worked, I wasn't surprised. He was pissed off at the idea of someone else making a profit. I was sure once Halton, Barney & Crabb got a toehold in Nantucket, the company would undercut all the remaining suppliers to the point of bankruptcy. From that day on, the world supply of quality candles would be controlled by the Crabb.

"Surely there are many other better-qualified staff members for this particular assignment," I stammered as I searched desperately for a way out. "I have absolutely no knowledge of candles or Nantucket. My schedule is terribly full at this time, as well."

The Crabb shook his heavy jowls. "No. It's well past time for you to start earning your keep. You'll do as I say, or you'll never see another farthing from this firm or me."

This last threat definitely caught my attention. Lately, I found it increasingly difficult to keep up with my bills at the club, let alone the incessant demands from my landlady and tailor. Without Uncle Crabb's benevolent hand-outs, I would be on the streets or worse.

I decided to play along, hoping that the old geezer would change his mind—anything to buy myself more time to come up with an exit strategy.

"Having our own factory sounds like a brilliant idea, uncle. Perhaps you give me some guidance on how I might go about fulfilling your wishes?" I asked hopefully.

"I don't give a rat's droppings how you do it," the Crabb snarled. "You have two important tasks to achieve in Nantucket. Discover their trade secrets and find me a vulnerable target. No excuses are acceptable. Don't even think about returning to London, ever again, unless you are successful with both of them. There will be nothing here for you."

"On the surface, it appears to me you're instructing me to do some things unfitting for a gentleman," I protested. "I'll have to give the matter some serious thought."

"No, you won't," the Crabb snarled. "You're booked passage on the Royal Mail ship tomorrow morning. Be on it, or don't come back."

With a careless wave of his hand, Rolland dismissed me. I slunk out of his office then headed for the warm and welcoming sanctuary of my club. After boarding a Hansom cab outside on the street, I sat back deep in thought, lulled by the monotonous beat of the horse's iron-shod hoofs on the cobblestones.

I didn't like my Uncle Rolland very much. Privately, I considered him to be a money-grubbing tightwad with no redeeming graces. He was a spiteful old man to boot. However, with no other income source outside of my job at the firm and a small monthly allowance,

I had no choice but to consider attempting to carry out my uncle's instructions.

When my carriage drew to a stop in front of the club, I threw my cape around my shoulders and tipped the driver a tuppence. Then, as I stepped out onto the muddy road, a swarm of begging orphans quickly besieged me with grubby hands outstretched. I threw all my loose change in the air before entering the club to a rousing chorus of, "Thank you, kind sir."

I felt sorry for the little beggars. Times were tough, forcing the young hordes to roam the streets of London at all hours searching for hand-outs.

The doorman, Bentley, took my top hat and cape before escorting me to the member's private gaming salon. The elegant room was thick with blue cigar smoke but not dense enough to hide the shapely figure of Constance Kingman. As usual, she was flirting with a table of card players.

She stopped abruptly when she spotted me, then excused herself from the men at the table, promising to return soon.

In an era when women were expected to be seen and not heard, Constance was an anomaly. From all outward appearances, her role appeared to be as a hostess for the club. I was one of the very few people who knew Constance was, in fact, a significant shareholder in the Mayfair. Over time Connie had become a wealthy woman.

I was quite fond of the lady, and possibly, in the future, it could lead to something more long-lasting. Connie was a beautiful, intelligent, and lustful woman. I knew she wanted more than a dalliance, but right now, my life was in too much turmoil to get involved in something long-term.

She advanced with a broad, flirtatious smile on her face. I met her halfway. She kissed me warmly on both cheeks before embracing me. She examined my face for a clue as to the outcome of my meeting with the Crabb.

"Was it bad, Jeremy?"

"Worse than bad, I'm afraid, my dear. It was downright disastrous."

"That sounds ominous. What did your uncle want?"

"The doddering old fool wants to send me the blasted colonies. I'm supposed to sabotage the Yankee candle-making establishment single-handed."

I was affronted when Connie broke out into uncontrolled laughter.

"Surely, you're jesting," she chortled. "It strains the boundaries of credibility to picture you as a secret agent."

"That's no way to talk to a man of my accomplishments," I huffed. "I came to ask for your advice. Now, I'm not sure I want it."

"Don't be a ninny," Constance said with a smile. "Come with me. We'll have a drink, then solve all your problems."

After Connie led me to a private table in a quiet corner of the club, she ordered a bottle of champagne and two glasses. When the bubbling concoction was served, she leaned forward to take my hand.

"Tell me what's happening. I'm worried about you,"

"I'm at a crossroads, Connie," I confessed. "There's no getting around it. The Crabb is a vile and ruthless man. He's ordered me to do some things that I think are quite dastardly. The problem is, if I don't follow his instructions to the letter, he's promised to dismiss me from the firm and discontinue any further allowances."

Connie poured more champagne then encouraged me to give her more details. I trusted her as a friend and a confidant, so I continued the sad story.

"In a nutshell, I'm to go to this God-forsaken Nantucket place on my own. When I arrive, he expects me to lie, cheat, and do whatever is necessary to steal information from the Nantucket candle suppliers. All to fuel his ultimate goal of driving them out of business."

I stopped talking when the waiter arrived to pour the remainder of the champagne. In response to the man's unspoken question, Connie nodded her head for another bottle.

"I believe in competition as much as the next fellow," I continued after the waiter departed. "But what the Crabb wants me to do is indecent. I don't want to end up hating myself for being a rotter."

"That won't happen, Jeremy. I know you."

"I appreciate your support, "I said quietly. "Still, I have to make a timely decision. What do you think I should do?"

I knew I could count on Connie to speak her mind. My friend was many things, but above all, she was a realist.

"Jeremy, it would appear you don't have much choice. If you fail to do as your uncle says, you'll end up here in London for the rest of your days. You'll still be a gentleman, but unfortunately, my dear, a penniless one."

I nodded. "So, I'm faced with an age-old dilemma. I have two choices, money or principles? But I'm not sure I could live with myself if I do as he wants."

"Unfortunately, there's no future here for a gentleman without prospects," Connie stated bluntly. "If you don't make the trip to the Colonies, I worry you might end up as a drunken wastrel or worse."

"I'm afraid I wouldn't have the funds to be a drunken wastrel," I said in jest. "In which case, I'll find out what you mean by 'or worse.'"

"When do you have to decide?"

"That's the bad news, Connie. Unless I choose to defy the Crabb. I have to sail from London on tomorrow's late morning tide."

Connie's delicate features darkened, mirroring her concern at the import of my words. We sat in silence, each thinking our own thoughts until she rose to her feet. She extended her hand to me while signaling to our waiter at the same time.

"Egbert," she instructed. "Please have the second bottle of champagne sent to my chambers. Make sure we are undisturbed for the balance of the day. Mr. Whitehall and I need to have a serious conversation."

Without disclosing too many salacious details, I can say that most of the serious conversation took place under the frilled canopy of Connie's comfortable bed. When the non-verbal part of our meeting ended, I lay back, struggling for breath.

"My goodness, Constance. You never fail to amaze me," I panted. "Even knowing full well what a lusty wench you are, that experience was beyond my wildest dreams."

"I wanted to make sure you would have something to remember," Connie grinned. "In case some native girl tries to entice you to stay in the colonies."

I looked at Connie lying stretched out beside me. I'm taller than any of my friends, but she was almost my height. Her full-bodied figure, long silky ash blonde hair, coupled with milky white skin, showed hints of a Nordic ancestry, no doubt inherited from some long-ago marauding Viking raid.

In vivid contrast, my coal-black hair, dusky complexion, and rapier slim body could be traced back to the Norman invaders. And, in all modesty, we were both considered attractive specimens by our many admirers. We always drew admiring glances when we entered any room together.

"You would be a difficult woman to forget under any circumstances, my dear. Besides, I haven't yet decided if I'm going to go to Nantucket."

Connie reached across to gently stroke my hair. "Why don't you stay here tonight? Perhaps after a good night's sleep, you'll know what to do."

Her suggestion surprised me. Up until now, one of Connie's unbending rules prohibited any overnight stay.

"Of course, my dear," I agreed. "What changed your mind?"

Connie looked into my eyes for a long, silent moment before she spoke. I could see she was fighting to hold back tears.

"I'm a realist, Jeremy," she said quietly. "I know full well this may be the last time I ever get to hold you in my arms, so I'm going to take advantage of it."

In the ensuing lapses between being taken advantage of, I lay in the darkness, turning over all the various possibilities in my mind. Then shortly after the faint light of dawn filtered through Connie's bedroom window, I made my decision.

● ● ● ●

I must have drifted back to sleep because I didn't awaken until the tantalizing twin odors of fried bacon and freshly brewed coffee assailed my nostrils. I quickly dressed then moved to join Constance in her drawing-room.

One of the club staff had set up the breakfast table with a sumptuous feast of crisp bacon, plump grilled sausages, scrambled eggs, and mushrooms. A plate of baked scones sat beside a mound of strawberry preserves and a jug of clotted cream.

Connie, glowing from a hot bath, sat smiling at the end of the table. She was enjoying a cup of Twinings tea.

"Good morning, sleepyhead. How are you this morning?"

"Tired and full of aches," I grinned. "I feel like a thoroughbred steed that has been ridden hard over a never-ending obstacle course."

"You're too soft. You need to toughen up," Connie said with a smile. "Now, come and join me before the food cools."

I took a seat at the table, then filled my platter from the extensive offerings. The night's sensual exertions had given me a raging hunger, so I refilled my plate. After the second cup of coffee, I sat back and smiled affectionately at my hostess.

"I say, Constance. One could get used to living high on the hog's back. It certainly beats the watery porridge I get from my miserly landlady."

"Don't get used to it," Connie laughed. "It was a one-night aberration. Besides, I have a feeling you won't be here long enough for a second visit, right?"

I nodded. "It was difficult, but I've made my decision. I'll go on the trip as instructed, and I'll try to do as the Crabb has ordered. But only if I can find a way to do it without causing significant harm. Maybe then, I'll be able to live with my conscience."

"That sounds like a good compromise," Connie said quietly, "You're a rogue and a wastrel, but you're also loveable and quite intelligent. I have a feeling everything will work out for the best in the end."

I reluctantly stood to leave. "I best be gone now, luv. Do take care of yourself. I'll miss your smiling face no end."

Connie rose from her seat, then moved over to give me a farewell hug. I could feel her shaking as she lay her soft face against my shoulder.

"Never forget," she sobbed. "No matter what fate may hold for you, if you ever find yourself in trouble, you'll always have a true friend waiting for you on this side of the ocean."

I squeezed her tightly, then turned and quickly departed before the sob rising in my throat could escape to join with hers. I felt overcome with sadness. I didn't want to leave, but I had little choice.

To avoid wagging tongues, I slipped out the club's side entrance and then made my way back to my lodgings. I still needed to pack my trunk, but I didn't want to run afoul of Mrs. Mildred McCabe. The old Scottish landlady and I didn't see eye to eye on the matter of rent. She unrealistically seemed to expect it would be paid in a timely manner.

Like clockwork, the old girl left for the shops at 11:00 a.m. as she did every day but Sunday. I skulked around the corner until I spotted her departure, then I hot-footed it for my rooms. I slipped up the stairs, opened my door, only to freeze on the spot.

"Grumbles," I exclaimed. "What the bloody hell are you doing in my room?"

"It weren't my doing," he whined. "Mister Crabb sent me with your ticket for the boat."

"Well, hand it over, then get the hell out of here," I demanded.

Grumble's shook his wizened head. "Can't. Mister Crabb's instructions. I'm to see you board the ship, then report back to him."

I seethed internally as I packed my belongings in a travel trunk. *Just like my blasted uncle to send a spy in case I change my mind.*

Grumbles watched my every move as I packed. When I finished, I made him drag the trunk out to the street while I hailed a passing carriage. After my luggage was aboard, I climbed in, then shut the carriage door in Grumble's face.

"Oi, what about me?" Grumbles grumbled.

"Find your own damned way," I snapped before giving the driver instructions.

We drove off, leaving the Crabb's spy standing in the dust.

The Royal Mail ship, *HMS TRENT*, due to sail on the morning tide, was in the final stages of departure when I rushed aboard. Before going below to my cabin, I searched the street for any sign of Grumbles. Fortunately, the road was empty save for the dockworkers loading last-minute cargo.

Good, I thought. *The Crabb will suffer in limbo. It will drive him crazy not knowing for sure if I departed on the ship or whether I'm hiding out in the city.*

Ten minutes into my unpacking, an urgent rapping summoned me to the cabin door. I opened it to see a smiling young seaman. "Sorry to bother you, sir," he apologized. "A man who claims to be your valet is here. He insists he must see you on an urgent matter."

Although my first inclination was to instruct the seaman to throw the caller into the harbor, I changed my mind when a better solution struck me.

"Very well," I said. "Show him below."

A few moments later, Grumbles arrived. He sauntered into my cabin, sporting a self-satisfied smirk on his ugly face.

"Urgent matter?" I demanded.

Grumbles fumbled inside his badly stained vest, then withdrew a long white envelope. I recognized the Crabb's distinctive scrawl, even from a distance.

"Mister Crabb said I was to give this to you but only after I saw you on the ship with my own eyes," Grumbles said smugly. "I'm supposed to wait on the dock to make sure you don't do a runner with the envelope before the ship sails."

My eyes widened when I opened the envelope to see fifty guineas, a princely sum. The note enclosed instructed me in no uncertain terms to use the funds exclusively for bribes. I was also warned that a strict accounting would be required on my return to London.

When the ship's horn sounded a blast signaling an imminent

departure, Grumbles headed for the cabin exit. Just before he reached the door, I snatched him by the scruff of the neck then deposited him behind the sturdy wardrobe door. I ignored the muffled screams for help, locked the wardrobe, then made my way up to the top deck.

Within a matter of minutes, the gangplank was retracted, and the *HMS TRENT* started to slowly move away from the dock. As I stood there watching the shoreline disappear in the morning mist, I wondered if I would ever see Connie and London again.

Then I headed below to deal with my 'valet.'

● ● ● ●

After all sight of the land had disappeared from view, I returned to my cabin. Even before I opened the door, I could hear muffled cries escaping from the locked wardrobe. When I opened the door, Grumbles stumbled out onto the cabin floor.

"Damn you, sir!" Grumbles exclaimed angrily. "Mister Crabb will hear of this despicable deed."

"It's far more likely Mister Crabb will conclude you've run off with his fifty guineas," I said with a grin. "In fact, I wouldn't be surprised if he's already contacted the coppers."

Grumble's face fell, "I must get to the office and set him right."

"Good luck, unless you can quickly sprout a set of wings. We must be several miles offshore by now."

"I'll have the captain turn back," Grumbles blustered. "I'll tell him I've been kidnapped, I will."

"A small problem with that, old chap," I drawled. "You have already mistakenly informed the crew that you were my valet."

"I had no choice," Grumbles sniveled. "The crew wouldn't let me come aboard."

"Well, you have a choice now. You can finish the voyage as my valet or be locked up for the duration as a stowaway."

Grumbles looked so distraught I almost felt sorry for him. At least

Spinning My Wheels

until I recalled how the sniveling coward took great delight in reporting every minor transgression of mine to the Crabb.

"Cheer up, Grumbles," I said. "At least you'll get a sea voyage out of it."

"What am I expected to do as your valet?" Grumbles asked fearfully.

"Oh, the usual. Wash my laundry. Keep the cabin clean, fetch and carry as I see fit, and generally make yourself useful."

"And where am I to sleep?"

"With the crew, of course. After you unpack my bags, you can search out the first mate and report to him. Tell him I sent you."

After Grumbles reluctantly departed, I went for a tour of the ship. Before long, I bumped into Captain Magnum Scott. I could see from his straightforward manner that he was well respected by the crew.

"Welcome aboard, Mister Whitehall," the Captain roared, "The TRENT is mainly a mail and cargo ship. We only have six passengers aboard. I've already made the acquaintance of the others, so that's how I knew your name."

"It's a pleasure to meet you, Captain. Please call me Jeremy if you will."

"The passengers eat at my table, Jeremy. Please join us at four bells sharp. I must excuse myself now. I have to make my rounds."

● ● ● ●

During dinner that night, I had my first stroke of luck. One of the passengers, Jack Grimsby, had spent most of his working life as a whaler out of Nantucket. Now retired, he was returning to the island after visiting a relative in London.

Like many of his ilk, old Jack loved to talk about his past glories. He was indeed a 'blue water' man, having gone to sea at the age of fourteen. I told him I was fascinated with whaling life and planned to write a book on the subject for the university. I felt terrible about lying to the man, but I needed to learn from him. The potential book was as good an excuse as I could think of.

I arranged to meet Jack at the stern the following morning after breakfast. When I showed up with a notebook, the old whaler was already at the rail. Fumes from his ancient pipe drifted through the cool morning air.

"I never tire of staring at the sea," the old salt said as he gazed out at the ship's turbulent wake.

"It does have a primeval beauty," I agreed.

"Aye, but it can be a cruel master too. I've seen storms at sea so frightening as to bring tears to the eyes of the most hardened of sailors."

"I'm sure you have," I agreed. "Now, tell me about your years as a whaler."

"I loved it, but it's a right-hard life."

"Well, why do men do it?" I asked.

Jack stared at me. He had that faraway look in his eyes that I would come to learn was the hallmark of an old salt.

"Have you ever heard of a Nantucket sleigh ride?" Jack asked softly.

"No."

"Until you experience one yourself, you'll never know real excitement, lad."

"Tell me about this sleigh ride."

Jack nodded. "We always hunt the whales in small boats. Once a big sperm whale sounds, our man jabs it with the harpoon. When the beast feels the bite of iron, it heads for the safety of the depths as fast as it can go. Our front man pays out the line as fast as he can. We all hold our breath praying like hell the spermer will surface before we run out of cable…"

"Why?" I interrupted out of a compelling curiosity.

"Sometimes, the rope is strung out hundreds of yards. If the whale is still heading for the bottom when the rope runs out, the crew only has two chances. Cut the line or be dragged down to Davy

Jones locker. I've seen many a man meet their death in the bosom of the sea when they couldn't cut the cable fast enough."

"So, if the wounded whale surfaces, the chase is over?"

"Mostly when the whale sounds, it's mortally wounded," Jack said softly. "But sometimes the harpoon isn't fully embedded. If that's the case, the beast will often take off at high speed, dragging the small boat behind it. It's the most frightening experience you can imagine. The men can only hold on for dear life, petrified the whale will head for the bottom at any moment."

"My God," I exclaimed. "Have you ever been on one of these rides?"

"Aye. Several times," Jack said. "On every occasion, we ended up being dragged miles away from the mothership. My first Nantucket sleigh ride almost cost me my life. We were under water four times before it ended. One lad was so frightened he actually shite himself."

Throughout our trip, Jack became an invaluable source of information. He had amassed a horde of books on Nantucket and the whaling industry during his years at sea. Eager to share his knowledge, he loaned me these treasures. I spent most of my days locked in my cabin, devouring the contents of the volumes.

I learned from my readings that Nantucket, in 1768, was the whaling capital of the world. Ships departed and arrived every day of the week. The voyages, sometimes stretching for years, combed the world's oceans in a constant search for the elusive sperm whale.

● ● ● ●

One day I had accumulated so many questions, I asked Jack to join me in my cabin for lunch. To my great surprise, Grumbles didn't object when I added the task of serving the meal to his list of jobs. In fact, the Crabb's man appeared to be taking a liking to life at sea.

At lunch, it wasn't difficult getting Jack to talk, especially after a few drams of brandy from my stores, when he became downright expansive.

"Tell me what happens after you harpoon a whale," I asked.

Jack nodded grimly, "That's when the backbreaking, filthy work starts. The black, smoke-belching fires are lit, then we start boiling the oil from huge chunks of blubber. Everything stinks."

"How much oil do you get from a whale?"

"Depends on the whale, you lubber," Jack laughed. "A big 'un might hit 100 barrels but on average maybe 40 to 50."

"Still, that sounds like it would make a large pile of candles to me."

"No," Jack said with a shake of his head. "Most whale oil goes for other uses. For the best candles, you have to use spermaceti."

Jack went on to explain that spermaceti was a waxy liquid substance harvested only from cavities inside the skull of the whale. Quite different from the common whale oil produced by rendered fat. He said it was the most valuable part of the whale.

"What makes it so valuable?" I asked.

"Spermaceti candles, lad," Jack explained. "Can't make a high-quality smokeless candle without the oil. Everyone wants them, even though they're expensive. They burn with a clear white, smokeless flame."

"Yes," I nodded. "They must be the candles we use at my club in London."

"Many a Nantucket seafaring man has become wealthy from spermaceti oil," Jack added. "Some fellers got so much money they stay ashore now and occupy themselves with ship building and candle making."

I needed clarification on a critical detail before letting Jack go. The Crabb was convinced our New England suppliers were creating an artificial shortage of spermaceti oil as an excuse for their exorbitant price increases on candles. Perhaps old Jack could shed some light on the subject.

"One last question, Jack. This spermaceti oil seems to be quite critical to making a quality candle. Is there an ample supply?"

"Well, son, let me tell you. The sea gives, and the sea takes. Many things have a bearing on the whaler's success. Weather, skill, the vagaries of the whale's food supply, pirates, and more. Sometimes there's a surplus of spermaceti, and at other times there's a dearth."

"How about now? Is there a surplus or a dearth?"

"There's a rumor of something terrible happening to the whaling fleet. I have no first-hand knowledge, and I'm not one to talk about rumors. I'm sure you'll find your fill when we get to Nantucket."

Despite my coaxing, Jack wouldn't say another word about the mysterious happenings. After he departed, I returned to my reading until I heard a knock on the cabin door. Grumbles entered, carrying a pot of hot tea from the galley. I was surprised as he did this without my asking.

"I must say, Grumbles, you're turning out to be a far better valet than one could have imagined. The Crabb will be impressed with the skills I've taught you."

"I'm not going back," Grumbles stated firmly. "I'll never work for that blood-sucking bastard again."

"That's surprising," I said. "What do you have in mind?"

"Captain Scott says there's a berth for me aboard the TRENT. I'm going to sign on for the duration."

From that day on, I looked at Grumbles in a new light. I hadn't quite realized the maligning influence he was exposed to working at the beck and call of the Crabb. For the balance of the voyage, I treated him more as a traveling companion than a valet, although he still preferred to take his meals with the crew.

On our last night at sea, before arriving in Nantucket, I made him share a table and a bottle of wine to celebrate his new life. I topped it off with half the contents of the Crabb's bribery fund.

He slept that night as a happy man.

● ● ● ●

Twenty-three days after leaving London, the Royal Mail ship, *RMS TRENT*, glided gently to a complete stop at the Town of Nantucket's main wharf. I stood at the rail and cast a jaundiced eye through the early morning mist at the small weathered town. I couldn't help comparing it in my mind to the magnificent city I had left behind.

Now, with the boat safely docked, I set off to explore the waterfront. My first challenge was to establish a base. Then, just a short distance from the jetty, I spotted the Seafarer's Inn on Water Street. It appeared clean enough, so I booked a single room with meals from the grubby landlord.

After changing into clothing more suitable for my mission, I ventured back out into the driving rain.

I wanted to assess the possibility of putting my uncle's plan into action quickly so I could return to the pleasures of London without delay. I had a slight difficulty in walking on the cobblestones after spending weeks on a pitching platform. Despite my mobility problem, I began to wander the maze of Nantucket's streets, looking for the factory district.

I soon found the area as the town wasn't that big. The first candle manufacturer I happened upon had a hand-lettered 'Help Wanted' sign posted prominently in the grubby front window. It was an old red, two-story, brick structure sitting on the tail end of Straight Wharf Lane.

The faded sign on the roof read, *RICHARD MITCHELL & SON*. The clapboard building looked severely in need of repairs.

I knocked briefly on the old warped wooden door and entered. The interior light was dim, but I could still make out the form of an attractive young lady sitting behind a roll-top desk. She looked up with a quizzical expression on her face. My face reddened when I realized I was staring.

I stammered, "Excuse me, Miss, would Mr. Mitchell or his son be available?"

She laughed. "Well, Captain Mitchell is down at the docks getting the *Sea Rogue* ready for her next whaling trip. But I should warn you if you go anywhere near him while he's so engaged, I guarantee he'll bite your head off."

"Would it be possible then to have a word with Captain Mitchell's son?"

The girl's face saddened. "You would have to go and find Davy Jones' Locker if you want to talk to our Ned. He was lost at sea two years ago."

I felt myself blushing as I became more tongue-tied by the minute. I was about to make a hasty retreat when the young lady took pity on me.

"You can deal with me if you like. My name is Betsy Mitchell. I'm in charge when my father's not here."

"I'm Jeremy Whitehall, just arrived from London," I said. "I'm hoping to write a book on the whaling industry for my university. I need to find employment while I'm here."

Betsy laughed again. "You certainly don't look like a candle maker, so I assume you're applying for the job as our bookkeeper."

I nodded as Betsy outlined the salary and other terms of the job. I thanked her then quickly accepted the position. At this point, I would have taken the job without pay. Luck was with me. Here I was on the first day of my assignment, and I already had a toehold.

Evidently, Betsy liked her new applicant's looks because she told me to report for work the following day. When she extended her hand to seal the arrangement, I found it incredibly soft and delicate. I quickly dropped my prolonged hold after her face took on a pretty pink hue.

After returning to the Seafarer's Inn, I unpacked my few belongings before joining a group of local sailors in the smoke-filled pub. I ordered a bowl of Nantucket fish chowder with a pint of ale, then sat quietly listening to the conversations. A few of the men had just returned from a long whaling voyage. When they lifted their glasses to toast four of their shipmates who had died at sea, I joined in.

"Could I ask how they perished?" I asked quietly.

"It was yon bloody '*King of the Seas*' agin," a grizzled old salt replied. "We had just stuck a small spermer with our 'poon when he attacked our whaleboats. We don't normally take the small 'uns, but we were desperate. Our holds were almost empty."

Another whaler joined in, "Aye, it was lucky any of us escaped from that killer to live to tell the tale."

I bought several rounds of dark rum for the sailors, encouraging them to tell the whole story of their voyage. In particular, I wanted to hear more about the creature they called King of the Seas.

"He's been given the name, King, but everyone knows he's the devil himself," said a colored man who called himself Dark Billy.

After listening and drinking, I soon discovered the *King of the Seas* was a gigantic rogue sperm whale creating havoc with the whaling fleet. According to my new friends, all the whalers lived in constant fear of running afoul of the beast. Lately, many men were refusing to sail.

Dark Billy slurred, "Aye, it's only a matter of time before the beast starts attacking the mother ship as well as the small whaleboats." The others all nodded in agreement.

"I won't be going back to sea," said one of the men as he crossed himself. "Too many dangers out there with the King just waiting for us to show up."

Although the Crabb was convinced the Yankee's were plotting against him, I was starting to see at least one reason for the shortage of spermaceti oil. Possibly the seafarers of Nantucket were telling the truth. With the *King of the Seas* on the rampage, some of the candle shortage could be legitimate, after all.

After a restless night, I showed up early at the old brick building. Betsy Mitchell was already at her desk. She gave me a complete tour of the operations. It soon became evident that Betsy was quite knowledgeable about all aspects of the delicate art of spermaceti candle making. However, I have to admit I found it difficult to concentrate.

Betsy's freshly scrubbed appearance and the delicate bone structure of her face were much more interesting to study than the factory's operations.

Over the next few weeks, against my instincts, I tried to concentrate on the spy mission the Crabb had forced on me. In my new position as the bookkeeper, it was crystal clear to me that the daily operations of *RICHARD MITCHELL & SON* were severely impacted by the shortage of spermaceti oil. Betsy and her father would be easy pickings for a greedy bastard like Uncle Rolland if something didn't change soon.

I had still not met Captain Mitchell in person. Betsy explained that her father was away on a trip to Boston to meet with his bankers, trying to line up desperately needed credit for his next voyage. Betsy said she hoped I could meet her father before he sailed on the *Sea Rogue* on July 5th for the north coast of Brazil.

Because Betsy was worried about the family business, she slowly started sharing her concerns with me. We had lunch together on a picnic table under a gnarled old apple tree almost every day. One particular day, Betsy was upset because she still hadn't heard from her father.

"I hope nothing has happened to him," she fretted. "Boston is a rough place these days. He should have been back by now."

In a friendly gesture of comfort, I took Betsy's hand. Then I dropped it quickly when I felt a jolt of electricity. Betsy must have felt the surge, too, because her face flushed. She abruptly stood and returned to her office.

I sat and tried to make sense of it all. Something about this vulnerable woman was getting to me. I was aware that Betsy aroused far different feelings in me than Constance Kingman ever had. I resolved to spend more time exploring the mystery of Betsy. In fact, I planned to spend as much time as possible.

Unfortunately, affairs of the heart sometimes travel a twisted path. My plans were soon derailed by an accidental misfortune.

• • • •

STOWAWAY

July 4th, 1768. The day I found myself running for my life, literally.

The highly agitated man on the other end of the wickedly sharp whaler's harpoon chasing me at full speed was none other than Captain Richard Mitchell, Betsy's father.

I was in imminent danger of losing my life, and it was all because of a slight misunderstanding.

Betsy had been giving me a tour of the new family barn. She innocently suggested I try the hayloft as a potential replacement for the expensive room I had at the Seafarer's Inn. To test the softness of the new-mown hay, I lay down and pretended to sleep. When she started to giggle, just as a jest, I had pulled her down beside me.

"I could become accustomed to this rather quickly," I said as I wrapped my arms around her soft body. Although my intentions were honorable, I can't honestly say they would have remained that way for long. Especially when she responded enthusiastically to my embrace.

Unfortunately, the innocent scene took place only moments before her father unexpectedly arrived. Obviously, the good Captain had badly misread the situation. This became apparent when he bellowed in rage, then turned and ran for the main house after seeing us entwined.

"Run!" Betsy panicked. "He's gone to the house for a weapon. If my father gets his hands on a harpoon, he'll kill you for sure."

"I'm staying," I protested. "Your father simply misread the situation. Surely, I can explain everything to him. I don't want to leave you right now."

She shook her head violently. "When he's in one of his rages, Papa won't listen to reason. Please, for my sake, go now."

I didn't want to go, but Betsy convinced me my life was in danger. Before I scampered, she took a chain holding an engraved, silver heart-shaped locket from her neck, then gently lowered it over my head.

"Keep this with you," Betsy panted. "It will protect you and keep you from harm until it's safe to return." Then she embraced me and kissed me full on the lips.

I swore I would return as soon as I could, then fled out into the rainy night with her angry father close on my heels.

I could almost feel the point of the harpoon on my backside when, with a sudden oath, Captain Mitchell slipped on the wet cobblestones causing him to fall face-first onto a pile of recently deposited steaming horse droppings.

I took advantage of this sudden break by quickly turning into a darkened alleyway leading down to the docks. I searched for a haven where I could hide from the wrath of my pursuer. Still, the area was devoid of any piles of cargo or any obvious shelter. Not far behind me, the sounds of rage echoed in the night air.

A long line of darkened ships were tied up in a row along the jetty. With no sign of any crew activity, I assumed they were all at the inn for their evening meal. I picked the third ship in the line at random, then quietly climbed the gangplank to the main deck. A wooden staircase led below decks through an open hatchway.

The stairs descended into a large open storeroom containing numerous sets of canvas sails. I burrowed beneath a pile of damp sails, lying quietly, trying to control the violent beating of my heart and muffle the sounds of my frantic breathing.

I froze as Betsy's father, cursing at the top of his lungs, banged the side of each ship with his harpoon. When he paused beside the boat where I was hiding, I could make out the words he was shouting.

"Come out, you little weasel, and face the music."

Although I was frightened, I tried to stifle my laughter. The captain reeked so terribly from his unfortunate encounter with the horse droppings that the noxious odor was drifting aboard through the open portholes. I pinched my nostrils and lay in darkened silence.

It took a long time before Mitchell abandoned his search. Now, thoroughly exhausted from the events of the day, I decided to stay in place until daybreak and then work out some plan to get things back to normal. It would be suicide if I chanced to meet him before he had cooled down long enough for me to explain what I was doing in the hayloft with his only daughter.

I smiled at the memory of the unexpected and enthusiastic kiss I had received from Betsy. I pulled the canvas sail up over my head, held her silver locket gently in my right hand, then slipped into a deep slumber.

• • • •

Footsteps pounding on the deck above my head woke me in a panic. Sunlight streamed through a pothole above my bed. I tossed aside my sail coverings and attempted to stand on the slanted floor.

Christ! I must have slept through the night, I thought.

I rushed to the porthole, peered out to see nothing but wave tops glittering in the morning sun. With nary a sight of land in any direction, my instincts told me I was in serious trouble.

I cautiously climbed the wooden steps to the main deck, then, exiting the hatchway, I collided with a rather large man who was rushing from my blind side. The chap smelled faintly of the essence of horse droppings. The man glared at me.

"Who the hell are you, and what are you doing aboard my ship?" he demanded

The faded captain's hat he wore, coupled with the scent of horse dung, alerted my sleep-deprived brain that I was in the presence of the infamous Captain Benjamin Mitchell. Unfortunately, also along with a shipload of deadly harpoons.

I was reasonably confident that the good captain hadn't had more than a tiny glimpse of me during my escape from the hayloft or at any time during our chase. I decided to bluff it out.

"Sorry, Captain, I came down to the ship late last night to sign on as a crew member, but no one was here. I decided to wait, and I guess I fell asleep."

I didn't realize it then, but the *Sea Rogue* was setting out on an extended voyage, painfully shorthanded. Despite offerings of increased pay, few regulars wanted to risk running afoul of the King of the Seas.

Mitchell stared at me for a prolonged time, trying to decide.

Although I knew from his eyes that I looked too well dressed to be an ordinary seaman, he wavered and finally decided to take a chance.

"All right, you blasted landlubber, get below and sign the crew book," the captain roared. "Mind you, this ain't one of those damned pleasure cruises. You'll work your backside off or get thrown overboard."

As ordered, I hurried below decks, signed the log, and then was shown my new berth in the forecastle, or fo'c'sle as it was known to the seamen. The cramped fo'c'sle was black and slimy with filth, small and hot as an oven—hardly suitable accommodation for a gentleman but preferable to dangling from the end of a harpoon.

Over the next few days, I received an ear full from my new shipmates. I ended up each day bone-tired, dejected and seasick. After learning that many of the whaling expeditions could stretch out over several years, I momentarily contemplated throwing myself over the side. My first ray of hope arose from the unfortunate death of another. It started when I overheard a sad conversation.

"Looks bad for old Mooney," Fred Langford muttered to Knobby, the barrel maker.

"Aye, he'll be over the side by morning, I fear. The captain will be right upset too. He and Mooney have been mates fer years. Still, Mooney had a good run for a man with a bad ticker."

If you never experienced a burial at sea, watching in somber silence as the grey shrouded, weighted corpse plunges into the dark waters of an endless ocean, you'll never know the depths of sadness it can cause. The unfortunate mortal, often thousands of miles away from family and friends destined to lie as an insignificant speck on the lonely ocean floor until eternity ends.

After poor Mooney met his fate, I noticed the captain move to the stern. He took a position there staring at the wake of the *Sea Rogue*. I left him to grieve on his own for over an hour, then I decided to approach.

"I'm terribly sorry about your friend, Captain Mitchell. Have you known him long?"

"Aye. Since we were lads. I've not only lost a good friend today, but I've also lost my only chess opponent as well."

"I play chess on occasion," I ventured.

Mitchell stared at me for a moment. "When you finish your last shift, stop at my cabin. Let's see what you're made of." He nodded, then turned back to stare at the sea.

The captain's invitation made me think again of the contrast between the harsh discipline and class distinction on a typical British ship compared to life aboard the *Sea Rogue*. Although the captain was still very much in command, the atmosphere here was closer to what one might expect in a family-run business.

Soon after showing up at the captain's cabin as arranged, we were engaged in a lively round of chess. The captain was a skillful player, but my many wasted hours at the Mayfair Club gave me a slight advantage. The captain seemed downright pleased when I won the match.

"At last, an opponent worth his salt. Old Mooney was a good counter but not much of a chess player."

"Counter?" I queried.

The Captain chuckled. "Aboard one of yer fancy British ships, Mooney would have held the position of Purser. On our vessel, he's the counter. It's an important job. I'm not sure how I'll be able to replace him."

"I'd be pleased to offer my services," I offered. "I'm good with figures. Best in my class at the university, in fact."

"You realize you'll be responsible for keeping tally of all the ship's supplies and barrels of oil from the hunt?"

"Yes," I nodded.

"We're terribly shorthanded, lad. You'll have to keep up your deck duties as well. Can you handle them both?"

"I'll do my best, Captain."

"I can ask no more from any man," Mitchell said sincerely.

After a week at sea, the *Sea Rogue* ran before the wind on a southeast course, bound for a stopover in Nassau. The captain wanted to top up his water and food provisions before making the long run down to the whaling grounds off the coast of Brazil.

I was on deck, taking my turn at the helm. We hadn't passed another vessel since leaving Nantucket. The salt air and the wind on my face almost made me forget my many troubles. My biggest concern was Betsy. I'm sure as a result of my sudden disappearance, she would assume I had abandoned her.

I was less concerned about Uncle Crabb. If Grumbles did as he professed, the Crabb wouldn't know if I remained in England or caught the mail ship to Nantucket. If I never saw his face again, it wouldn't faze me a bit.

I loved the changing color of the sea as the ship drew closer to the Bahamas. The beautiful shades of emerald green reminded me of Betsy's eyes. In the depths of my daydreams, I failed to hear the captain talking to me.

"Pay attention, you damned lubber!" The Captain barked.

"Sorry, sir, what did you say again?"

"I said, I don't like to spend too much time in Nassau. It's a den of thieves and full of rogues and pirates, too."

"Are we in any danger?"

"Not at the moment," Mitchell said. "The real threat from those blasted pirates will be on our return voyage to Nantucket."

"Why is that?"

"Those damned scavengers wait until the whaling ships have a full cargo of whale oils before they attack. We do all the work, and these blasted heathens take all the profits. But what they are really looking for is any ambergris we might have on board."

"Ambergris? Is that another name for spermaceti?"

"No, it's far more scarce and immensely more valuable. Sperm whales put a slurry from their insides into the ocean. Usually, it sinks, but sometimes it hardens into a ball of ambergris on top of the water. It's even been known to float ashore."

I was puzzled. "Why is it so valuable, Captain?"

"It seems those French fellows can't make their expensive

perfumes without the ambergris," Mitchell chuckled. "I wonder how many of those fancy women know they're spraying themselves with whale shit?"

We approached New Providence Island in the early dawn. After rounding Lighthouse Point, the open harbor lay ahead, its sheltered waters dotted with sailing craft from all parts of the world. With the *Sea Rogue* safely secured to the main wharf in downtown Nassau, the captain invited me to join him later in the day for dinner at the Green Parrot Inn.

Although the small inn, located on a side street off the waterfront, was unofficially recognized as neutral ground, numerous fights had often broken out if pirates and whalers happened to find themselves dining at the same time.

Fortunately, that night, the inn was almost empty. As the evening progressed, Captain Mitchell consumed a large quantity of dark rum. As his mood darkened, he began to talk about the unfortunate death of his son.

"May I ask what happened?"

"Jed was a fine lad. He was in the leading whaleboat that morning. They had just harpooned a small spermer when the cursed *King of the Sea* rose out of the water to smash Jed's boat to splinters. My boy sank like a stone. He didn't have a chance. I'll destroy that beast if I ever get the chance."

"Do you know why the whale attacked them?"

"Who can read the mind of a monster? Something seems to trigger the beast. Maybe, if I ever get close enough, I'll ask him, right before I drive my harpoon between his eyes."

The captain laughed, but I could see tears in his eyes as he spoke. His voice hardened when he talked about Betsy.

"My son is gone, but I still have my wonderful daughter, Betsy. She's my treasure. If I ever find the bounder who was trying to do her wrong in my hayloft, I'll wring his neck without mercy."

Being the bounder in question, I wanted to try and explain the misconception. Still, in the captain's current state, I didn't think it advisable. Instead, I helped him to his feet and escorted him safely back to the ship.

We left the Port of Nassau at daybreak bound for the whaling grounds off Brazil's northern coast. With fair seas and favorable winds, Captain Mitchell told me he expected to be whale hunting within thirty days. I moved slowly up to the bowsprit at the front of the *Sea Rogue* and stared down at the surging white waters streaming off the hull.

"I wonder what dangers await us, out there in this vast and untamed ocean?" I thought.

REVENGE OF THE KING

It had taken the better part of a year foraging off the wild coast of Brazil. Still, the Sea Rogue's holds were now almost full of old oak barrels containing different grades of processed whale oil. The men were tired and ready to see the waiting faces of their loved ones again.

Although we had more than our share of difficult days and despite our ranging over a broad swath of ocean, no sightings of the infamous *King of the Seas* had taken place. I began to wonder if he had fallen victim to another boat's harpoon. Or, perhaps, the King was only a myth after all.

I hardly recognize myself anymore. I boarded the ship as a misfit of little talent. Now, gone was the soft pasty skin of a pampered London dandy, replaced by a sun-bronzed, muscular, competent seaman. I even wore my long black hair in a tarred pigtail like the others.

Over time, Captain Mitchell had grown quite fond of me, almost treating me as a surrogate for his lost son. Although I had grown increasingly fond of the man, I still hadn't broached the subject of my involvement with Betsy. I pledged to myself to have a talk on the return voyage. He entertained me almost every night with tales of his adventures at sea over the years.

"Aye lad, I've had some close calls with rogue whales, foul weather, and even a pirate attack. But when all is said and done, I still love the sea and couldn't picture living any other life."

"A pirate attack? This begs for more telling."

"We were homeward bound with a full cargo when we spotted *The Skeleton Lady* shadowing us off the Bahamas. The crew was petrified because that ship is famous for the cruelty of her master, Black Bart Upton. He leaves no survivors unless he comes across a woman passenger or two." Mitchell grimaced. "In that case, the women would be better served had they died."

"How did you escape?"

"We loaded on all sails, but we were no match for *The Skeleton Lady* heavily loaded as we were. We kept ahead of them through the night, then in the early morning, a British frigate out of Nassau forced Black Bart to flee the scene."

• • • •

At the end of the month, early in the morning, we sighted a school of sperm whales about a half-mile off the starboard bow. Captain Mitchell was in a good mood. Our holds were almost complete, and we planned to turn northwards for home this very day.

"I haven't had a chance to get one of these spermers by myself for a long time," Captain Mitchell chuckled. "The crew usually has all the fun. Come with me. I'll show you how an old salt does it."

"Perhaps I should stay behind," I responded. "I want to do a final inventory count before we head for home."

"Nonsense, lad. You can count barrels any time, but the chance to go on the hunt only comes on rare occasions. Get yourself into the boat."

After our small whaleboat dropped into the choppy sea, we proceeded to chase the pod of sperm whales frolicking on the surface ahead. Mitchell stood poised on the bow; razor-sharp harpoon held at the ready. I smiled because it was evident the captain was enjoying the hunt immensely.

"There's a small 'un ahead. It should be easy pickings," Mitchell drawled. "We'll get this one, boys, then head for home."

I spotted the small whale swimming slowly on the surface, dead ahead. Something about this whale's size kept nagging me in the back of my mind. I tried to recall, knowing the information was quite significant.

Then it dawned on me.

The sailors in the Seafarer's Inn in Nantucket talking about their dead shipmates and Captain Mitchell telling me about the death of his son, Jed. In both cases, the *King of the Seas* had attacked the tiny whaleboats immediately after they harpooned a small whale.

Is it possible that the old sperm whale was only trying to protect the small ones in his herd from danger? I asked myself.

"Captain! Don't do it!" I shouted, just as the captain was about to hurl the harpoon into the exposed flank of the small whale ahead.

I grabbed the line attached to the harpoon, pulling back as hard as I could. Because the captain turned when I shouted, he didn't see the monstrous sperm whale surge from the sea immediately between our boat and the calf.

I couldn't believe my eyes. The giant was close enough for me to have touched him from my seat. The *King of the Seas* was old. He bore numerous scars of past encounters with the whaling fleet. His aged skin was a mottled gray and white and covered with barnacles. The whale kept his position alongside our boat, sheltering the young one with his bulk.

Captain Mitchell was furious. He was helpless to throw the harpoon as long as I kept the line pinned down with my boot.

"Let me kill that damned monster!" Mitchell raged. "That's the devil that took the life of my son."

Still holding the line to prevent the harpoon from being released, I found myself looking directly into the large bloodshot eye of the whale as it swam alongside our boat. The mammal's returning gaze stunned me.

I felt like I was staring into the wisdom of an eternal sea. I could feel the pain radiating from the *King of the Seas*. I know it defies all sense of reason, but, in some subliminal way, it was almost as if the animal knew I had prevented the captain from killing the baby whale.

With a giant flap of his tail, the King turned away from our boat, escorting the small whale into safer waters. The whale's tail movement didn't appear to intentionally cause harm. Still, the unintended surge of the sea caused our small boat to rock violently from side to side.

The sudden motion caused Captain Mitchell to lose his footing and fall. The weight of his fall, combined with the boat's movement, caused the Captain to land heavily on his right side, directly onto the razor-sharp harpoon that lay under him. I rushed to his aid.

"Forget about me," he screamed in pain. "Don't let the beast escape."

When I spotted blood pooling beneath the Captain, I ignored his orders, then instructed the boat crew to head back to the *Sea Rogue* as fast as possible. On the way, I attempted, as best I could, to stop the flow of blood gushing from the captain's side.

The captain screamed in agony as we moved him down the hatchway stairs to his cabin. We doused the wound with rum, then bound it tightly with torn remnants of a bedsheet.

Then, a second disaster happened.

• • • •

When we were hoisting the heavy-set man onto his bunk, the strain caused my shirt buttons to break loose. Now free of confinement, Betsy's unique engraved, heart-shaped locket hung loosely from my neck, in full view of her father.

I tried to hide the locket, but I wasn't quick enough. Recognition flashed in the Captain's eyes. His face glazed over with disgust.

"Oh no, you're the blackguard who took advantage of my Betsy in the barn," he snarled. "I treated you like a son, and this is my repayment. May God curse you forever, Jeremy."

I tried to explain the locket, but the captain couldn't hear me. He had passed out from the pain of his wound. My heart ached from the words of his curse.

For the next several days, Mitchell alternated between episodes of raving delirium and moments when total sanity returned. I remained at his bedside, applying cool cloths to the ailing man's forehead. Even while he slept, I continued to murmur to him about Betsy, what had happened in the hayloft, and my deep feelings for his daughter.

One morning, I awoke instantly aware of the foul odor of gangrene in the cabin. There was no question now. The Captain's wound had become infected. I feared he was close to death. As the day passed and that final moment drew nearer, the captain seemed to regain a little of his old strength. He slowly sat up on his bed, then motioned me to come closer. His voice was low but still understandable.

"I know now that I misjudged you, lad," he whispered. "I'm sorry for my mistake. You must forgive me for that terrible curse. I know my end is near, but I want you to promise me you will get the *Sea Rogue* safely back to Nantucket."

I said nothing to interrupt his thoughts.

"When you make it to port, you must try and help Betsy," he groaned. "Our business is in serious trouble. If it goes under, I don't know what will happen to my little girl."

I wasn't sure I could honor his last wishes, but I nodded my assent.

The captain relaxed on seeing my agreement, then, a short while later, the master of the *Sea Rogue* closed his eyes for the last time. I tried to be stoic, but I couldn't stop my tears from flowing.

• • • •

The following morning the *Sea Rogue* hove to. It was a beautiful sun-filled day with calm seas. All hands assembled to witness Captain Mitchell's mortal remains committed to the deep. I read a passage from the Bible, then told the crew how fortunate they were to have had him as their leader.

They were tough, hard men, but many wept openly when we finally raised our sails, headed due north, leaving our captain to his eternal rest.

After the burial, I returned to the captain's cabin, intending to discard the foul-smelling bed linen. I was hard at work when I heard a tentative knock on the door. Freddie Langford, the sailing master, entered. He took off his cap. He looked nervous and unsure but spoke in a respectful tone.

"Excuse me, Jeremy, we all know you ain't a real seagoing captain, but the crew has asked me to tell you that we all accept you as our leader aboard the *Sea Rogue*. We can handle the ship and find our way home, but all of the decisions the captain would have made must come from you."

I was overwhelmed at the idea of becoming the ship's captain, albeit temporarily. Still, I had promised Betsy's father to get the vessel safely back to Nantucket. Other than navigation, I felt confident in my handling of the ship.

I thought about the proposal for a few minutes then went on deck to address the crew. I told them the pledge I made on the captain's death bed to get the ship safely home. They cheered, and to a man, they shook my hand.

The winds continued to blow fair, and the sea conditions favorable for a fast passage home. During the long sea days, I had time to dwell on Betsy's situation. The better part of a year and a half would have passed by the time we moored in Nantucket again. I had no idea what dire straits the family business was experiencing. I also hated having to tell Betsy about the death of her father.

Eventually, the sailing master reported we were approaching the southeast corner of Andros Island in the Bahamas. All going well; we should sight Nantucket in the next ten days. I was checking the charts for Bahamian reefs when the lookout yelled an urgent warning.

"Sail ho, five points to starboard!"

A mystery ship, under full sail, appeared to be rapidly overtaking our heavily laden vessel. When I trained the telescope on the boat, I was stunned to see the Jolly Roger pirate flag streaming from her mainmast. The coal-black pirate ship was considerably bigger than the *Sea Rogue*. Everything about its appearance reeked of malicious intent.

Over the next several hours, the intruder steadily closed the gap between our ships. When we were within range, the pirate ship opened fire. The steaming cannon shot bounced off the surface of the ocean only a short distance in front of our vessel. I knew the next one would be through our hull.

As acting captain of an unarmed ship, I had no choice. I ordered the *Sea Rogue* to heave to and await her fate. I hoped I could reason with her captain, but when the writing on the other ship's bow revealed her to be the infamous *Skeleton Lady*, I felt a sense of dread.

I was well aware of Black Bart Upton's vicious reputation. Still, I had no options. My crew only numbered twelve seamen, with few weapons other than harpoons to defend our ship.

We lowered our sails and waited for our destiny.

• • • •

Aboard the *Skeleton Lady*, Captain Black Bart chortled with glee. He had a fully laden unarmed victim in his gun sights, just waiting to be plucked. The problem was his holds were already overflowing with booty.

"Avast, ye blackguards, lower the boats. I want everyone aboard for the plunder. Kill the crew but leave the ship unharmed. We'll sail her behind us to save unloading."

"Who shall we leave aboard our ship to man the helm, Captain?"

"One man is more than enough," Black Bart said. "Leave old Rollie to man the ship. He's too fat to fight anyway."

The pirate crew boarded their small boats, armed to the teeth, and headed our way.

I was filled with remorse. I had promised Captain Mitchell on his deathbed to get the *Sea Rogue* safely back to port. Now I had two cutters, fully loaded with armed pirates, approaching quickly. I could see Black Bart standing in the bow of the leading boat. Sunlight sparkled off the pirate's cutlass. The pirate captain wore an evil grin on his weathered face. His smile widened as they drew closer.

My crew grabbed harpoons and whaling knives, although I knew it was in vain because we were vastly outnumbered. Our situation was desperate. I took one of the remaining harpoons. I knew we were all dead men, but I planned to try to take Black Bart to the bottom with me.

I learned a lesson that day. One that I've never forgotten. Even if a situation seems hopeless, there is always the possibility of a reprieve. Our miracle arrived without warning from a most unexpected quarter.

Only moments before the first pirate cutter reached our side, the surface of the sea erupted in a giant, turbulent wall of water. A colossal shape shot high into the air, hovering for seconds before falling with a resounding crash directly on top of the first pirate boat. The wooden craft was instantly smashed into splinters. The heavily armed pirates quickly sank beneath the waves, too encumbered to even attempt to swim.

The avenging beast then sounded a water spout and submerged under the second pirate boat, the one with Black Bart aboard. Everyone aboard the *Sea Rogue* waited in horrified silence, but nothing happened. Minutes passed. We prepared ourselves for being boarded.

Then, before our eyes, the last pirate boat was propelled straight up in the air on the back of its attacker. It teetered there for an instant before receiving a devastating blow from the tail of the *King of the Seas*.

Although most of his men sank without a trace, Black Bart had managed to stay afloat by seizing a damaged plank from the first pirate boat. He looked up at me.

"For God's sake, throw me a lifeline,' he pleaded.

But Captain Mitchell's story of the many innocent seamen condemned to death by this evil man flooded back. I'm not a heartless man, but I stared back at Black Bart, then slowly shook my head.

Upton's end was bloodthirsty. When several dorsal fins surfaced, indicating the arrival of some hungry great white sharks, my crew cheered. The pirate captain had caused the death of many innocent whalers over the years. Now, he and his few remaining men were about to taste the revenge of the sea.

Minutes after the carnage ended, the old giant sperm whale surfaced atop the debris-strewn ocean. He swam slowly, circling our ship several times. Again, I had an eerie feeling the *King of the Seas* was trying to communicate with me. I could almost imagine his mental message.

"Now we're even. The slate is clean."

Finally, with one last lazy wave of his tail, the whale sounded, then headed for the deeps. In a few more moments, the sharks departed as well. Other than the floating debris, it was almost as if nothing out of the ordinary had taken place here that day.

After training a scope on the *Skeleton Lady*, I could see the ship was crewed by only a single crew member. I quickly ordered a longboat lowered and, accompanied by four harpoon-bearing shipmates, made my way to the pirate ship.

The lone pirate helmsman surrendered quickly to our superior force. We tied him up, then moved him to our longboat. After I ordered the Jolly Roger flag lowered, we set off to explore the captured ship. The pirate ship was much larger than the *Sea Rogue*.

A heavy padlock secured the hatchway door to the lower cargo deck. Using one of the harpoons as a lever, I managed to force the lock. At first, I was hesitant about going below. Black Bart had such a reputation for savagery, anything might be waiting.

I called for Freddie to bring two harpoons and a lantern, then join me for the search.

As we descended into the darkness, a sickening odor almost forced our retreat. I found some cloth scraps hanging on the back of the hatch door. We used the leftovers to cover our noses so we could continue to investigate the lower hold.

The lantern's feeble light was just strong enough to reveal the horror that lay in front of us. I gagged, and Freddie moaned when the light beams fell on a mutilated corpse, nailed to the wall beside a thick oak door. The desiccated body had a sign handwritten in dried blood hanging from its neck. Its message was clear.

"HERE BE A THIEF."

My sailing master wanted to escape, but I ordered him to stay put even though the stench was overpowering.

"This man and that sign is a warning," I said softly. "We must find out what lies behind the door."

Again, we used our heavy-bladed harpoons to a good end. The old lock on the door finally broke, allowing us to enter the mysterious space behind the door. I entered ahead of Freddie then halted so abruptly he crashed into my back.

I'll never forget that day. The contents of the locked area were astounding. Accumulated loot from several seasons at sea flowed out of chests onto the deck itself—gold, silver, diamonds, and jewelry of all kinds in abundance.

A king's ransom, I thought to myself.

Obviously, Black Bart had felt the locked storage area, guarded by a macabre corpse, was safer than storing his vast plunder somewhere onshore.

At the far end of the hold, several shelves contained numerous heavy-duty burlap bags. I told Freddie to open one of the bags to check out the contents while I tried to count the chests of coins. Freddie did so and returned to me with a stunned look on his face.

"You won't believe this," he said breathlessly. "I think these bags are worth more than all this stolen treasure and the value of this ship as well."

"Are you daft, Freddie?"

"No, Captain. Every one of these bags is full of ambergris."

Ambergris! The burlap bags held the dried substance in such high demand by the perfume makers of Paris. The find was far more valuable than gold. I cautiously examined the material. The lumps of ambergris emitted a strange marine-like odor, not totally unpleasant to the nose.

With the exploration complete, I assigned half the crew to the *Skeleton Lady*. After *we* removed and buried the old corpse at sea, I ordered the men on the *Skeleton Lady* to take up a position astern of the *Sea Rogue* for the voyage back to Nantucket.

I knew Black Bart wasn't the only pirate operating in the area, so we maintained a continuous watch around the clock for any suspicious craft. The sailing master estimated ten more days at sea. One night, while we sailed smoothly under star-speckled skies, he passed on some information he had heard on his last trip to Nassau.

"In addition to the value of the *Skeleton Lady's* cargo, they say the British have posted a large reward for the capture of Black Bart as well. We may not have his body, Captain Jeremy, but having his ship should prove our claim without a doubt."

I knew my crew was ecstatic. Their share of the bounty would make my men wealthy beyond their dreams. I knew the team held me in high esteem because many of them were now calling me Captain Jeremy without hesitation.

I was happy too, but as we drew closer and closer to Nantucket, my thoughts headed in a more personal direction. I was dreading the task of having to tell Betsy about the death of her father.

• • • •

HOME TO NANTUCKET

During the last few days of the voyage, the spare crew aboard the *Skeleton Lady,* on my instructions, fumigated the holds and painted every surface they could reach. We did the same with the *Sea Rogue,* so our two vessels made an impressive sight as we sailed into the harbor at Nantucket, one year and six months after our departure. People on the docks scattered quickly with news of our arrival.

When the two ships were tied safely up to the Nantucket main wharf, I left Freddie in charge and headed up to the Seafarer's Inn. I wanted to get cleaned up before I went to see Betsy. As I made my way along the street, I heard the constant ringing of the central church bells. I stopped in the pub area of the inn to ask Sally, the barmaid, what the ringing was about.

"Did someone die, Sally?"

"Oh, no, sir," she said. "Probably worse, I reckon."

"Don't keep me waiting, girl. I've got a shilling for the news."

The barmaid laughed. "It's worse than death for poor Betsy Mitchell. She's getting married today."

"What?" I exclaimed with my heart sinking.

"It's some old geezer from London. They say he forced her into the marriage by taking over the debt of the family business. It was the only way she could keep the thing afloat until her father returned from his voyage."

I tossed the shilling to the girl, turned, and ran back to the *Sea Rogue*. I gave Freddie instructions to arm six crewmen with harpoons and meet me at the church. Then I went below decks to arm myself with a secret weapon.

When I led my crew of harpooners crashing through the church's closed front doors, the Vicar stopped in mid-sentence. I immediately spotted Betsy. She was standing at the front of the church, her stricken face as white as the wedding dress she wore. Her expression turned quickly to joy when she realized it was me.

Standing beside her in a black, rumpled, ancient formal outfit was the familiar and detestable figure of my uncle, Rolland Crabb. The Crabb gasped when he saw me.

"I thought you were dead, lost at sea, they told me."

"An untrue story, as you can plainly see," I barked. "Now, get the hell away from that young lady."

The Crabb shook his head. "I'm not going anywhere until the debts owed to me by *RICHARD MITCHELL & SON* are paid in full, either by marriage or by cash in hand. And as for you, you useless slacker, get your worthless body on the next boat to London. I'll decide how to deal with you after my honeymoon."

Obviously, the Crabb failed to realize he was dealing with a much different individual than the one he had sent from England to do his dirty work. My time at sea had toughened me considerably, both physically and mentally. I left London as a callow youth, but now I was a hardened, seasoned sea captain. And a damned wealthy one to boot.

The Vicar and the assembled guests watched in stunned silence as I emptied the contents of my seabag at the Crabb's feet. I could tell by his gaping mouth that he recognized the valuable ambergris.

"There's another hundred-weight to follow," I said confidently. "This should more than cover any debts owed, you doddering old buzzard. If there is any marriage taking place today, it sure as hell won't be to you."

The Crabb sized up the situation. He stared at Betsy, then looked at the fortune in ambergris that lay at his feet. As a trader, my uncle knew how valuable the dried material was in Paris. He had to make a choice. He looked at my harpooners and me, another furtive glance at Betsy, and then again at the treasure. Finally, greed triumphed over lust.

The Crabb decided on the ambergris.

I ordered my harpooners to escort the Crabb back to the inn. From there, he would be transferred to the waiting Royal Mail ship, which was due to sail on the morning tide back to London. I waited for a parting word, but he said nothing. Just clutched the ambergris and stared ahead.

Betsy ran to my side then threw herself into my waiting embrace. For several moments we remained that way before I reluctantly broke loose and spoke to the Vicar.

"Reverend, you might as well tell these folks to go home. I'm sorry, but there won't be a wedding here today."

I took Betsy into the registry office, then reluctantly told her about her father's accident. I held Betsy tight while she cried desperate tears. When she stopped, I told her of the vow I made to her father as he lay dying.

"I promised your father I would look out for you and the family business, Betsy. I'll do what I can to help you. Your future is important to me."

"I'll never be able to repay you, Jeremy, for saving me from that terrible man. I can't imagine what my father would have done if he returned to find me forcefully married."

"Nothing, your father's sharp harpoon wouldn't have settled," I said with a grin.

Over the next several months, I worked side by side with Betsy to put the family business back on a firmer foundation. I gradually liquidated the pirate's treasure, ensuring at each step that all the crew received a fair share.

Because her father had died before the capture of the treasure, he theoretically was not entitled to a share. Still, after securing the crew's agreement, I made sure a substantial sum went to Betsy's bank in Boston.

With the business of *RICHARD MITCHELL & SON* running smoothly, I finally had to face up to my dilemma. My feelings for Betsy were intense and genuine. Still, I could never entirely forget the beguiling memories of Constance Kingman back in London.

I faced a difficult choice. Stay in the Colonies, marry Betsy, and start a new life, or return to London and take up where I left off with Connie. It was a difficult choice. Betsy was sweet but naïve, where Constance was worldly and experienced. I felt I could be happy with either of the women in my life.

But each road led to a completely different future. I sat outside the inn all night, smoking cigar after cigar until I finally made the fateful decision that would impact the rest of my life.

I prayed it was the right decision—As it turned out, it was.

• • • •

EPILOGUE

Betsy Mitchell and Jeremy Whitehall had a very happy marriage that included a wonderful family of six healthy children. Jeremy never went whaling again. Instead, he and Betsy worked diligently to turn the small family business into the world-famous New England Candle Company.

They were generous with their vast wealth. In addition to charities, they founded the Nantucket Marine University. This educational institute specialized in programs devoted to sustainable and humane whale harvesting. It eventually became world-famous.

Shortly after their marriage, Betsy and Jeremy returned to England. On that trip, Jeremy used a small part of his fortune to purchase control of the London-based trading firm Halton, Barney & Crabb. He used his ownership of the firm to ensure a system of fair-trading practices was put in place for dealing with suppliers in the Colonies.

Uncle Rolland Crabb continued to work at the firm, as a clerk, until his death at the age of ninety-four. His previous clerk, Grumbles, spent his life at sea and never reencountered his old master.

With some trepidation, Jeremy introduced his bride to Constance Kingman. He needn't have worried, as the two had an instant rapport and, over the years, became good friends. They corresponded until the end.

After the final deadly rampage on the pirate boats, no sighting of the *King of the Seas* was ever reported again.

As a gesture of goodwill, the whaling industry agreed that there would be no harvesting of whale calves.

It was too little and too late.

SNOWFALL IN VENICE

CORTINA, ITALY - THIRTEEN YEARS AGO

He had made good progress—more than he ever thought possible when he first set out on this futile trek from the lonely log cabin high in the dense woods of the Dolomite mountains.

But the starving man knew death hovered over him as his weary body teetered on the edge of surrender. Only human resilience kept him moving forward down the mountain slope, plodding knee-deep through freshly fallen snow.

The swinging bridge loomed within sight when the man who would eventually become known as the 'hermit' finally reached the limit of his endurance. He could go no further.

A comfortable bed of soft white snow seductively beckoned him to rest, even if only for a brief respite. The hermit slowly lay on his back, letting the falling snowflakes gently cover him with a thick blanket of white. As the numbness gradually invaded his body, a sense of peacefulness ensued.

His last coherent thought before the darkness overtook him:

"Forgive me, Father, I meant well, but I know I have done wrong. I may have failed, but at least my sin was only trying to help the less fortunate of your flock."

As the relentless snowfall continued to descend from the heavens, the hermit's inert form soon became no longer visible to the naked eye. The silence of his snowy grave would not be disturbed for several days. Then, one of the mini avalanches so prone to this area would sweep down the mountainside in the dark of night. It would carry the frozen body of the hermit, in a wave of rolling ice and snow, deep into the lonely canyon that lay waiting for him, far below the old swinging bridge.

NEW YORK CITY-TODAY

I was pissed off.

After a day of working on what I considered to be a medical assembly line, I wearily removed my mask and gown before retreating to the staff room for a welcome coffee and a chat with Gayle Wellington. Gayle was my operating room nurse, general assistant, confidante, best friend, and lover. She was also going to be my bride in five more days.

"Gayle, I'm sick and tired of doing the same old stuff, day after day." I groused. "I've done more butt lifts, tummy tucks, nose jobs, and lip enlargements than I can count. Why the hell can't I just concentrate on what I'm good at?"

Gayle moved over to my side, kissed my cheek softly, then began to give me a badly needed shoulder massage. I found her gentle, sympathetic voice soothing on my frazzled nerves.

"Sorry, Mark, you know that's never going to happen as long as we remain employees of the Kingston Center for Cosmetic Surgery."

I was unhappy, but I knew her evaluation was accurate. The Kingston Center had turned into the medical equivalent of an old-fashioned sweatshop. Nothing mattered to the new owner but increasing the flow of profits.

With some modesty, I can say that some people considered me to be a genius at reconstructive surgery, particularly for kids with severe deformities. I tended to favor children from the less fortunate financial community when I could. I had pioneered some radical new approaches to cleft palate reconstruction with a great success rate.

Some people in New York medical circles considered me brilliant at my work. The jealous ones spread the rumor that Doctor Marcus Gunderson was grandstanding by using unorthodox surgical approaches.

Although we had helped numerous low-income families with the new procedures, the blunt truth was Gayle and I were gradually going broke. The private clinic owner would only permit us to do charity operations if we agreed to reimburse the Kingston Center the going rate for operating room time out of our own pockets.

I vividly recalled my last heated conversation with Donald Kingston, the sole owner of the Center. Kingston was adamant.

"Damn it, how many times do I have to tell you?" Kingston had snarled. "This clinic isn't a charity operation. I'm only interested in turning a profit, period. If you want to keep taking on all these poverty cases, be my guest, but only if you keep paying the going rate. If you don't like it, you can get the hell out and start your own business."

At this point, I stalked out of the meeting. *No use arguing with a turd with a heart of stone,* I mumbled to myself. I unloaded on Gayle.

"Shit. Kingston refuses to budge, even though he knows we have a backlog of desperate cases. Unfortunately, I'm just about tapped out, so those poor kids will have to wait a little longer. To be frank, at this point, we barely have enough cash on hand to finance our honeymoon trip. Thank God, your old man gave us the first-class airfare as a wedding present."

Gayle nodded, "That's okay, honey. Both of us are badly in need of a break. Let's get the wedding out of the way and do some skiing. We can take another crack at that cheap S.O.B. Kingston when we get back."

We were both passionate about skiing. We met while waiting for the lifts at the resort town of Whistler, British Columbia, and it was love at first sight. After working together at the surgical center for several months, we decided to get married. I wanted to return to Whistler for our honeymoon, but Gayle had her heart set on spectacular Cortina, Italy. We planned to enjoy two fabulous weeks skiing over Christmas and New Year in Cortina before returning to the grind in New York.

● ● ● ●

Five days later, an old aunt told us that Gayle and I had made a lovely sight when we walked hand in hand into the church. Supposedly I inherited my coloring and physique from some distant Viking ancestor. I'm well over six feet in height, with a muscular build and a slight reddish tinge to my fair hair. Gayle only reached as high as my shoulder, but she is a rare beauty. Her raven dark hair frames a very expressive face, set off by luminescent eyes. It was her spectacular eyes that had first attracted my attention.

Gayle's mother cried as she watched us exchange our wedding vows in the small candlelit chapel before an intimate gathering of friends and family. Most of the guests were also in tears by the end of the ceremony. Gayle was happy, crying tears of joy. Heck, I might have had a little moisture flowing myself by the time it ended.

Gayle's brother, Tom, rented a stretch limo for the occasion. It was already packed with our baggage and ski gear, ready to go. After a sumptuous light meal of cold poached salmon and assorted salads, we bid the guests farewell then headed to the airport for the official start of our honeymoon. Traffic was light for New York, so we made good time.

After clearing airline security, we worked our way through to the Delta first class lounge for a departing drink. I raised my glass and winked at my new bride.

"Here's to you, Mrs. Mark Gunderson. You are one lucky woman."

Gayle shot back, "If you keep that up, buster, I'm going to revert to my maiden name."

We both laughed then strolled hand in hand to the departure gate. The scheduled Delta flight was being operated by Alitalia Airlines, substituting the enormous Airbus A330 for Delta's smaller Boeing 767.

● ● ● ●

For the first hours, the flight was uneventful. I was enjoying the comfort of my first-class seat to the fullest when the flight attendant approached.

"More chilled champagne, Doctor Gunderson?"

I checked my watch—ninety minutes before our scheduled arrival in Venice, Italy. "Don't mind if I do, Maria. My first wife will probably join me as well."

Gayle didn't like my use of the word 'first.' In fact, she stuck her little pink tongue in my direction. I grinned. For the first time in ages, I felt utterly relaxed.

The flight attendant smiled at us before pouring two large glasses of the bubbling concoction.

I raised my glass to Gayle. "May the rest of our honeymoon be as pleasant and smooth as this flight…"

The words froze in my throat when the massive aircraft hit a patch of severe turbulence. The seatbelt sign flashed on. I knew Gayle was a nervous flyer, so I reached over to hold her hand. Then suddenly, without warning, the Airbus A330 began to experience a violent, yawing motion. The wingtips rose and fell in rapid succession before the nose dropped, then the ailing craft started a terrifying, freefall plunge toward the dark, cold ocean below.

For moments that seemed like an eternity, the Airbus continued its chaotic plunge. Champagne glasses rolled in the aisles. Loose pillows, handbags, and assorted meals flew through the cabin before landing on screaming passengers. It was total bedlam in the air.

Multiple alarms screeched from the cockpit area. My heart was in my throat. I couldn't believe our married lives were ending before we began. But then, abruptly, the aircraft leveled out and started flying smoothly again, almost as if nothing had happened.

"We have a medical emergency on the flight deck," the captain croaked breathlessly. "If there's a doctor or anyone with medical training aboard, please push your call button, now."

Our flight attendant motioned frantically to me. I unbuckled my seatbelt and ran forward. Maria was already unlocking the cockpit door by the time I arrived.

Captain Victor Moretti seemed calm and in control, but his complexion was pasty. His voice wavered as he said, "My First Officer, Gino, started choking—he's still unconscious. Can you do anything?"

My years of emergency room training came into play. I noted Gino's skin had a bluish tinge with a faint and irregular heartbeat. The man was at the critical stage of oxygen starvation. A few more minutes and the damage would be irreversible. I scanned the cockpit before spotting a cheap Bic ballpoint pen secured to the captain's clipboard.

I grabbed the pen and removed the internal ink assembly, leaving only a hollow plastic tube. To Captain Moretti's dismay, I plunged the hollow tube into Gino's inert throat, just below his Adam's apple. The quick intake of air through the tube showed me that the emergency tracheotomy was working.

"What happened?" I asked.

"Gino was finishing his meal when we hit the patch of turbulence," Moretti answered. "I've told him many times to never eat that damned airline beef. He must have swallowed a chunk whole when we hit the rough patch."

"What happened then?"

"He started choking and wildly thrashing around. When his foot hit the autopilot control, it disengaged the system. After he fell forward on the controls, we went into that deep descent. I was damned lucky to push him back and regain control when I did."

I opened the first aid kit, found a roll of adhesive tape then used the tape to secure the makeshift breathing tube in place. Gino appeared to be getting enough oxygen but still remained unconscious.

"Captain, I'm going to have to remain here with Gino until we land," I said. "He needs to get to a hospital as soon as possible."

Moretti called Marco Polo airport control and advised them to have an ambulance waiting for our arrival. After the tower gave us a priority clearance to land, the captain, aided by the Airbus's latest technology, managed a smooth unassisted landing.

When the aircraft was secure at the gate, Captain Moretti stood and stretched. I could see the back of his shirt had soaked through with sweat from the stress of the ordeal. He gave me a huge grin.

"Thanks, Doctor. Not only did you save my first officer, but you also saved my best friend. Gino and I went to grade school together. Don't tell him I said so, but he would be a hard guy to replace."

The captain picked up the intercom. "Ladies and Gentlemen. Sorry for the scare earlier as a result of a medical emergency on the flight deck. Fortunately for us, Doctor Mark Gunderson was on board. His quick action saved our first officer's life."

The passengers clapped loudly enough for me to hear them through the cockpit doors. I was gratified but also slightly embarrassed as I made my way back to join Gayle.

After we deplaned, an airline official helped us to proceed quickly through the customs and immigration formalities. "The airline has arranged for a limousine to take you to your hotel in Cortina at our expense," she explained. "It's the least we can do."

With the luggage loaded, we set off for the two-hour ride to Cortina, a picturesque old town nestled for over a thousand years at the base of the Dolomite Mountains. A peaceful honeymoon was all we had planned.

But sometimes fate has other ideas.

● ● ● ●

CORTINA, ITALY

As the limo rounded the steep mountain highway curve, Gayle had her first glimpse of the sparkling, snow-covered, enchanting village of Cortina.

"Oh, honey, it's just like a winter fairy tale."

I had to agree. The sight was stunning. A short time later, our car pulled into a wide circular driveway. We thanked the driver before entering the ancient hotel through large double doors. The hotel was everything we could have wished for. Built in 1826, it featured large wooden outdoor balconies, hand-carved ceiling beams, and a very romantic bridal suite.

"I'm exhausted," I said. "But I'm still wound up from that flight. How about joining me for a nightcap in the hotel bar?"

"I don't know why you're exhausted, you lazy lump. I did all the unpacking."

After I gave Gayle my 'little boy lost' look, she relented and agreed to join me.

The main lounge located just off the hotel lobby was still open but empty of patrons. We opted for two comfortable leather seats at the long, hand-polished mahogany bar. Gayle ordered two glasses of the house merlot in her fluent Italian.

Roberto, the bartender, having assumed we were American tourists, seemed impressed with Gayle's mastery of the language. Gayle noticed Roberto's expression, so she explained.

"I've always loved everything Italian. I started with immersion classes before going on to advanced studies. Actually, I almost became an interpreter for the U.N. before I decided on nursing as my career choice."

Roberto smiled. "Your accent is to perfection, Bella Donna."

After exchanging pleasantries in Italian, they switched back to English to include me in the conversation. After talking about the weather and local politics, Roberto asked about our plans for the next day.

"We thought we would have an early breakfast and head right out to the lifts."

"Are you both good skiers?" Roberto asked.

I grinned. "We manage to keep up with most people."

The bartender thought for a moment. "I have an interesting idea for you. Because you are here for the first time, you should do something special always to remember your holiday in Cortina."

"What are you suggesting?" Gayle asked.

"The ski shop manager, Mario Romano, has designed a unique package of back-country ski adventures. All the advanced skiers raving over his tours. If you would like to talk to him, I will call. Don't worry, he'll treat you well—he's my wife's brother."

I looked at Gayle. When she nodded with a smile, I said, "Thanks, Roberto. Please tell Mario we'll be happy to meet with him after breakfast tomorrow."

"Si, tomorrow after breakfast," the bartender confirmed.

We finished the wine, said goodnight, and departed for the honeymoon suite.

• • • •

The following morning, Mario Romano approached our breakfast table just as we were finishing our second cup of espresso. He introduced himself and joined us for a cup. Mario was a nice-looking middle-aged man with swarthy skin, dark hair, and a friendly smile.

"Roberto tells me you maybe have the interest in my special trips?"

Mario's English was passable but not nearly as good as Roberto's. He talked slowly, giving us the details about his best-selling deluxe trip called *The House of the Hermit*.

He said, "To get there, you must be taking the special snowmobile. All fix for carry your skis and stuff. I gave you the detail map and other things. The map lead you to Hermit's House."

At this point, much to Mario's relief, Gayle switched to her fluent Italian. With Gayle translating, I learned that the snowmobile trip would take us up the far side of the mountain to an area of extreme snowfall. Our destination would be at an old log cabin nestled in a beautiful area of back-country skiing. This year, about two kilometers north of the house, a temporary landing area had been created for a helicopter. Part of the package included helicopter lifts to the top of the runs for an entire afternoon of downhill mountain skiing.

Mario began speaking more rapidly, so Gayle paused before continuing. "Mark, he says it's important that we take some food from the hotel in case we get snowed in. Also, if we get stuck, the cabin is rough but habitable enough to stay overnight if we must."

"Oh, boy. Another honeymoon locale. I can't wait for an encore."

Gayle grinned at my remark before turning serious. "It looks like we have to cross a deep canyon over a narrow suspension bridge. Mario says to cross the bridge with only one person on the snowmobile because the bridge is so old it will not support too much weight. After that, the other person is to cross on foot."

"I'm not sure I like the sound of that," I said dubiously. "But ask him how much if we decide to go."

Gayle laughed at the look on my face when I heard the quote for the trip. But what the hell, you only get married once. I gulped and agreed with the deal. Mario stood, saying he would have everything ready for a noon departure. He shook hands with me, then said something quietly to Gayle with a smile.

I waited until Mario departed. "Gayle, the only two words I caught were a hermit and haunted. Did he say anything else?"

Gayle laughed. "Mario did say that some of the skiers return from the trip convinced the ghost of the missing hermit still haunts the old log cabin."

"Sounds like marketing bullshit to me."

On our way back to the room, I spotted Roberto at the elevator, crossing the lobby. I called him over and asked for more details about the ghost of the hermit.

Roberto chuckled. "I see Mario's been at it again. I think he says that story just as a way to get more tourists out searching for the hermit. The real story is that the cabin was inhabited for about ten years by a mysterious stranger. The man kept to himself and rarely made a trip down to the village. Then, about three years ago, he just vanished from sight. Some skiers swear they can hear him walking around the cabin, but I think it's just too much vino talking."

"I agree, Roberto. I'm not much of a believer in ghosts in the night."

After lunch, we met with Mario to go over the details of the trip. He gave us a hand-written map of directions. Then, after making sure we were comfortable with the snowmobile controls, he waved goodbye and sent us on our way up the mountainside.

The Ski-Doo, Expedition SE 900 ACE, packed with a picnic hamper from the hotel, purred nicely when we finally made the turn onto the trail and started the climb. As we climbed higher, the scenery became even more spectacular. Sunshine sparkled on boundless fir trees, all draped with a heavy blanket of newly fallen snow.

Down below, the village started to resemble a child's collection of toy houses.

"The old suspension bridge should be coming up anytime," Gayle said after double-checking the map.

Sure enough, around the next bend, we drew up to the edge of a narrow but deep canyon. The base of the ancient suspension bridge consisted of a layer of snow-covered wooden slats. The bridge looked barely wider than the width of the snowmobile.

"Honey, this bloody thing doesn't look safe to me. You stay here. I'll walk across the bridge first to make sure it's okay for you to cross. Then I'll bring the machine over after you reach the other side."

Gayle watched as I cautiously walked across the structure and back. I could tell she was nervous, so I gave her a reassuring hug.

"Okay, it seems to be safe. Just don't look down when you cross."

Gayle crossed the deep canyon warily, then she waited anxiously on the other side for me to join her. Mario's instructions implied the bridge was safe but only for a snowmobile and driver, no passengers. I hoped he was right.

As I started to ease across the bridge, the structure creaked and groaned, then started to swing slowly from side to side. The movement concerned me but with no room to turn around. I was committed. I flashed a reassuring grin at Gayle then continued, trying all the while not to look down at the jagged rocks lying in wait for me below.

It was challenging to keep the snowmobile on track with the clearance only inches on each side. When I finally reached the other end of the bridge, I pretended it was no big deal, but the perspiration was running down my back, and my legs felt shaky.

The snowfall turned gradually heavier as we continued our climb. Then, around an hour's travel from the bridge, the old House of the Hermit finally came into view. It was an ancient structure built from rough, hand-hewed logs. The cracks where the logs joined were deeply filled with moss that had blackened with age.

A stone chimney jutted jauntily out of the steep, snow-covered roof. The glass panels of the small windows were dirty but intact. The rusted hulk of a long-abandoned snowmobile lay on its side by the path to the front door.

"Any ghosts at home?" I said in a mock shaking voice as I knocked on the weather-beaten front door.

Gayle laughed, but I could tell she was uneasy.

The stale air inside the cabin seemed musty but dry. A stack of firewood lay piled haphazardly by the stone fireplace. There was a red switch on the wall marked GENERATOR. I threw the switch, and, after a few coughs and burps, an outside generator started up. The lights came on, then the motor on the old refrigerator began to hum. We checked the interior—no food but numerous bottles of frozen water.

"Come on, honey,' Gayle urged. "We came up here to ski. Let's get started."

After we unloaded the food from the snowmobile to keep it safe from the local animal population, we fired up the machine, then departed for the temporary helicopter landing. The chopper was waiting when we arrived.

The back-country skiing was exhilarating but exhausting. I was becoming concerned about getting back to the hotel as the snowfall was getting heavier by the minute. The helicopter pilot wanted to leave, too. After a quick hop, he dropped us off at the temporary landing spot. Our snowmobile was covered with an accumulation of snow and ice, but, fortunately, it started on demand.

"We should go back to the cabin, Gayle. I think we should plan on staying overnight, too. I'm not a chicken, but I don't feel like tackling that bridge in this heavy snowfall with night coming on fast."

She agreed, and we left for the cabin. I breathed a sigh of relief when our refuge finally emerged through the haze of the heavy snowfall.

● ● ● ●

LA CASA DELL'EREMITA

"If the legend is true, Gayle, it must have been a lonely life for the hermit, living up here in this isolated cabin."

"I can't even imagine it. I think I'd go crazy."

I paused to put another log on the roaring fire. "The real mystery is why anyone would do it in the first place. The legend doesn't give many details, so I can't even hazard a guess."

Gayle nodded as she worked on setting up the old wood plank table for our evening meal. The cabin had warmed up nicely from the heat rising from the stone fireplace. With the candle stubs flickering, the room began to take on an inviting glow.

I arranged the bedding around the fireplace to reduce the dampness accumulated from the long period of disuse. Gayle laid out the sumptuous spread the hotel had packed for our trip.

"Something smells good, honey, and I'm ravenous."

"At least wait until I have everything unpacked. Don't be a pig."

The hamper contained a large bottle of local merlot and the bottle of Chablis. An entire loaf of freshly baked, crusty Italian bread nestled in the hamper alongside an ample supply of unsalted butter and Cognac paté. Cold poached Scottish salmon, large marinated shrimps, smoked oysters, assorted cold cuts, and tossed greens completed the spread.

Gayle smiled. "I never thought we would be spending our honeymoon in a haunted cabin, but this is great."

I nodded. It was great to be away from the clinic. Just the two of us deep in the woods on a snowy night. What could possibly go wrong?

We were both tired from our skiing, so Gayle welcomed my suggestion to make it an early night. I turned out the light and joked as we snuggled down in the old but comfortable, hand-crafted double bed.

"Goodnight, Mrs. Gunderson, now get over here. I've got a honeymoon gift waiting just for you."

The first response from the darkness was a giggle followed by, "Who the hell wants an old, previously used, very tiny, wrinkled up honeymoon present anyway?"

I delivered her honeymoon gift despite the jibes, and her laughter soon subsided.

Between the large meal and the heat from the fireplace, I fell into a deep sleep. Then, sometime during the night, I began to have a vivid dream. It was so real; I can still recall every frightening detail.

In my dream, I found myself in the woods outside the cabin. Everything seemed strange because, despite the heavy snowfall, I didn't feel the cold. I was following in the footsteps of an older man, wearing a hooded snowmobile suit of old-fashioned design. The specter turned and beckoned me to continue following him. I couldn't see his face because of the hood.

The man reached the cabin entrance and went in. Again, he beckoned for me to follow him. The inside of the cabin was the same, but it was also vaguely different. The changes were too subtle for me to recognize. The figure I was following moved silently to the center of the room, then pointed at an antique woven rug. The rug depicted an alpine winter scene with snow-peaked mountains and numerous skiers. A skating rink lay off to the side of the ski runs.

The man motioned for me to come closer, then gestured down at the figure of a young female skater woven into the carpet's center panel. I tried to speak, but no words would come out of my mouth. The man shook his head, pointed directly down again at the girl, and then simply vanished in a shimmering haze.

● ● ● ●

I woke with a gasp, sweating heavily. I shook my head to try and clear the dream while sitting trembling until the first rays of early morning light filtered into the room. Because Gayle was still sleeping so soundly, I left the bed quietly and moved to the window. Flakes of heavy snow continued dropping from a leaden sky. The fire had died during the night, leaving the room blanketed with an early morning chill.

On my way to the wood supply, I froze in my tracks. The old rug in front of the fireplace was identical to the carpet in my dream. Even the young female skater was just as I remembered. I shook my head. *Obviously, I must have looked at the rug when I was building a fire last night, and that's why I remember the girl.*

I sat at the table, trying to make sense of it all. Gayle woke up and joined me. She was troubled by the strange look on my face.

"Is something wrong, Mark?"

I hesitated. "Honey, I had a weird and disturbing dream last night. It's bothering me. I'm still shaking because It seemed so damned real."

"Tell me."

I told her about my dream. When I got to the description of the old man pointing down at the girl in the rug, Gayle said she felt a chill traveling down her spine. We moved over to the carpet and took a closer look at the girl on the skates.

We studied the figure from all angles but could find nothing out of the ordinary. We sat in silence for a few minutes until I said, "I've got a hunch, Gayle. Let's roll up the rug."

Gayle gave me a hand to roll the old rug. It needed two of us because it was heavy and full of dust. The carpet obviously hadn't been moved in years.

The wooden floor under the carpet was much lighter in color, resulting from being protected from the effects of sunlight over many years. The flooring consisted of hand-hewn planks about four feet long and ten inches wide. No nails were used in the construction. Instead, the planks were secured in place by two wooden dowels at each end of the board. I studied the flooring intently, but again I was unable to spot anything out of the ordinary.

Gayle was just about to start rolling the rug back when I said, "Wait for a second, honey, something is different here. This one plank has the grain running in the opposite direction to all the others. I think if we measure it, we might find that this plank lies directly under the skater."

I scoured the cabin for any makeshift tools I could find, but it still took over an hour of hard effort before the plank loosened. Gayle was becoming increasingly skeptical.

"This is a lot of work for nothing," she groaned. "It was probably only a dream. Maybe you shouldn't have eaten so many smoked oysters last night."

I laughed at the jibe. "This sucker will be up in a few more minutes. If it all turns out to be a pipe dream, we can pack up and head back to the hotel."

Finally, the reluctant plank broke loose. I peered down into the darkness but could see nothing.

Gayle was becoming miffed. "I told you this was a waste of time, bub. We could have been out skiing."

I was reluctant to give up. The dream was still too vivid in my mind. I was directed here for a reason. I knew if I didn't find out why it would always bug me.

"Gayle, light one of the candles for me, please. I want to take one last good look before I put the plank back in place."

The candle she reluctantly gave me threw off a faint light. I held it down the hole, but there was nothing to see. I needed to be able to reach further into the darkness. An idea popped into my head—I didn't think Gayle would like it.

"Grab my ankles so I can reach in further," I said with a smile.

"How do you know I won't push you in then replace the planks and go skiing?"

"This is our honeymoon," I laughed. "I'll take my chances."

With my ankles held, I was able to reach down far enough for the candle's rays to penetrate the gloom. I could make out the shape of an old burlap bag, sitting tantalizingly just out of reach on the dirt cellar floor. We needed something long enough to catch the burlap.

An old wire coat hanger from the bedroom closet solved the problem. Gayle bent it to produce an extension with a hook. Then after a few attempts, I managed to snag the bag. I pulled it through the opening in the floor and set it down with a clunk.

"After my disturbing dream, I'm almost afraid to open it," I said.

"If it contains body parts, I'm out of here," Gayle joked nervously.

The dusty burlap bag was secured so tightly with a knotted string that I had to use a knife to gain access. I reached slowly down into the bag until I felt something covered with a silky material. I brought it to the surface then gently removed the covering.

Gayle gasped at her first sight of the exquisite object. It was a stunning Murano glass piece. The multi-colored work of delicate art depicted a woman and a young girl in an embrace of love.

"Mark, this is gorgeous work. It must be worth a fortune," Gayle said softly. "Murano glass is famous, but I've never seen anything remotely as beautiful as this."

I didn't answer her. I was busy retrieving a large brown envelope from the bottom of the bag. Because it was addressed in Italian, I handed it to Gayle to read.

Gayle took the sealed envelope marked PRIVATO E CONFIDENZIALE from me. It was heavier than one might expect for just a letter. I noticed her hands trembled as she broke the seal and removed the contents, one item at a time.

Both our eyes widened when she removed a gleaming, highly polished flawless diamond of about two carats in weight. It sparkled mysteriously in the reflected light from the candle.

An intricately woven gold chain followed the diamond. The chain was of antique design and appeared to be quite old. There was also one half of a torn five-euro banknote.

The last item out of the bag appeared to be a letter, written in Italian in beautifully free-flowing longhand.

"Honey, this whole thing scares me," Gayle whispered. "I almost feel like we should just put it all back in the bag and get the hell out of here while we still can."

"Nope, read that damned letter," I coaxed. "My curiosity has reached the point of no return. We have to get to the bottom of this, or we might regret it forever."

As Gayle moved closer to the fireplace, I put my arm around her for moral support. Then she started to translate.

'My name is ANTONIO FONTANA, and this is my last confession:

I was an artisan glassmaker on the Venetian island of Murano for many years. Although the craft had been practiced on the island for centuries, I was considered one of the best artists.

My unique colored glass designs have always been prized by collectors. So I was not surprised to be commissioned by a wealthy businessman to produce a special piece to commemorate his first child's birth. Because I knew the man to be the head of the local Mafiosi, I did not refuse. The unique piece you now hold in your hands is the work of art I designed for him. I titled it simply, The Birth.

I was instructed to personally deliver my finished work to his villa on December 23rd so that he could present it to his wife as a Christmas present. I planned to do so, but when I arrived at the villa, I saw two ambulances leaving the building at high speed with sirens blaring.

To my surprise, no one answered my knock on the door. I checked, and it was open. The house was empty when I entered. I can only surmise that a medical emergency triggered their immediate departure. I decided to leave the statue along with a note for the owner, Don Lorenzo Benedetti.

I found a room that I assumed was the Don's private study. Upon entering, I immediately saw that the full-length vault door was slightly ajar. I was frightened that someone would return and find me there, but my curiosity got the better of me.

I entered the vault intending only to take a quick look, but the contents of the secured room held me transfixed. It was the wealth of ages. Gold and silver bars stacked to the ceiling, box after box of assorted gleaming jewelry, and an untold fortune in diamonds.

I was about to exit the vault when an all-consuming rage struck me at the injustice of it all. This great wealth must have been accumulated on the backs of poor, hard-working people worldwide. Surely, I thought, there must be some way to use some of this wealth to help the less fortunate in life.

It was then that I lost all reason. Knowing full well that this was a Mafiosi leader's property, I decided to steal back some of the bounties and put them to good use.

There were sixteen heavy bags of diamonds, eight red bags, and eight blue bags. The stones were sorted so that the red bags contained uncut diamonds, and the blue bags were full of polished stones. I stole five of the blue bags and two bags of heavy gold linked chains, along with several smaller gold bars.

There was an old red leather suitcase embossed with the Swissair logo sitting next to the desk. It was empty, so I used it to pack the valuables.

When I left the property, the villa was still empty. To my knowledge, no one had seen me arrive or depart. I did not deliver the unique glass piece, The Birth, as I had been instructed to do. I also did not sleep well that evening.

The following morning, I went to Banco San Paolo's downtown branch, located just behind the Piazza San Marco in Venice. I rented one of their new sizeable ultra-secure safety deposit boxes.

To open this new type of box requires the holder to have a safety deposit box key in addition to the key the bank always keeps. The key given to me was engraved with the letter "C" for the customer. The manager, Angelo Cavallo, then showed me a second level of security, recently introduced by the bank.

He took a five-euro banknote then cut the note into two equal parts in front of my eyes. Each half of the banknote had an identical unique serial number. He passed one of the half notes to me.

He assured me that my box could not be opened by any living person unless the key marked C and the half euro note was presented to the bank. The manager would check the serial number against the bank's retained half of the euro note on presentation. If they matched, the box would be opened with no further formalities.

He explained they were doing this because they were no longer assigning names to each box in the interest of anonymity. I prepaid a fifteen-year lease for deposit box #888. It was the longest available at that time.

I decided to keep one of the largest diamonds and a gold chain as a lucky charm on a whim. I then went home and hid the gold chain and the diamond inside the lining of my traveling suit in the attic. I kept the safety deposit box key on me for safekeeping.

When I arrived back in Murano, I was late for work. The maestro who manages the glassworks was furious with me. I told him I had been sick overnight.

This was the day I was due to complete another masterpiece I was working on. It was a multi-colored, beautiful depiction of The Madonna at prayer, commissioned by the Church of San Pietro to celebrate their anniversary. The rumor was that Don Benedetti was paying for The Madonna's cost as a gift to his church to atone for some of his many sins.

I had just begun the final firing of The Madonna when I heard loud, rough voices coming from the showroom out front. Three large hard men were demanding to know my whereabouts.

I don't know if I had been seen leaving the villa or if Don Benedetti was investigating all possibilities. The maestro told the men that I was at the final delicate stage of completing an expensive piece of glass, and they would have to wait until I was through.

I panicked. From my position in front of the furnace, there was no hiding place for the key. I knew if the men found the key and the safety deposit box receipt, they would kill me without mercy. I threw the ticket into the fiery furnace.

Then, I made a decision that broke my heart. I prematurely withdrew The Madonna from the heat of the fire. The resulting stresses caused the lovely face of the lady to warp horribly out of shape.

The figure was probably the most delicate piece of my career as an artisan, and it was now unfixable. The base of The Madonna was still flexible from the heat, so I pressed the safety deposit box key deep into the soft glass of the bottom then placed the whole piece in the cooling tank.

The rough men from the villa became impatient and bullied their way into the back workshop. They searched me and interrogated me for over an hour. Still, I stuck to my story that I had been unable to make *the Christmas gift's planned delivery to the villa because I was ill. The maestro backed up my account. The men left, but they were unhappy. So was the maestro when he saw my ruined work.*

He called me many unflattering names as he stared at what he now referred to as The Flawed Madonna. When the piece had sufficiently cooled down, he made me place it on a long shelf that was known to all as The Shelf of Shame. If an artisan ruined an expensive piece, it was placed there as a constant reminder of the cost of failure. I reasoned that I would have plenty of time the next day to retrieve the key hidden in the base of The Flawed Madonna. As it turned out, I was wrong.

When I reached home, my neighbor, Nicholas Fermi, rushed out to meet me. He was excited when he told me there had been rumors of a grand theft from the villa of Don Benedetti. He also said the men from the estate were starting a house-to-house search for the missing valuables. He also told me the head of the Esposito family had been found dead. Rumors were spreading that The Don blamed him for the theft and had ordered his death.

I then knew I had to escape Murano immediately. I took only the red Swissair leather bag from my home. In my pocket, I had my lucky diamond and the gold chain. I then hastened back to the glassworks to retrieve The Flawed Madonna, still holding the safety deposit box key in her secret embrace. To my dismay, the door to the glassworks was locked, and the maestro nowhere in sight. There was no way for me to free the safety deposit box key from the premises.

With no other choice, I had to leave The Flawed Madonna behind. I abandoned my car at the docks and took the last water taxi to Venice. From there, I traveled by train to the village of Cortina. I knew of this area from early ski trips taken with my late beloved father, Giovanni Fontana. I planned to hold a meeting with an old friend of the family before seeking refuge in the mountains above the town in a log cabin where I had spent many happy childhood days.

And now, I come to the end of my confession. I have lived alone in my tiny cabin for almost ten years. Although I only make trips into town for supplies as little as possible, I know that I have been noticed.

Some of the people even refer to me as the hermit. Now I have an unexpected and unsolvable problem that forces me to decide my ultimate fate.

Heavy snowfall has been blanketing the mountain for two weeks without letup. A small, unnoticed fuel leak has left my old snowmobile inoperable, and I have been without nourishment for almost ten days. I will attempt to reach the town on foot, but inside my heart, I know this will be a futile gesture.

For this reason, I am writing my confession before I begin my final trip. The glass figure in the burlap bag is The Birth. It is the one that I was supposed to deliver to Don Benedetti on Christmas Eve. This glass figure, along with the gold chain, my lucky diamond, and the torn euro note, will confirm my story's authenticity.

I am not sorry that I stole from the Mafiosi. My only regret is that I was never able to use the proceeds to help the less fortunate, as was my original plan. The failure to do so grieves me to this day.

It is my dying wish that my confession and all it entails will eventually be discovered by someone with a heart of kindness who will use the stolen fortune to complete the mission of mercy in my memory.

To retrieve the fortune will not be easy. The Banco San Paolo will not open the safety deposit box unless the applicant produces the key marked C and the missing half of the five euro note. I was never able to retrieve the key because of my fear of the Mafiosi.

The euro note is now safely in your hands. You will have to retrieve the key at great peril. To the best of my knowledge, it is still embedded in the base of The Flawed Madonna. It was last seen sitting on The Shelf of Shame at my workplace in Murano.

Perhaps the Good Lord will look kindly on me as a sinner who tried his best, and I pray He will protect you as you take up my quest for justice.

BY MY HAND-
Signor Antonio Fontana

Tears rolled down Gayle's face as she finished translating the hermit's confession. She silently set the pages on the table.

"That poor man. Imagine living up here all those years, alone and afraid for his life," Gayle said softly. "What should we do now?"

I shrugged. "I don't think we have any choice, honey. The story must be true because the statue is real. So are the gold chain and the diamond. The hermit states that the Banco San Paolo in Venice will not open the box without the key and the matching half of the five euro note. We have the banknote but not the key. Unless the Mafiosi have found it, the key is still hidden in the base of the Flawed Madonna, at the workshop in Murano."

"I don't know, Mark. Do you actually think we have a chance of getting to the fortune in that deposit box without being caught? I feel like we are embroiled in a dead man's dream. A dream that could turn into a nightmare. Maybe we should just get out of here and pretend we never found the confession."

I hesitated before answering. "The theft took place over ten years ago. There's an excellent chance that this Benedetti guy has given up the search and moved on to greener pastures."

"Maybe. Maybe not."

Gayle was dubious, but I forged ahead. "I don't know why I feel so strongly about this Gayle, but it's almost as if it is our destiny to fulfill the hermit's quest. If we can put that stolen fortune to good use, Antonio Fontana will not have died in vain."

"Okay, honey. If you want to do it, I'll support you as best I can, but I have a feeling this will all end badly."

We hastily wrapped the glass statue and diamond in an old towel then securely packed the valuables deep in my backpack. Gayle placed the gold chain around her neck for safekeeping. I stuffed the partial euro note in my wallet. We donned our snowmobile suits and left the cabin, hoping to reach our hotel in Cortina before the fall of darkness.

Although it was still early afternoon, I knew that it would be a close call as soon as we went outside. The snow still fell heavily in a slant, driven by buffeting, frigid winds. The sky was dark, menacing, and occasionally punctured by jagged bolts of lightning, a harbinger of the violence hidden in a severe winter storm. I knew we were taking a chance but, with no food left, we couldn't wait out the storm in case we ended up marooned as the hermit had been.

I breathed a sigh of relief when the Ski-Doo fired up without a problem. "Hold tight, Gayle. We have to go like a bat out of hell to get ahead of this storm."

I couldn't hear her response over the howling winds, but her reassuring hug told me she understood. I opened the throttle and started the descent to the canyon and the waiting suspension bridge.

Although the bucking motion of the snowmobile moving at high speed was uncomfortable, I was satisfied with our progress. I estimated the bridge was only a few minutes away. Distant rumblings of thunder, generated by a severe storm in the distance, rolled down the mountainside.

A dagger of fear hit me hard when I realized the thunder was not only getting louder, it was also continuous and approaching rapidly from our rear.

• • • •

AVALANCHE!

As a skier, I knew we were in trouble. The avalanche probably triggered by a lightning strike could be traveling at speeds as high as a hundred miles per hour. Like an out-of-control freight train, it was barreling directly downhill behind us. I could tell from Gayle's frightened grip she understood what was happening, too. Our only hope was to make it to the other side of the deep canyon before the tidal wave of snow and debris engulfed us. I went to maximum power and forged ahead.

By the time the swinging bridge's outline appeared through the densely falling snow, my heart was in my throat. I realized we wouldn't stand a chance if we stopped to cross the bridge safely, one person at a time, as instructed by Mario Fontana. Heavier pieces of snow were now hitting the machine, plus the roaring in my ears confirmed the main thrust of the avalanche was only seconds behind.

I had no alternative but to go for it.

I aimed the machine at the center of the bridge. My only hope was that our high-speed momentum would carry us across the structure before it snapped. Otherwise, it would be a violent end on the jagged rocks scattered across the bottom of the deep canyon far below.

I was painfully aware of the scant few inches between the snowmobile and the bridge's sides as I maneuvered the heavy machine onto it. Gayle held on so tight I could hardly catch a breath. As soon as the treads hit the snow-covered slats of the bridge, the whole structure gyrated wildly.

I kept the throttle wide open, crossing at full speed. Then, only moments from safety, the avalanche struck the side of the bridge behind us, snapping the support cables like dry twigs.

The bridge began to collapse just as the front of the snowmobile touched the hard ground on the safe side of the canyon. With the engine screaming at high revs and the snowmobile treads clutching for traction, we hovered on the edge for what seemed an eternity.

Then the treads caught solid earth, and the machine bounded forward, taking us to a fragile safety. We dismounted, and I held Gayle tightly. She was shaking so badly it was difficult to stand. For several minutes we watched the avalanche cascade down into the depths of the canyon.

Gayle's face was as pale as the new-fallen snow. I took a deep breath then helped her back onto the machine.

"C'mon, hon, let's get you back to the hotel and a warm bath. You sure look like you could use one."

Myself, I felt like I could use a stiff drink instead of a bath.

Although I was putting on a brave front for Gayle's benefit, my hands were also shaking. I realized now just how close we had come to spend the rest of eternity as silent companions of the hermit, Antonio Fontana. We made our way cautiously down the mountainside until the welcoming lights of Cortina lay beckoning ahead.

The snow continued to fall around us.

● ● ● ●

A SMALL THEFT

Gayle sank back in the deep old-fashioned bath, hoping the warm, comfortable embrace of the scented water would restore a sense of inner calm. She considered herself a brave and adventurous soul, but she had to admit the events of the last twenty-four hours had taken a hefty toll. After escaping near-certain death by microseconds, the thought of now pursuing a stolen fortune under the noses of the Mafiosi filled her with dread.

Her thoughts were interrupted by me knocking on the bathroom door. "Gayle, the cleaning lady will be back in fifteen minutes to make up the room. Why don't we go down for a meal while the place is being cleaned up?"

Gayle replied in the affirmative, pulled the plug, and watched the water of her quiet refuge drain slowly away. She put on a bathrobe then called to me through the door.

"I want to read Signore Fontana's final confession one more time before we go for dinner."

While I was busy checking Venice's train schedule on my computer, Gayle sat and read the handwritten document, carefully studying each line. When she finished, she placed the confession in her purse and then put her bag on the floor at the back of our closet. The gold chain still hung around her neck.

"Let's go, Mark," Gayle said, her voice sounding troubled. "I need a drink, and we both need to talk."

As we walked silently to the lift heading down to the elegant dining room on the ground floor, we passed the cleaning lady on her way to freshen our room for the evening. The night maid stood to one side to allow us to pass by, a neutral smile on the maid's face masking the true feelings she held back.

• • • •

Marta Rinaldi, the maid, unlocked the recently vacated suite with her master key and stepped inside with her cleaning materials. She stood for a moment surveying the room, barely holding her resentment back.

She muttered under her breath, "For twenty-two years, I've been cleaning the rooms of these rich tourists who barely acknowledge my existence. Even though I leave the 'Thank You' tip envelopes to remind them, most just throw them in the garbage."

Over the years, Marta had developed her particular form of revenge. She had become a master at what she referred to as the art of 'Piccoli Furti,' or small thefts.

Her strategy was simple. As she cleaned, she watched for any signs of a wallet or purse that might contain currency. Because the hotel was an old structure, it didn't feature some of the newer amenities like in-room safety deposit boxes. If Marta located a wallet or purse, she would only remove a few notes depending on the amount of currency. By making a minor theft and never under any circumstances taking it all, no one had ever complained. The thefts went undiscovered, and most weeks, she managed to at least double her salary.

She quickly found my wallet and passport in the bedside drawer and removed three small denomination bills from the dozen or so in the wallet. Marta remembered that the lady who had passed her in the hall was not carrying a purse. It had to be hidden somewhere in the room. She looked in the other bedside table and under the bed itself before deciding to check the closet.

Marta didn't have to rush. She knew we would be gone for at least an hour having our dinner. She opened the closet and immediately spotted the purse partially hidden in the shadows at the back. She rubbed her hands in glee when she opened the bag and saw the large roll of bills just waiting to be plundered.

Marta rapidly calculated that she could remove several bills without making it evident that a theft had occurred. She did so and was about to return the purse to its original hiding place when she noticed the carefully folded sheets of paper. Out of curiosity, she removed the confession from Gayle's bag then took it over to the bedside to read it under the table lamp.

Marta read the story of Antonio Fontana's daring theft years ago from Don Lorenzo Benedetti's villa. She was not an educated woman, or even a particularly worldly one. Still, she knew immediately that the information contained in the confession was of great value. She thought, *perhaps if I do the right thing, my days as a cleaning person will be over for good.*

She remembered that her favorite second cousin, Alba Bianchi, a cleaning lady, lived just outside Murano. Maybe Alba would know if there was any reward offered by The Don.

She dialed Alba's number from the contact list on her phone and waited. The ringing was finally answered by a young man who identified himself as Gino.

"Gino, this is your Aunt Marta calling from Cortina. Is your mother there to speak with me?"

"No, Aunt Marta, my mother is not here. She's at work."

Marta thought for a moment and asked, "Alba must be working very hard to be still cleaning houses at this time of night."

Gino laughed. "No, she's not a cleaning lady any longer. She managed to get a full-time job as a servant at a villa in Murano. She only comes home on weekends now."

Marta had to ask. "Do you know the name of her new employer, Gino?"

"Of course, Auntie. She works for an important wealthy man by the name of Lorenzo Benedetti."

Marta's face lit up. "Tell your mother to call me back as soon as possible as it's an urgent matter." She hurried to finish up the room before the occupants returned.

● ● ● ●

The dining room manager smiled. "Buona sera, Doctor Gunderson. As requested, I have reserved a lovely quiet table for you and Signora Gunderson by the fireplace." He escorted us to a candlelit table, beautifully adorned with fresh-cut flowers.

Before the man could return to his station, Gayle blurted out, "I'll have an extra dry gin martini right now—in fact, make it a double."

I was surprised because Gayle was not a heavy drinker. I asked for the same drink, but I said a single would be enough.

Gayle remained uncharacteristically silent during the entire meal. Although the seafood linguine was delicious, she hardly touched her dish. I knew she was troubled.

"Okay, honey, what's up?" I asked.

Gayle looked directly at me for a few seconds and then burst into tears. "I've never been this frightened in my life. First, the avalanche and now the thought of going after the hermit's treasure under the noses of the mafia scares me to death. All I want to do is go home and start taking care of all those poor patients waiting for our help."

I tried to reason with my wife by pointing out the tremendous amount of good we could do if we had access to the financial windfall that the treasure could provide.

Gayle was adamant. "The risks are just too high. We would have to take tremendous chances just to retrieve the missing safety deposit box key. Even if we do manage to get the key, there is no guarantee the bank would grant us access to the box."

I tried to reassure her by saying the bank was obligated to open the box to anyone who showed up with the deposit box key and the matching half of the five euro note. Gayle was still not convinced.

I tried my final argument. "Honey, I feel strongly that we have a moral obligation to the memory of Antonio Fontana to try and fulfill his dying request."

Gayle got up and threw down her napkin. "Damn you, Mark. You care more about an obligation to some dead man than you do for the safety of your wife."

She turned and stalked out of the room, leaving me sitting open-mouthed at the table. The other dining room guests pretended not to notice the outburst.

After walking around the grounds of the hotel to cool down, I returned to our room. The hotel had given us the honeymoon suite, consisting of a sitting area and a separate bedroom. When I entered, the first thing I saw was a pillow and blanket thrown haphazardly on the sitting room sofa.

The door to the bedroom was closed. I gently tried the handle but found the room locked. I decided it would be better to wait until morning before trying to reason with Gayle again.

I undressed and made up a makeshift bed on the sofa. For several hours I tossed and turned while my mind kept reviewing the various possibilities ahead. Finally, just before dawn, the combination of physical and mental stress kicked in, and I fell into a troubled sleep.

I eventually awoke to a loud knocking on the suite entry door. It was the maid wanting to make up the room. I told her to come back in an hour. I went to the bedroom door and knocked gently. No answer, so I tried the handle. The door opened, and I saw that Gayle was not there.

At first, I thought she was in the shower or possibly had gone down for breakfast, then I noticed the small untidy pile on the center of the unmade bed. It was the hermit's handwritten last confession and his lucky diamond, along with the gold chain last seen around Gayle's neck.

A brief, tear-stained note written on the embossed hotel stationary said:

Mark, I'm sorry - I can't do it. I am taking the early morning train to Marco Polo Airport and catching the first flight home. Do what you must, but be careful and, above all, be safe. Gayle.

I glanced at my watch. The early train to the airport had departed over two hours ago—there was no way to stop her now. I sat with my head in my hands for several minutes, thinking of my ruined honeymoon and the dilemma facing me. Finally, I got up and went in for a shower.

I guess the honeymoon is over, I thought sadly.

● ● ● ●

VILLA OF DON BENEDETTI

Don Lorenzo Benedetti sat slouched behind his massive desk. Blue smoke from his Monte Cristo hand-rolled cigar partially obscured his weathered face. In front of his desk, shaking in her shoes, stood his new housemaid, Alba Bianchi.

"All right, Alba, please tell me what's so important."

"Si, Signore," she responded, her voice quivering. "My cousin Marta Rinaldi called me from Cortina, where she works as a maid in the hotel. She said she had important information about a great theft from this villa several years ago."

The Don waited for a moment. "And what is this important information?"

"My cousin said I was not to release the information until you agreed to pay us a reward of ten thousand US dollars."

Don Benedetti laughed then beckoned to his houseman, Carlos. "Go bring me a knife from the kitchen. Make sure it's a sharp one."

Carlos nodded and went off to do his master's bidding. He returned moments later with a wood-handled carving knife.

"Now, Alba, one of two things is going to happen here," the Don said softly. "If you tell me this information and I do indeed find it valuable, you and your cousin will get a reward. If you fail to tell me the information or if I think it's a hoax, Carlos is going to remove one small finger from each of your hands."

Alba blanched. She hastily retrieved the notes she had jotted down after the early morning conversation with her cousin. She stumbled over the words as she told Don Benedetti of the details revealed in the hermit's confession.

"And who has this confession and euro note now?"

"Marta says a doctor and his wife. They are the occupants of the suite where she saw the confession. She also says that early this morning, she saw Signora Gunderson—the wife—asking the concierge to arrange transportation to the train station to catch the morning express to the airport. She was alone."

Don Benedetti stared at her moodily for a few moments. "Alba, I believe this story has a ring of truth to it. If, and when, I recover the safety deposit box key and my missing goods, you and your cousin will receive a reward."

He dismissed the maid and called Carlos. "Get me Marco Polo Airport immigration control on the telephone. Quickly!"

• • • •

GAYLE GUNDERSON

Gayle cried quietly to herself for most of the lonely train trip to the airport. She had no idea what the future might hold for her and Mark. One thought repeated in her troubled mind like a mantra.

If only we hadn't found that damned confession, everything would have been okay.

With her newly purchased economy class Delta flight ticket and her passport in hand, she waited in line to go through the passport control exit formalities.

The young man behind the counter scanned her passport, hesitated a moment, then said, "Signora, please to stand to one side. There is a message waiting for you." Gayle immediately assumed I was trying to reach her.

An armed man rapidly approached from a small office to the left of the control desk. "Please to follow me, signora."

Gayle had little choice since the burly police officer had grabbed her upper arm, forcing her to follow. He escorted her into a small office then told her to wait for his superior. Gayle sat on the hard-backed chair, wondering why they didn't just give her the message. After a lengthy wait, a well-dressed senior officer entered the room.

He came right to the point. "Signora Gunderson, your passport is being held pending your hearing before a local judge."

Confused and frightened, she said, "I haven't done anything. Why would I have to appear before a judge?"

"You're being held on suspicion of being an accomplice, after the fact, to a robbery from the villa of Don Lorenzo Benedetti." Gayle went numb when she heard the name. The officer continued, "A car will arrive shortly to take you to the station." Gayle said she wanted to contact the American Embassy, but the officer just smiled and shook his head again.

The police vehicle drove rapidly away from the airport with Gayle securely belted in the backseat. The two policemen in the front seat were conversing in rapid Italian. Obviously, they didn't realize Gayle was fluent in the language because they made several obscene remarks about her shapely figure.

She was straining to catch the drift of their conversation when she heard the words Benedetti and reward repeated several times. Gayle was not surprised when the police car stopped at the boat dock for the water taxi to Murano instead of the police station.

She had a pretty good idea of where they were taking her.

• • • •

MARK GUNDERSON

With a heavy heart, I packed my bag and checked out of the hotel. I had given the whole situation some serious thought. *I'll give myself forty-eight hours to try and recover the hermit's stolen treasure. If I don't find it, I'll book the first available flight back to New York and try and patch things up with Gayle.*

After booking a first-class seat on the early afternoon express to Venice, I sat back on the soft leather seat, ordered a glass of red wine from the attendant, then started to plan my strategy. First, I decided to head for Murano to visit the glassworks where the hermit had worked, hopefully before they closed for the day.

Assuming the Flawed Madonna was still at the glassworks with the safety deposit box key embedded in the base, I would have to find some way to purchase it without arousing suspicion. I knew that once I set foot on the island of Murano, I would be entering dangerous territory, closely controlled by Don Benedetti. I couldn't take a chance on being searched or caught with the half euro note, the diamond, the hermit's confession, or the gold chain in my possession.

As a safeguard, I put the items in my suitcase and buried them deep under my clothing. After departing the train, I checked the suitcase into the secure luggage storage area. In return for a small fee, I received a purple claim ticket. I stuffed the claim ticket down into my sock.

A waiting cab took me to the wharf where the water taxi to Murano was getting ready to depart.

As I crossed the open waterway, I marveled at the sights of Venice and her sister islands, perched precariously on an endless sea. The impatient body of water always seemed to be trying to reclaim the wonders of Venice to her depths. Even this late in the afternoon, gondolas, water taxis, freighters, and cruise ships crisscrossed the canals in a never-ending stream. The water taxi finally bumped against the Murano dock, and the passengers flooded out. I quickly hailed a local cab.

"Ciao," I said to the elderly driver as I entered the decrepit automobile. "Do you speak English, signore?"

The driver held up his fingers a few inches apart to indicate that he spoke a little.

"I want to go to the glassworks as quickly as possible."

The old man laughed. "There are many, many glassworks. Which one you wish?"

I hadn't realized that blowing glass was such a big industry on Murano. I was about to give up and head back to the boat when I remembered a name from the hermit's confession.

"The glassworks I want has a manager known as, The Maestro."

The driver nodded and started down the narrow road. As he drove, he thought to himself, *this rich tourist's wallet will be much lighter after the Maestro sells him one of his lower quality pieces at prices to the sky.*

The taxi pulled up in front of an impressive glass-fronted showroom. An array of spotlights shone down on spectacular multi-colored pieces on display in the windows. I gave the driver a large tip and asked him to wait. I assured the old man that I wouldn't be too long before I needed a ride back to the wharf for the water taxi to Venice.

As soon as I entered the premises, a smiling, middle-aged man approached me, hand outstretched. The man wore a starched, old-fashioned white shirt, adorned by a gigantic black bow tie. Although the man's black striped suit showed the shiny surface of age, his thinning silver hair and shiny black shoes combined to give him an air of gentile elegance. I correctly assumed that he was the Maestro.

"Is there something special signore wishes to see?" The Maestro asked.

"Perhaps I will browse for a few minutes first. There are so many pieces to see."

"Of course, signore, perhaps I could offer you an aperitif as you shop?"

I replied that I would enjoy a glass of red wine if it were available.

I examined a dozen or so assorted works of art before he returned with the wine. He hovered over me.

"Have you discovered anything to your liking, signore?"

I decided to go with the story I had concocted on the train. "To tell you the truth, these are all beautiful pieces. They would be a significant gift for any loved one. However, my wife and I are in the middle of a nasty divorce. I was hoping I could find something ugly to remind me of what a warped woman she is."

The Maestro's internal antenna went up. He had earlier received a call from Don Benedetti's villa, advising him to watch for a tourist looking for anything unusual.

"Signore, on a rare occasion, one of our artisans has a failure. We keep the ruined pieces in a special place known as the 'Shelf of Shame.' Normally, these ruined pieces are not for sale, but perhaps I could make an exception in your case."

The Maestro beckoned for me to follow him into the back room. From the hermit's confession, I immediately spotted the Flawed Madonna. Still, I took some time examining all the samples, so The Maestro would not be suspicious.

I pretended to show interest in one ugly piece but backed off when he suggested an outrageous price. Finally, I picked up the Madonna.

As I ran my finger under the base, I felt the outline of the key. Good, it was still there, just where the hermit left it.

Other than the ruined face, it indeed was a beautiful work of art. We agreed on a price after some serious haggling, but I didn't have enough cash to cover the purchase price.

"Do you take credit cards?"

The Maestro indicated that he took Visa, but the price would have to be increased by ten percent to cover the handling fee. I knew I was being ripped off, but under the circumstances, I had no choice. When I handed my card over, he carefully examined the name on the card and the signature on the back.

"Grazie, Doctor Gunderson. I do not have the Visa machine, so I will have to make out a slip by hand. I am sure you understand. I will also have to call the Visa office for authorization of the amount. Please to have another glass of vino and look at the rest of the showroom. I will only be a few moments."

I accepted the second glass of red wine and walked casually through the showroom. I could hear The Maestro faintly from his office talking rapidly in Italian on the telephone. *I wish Gayle were here so that she could translate the conversation for me*, I thought to myself.

Finally, he returned and began the meticulous packing of the *Flawed Madonna*. He tried several cartons before finally selecting the right one. I wanted to hurry him up because I knew the last water taxi to Venice was due to leave shortly. The Maestro finally shook my hand before handing over the carefully wrapped package.

He gave me a sly smile. "Arrivederci, Doctor Gunderson."

I stepped outside into the night to find my taxi gone. A long black limo waited in its place. Two large and menacing men motioned for me to get into the backseat. I didn't have much choice, so I went along, hoping for the best.

THE FLAWED MADONNA

The maid, Alba Bianchi, once again stood at attention in front of the massive desk of Don Benedetti. Once more, she was visibly trembling.

"Relax, Alba. You have done a good thing. I know many of the local people believe that I am a cruel man, and that may be true. But above all, I am an honorable one."

Alba nodded, then remained silent.

The Don took a puff of his cigar before continuing. "In this bag is the ten-thousand-dollar reward that you asked for. It's yours to keep, but if you or your cousin Marta Rinaldi ever breathe a word of this matter, Carlos will retrieve the reward along with both of your little fingers. Do you understand?"

"Si, signore," Alba said as she turned to leave.

Don Benedetti stopped her. "Go check on the woman. Make sure she is okay and offer her some refreshments."

Alba unlocked the door to the luxuriously furnished guest apartment and entered. Gayle sat on the bed. She had been at the villa for several hours after the local police delivered her but still had not seen Don Benedetti.

"May I get you something, signora?" Alba asked in Italian.

Gayle replied in the same language. "Please, just let me go. I haven't done anything, and I just want to go home." She broke out in tears. Alba wasn't sure what to do, so she left the room, locking the door carefully behind her.

Outside, heavy rain had started to fall. Gayle went to the window and stared out just as a long black limo pulled up in front of the villa. The driver-side door opened first, and the massive figure of Carlos the houseman emerged. He was carrying a parcel wrapped in heavy brown paper. He opened the passenger door with a key, then a figure stepped out into the rain.

Gayle's heart rose in her throat when she realized that the man was her husband. Her emotions were conflicted. Terrified at seeing Mark, a prisoner, but elated because she knew her husband was a smart and resourceful man.

If anyone could get them out of this mess, it would be Mark.

● ● ● ●

Spinning My Wheels

Carlos pushed me through the villa entrance and then knocked on the door to Don Benedetti's office before entering. The Mafiosi leader continued a low conversation in Italian with a young girl sitting on his red leather couch. I assumed it was a young girl. I could barely make out her figure under a long black outfit that covered her from head to foot.

Finally, Benedetti pointed to one of the two chairs in front of his desk and motioned for me to sit. Carlos handed the wrapped package to his boss and then took up a position by the doorway, standing guard.

The Don still did not speak to me but smiled as he unwrapped the package. I was in a quandary. Not aware, Alba and her cousin had already passed on all the details of the hermit's confession to Benedetti. I decided to bluff it out.

"I have no idea why I am here," I blustered. "Your man kidnapped me while I was trying to return to Venice for my flight to the USA."

The Don ignored me and continued to unwrap the package. Finally, the last of the wrapping fell away, and he held the beautiful but flawed, multi-colored statue of the Madonna in his hands. The Don paused to light a cigar then posed a question in flawless English.

"Could you tell me, signore, why an American tourist would come all the way to Murano just to purchase a piece of ruined art?"

I continued with my bluff. "Just as I told the Maestro, I wanted something ugly to present to my ex-wife to celebrate our divorce." Don Benedetti laughed sadly and nodded to Carlos.

Carlos left the office but soon returned. I gasped when I saw Carlos holding Gayle. Carlos pushed Gayle roughly onto the seat beside me. She looked frightened but unharmed.

"Now that your *ex-wife* is here, perhaps you would like to give her the present you selected to celebrate your divorce," the Don growled.

Benedetti sat back, waiting for a response from me. I was still in shock over seeing Gayle here at the villa. I remained silent as my mind raced as I searched for a way out.

"I thought you might have a change of heart, signore. Why don't I tell you the real story of the Madonna?" He pointed to the statue.

"This is the masterpiece that I commissioned Antonio Fontana to create as a gift to my church. As you can see, he ruined it."

The Don paused to knock the ash off his cigar. "Fontana was also commissioned by me to create another piece as a special Christmas present for my dear wife, Maria, to celebrate the birth of our first child. The bastard was ordered to deliver The Birth to this villa on Christmas Eve. Before he arrived, Maria suffered massive bleeding. We rushed to take her by emergency ambulance to the hospital. That cretin took advantage of our unplanned absence and stole a fortune from my vault…"

Benedetti paused to gain control of his emotions. "This unforgivable outrage took place while my entire household waited at the hospital for news of Maria. Unfortunately, the news was not good. My beloved wife died in childbirth."

Gayle and I remained silent, although we heard muffled sobs coming from the girl on the couch.

Don Benedetti shook his head sadly, then stared down at the statue. I could have sworn there was a tear in the corner of his eyes. In a quiet voice, so low we could hardly hear, The Don murmured, almost for his own ears.

"Now, I have no wife, a missing fortune, with only a flawed Madonna to remind me of the days gone by." Then, almost trancelike, he muttered, "That is not correct. Now I have two flawed Madonna's."

Without warning, The Don stood up, raised the Madonna statue high over his head, and hurled it down on the hard tile floor. The glass piece shattered in all directions. The girl in black jumped from the couch and fled the room. Carlos let her go and then walked over to the pile of debris, picked up an object, then placed it on the desk in front of Benedetti.

I looked at the item, then at Gayle. It was the safety deposit box key. The Don motioned for Carlos to call for Alba to clean up the mess. He picked up the key and scrutinized it.

"I know that the Banco San Paolo in Venice has my fortune. I now have the safety deposit box key in my possession. That only leaves one-half of a five euro note left to be found. Would either of you know of its whereabouts?"

When we both professed to know nothing of the missing banknote, Don Benedetti sat back in his chair. "One of two things are going to happen here. You are going to tell me the location of the euro note. In which case, you will not be punished. Or, if you fail to do what I ask, Carlos will remove one small finger from each of your hands."

Gayle was petrified, but I thought The Don was bluffing. "I'm sorry, Don Benedetti. While It's true that we found the hermit's confession, there was no sign of any euro note."

The Don snorted. "Carlos, take the fingers. Start with the doctor."

When the houseman approached us with a gleaming kitchen knife he had been holding, hidden by his side, Gayle quickly took a protective stance between the knife-wielding Carlos and me

"Don Benedetti, you must not do this," Gayle pleaded. "My husband is a gifted doctor. Mark has a worldwide reputation for helping many people. Please, take my fingers instead."

The Don motioned for Carlos to stop. "And what is it about this man that makes him so special?"

Gayle resorted to her fluent Italian to try and make Benedetti understand. "My husband has many talents. He has perfected his own surgical techniques. He's one of our country's finest reconstructive cosmetic surgeons."

The look that flooded over the Don's face was genuinely frightening. "Butchers. You are all butchers!" he screamed in a tortured voice. "Carlos, bring Angelina here to me at once."

The Don paced the room back and forth, waiting for Carlos to return. I took Gayle's hand, trying to comfort her fears. Finally, Carlos returned with the girl clad in black. She took up her original position on the red couch. We had no idea what was happening.

Don Benedetti stood, his voice shaking with rage. "When my wife Maria died, Angelina was all I had left. As a child, she had a large birth defect of her upper lip. We hired the finest surgeon we could find. He assured us that the operation would be a complete success.

He failed to tell us of his fondness for the cocaine, which he indulged in before the operation. The results were a total mess. Now that man will never operate again as he has no hands."

Don Benedetti lowered his head in grief and then continued. "Three more specialists each tried to repair the damage of the other. Each made the situation worse, not better. Butchers, butchers, you are all the same."

By now, Benedetti had uncontrolled tears flowing down his face. "Angelina, come over here to me, my angel." Angelina moved to her father's side. "And now, you will see that I truly have a Flawed Madonna of my own flesh and blood."

With that, The Don pulled sharply on a ribbon, and the black coverall fell to the floor.

Gayle tried not to gasp, but the young girl's face was truly grotesque. I was shocked, too. I'd seen some bad ones in my career, but this was the worst I had ever encountered. Our hearts went out to the young girl as she stood there in her simple cotton dress. She had beautiful hair and a slim, youthful body. Other than her ruined countenance, she was perfectly normal.

Seeing his lovely daughter's tragic face seemed to enrage Benedetti even further. "Carlos, forget the fingers. Cut off his hands now so that he may never hurt another man's daughter in the future. Take the woman to the basement. She will tell us where the euro note is eventually."

Gayle shrunk back in horror, but I decided to take a gamble. "Wait, Don Benedetti. I will freely tell you where the missing half euro is if you will grant me one small request."

The Don reluctantly asked, "And what is this small request you wish for?"

I reached into my sock and retrieved the baggage claim ticket. I placed the purple ticket on Don Benedetti's desk and looked at the man square in the eyes.

"The half banknote is in my luggage at the train station in Venice. In return, I ask your permission to make a thorough medical examination of Angelina. I simply want to see if there is anything I can do to help the poor child lead a more normal life."

The Don slumped back into his chair as he fumbled for another cigar. He appeared to be in deep thought for several moments before he responded.

"Very well, I will sleep on this matter. You will have my decision in the morning. Now, Carlos will show you to your quarters."

Carlos led us up a long, richly carpeted staircase to an immaculate suite of rooms at the far end of the villa. He motioned for us to sit before telling us our luggage would be retrieved as soon as possible. As he left the room, the sound of a secure lock reminded Gayle and me that, although we had a reprieve, we were still prisoners. A few minutes went by, and then Alba, the maid, informed us that she would deliver a meal to our room.

Almost an hour passed by before Alba returned bearing two freshly decorated trays holding the main dish of piping hot fresh pasta and lobster, broiled in a pungent butter/garlic sauce. Newly baked rolls, along with two bottles of wine, accompanied the meal.

I tried to lighten the scene. "This almost feels like our proverbial last meal."

Gayle, unfortunately, was not in a mood for jokes. "What the hell are we going to do, Mark? There is no way you can repair the damage to that poor girl's face."

I took a moment before replying. "Gayle, I know I can't perform miracles, but I'm sure I can make that face look a hell of a lot better than it does now."

We finished eating then retired to the comfort of the old-fashioned four-poster bed. Just after the lights went out, Gayle turned to me and murmured, "Honey, I am so sorry I abandoned you in Cortina. I was petrified of being caught up in troubles with the Mafiosi."

I returned her hug as I told her everything would be okay. I hoped I was right in my heart, but, in my brain, I was afraid for our safety.

At times tonight, the Don had appeared to be almost deranged.

● ● ● ●

THE DECISION OF DON BENEDETTI

The following morning Carlos escorted us to an elegant dining room for breakfast. Two well-dressed servants offered steaming platters of breakfast meats, eggs of all types, and baskets of freshly baked rolls and crusty bread.

We were finishing our second cup of coffee when Benedetti finally joined us. He sat at the head of the table then asked the servant for a double black expresso. I thought the Don looked like he hadn't slept a wink.

"Doctor Gunderson," he began. "I have made my decision. Despite the trauma and many disappointments my daughter Angelina has already suffered, I will allow you to make one last medical examination of her condition."

I thanked him and attempted to shake hands, but the Don just stared at me with those cold dead eyes of his.

He pointed to his office. "Go, now, and do your examination. Angelina is waiting for you."

We left the breakfast table and moved to the office. Angelina was there, covered from head to toe as she had been the previous night.

At first, the girl was reluctant to remove her facial covering. Gayle talked soothingly to her in Italian, and, finally, she removed the veil. Up close, her condition was even worse than I thought. After an exhaustive examination, I was ready to talk to her father. I found him still at the breakfast table.

"You mentioned that three doctors have tried to restore Angelina's face," I said. "Can you remember how many operations they performed?"

"Si. Each of the butchers did one operation before giving up."

I nodded. My hunch was correct. "Don Benedetti, I want to take some pictures of Angelina's face for a more thorough review. Then, if you will grant me some time, I will present my professional opinion to you later this evening."

Benedetti agreed, allowing me to spend the next hour taking

close-up photos of Angelina's face from all angles. I spent the rest of the day in the solitude of our suite, making copious notes and diagrams based on my evaluation of the pictures. Occasionally I bounced an idea off Gayle to test my assumptions.

Finally, I said to Gayle, "I think I have everything I need. Let's go see the Don and hope we survive the meeting."

• • • •

We found Benedetti in his study sitting in front of the fireplace. He wore an old-fashioned smoking jacket with black lapels and soft leather slippers on his feet. The Don held a glass of cognac in one hand with the ever-present cigar in the other. He stared broodingly at the flames with the hermit's last confession resting on the coffee table at his side. He motioned for us to sit in the two stuffed chairs opposite him.

I took a deep breath and started. "Don Benedetti, I have to be honest with you. Angelina will never have the face of the Madonna again. The damage is too severe."

When the Don interrupted with a groan of anguish, I held up my hand and continued. "But, in my professional opinion, with the proper reconstructive surgery and a little makeup as she grows older, Angelina will look substantially better. At the very least, she will no longer have to wear a cover over her face every time she goes out in public."

Benedetti took a long pull on his glass of cognac and then said, "Why should I believe you? Every attempt has failed. Each time my poor daughter's face became more ruined."

I knew it was now or never. If I failed to convince the Don, it would be game over for us both.

"The missing ingredient that caused the past failures was simply lack of time," I explained. "The others tried to correct the problem with only a single operation. That approach was wrong."

The Don glared at me. "I have already told you everything was wrong."

"You must understand," I responded. "To do a proper reconstructive repair on severe damage requires not one, but several small procedures. Each operation must build on the success of the previous one. Like an artist slowly layering color to produce a masterpiece."

Benedetti stood up abruptly. "You have given me much to think over. Please go now. I will take up this matter with you again in the morning."

■ ■ ■ ■

We both spent a restless night wondering what decision the Don would make. We finally fell asleep just before daybreak, and, soon after, we were woken by Carlos's knock on the door.

"Don Benedetti is ready to see you now in his office," he growled.

We had a hasty shower, dressed quickly, then headed for the meeting. The Mafiosi clan leader sat slumped behind his desk; a lack of sleep apparent on his lined face. He said nothing until Alba had served coffee to the group.

After a long, uncomfortable silence, he finally spoke. "Your explanation of the previous failures makes sense to me. Although I am fearful, I feel that if there is a chance for my daughter to live a normal life, we must take it."

I was ecstatic. "Don Benedetti, you have made the right choice. We are so happy about this new chance for Angelina. Gayle and I will start immediately to write out detailed surgical notes with our recommendations to leave for her doctor …"

My voice trailed off as I saw Benedetti shaking his head. "No signore. You misunderstand me. The only person who will be allowed to operate on my Angelina is you."

I was stunned. "Don Benedetti, to perform these reconstruction surgeries could take a year or more. Gayle and I can't stay away from home that long, and, even if we could, I'm not accredited to do surgery at any hospital in Italy."

The Don gave me a benign smile. "Don't worry about the minor details. First, the chief of police in Cortina is an associate of ours. He will issue a bulletin announcing that you and your wife were, unfortunately, caught up in an avalanche. To date, no bodies have been recovered. The police bulletin will explain your absence to your families and friends."

I desperately interjected. "That doesn't solve the problem of my medical accreditation in Italy."

The Don continued as if he hadn't been interrupted. "The operations will be done privately here at the villa. We rarely use the ballroom in the west wing, so we will convert it into a state-of-the-art operating theater. You will give Carlos a detailed list of your medical requirements, and he will make it happen."

Gayle finally found her voice. "Mark can't do these procedures without a highly trained assistant, and I refuse to help. I won't be kept a prisoner in this place for a whole year."

Benedetti motioned to Carlos for more coffee before replying. "Perhaps I should have explained the entire plan to assist you in making your decision. Let me tell you that one of two things will happen here."

Benedetti stopped to light a cigar before continuing. "First, if you refuse to do the procedures or if they fail in any way, you will wish you died in that avalanche."

Gayle's blanched then held both my hands in a death grip. I looked at the Don. It was clear from his expression that the threat was genuine.

"If we do the procedures successfully, will we be released to go home, or will we end up as fish bait in a canal somewhere?"

The Don looked affronted. "I may be Mafiosi, but I consider myself to be a man of honor, so I also swear to you this. If you do what is necessary for my daughter successfully, I will reward you with the entire contents of the safety deposit box at the Banco San Paolo. You will also earn my personal gratitude, which means you both will be under my protection, anywhere in the world, for the rest of your lives."

Benedetti rose to his feet, then gestured for us to leave the room.

"Please, take the rest of the day to consider the options I have presented to you. Join me for the evening meal, and we will discuss everything then."

For the next several hours, we hashed over the pros and cons of our situation. I finally said, "Honey, I don't think Benedetti is making an idle threat. We could both end up mutilated on the side of some backroad if we don't see this thing through."

Gayle was petrified, but she was also a practical lady. "What happens if you use every skill you have at your disposal, but the result doesn't satisfy the Don?"

That possibility was a serious concern and one that had been bothering me all afternoon. The final judgment would have to be subjective. Success to me might appear a failure to another.

"We'll have to make Benedetti understand that Angelina will never be a raving beauty, period. As far as I'm concerned, if we can get her to the point that she doesn't need her veil, that should satisfy everyone."

Gayle nodded. "It's time for dinner. We might as well go and get this over with."

• • • •

ANGELINA

When we entered the elaborate dining room, I was surprised to see Benedetti already sitting at the end of a long, heavy wooden table. A vast array of silverware sparkled in the light of numerous tapered candles. Benedetti was wearing a formal white dinner jacket with a crimson bowtie and matching waistband. He stood and formally welcomed us.

"Please, take a seat," he said softly. "You're just in time for the first dish, Linguine al Nero di Seppia."

Alba and Carlos placed steaming hot platters of the fragrant black pasta, tossed with jumbo prawns in front of us.

"This is a specialty of the villa," the Don said with a smile. "Pasta colored with the black ink of the squid. Please to enjoy."

Gayle and I looked at each other. We both recognized how surreal it was to be dining this way with a man who could have our hands removed with a simple nod. Oblivious to our concerns, Benedetti rolled his eyes in enjoyment with the first taste of the house specialty.

I took a deep breath. "Don Benedetti, Gayle, and I will agree to do the reconstructive surgeries for Angelina, but we have one problem."

Benedetti stopped eating. "And what would that problem be?"

"I'm sure you've heard the old saying, 'beauty is in the eye of the beholder?'"

When the Don nodded, I continued. "Our concern is that you may have such high expectations that you will be disappointed with the results. This might happen even if Gayle and I are satisfied that we have done everything possible."

Our host put down his wine glass. "Signore, you are mistaken. I will not be the judge of the success or failure of your efforts. That decision will rest solely with my daughter, Angelina."

Gayle asked, "Angelina, alone?"

"Si, it is already decided this way. Every Christmas Eve, we always participate in the town square's festivities before returning to the villa for the feast of the seven fishes. Each year since she could walk, Angelina has taken part in the parade but always wearing the veil over her face. Now, she alone will decide if she will attend the Christmas festivities this year with her face uncovered."

The Don paused before continuing, "I swear to you on my honor, if Angelina stands in the town square on Christmas Eve without her veil, you will receive the rewards I promised you. I have sealed the safety deposit key and the euro note in an envelope in my vault. It will be yours if you are successful."

We ate the rest of the meal in silence. I had a lot to think about, so we said goodnight and retreated to the safety of our room for the night.

● ● ● ●

The next few weeks went by in a blur. Obviously, Don Benedetti was well connected because, each day, a truck would arrive loaded with the latest medical equipment, exactly as I had ordered. Carlos supervised the unloading while Gayle and I both directed the installation of the newly arrived hospital gear.

The previously unused ballroom in the west wing of the villa was gradually transformed into a first-class operating theater. Electricians and other specialists seemed to show up as if by magic. I couldn't help being impressed by Benedetti's organizational skills. He had even managed to convince the local hospital's best anesthesiologist, Doctor Anthony Cosmo, to 'volunteer' his services whenever required.

As the date of the first of the planned series of operations approached, Gayle was surprised to see Alba, the housemaid, busy at work covering all the mirrors in the villa.

"Why are you covering all the glass mirrors, Alba?"

"Signora, this is at the special request of Angelina. She refuses to see her image until all of the operations are completed."

Gayle could understand the young girl's concerns, but she was concerned herself. If Angelina didn't look at her face after each procedure, it would be impossible to get any indication of her thinking of the facial changes taking place.

• • • •

On the morning of the first operation, Gayle escorted Angelina into the operating room, gently holding her hand. My wife had worked hard to develop a good rapport with the young lady by spending some time each day getting her to understand what would be taking place.

I murmured to her as she lay on the table. "Angelina, in a few moments, Gayle will give you a gentle injection. It will not hurt, but you will be asleep in a short time. Doctor Cosmo will make sure you are kept safely asleep for the entire time."

The girl turned her ruined face toward me and said, "I have great faith in you, Doctor Mark. I may only be a young girl, but I know a good person when I see one. Gayle has told me of your work on poor children, and I believe God has sent you here to change my life forever."

As I nodded for Doctor Cosmos to put Angelina under, I reflected on her words and hoped that her God would indeed help guide my hands. I sincerely wanted to help Angelina, but I also had a selfish motive. I've grown fond of my hands over the years. They have helped many people, and I wanted to keep them attached to me forever.

After an hour or so, I was sweating profusely. The scar tissue from the previously botched procedures was worse than I had expected. I worked delicately at shaving the old tissue while keeping a close eye on Doctor Cosmo's efforts. Everyone involved in the operation fully understood the consequences if Angelina should suffer a tragedy caused by the anesthetic.

Finally, the first operation was complete, and Angelina was wheeled off to the recovery room. I was happy about the covered mirrors because Angelina's face would continue to look worse until the final procedure took place. I washed up and went to report to the Don.

Don Benedetti looked up anxiously as I entered his office. "Tell me quickly, signore, how is my daughter?"

I reassured him that Angelina was in the recovery room under Gayle's care and that everything had gone as planned. Benedetti sat down, looking relieved. He lit a cigar and offered one to me, which I declined with a shake of my head.

"I need to ask you a favor," I said.

"What is it, you wish?"

I decided to be blunt. "The first procedure on Angelina's face is now finished, but there are still several operations left to go. We also must allow for recovery time between each stage, and there are still more than ten months left until Christmas. The problem is that Gayle and I will go crazy if we must stay only in the villa for the duration. We would only ask to be able to live a more normal life until this is all over."

The Don lazily blew a smoke ring before responding. "I, too, have given your situation some thought. Suppose you give me your solemn oath that you will not try to disappear before the operations are complete. In that case, I will agree to allow you some personal freedoms."

I reached out to shake his hand, but the man said, "I'm not finished quite yet. If you swear your oath, I will put Carlos and a car at your disposal. You may travel anywhere within the Venetian Islands, but you will require my permission to go beyond those boundaries."

"Thank you," I said sincerely. "I'm sure Gayle will enjoy getting out."

Benedetti held up a hand. "However, I must warn you if you attempt to escape, you will be found and punished. We have a long reach. There is nowhere in the world where you will not be looking over your shoulders every day."

I knew Benedetti was deadly serious, so I agreed to the terms and went to tell Gayle the excellent news.

● ● ● ●

EMERGENCY!

With our newfound freedom, Gayle and I set about exploring the wonders of the Venetian Islands, but always under the watchful eye of the hulking Carlos.

"I don't think Carlos likes us," Gayle said.

"What makes you think that?'

"Every time he looks at us, I have the feeling he can hardly wait to take a knife to our hands."

I laughed. "I know the guy looks sinister, but as long as Benedetti needs us, we should be safe enough."

We were enjoying a lazy early spring day at a small café on the edge of Piazza San Marco. I had ordered a whole bottle of chilled prosecco, the contents of which were making us a little reckless.

I whispered to my wife, "Let's see if we can ditch our shadow for a few minutes and have some fun."

After paying the bill, I rose and took Gayle by the hand. We started to walk away from the café. Carlos had been leaning against a nearby wall, keeping an eye on us. When he saw us start to leave, he immediately began to follow. I silently nudged Gayle in the Grand Canal direction, where several gondolas were bobbing gently at the dock.

When we got within twenty paces or so of the dock, I broke into a run, and we jumped onto the nearest waiting vessel. The startled gondolier stood speechless until Gayle instructed him to depart quickly, in Italian.

The man immediately pushed off from the dock, but not before Carlos took a running leap to try to board the departing gondola. Although Carlos was a large man, he was agile for his size. For a split second after landing on the railing of the boat, he teetered back and forth precariously, trying to find his balance.

Finally, the forward momentum of the gondola was too much to overcome. With a loud resounding splash, Carlos fell backward into the canal's fetid-smelling, polluted water. Gayle and I roared with laughter. The sight of Carlos hurling curses while splashing his way toward the boat drew a small crowd. When they started taking photos, the gondolier joined in by doffing his cap.

We finally pulled the soaking wet Carlos into the boat. He repaid us with another stream of Italian curses that continued for the balance of the boat trip and the drive back to the villa as well.

• • • •

That evening the Don invited us to join him for a pre-dinner cocktail in his office retreat. We found him sitting in front of a roaring log fire, drink in hand, reading a report. He stood as we entered and, in a courtly gesture, took Gayle's hand and gently kissed it on the back.

Both Gayle and I had noticed since the first operation on Angelina, the Don was treating us more like honored house guests than reluctant prisoners.

Carlos was not standing in his usual spot by the door. Before I could say a word, Benedetti said, "I understand Carlos decided to take a swim in the canal today. He will be back shortly. He has gone to his sister's house for a change of clothes."

Although the Don had a severe look on his face, his eyes were smiling.

"We know very little about Carlos," Gayle said. "We spend a lot of time with him, but he doesn't talk much. Is he married, Don Benedetti?"

Benedetti nodded. "Carlos is, indeed, a silent man. He has worked for me for years. He's a loyal and trusted associate. He is not married and only has his sister and her young son as his family. He loves his nephew, Gino, with a passion. I truly believe Gino would die for the boy if necessary."

The evening meal that night was quite enjoyable. The Don was in an expansive mood. The man was a born storyteller full of colorful tales of the history of Venice. Although Angelina usually dined alone, she had joined us for coffee and a chocolate treat. We assumed the girl was embarrassed eating with others because of the veil.

That night a central storm system hovered directly over the Venetian Islands. Even from the dinner table, we could hear the threatening sounds of high winds and rain buffeting the villa's walls.

The Don called for Alba to ensure that all the windows were shut tightly against the storm. He remarked, "Usually Carlos would be doing the storm checklist, but he still hasn't returned from his sister's house. Perhaps, because of the storm, he will spend the night there."

We thanked Benedetti for his hospitality before heading off to our suite for the balance of the evening.

• • • •

My deep sleep ended up shattered by a violent hammering on the bedroom door. Our beside alarm showed it was just before 3:00 a.m. Gayle also woke and hurriedly donned a robe. Before either of us could respond to the loud knocking, the door flew open. Carlos stood there, sobbing. He was soaking wet, a look of extreme anguish on his rugged features.

I couldn't understand a word of the rapid flow of Italian, but

Gayle did. "Mark, we have a medical emergency. Carlo's nephew is in severe pain. They couldn't get him to the hospital because of the storm. The boy is out in the car."

Although I didn't know any details of the boy's condition, I blurted out, "Gayle, go and get the operating room prepped. Carlos can help me get the lad into the house."

After reaching the car, it took me only a few moments to diagnose that the boy was suffering from a severe bout of appendicitis. Between us, we managed to get young Gino out of the car and down to the operating theater. By now, the boy was screaming in pain.

After assessing the situation, I whispered to Gayle, "I'm worried that he's on the verge of having a burst appendix. I don't want to fiddle with a laparoscopic approach if that's the case, so prep him for an open procedure."

By now, the Don and most of the household staff had joined with the sobbing Carlos, all pushing to get closer to the boy. I held up my hand to hold them back.

"Don Benedetti, please take these people with you and leave immediately. We don't want to take a chance of contaminating the area. Please take Carlos to your office and give him a cognac. We will report to you as soon as we can."

I could tell the Don didn't like taking instructions, but he saw the wisdom of my order and silently complied.

Although I hadn't done an appendectomy for some years, my early training kicked in, and the procedure went smoothly. I smiled at my nurse. "Just in the nick of time, Gayle. Look at how swollen this appendix is. It could have ruptured any minute."

We both knew the severe consequences if the organ had released bacterial infection into the abdominal cavity with a resulting high risk of peritonitis. The quick removal of the boy's appendix intact had avoided this potentially fatal condition.

Gayle wheeled Gino into the recovery room while I washed up. After we finished cleaning up, we double-checked on Gino and then headed up to Benedetti's office.

We were totally unprepared for the reception we got. Upon entering the office, I saw Carlos with his head down being consoled by the Don. A half-empty bottle of aged cognac with two glasses sat on the edge of the desk. On spotting us, Carlos jumped to his feet, a mixture of hope and despair on his tearful face.

I decided to address my remarks to Carlos with Gayle translating. Benedetti leaned forward to hear the results.

"Signore Carlos," I said. "The operation was a great success. We safely removed Gino's appendix. The boy should be just fine in a few more days. We recommend that he stay at the villa until he is completely recovered…"

I couldn't continue because Carlos seized me in a giant bear hug then covered my face with slobbering kisses. When I finally escaped the embrace, Gayle got the benefit of a second repeat performance. The Don was standing behind his desk, handing out cigars to everyone. Only Gayle declined his offer.

From that day on, Carlos was like a lapdog. We could do no wrong in his eyes. He even participated in the daily English lessons Gayle was giving to Alba and Angelina. I was also studying Italian, gradually becoming conversational, if not quite fluent. We also found ourselves becoming much more involved with outside medical activities.

When word of Gino's operation spread through the village, ailing residents started dropping in at the villa. The numbers grew to the point that it was necessary to open a full-day clinic every Wednesday. I completed three more procedures on Angelina in between clinics, finding each one increasingly delicate and time-consuming.

• • • •

THE VENDETTA

As time passed by, I found myself developing a morbid fascination with our captor. Since Gino's emergency operation, Benedetti had become increasingly friendly. He frequently asked me to join him for a drink before going to bed. Sometimes we played a game of backgammon as we discussed events taking place around the world.

Contrary to popular misconceptions, the Don was not some thuggish mafia brute. He was well educated, well informed, and a genial host. As far as I could tell, Benedetti spoke several languages and had business interests worldwide. He was also known to the household staff as an incurable practical joker.

As time passed, I became convinced that I was dealing with two very different Don Benedetti's. In one persona, he was a thoughtful, kind, and benevolent family man. In this role, he arbitrated disputes and handed out advice and sometimes money to any of the numbers of Murano residents who requested a personal audience.

But many times, particularly regarding his business dealings, the other Don Benedetti emerged. In this role, he could be cold, calculating, and sometimes even quite violent. This trait was particularly true in the strange case of Pietro Esposito.

It happened this way:

Gayle and I were lounging in the villa's library drinking espresso, reading the latest copies of the New York Times. The Don had kindly arranged for the papers' procurement to help us keep in touch with news from home. Suddenly we heard loud voices coming from The Don's office, followed by the sharp report of a gunshot.

Being native New Yorkers, we both were all too familiar with gunshots. When we burst through the office door, the pungent smell of gunpowder overpowered the confined close quarters. Don Benedetti was standing behind his desk with blood streaming from a shallow cut on his hand. Carlos stood over a prone man pointing a revolver at the man's head. The man on the floor was still alive but bleeding profusely from a bullet wound to his upper right arm.

"Gayle, grab some towels from the bathroom!" I yelled.

I quickly evaluated both wounds. When the towels arrived, I bound Benedetti's hand tightly and then made a makeshift tourniquet around the wounded man's arm.

"What happened to...?"

My question was interrupted by Benedetti barking orders at Carlos. The Don's face mirrored a strange mixture of fear and fury.

"Get that piece of filth out of my office," Benedetti commanded. "He's ruining my carpet. Dispose of him outside."

While Gayle took the Don onto the adjacent washroom to cleanse his superficial wound, I helped Carlos get the wounded man to his feet. The young man half walked and half staggered. Carlos was heading for the outside doors, but I convinced him we should take the man to the surgery first.

I had just finished cutting off the young man's shirt sleeve when the Don burst into the operating room. Gayle had applied fresh bandages to Benedetti's hand—the bleeding appeared to have stopped.

I turned to Benedetti. "It appears this man is quite lucky. I'm pretty sure we can save his arm..."

"Stop!" Benedetti shouted.

"But I need to...."

"This piece of garbage has a vendetta against my family," Benedetti interrupted. "Tonight, he tried to kill me with a knife. Only Carlo's quick action saved my life. You will not save the assassin's arm. You will amputate it so that he may never hold a knife against me again."

I stared at Benedetti. I knew I had to take a stand, or I would forever have to follow the Don's orders, no matter how despicable they might be.

"I know from our conversations that you are a great believer in loyalty and the value of binding oaths," I said softly. "But as a doctor, I too took an oath. I swore above all to do no harm to my patients. I will not break this oath for you or anyone else. This man's vendetta is against you, not me. If you want to cut off his arm, be my guest."

I moved across to Benedetti then silently handed him a scalpel. As he held the sharp instrument in his hand, the rage behind his eyes seemed to cool. Without a word, he dropped the scalpel and abruptly left the room with Carlos following a step behind.

Gayle quickly proceeded to put Pietro under so I could remove the bullet from his arm. It was difficult, but I managed to complete the operation without further damage to nerves or muscle tissue. As I worked on the wounded man, I couldn't help wondering what fate Benedetti had in mind for my patient.

● ● ● ●

Two full days passed with no sign of Don Benedetti. He remained in seclusion in his office. We had just completed a dressing change on young Pietro's arm when Carlos came into the recovery room holding a pistol.

"Get up. The Don wants you in his office." Carlos spoke in Italian.

Gayle tried to talk Carlos out of moving Pietro, but he persisted. After Pietro left the room at gunpoint, we spent the next anxious hour waiting for the sound of a shot to break the eerie silence of the villa.

Inside the office, the young man sat on a chair in front of the Don's desk, where Carlos had roughly dumped him. Pietro started to speak, but Benedetti held up his injured hand for silence.

"You would be sitting here with only one arm if Doctor Gunderson hadn't intervened on your behalf."

Pietro said nothing.

Benedetti continued. "I know you hold me responsible for the death of your father. He was murdered while I sat at the bedside of my dying wife in Venice. That was the night my villa was robbed of a great treasure. Someone started a false rumor that I blamed your father for the theft and ordered his death."

"Did you?" Pietro murmured.

"No. This rumor was not true. I had been friends with the Esposito family for many years, and I knew your father did not commit the robbery. We knew the thief had to be the glassmaker, Antonio Fontana, because he fled from Murano when we started the search."

The Don stopped to light up a cigar. "Pietro, this vendetta between our families has gone on long enough. It is time to end it now." He motioned for Carlos to approach the desk with his pistol.

"Give me the gun, Carlos, and go back to your station by the door." Carlos did as he was instructed, then Benedetti put the gun in his desk drawer. At the same time, he brought out a long, wicked-looking stiletto which he placed, handle first, in front of the confused young man.

"Pietro, I know who stole my treasure, but I do not know who killed your father. In this world, we all have many enemies. Perhaps we will never know who is responsible. But I swear to you this, I did not kill your father, nor do I have any knowledge of who might have done it. If you want the vendetta to continue, then pick up the knife and kill me. Carlos will not stop you. Otherwise, go with my blessing, the vendetta will end, and I will forgive you for the recent attempt on my life."

Pietro picked up the stiletto.

● ● ● ●

Gayle and I waited anxiously for the outcome of the meeting in the office. "It's now been over an hour. What the hell could be happening in the office, Mark?"

Before I could respond, the bell rang to announce visitors at the front door. Alba was cleaning upstairs, and Carlos was still in the office, so I decided to answer the door. Outside, a long black town car waited at the curbside, the engine still running. Two husky men approached and announced they were assigned to pick up Pietro Esposito. The men appeared friendly enough, but I couldn't help but notice the telltale bulges under their jackets.

However, my concern was short-lived because the door to the Don's office opened, and Pietro emerged smiling and unharmed. He walked directly over to me.

"Doctor Gunderson, I want to thank you for saving my arm and possibly my life. Don Benedetti has told me of your intervention. I owe you and your wife a debt of gratitude. I hope one day to be able to repay that debt."

He shook hands awkwardly with his uninjured arm and departed.

Benedetti motioned to us to join him in the office. Once inside, he said, "Mark, you have done me a great service. Because your actions spared the boy's arm, I decided to spare his life. Without your intervention, I would have very likely had him eliminated to make sure he was no future threat. In that case, the vendetta would have continued for generations, perhaps even bringing harm to my beloved Angelina."

Gayle noticed that Benedetti had addressed Mark by his first name. It was the first time he had done this since they arrived at the villa. Benedetti poured us both a glass of red wine and told us all about his meeting with Pietro.

"For a few minutes, I thought that Pietro might actually use the knife to kill me, but then I looked at Carlos. He was glaring so hard at Pietro's back I thought the young man's jacket would catch fire."

We all laughed, with even Carlos reluctantly joining in.

• • • •

THE UNVEILING

One evening after dinner, the Don asked us to join him in his office for cognac and a chat. As we sat warmed by the open fire, The Don asked us a question.

"If Angelina's operation is a success, and you receive your reward, what will you do with it?"

"We haven't talked much about it, but Gayle and I want to spend our lives helping as many people as we can. Our goal is to organize a charity focusing on medical care for injured children."

The Don nodded and made notes on his pad.

Nothing else was mentioned about the reward or our future plans, so we discussed Italian politics until it was time for bed.

Between outings with Carlos and our weekly clinics, time passed by quickly. Soon it was the middle of November and time for the final and crucial operation on Angelina's face. As far as Gayle could tell, Angelina had kept her pledge to not look at her face in a mirror until all the procedures were done.

While the young girl waited on the table for the operation to proceed, we carried on a lively conversation, switching effortlessly from Italian to English and back again. Angelina kept inquiring about Pietro's arm, wondering if he had fully recovered. Both Gayle and I suspected a hidden motive behind the inquiries because Angelina had confessed that she thought him quite handsome when she saw Pietro leaving the villa. I was oblivious to their conversation; I was anxious to get started with the operation.

The procedure took much longer than I had anticipated. I knew by instinct that I was trying for a level of perfection that just wasn't achievable.

Finally, I finished and turned to Gayle. "Now we have to wait for the healing to see the final result. I know she'll never win any beauty contests, honey, but at least I think we've improved on the worst of the botched operations."

With six weeks left before Angelina had to decide if she would participate in the annual Christmas town square parade, Gayle decided to take one more step. She met with Angelina several times each week, showing her how to do her hair and how to apply makeup. She did the cosmetic lesson by having Angelina watch as Gayle applied makeup to her own face.

Angelina had finally stopped wearing her full-length black robe. Most days, she moved around the villa with a black veil covering only her face. Gayle and I both noticed that the young girl was rapidly transforming into a slim-figured young woman.

The night before the Christmas festivities were scheduled to occur, we had a deep discussion in our suite. Both of us were experiencing severe tension—Gayle more than me on this occasion.

"What happens if she won't remove her veil? Benedetti said he would remove our hands if Angelina's operation failed to meet her expectations."

"I honestly don't think he would do it, honey. Look at the way he's been treating us lately. It's almost as if we've become part of the family."

"Don't kid yourself, Mark. Benedetti took an oath, and he was deadly serious. Carlos loves us both, or at least he loves me anyway, and he confessed that he would have to carry the threat through if the Don ordered him to do it."

● ● ● ●

I tried to calm her down. "Look, sweetheart, we've done the best we could do. Let's look at the bright side. If Angelina is brave enough to take part in the parade without her veil, we get the reward from the Don and can finally get on with our lives again."

I tossed and turned all night long. Gayle wasn't sleeping much better. She occasionally emitted noises that were seemingly driven by a series of nightmares. I knew instinctively I had called on every ounce of experience and talent during the reconstruction of Angelina's face. I could only hope now for the best.

Finally, daylight filtered gently through the bedroom windows. I dressed quickly and went in search of a badly needed coffee. I was surprised to see Benedetti already seated at the breakfast table, dressed in a purple satin dressing gown and smoking the first cigar of the day.

"Buongiorno, Mark, did you sleep well?"

I stared at the Don, wondering again about the perverse nature of my relationship with this enigma of a man. I thought to myself, *by nightfall, the man could be cutting off my hands, but here in the morning, he seems concerned whether I had a good sleep or not.*

I decided to be blunt. "No, I did not have a peaceful night, nor did my wife. We're both very concerned about the threat hanging over our heads."

Benedetti looked solemn as he stood up and started to leave. He stopped at the door long enough to make a sobering remark.

"It is my sincere hope that today ends happily for my daughter—for both our sakes."

● ● ● ●

We stood in the front of a large crowd of local folks at the town square, having arrived earlier by car with some of the house staff. Don Benedetti and Angelina were due to arrive at 3:00 p.m. for the start of the Christmas parade. Although the day was bright and sunny, the temperature had been steadily dropping since morning.

You could almost cut the tension in the chilly air with a dull knife. Rumors had been spreading for months about Angelina's operations and the Don's threat to mutilate the two Americans if the operations' results were not acceptable.

Over time, we became popular with the town inhabitants because of the charity medical work we had performed at the clinic in the villa. One older lady, dressed all in black, hobbled slowly over the cobblestones leaning heavily on her cane. She took me by both hands, then spoke Italian in a low quivering voice.

I tried to understand her, but I couldn't quite make out what she said above the crowd's noise. I turned to Gayle for a translation. At first, she didn't want to tell me the message, but I insisted.

"The old lady says the whole village is praying to the Virgin to save your hands from the Don's revenge," Gayle mumbled.

I wished I hadn't asked.

Promptly at 3:00 p.m., two long black limos with darkened windows pulled up then stopped in the center of the brightly decorated town square. After the first vehicle's doors opened slowly, Carlos and three other bodyguards emerged warily, scanning the crowd for any signs of obvious danger.

Carlos nodded his approval to the driver of the second car. The uniformed man then immediately jumped out and opened the back door for Don Benedetti. The Don looked quite dapper, wearing a black tuxedo. He carried a silver-tipped walking stick under his left arm.

We waited, but there was no sign of Angelina.

The silence in the square was unnatural. The entire crowd stood quietly, holding a collective breath, waiting to see if Angelina would emerge with her face uncovered or not. Even Benedetti was nervously pacing back and forth, fidgeting with his walking stick. Finally, we could see some movement from the backseat, then Angelina emerged into the sunlight.

A loud disappointed moan rose from the crowd when Angelina emerged, still dressed from head to toe in her traditional black garb. Even from my position at the edge of the group, I could hear Angelina's loud sobs of despair coming from under the veil.

When he saw her, the Don shook with rage. He threw the silver-tipped walking stick onto the cobblestoned surface with such violence that it shattered in three jagged pieces. Benedetti motioned for Carlos to join him and began issuing a string of orders. The Don turned and pointed angrily at us.

Carlos approached us. He was apologetic but firm, "The Don has ordered me to take you back to the villa, but first, he wants to speak with you."

Carlos took a firm grip on our arms and steered us to the center of the square. Benedetti, hunched over the hood of the limo, had his back to the crowd. His torso noticeably shaking with rage.

Angelina's sounds of despair were still quite audible. I desperately tried to formulate a plea that would at least spare Gayle from the amputations when Benedetti turned and faced us.

To our astonishment, The Don had tears running down his face. He was shaking, not with rage, but with barely controlled laughter. Without a word, he walked over to Angelina and pulled on a drawstring. The black robe fell to the ground in a silent shroud. The covering had been concealing, not Angelina, but Alba, the housemaid. She was also doing her best not to laugh out loud.

I was bewildered until some other movement became apparent behind the darkened car windows. The Don personally opened the back door with a flourish, causing a deafening roar from the crowd. Looking back on what took place on that fateful day will always remain in my most cherished memories. It was like watching a rare and delicate butterfly emerging in slow motion from a long-dormant cocoon.

Angelina gracefully stepped out into the fading sunlight in full view of the cheering crowd. She wore a full-length white lace dress, accented with silver and gold piping on the sleeves and hemline. The dress highlighted her youthful but striking figure. Her raven black hair was artfully cut to frame her delicate features. She had a serene smile on her face exposing perfect white teeth. Angelina had applied makeup, and it was skillfully done.

Gayle couldn't hold back her tears at the sight of the brave young woman making her debut in front of the whole town. I had tears in my eyes too.

Both Benedetti and Angelina hugged Gayle first and then me, with obvious affection. The Don gave me a formal bow, shook my hand, then spoke in a voice quivering with emotion.

"Signore Mark, I apologize for making you suffer because of my little joke with Alba. You and your wife have given life back to my only daughter. I will be eternally in your debt. From this day forward, you are under the protection of the Benedetti family."

I hardly heard his words. I was still stunned by Angelina's appearance. I had seen her many times during the operations but never as the lovely vision that she now presented. It was indeed my best work of art.

I struggled to find my voice. "Thank you, Don Benedetti," I said formally. "Gayle and I are so pleased for Angelina."

"No, no, you must call me Lorenzo," Benedetti laughed. "After all, you are family now."

Benedetti signaled for the band to strike up a tune in preparation for the start of the parade. Then the Don, Angelina, Gayle, and I linked arms and led the procession as it circled the square. Carlos and Alba followed close behind. The crowd roared their approval as Angelina continued to wave and blow kisses.

Standing in the crowd waving back madly, with a foolish but infatuated grin on his face, was none other than young Pietro Esposito. He had come to watch the parade, but afterward, he could remember seeing only one thing.

The captivating form of the enchanting Angelina Benedetti.

● ● ● ●

AN UNEXPECTED SNOWFALL

Although her four-poster bed was warm and comfortable, Angelina was too excited to sleep. A multitude of memories of her triumphant debut in the town square still played in her mind. The most exciting and vaguely disturbing of the flashbacks was recalling the look on Pietro's face when she emerged from the car.

I have a feeling that Pietro Esposito finally saw me today for the very first time.

After another hour of futile tossing and turning, Angelina gave up. She rose, donned a flannel nightgown and her fuzzy pink slippers, then departed for the kitchen in search of a warm glass of milk. It was always a sure-fire antidote for her restlessness.

The heavy curtains on her full-length bedroom windows were closed except for a small gap where the two sides met. As she passed the window, something caught her attention. A faint suggestion of something moving in the outside air. She pulled the drawstring, opening the curtains to investigate.

Angelina was stunned. The whole night sky twinkled with the reflection of gently falling snowflakes, caught in the beams from the garden security lights. Angelina had seen snow a few times before, but always only a slight dusting of the land before quickly melting away.

This was different. The cold front that had been building all day ensured the flakes were preserved. The outside lawn had already accumulated a significant build-up. Angelina left her bedroom and ran to the stairs thinking, *I must tell Papa about the snowfall before it melts. It is just like a Christmas miracle!*

The door to her father's office was opening as Angelina approached. She was surprised and a little flustered to see the lithe figure of Pietro Esposito emerge, closing the office door behind him.

"Pietro, what on earth are you doing here so late at night?"

The young man was caught off guard. "Oh, Angelina, I'm sorry if I startled you. Your father asked if I could meet with him and Carlos about some business opportunities for the new year. He's a busy man, so you have to meet him when you can, I guess."

"That's all right, Pietro," Angelina said shyly. "Did you see the snowfall outside?"

"It was snowing when I arrived, but I thought it would all be melted by now. Is it still hanging around?"

"Come and see for yourself." Angelina led him by the hand to the expansive dining room windows.

Pietro was caught off guard by the heavy white blanket that covered everything in sight. He was also desperate to find an excuse to spend more time with Angelina. "This is a wonderful surprise, Angelina. Let's go outside and try to make a snowball. I've never done it before."

At the mention of outside, they both became acutely aware that Angelina was still wearing her nightclothes. Angelina, her face flushed, said, "Wait for me, Pietro. I'll only be a few minutes while I dress into something more suitable for an outdoor excursion."

The maid, Alba, smiled as she passed Angelina in the upstairs hallway. She thought to herself, *Miss Angelina must have discovered that young Pietro is in the vicinity judging by the look on her face.*

Alba was carrying a tray of hot chocolate and snifters of cognac to the guest quarters for us as a treat. She knocked on the guest room door and entered.

"Buona sera, signore e signora Gunderson. I have for you a nice treat, compliments of Don Benedetti." She placed the tray on the side table. "Have you seen the snow? It's still coming down, covering everything."

Gayle rushed to open the bedroom drapes.

"Alba," I said. "I wouldn't have believed that you would experience snow in a warm place like Venice."

"I've seen the snow a few times, signore, it always melts. But I have never seen a sight like this before. Perhaps it will remain for the holidays. The children will love it."

After the maid left, I joined Gayle at the window. "That's quite a sight, hon. Who would have thought we would ever miss snow after living in New York all our lives? I feel a little homesick looking out there."

"Me too, honey. Why don't we go outside and make a snow angel? I haven't done anything like that since I was a kid."

I laughed then started to search for some outdoor clothing.

By the time we arrived at the back lawn, Angelina and Pietro were in the final stages of shaping the head for their snowman. They had done an excellent job building a man-like snow creature almost as tall as Pietro.

Gayle giggled. "Wow, Angelina, for a moment, I was frightened when I saw it."

I thought the snowman, with only a portion exposed to the garden lights, did look a little scary. I had a sudden thought. "You know, your father is always playing practical jokes on us. Why don't we give him a taste of his own medicine?" I quickly explained my idea to the others.

Angelina laughed. "This is a good plan. I will retrieve one of my father's cloaks and a hat from the hall closet. When it is on the snow person, we can play the joke."

With the snowman fully dressed, it did indeed vaguely resemble a sinister stranger standing hiding in the shadows. Gayle and I, along with Pietro, took refuge behind a corner of the villa, waiting to pelt Don Benedetti with snowballs after Angelina completed her part of the plan.

Angelina, in turn, raced up to her room to change back into her nightclothes. Still slightly breathless from her exertions, she ran down the stairs and, without knocking, burst through the doors of her father's office.

"Help Papa!" she screamed. "I saw an intruder on the back lawn. I'm afraid he's heading for the house!"

Don Benedetti and Carlos were sharing a nightcap after a long day of meetings. As expected, he leaped to his feet, knocking the coffee and brandy flying in his haste. "Quickly, Carlos, follow me."

Because she was running behind her father, Angelina didn't see Carlos rummaging in the desk drawer for a weapon.

We were ready with our snowball ammunition when the Don,

followed by Angelina, arrived on the run. Angelina pointed to the snowman and screamed, "There he is, Papa."

Gayle was preparing to fire the first snowball at Benedetti when our good practical joke turned terrible. Before she could throw the snowy missile and reveal the prank, Carlos arrived on the scene, gun hand extended.

"Everybody, get down, now!" Carlos yelled.

His scream startled Angelina, but before she could say anything, Carlos fired his pistol four times in rapid succession, directly into the chest and head of the intruder. The high-velocity shells ripped the cape and blew the hat off the figure, exposing the naked snowman to view.

"Oh, shit," I whispered to Gayle. "Now we're in trouble."

The Don took a deep breath then stalked angrily toward the dead snowman. He held up his favorite cloak, poking his fingers through the bullet holes, then retrieved his ruined top hat. Angelina was petrified, and so was Pietro. Benedetti was known throughout Italy for his mercurial temper.

To the astonishment of everyone, he began to laugh. And not just his regular chuckle but a full-throated belly laugh. In all her years, Angelina had never seen her father laugh so hard. As a connoisseur of practical jokes himself, the Don appreciated the finesse and meticulous planning of the trick we had played on him.

As he continued to roar with laughter, the mirth became contagious, and soon everyone, including Carlos, was laughing as well. Gayle, still holding her snowball, spotted a likely target and fired her shot at the back of my head. That set off the war, and within seconds, dozens of snowy projectiles filled the air. When her father, still laughing, hit Carlos's square on the end of his prominent beak, Angelina thought he looked like a happy man.

Eventually, the snow fight ended, and Pietro, looking at his watch, thanked everyone and said it was time for him to leave. Although it was quite late, Benedetti invited us to join him by the fire for a nightcap before going to bed.

Benedetti led the procession into the villa, while Angelina

remained behind to say goodnight to Pietro. She held out her hand for the young man to shake but was both surprised and delighted when he kissed her instead.

When she returned to the bed she had earlier abandoned, Angelina reflected on the many happenings of the day. She remembered her thrill at finally taking part, unveiled, in the town's annual Christmas parade. And her father's practical joke, pretending Alba was her and, of course, the delightful snowball fight. But most of all, she dwelt on the strange sensations she felt when she shared her first kiss with Pietro.

Angelina turned off the light and snuggled down under the warm blankets. Her last thought before drifting off was, *this has been the best day of my life. I will never forget it ever.*

Outside the villa, the snow continued to fall.

• • • •

BANCO SAN PAOLO

With the Christmas festivities finally over, several days had passed by with no mention of the reward. Gayle and I were starting to wonder if Don Benedetti had changed his mind when Carlos told us he wanted to see us in his office.

We found our host hard at work in his walnut-paneled office. He looked up from a pile of papers and smiled as we entered.

"Please, make yourselves comfortable. I apologize for not talking to you sooner, but several matters needed to be arranged first." We took our usual seats in front of the large desk and waited.

Don Benedetti lit another cigar. "Tomorrow, Carlos will drive us to the ferry, then we'll go to the Banco San Paolo. We will take the safety box key and our euro note. Roberto Farina will join us. He is the leading evaluator in Venice."

I looked at Gayle and smiled. It was finally happening as the Don had promised.

Benedetti continued. "It occurred to me that it would be impractical for you to try and take the contents of the deposit box back to the USA in physical form. Roberto will assess the contents and determine a total value in US dollars. We will then have a certified check made out for the amount. This check will be payable to your newly formed charity. By doing this, you will not be liable for any USA taxation."

We shook hands with Benedetti then returned to our suite in a state of high excitement. Finally, after all this time and worry, we would be on the way back to New York in a matter of days. We were both looking forward to reuniting with friends and family, although we knew everyone would be shocked to find out we were still alive.

"I can hardly believe it, Mark. With the Benedetti donation, we have a good chance of getting our new charity off the ground. Do you have any idea how much it might be?"

"Honey, I haven't got a clue. But from the hermit's description of the stolen treasure, I wouldn't be surprised if it was over a hundred thousand dollars. Maybe, even more."

• • • •

The gray skies and pouring rain the following day didn't dampen our spirits. We joined Benedetti and Angelina for breakfast, chatting happily over coffee until we heard Carlos report that the limo was ready. Angelina was not joining us on the Banco San Paolo trip because young Pietro had called and asked her to join him for lunch.

When the small water taxi from Murano arrived in Venice, Carlos helped Don Benedetti and Gayle up the stone steps to the wharf. The waiting limo quickly took us to the Piazza San Marco location of the stately Banco San Paolo.

Inside the bank, Benedetti made an imposing sight. He wore a long black cape and a top hat. The Don also carried his recently repaired silver-tipped walking stick. He strode in a straight line across the marble floor, heading directly for the manager's office. As he forged past the receptionist's desk, she jumped to her feet to stop him.

"Excuse me, sir. You can't go back there without an appointment."

The Don just glared at her and continued with us trailing in his wake. He pushed open the door without knocking and entered. A small thin man, wearing a starched white shirt and a pin-striped suit, was sitting at the massive desk, working on some papers.

Benedetti stared at the man and then rapped the desk with his walking stick. "Who the hell are you? Where is Angelo Cavallo, the manager?"

The man jumped to his feet. The young receptionist may not have known who this important customer was, but the flustered assistant manager certainly did.

"Oh, excuse me, Don Benedetti, I had no idea you were coming to our offices today. My name is Gino Durante. I am the assistant manager. I'm filling in for signore Cavallo while he is enjoying an extended Christmas holiday with his family in Bermuda."

The receptionist came to the door to announce that Roberto Farina had arrived, looking for Don Benedetti. Benedetti smiled. "Good, my evaluator has arrived. We can now get started."

The Don turned to the assistant manager and threw one half of the five euro note on the desk. "You have a deposit box registered in the name of Antonio Fontana. I have with me the key. You will now open the box and then leave us in privacy."

"With all due respect Don Benedetti, if the box is registered to Antonio Fontana, it would not be proper to open it without his presence," Durante said shakily.

Benedetti glared at the frightened man. "Fontana is dead. He left his estate to me. Now, take us to the box."

The assistant typed the serial number of the euro note into his computer. "Si, Don Benedetti, we have a confirmed match. The safety deposit box is #888."

Moments later, we all assembled in the safety deposit box vault. Box #888 was massive. The stainless-steel front showed two different keyholes. Gino Durante inserted the key held by the bank into the first slot and then left the room. Don Benedetti, with a flourish, bowed, then turned to Gayle.

"This key has rested safely in the base of the Madonna statue for many years. I believe it is only fitting that it be finally used by another Madonna." He handed the key to Gayle.

Gayle took the key with trembling hands then softly kissed Don Benedetti on the cheek. Roberto Farina moved closer in anticipation of the first sight of the items he was expected to value for the Don.

I held Gayle by one hand as she inserted the key and opened the box's outer door. Inside was a closely fitted steel container, almost as large as the safety deposit box itself. Carlos removed the container and placed it on the examining table in the center of the room.

On a whim, Gayle said, "For good luck, why don't we all open the box together? Everyone put a hand on the top. I'll count to three, then we open the lid."

Benedetti thought this was a good idea. He placed his hand on the container, as did Gayle and myself. Carlos and Roberto Farina abstained.

From Gayle's beaming smile, I could tell she was thinking of the bright new future for the children's charity with this box's contents. She slowly counted to three, and we lifted the lid together.

The color left my face as I stared. Benedetti looked like he was going to have a stroke. The safety deposit box on the table in front of him was empty, except for an envelope that lay waiting on the bottom of the container. The yellowing edges of the envelope indicated that the paper was quite old. It was addressed to Don Benedetti. I recognized the handwriting immediately.

It was identical to the writing on the hermit's last confession.

A HERMIT'S REVENGE

When Don Benedetti finished reading the letter, his face tightened into a rigid mask. He handed the document to Gayle to interpret for me. Gayle's voice quavered as she interpreted the letter into English.

To: Signore Don Benedetti

If you are the person reading this document, my worst fears have come to pass. It will mean that, somehow, you have recovered the key and the euro note and have accessed this box.

But, if someone other than Don Benedetti is reading this letter, then perhaps my prayers have been answered. Possibly now, my hope that the treasure I stole would be used for the benefit of humanity will be fulfilled.

Why is box #888 empty? And where is the treasure?

On the day that I fled Murano, I came to this Banco San Paolo branch and rented this box. After the manager left the room, I intended to deposit the treasure in the box. Still, I started to worry that Benedetti or his men would somehow discover what I had done.

I decided against my original plan and left only this letter in the box. I was not sure I could ever return to Venice without risking discovery by the Don. This meant I had to hide the treasure in such a manner that he would never find it but that it could still be available to someone of good heart if it were the will of the Lord.

On leaving the Banco San Paolo, I took the train then proceeded directly to the law offices of Marco Amodeo in Cortina. Signore Amodeo had represented my father for years, and I knew him to be an honorable man. Together we worked out a plan to safeguard the valuables. I then departed for the old cabin high in the mountains of Cortina. I planned to seek refuge there until enough time passed for me to try to safely recover the treasure myself.

If someone is reading this letter, it means that I will never be returning to Venice in this life. By taking this letter along with the key to the safety box to Marco Amodeo's offices, you can start the process of recovering the treasure. Signore Amodeo is only authorized to release information if he is convinced the proceeds will not fall into the hands of Don Benedetti of Murano.

I pray again that the treasure will be recovered by the hands of someone with a good heart who will take up my quest to help those less fortunate in life.

Signed: Antonio Fontana
Artisan First Class

Gayle finished reading the letter. "What do we do now, Mark?"

I looked to Don Benedetti for guidance. His face was cold as granite. He remained silent for a few moments before barking orders.

"Carlos and I will return to the villa. Mark, you and Gayle must take the express train to Cortina and search out this lawyer, Marco Amodeo. Take with you the original confession of the bastard, Antonia Fontana. If you give to the lawyer that confession, this new letter, and the deposit box key, he should be convinced."

The limo dropped us off at the Venice Central Rail station before taking Benedetti and Carlos back to the Murano water taxi dock. Once on the train, I searched the internet for information on the lawyer, Marco Amodeo. I located the telephone number, called, and made an appointment for one hour after arriving in Cortina.

The offices of lawyer Amodeo were old, dusty, and frayed around the edges. Something like the lawyer himself. He was gaunt with skin like aged parchment. He stood when we entered his office, shook hands, then invited us to sit. He spoke passable English.

"How may I be of service, Doctor Gunderson?"

"Signore Amodeo, we are here on a matter that concerns the late Antonio Fontana."

The lawyer's ears perked up at the name. "Please continue, signore."

I reached into my jacket pocket then placed the contents, one at a time, on the desk in front of the lawyer.

Amodeo started with the confession Antonia Fontana had left hidden in the old log cabin. Then he carefully read the letter from the safety deposit box. Lastly, the old lawyer picked up the key from box #888. He took his glasses off and turned to me.

"Please, Doctor and Mrs. Gunderson, tell me the entire story of how you came to have these items in your possession."

Between us, we told the whole story beginning with finding the Hermit's confession, to the key hidden in the Madonna statue, to the involvement of Don Benedetti and his daughter Angelina. It was a long story, broken only by a stop for some fresh coffee.

"Antonio Fontana expressly forbids me to disclose any information if it would benefit Benedetti," the lawyer said. "You say Benedetti is going to give you a check equal in value to the goods stolen by Fontana. How do you know the Don will honor his promise and make this donation to your charity?"

"Signore Amodeo, Don Benedetti was present when we opened box #888. He fully expected the stolen valuables to be there. He had even arranged for a valuator to be present to determine the total value for his donation. Gayle and I are absolutely convinced he will keep his word."

The lawyer sat for a few moments, then rose from his seat and walked painfully over to a full-length office safe. He fumbled with the combination before he retrieved a large brown envelope and returned to the desk.

"My friend, Antonio Fontana, was a good man who did a bad thing. I know he would rest more easily if he knew his deed would help injured children for many years to come. I am satisfied that I can release the information to you."

With that, he opened the envelope and took out a safety deposit box key and one-half of a five euro note. The crest on the key was for the Banco San Paolo in Venice. The key had a self-stick label marked Box #777.

Gayle shook her head and stared at the key. "I don't understand, signore Amodeo. The key we had was for box #888 at the same bank as before?"

The lawyer nodded. "There is an old Sicilian saying. The best place to hide a stolen chicken is in a chicken coop."

He explained that they had decided the best place to hide the stolen goods was right back at the same bank but in a different safety deposit box.

"After Antonio left to hide at his isolated cabin, I took the train to Venice and opened a box at the Banco. I dealt directly with the branch manager. He seemed interested in the red Swissair suitcase I was carrying. This scrutiny worried me because I thought he might have remembered Antonio carrying the same suitcase when he opened box #888. He said nothing, so I assumed it was just my imagination."

We thanked the old lawyer profusely then took a taxi to a hotel by the train station. I phoned Benedetti to tell him of our conversation with the lawyer.

"We will be on the morning train, Don Benedetti. If you can arrange for the evaluator, Roberto Farina, to join us, we could meet you at the Banco San Paolo at 11:30 a.m."

● ● ● ●

We met Benedetti as scheduled at the bank the following day. I was armed with a letter of authorization from Marco Amodeo, granting us access to safety deposit box #777. The Don was in a foul mood. He didn't like the water taxi from Murano and resented having to take it twice in one week.

He yelled at the assistant manager. "Where the hell is Angelo Cavallo? As a manager of this bank, he is a shit!"

"I apologize, Don Benedetti. Signore Cavallo is still in Bermuda with his family. He is expected back in Venice late tomorrow night."

Still fuming, Benedetti led our small group back into the safety deposit vault. Once again, the assistant manager inserted his key in box #777 and hastily departed. Gayle then inserted the key that had been given to us by the lawyer.

We didn't bother with ceremonies this time. Instead, Carlos just lifted the internal container to the examining table on his own. The Don pushed past him and quickly lifted the top of the container.

When faced with yet another utterly empty deposit box, Benedetti lost his temper. With one sweep of his arms, he pushed the box off the table onto the pristine marble floor. It landed on its side with a resounding crash. The impact dislodged a small item stuck at the back of the container.

Gayle quickly crossed the room and picked up the item. She held it up to the light for all to see. It was a flawless, sparkling diamond around two carats in weight. It was apparent the deposit box at some time had held the treasure. Roberto Farina, the evaluator, asked to examine the stone. He addressed his remarks to Benedetti.

"Assuming the balance of the missing material consists of diamonds of this superior quality, I am certain you would have no difficulty in disposing of them at an excellent price."

Benedetti didn't listen to a word his evaluator said. He stormed back to the manager's office to confront poor Gino Durante.

"Durante, listen to me carefully. If you value your miserable life or those of all your relations, you will say nothing to anyone about the events of today. You will give me the details of Angelo Cavallo's flight from Bermuda. If he contacts you before tomorrow night and you reveal anything, you will sleep with the fishes."

With that, Benedetti stalked out of the bank then boarded the waiting limo. Carlos tried to explain his boss's behavior.

"The Don is frustrated and feels he is being taken for a fool. He doesn't blame you, but he needs some time alone to decide on a new approach. Please come with me back to the villa. I'm sure he'll give us details of the new plan."

● ● ● ●

By the evening meal, the Don had calmed down and was able to talk about the situation in a measured manner. "I have thought about all the possibilities. I now believe that cretin, Angelo Cavallo, is the culprit. Carlos will meet his flight from Bermuda tomorrow night and bring him to the villa. We will have the truth, believe me."

The following day dragged on endlessly because the bank manager's flight was not due to land until almost ten in the evening. Carlos had left for the airport two hours earlier, and Gayle and I waited in the office with The Don for Carlos's return.

Hour after hour, we waited in vain for Carlos to return with the Banco San Paolo manager. Then gradually, the unthinkable began to permeate the room, like an odious unwanted visitor.

Could the stalwart, loyal, and dedicated Carlos have given in to temptation and joined ranks with Cavallo in the theft of the treasure?

The morbid speculation ended when the front door opened. Two uniformed men entered, supporting a blood-stained Carlos between them. The injured man was bleeding badly from a cut to the back of his head.

One of the officers spoke. "My respects Don Benedetti. We found your man lying on the water taxi dock in Venice. He refused to go to the hospital and demanded we bring him directly to you."

Benedetti stood, thanked the two men, and shook hands. Mark noticed that several euro notes changed hands at the same time. After they saluted and departed for the waiting police car, the Don issued instructions.

"Mark, please take Carlos to your clinic to see if you can help him here or if we need an ambulance."

As with many scalp wounds, the copious flow of blood was more of a visual issue than the seriousness of the underlying damage. Gayle and I cleaned and stitched the wound and gave Carlos a painkiller. Afterward, we returned to the Don's office, where coffee and cognac were waiting.

"Take your time. Tell me what happened," Benedetti said softly.

"Si, Don Benedetti. I waited at the airport for Cavallo as instructed. When he departed the airplane, I told him you needed to see him on an urgent matter. His wife and children took a taxi with their luggage. Cavallo had a duty-free bag containing a bottle of expensive cognac. He asked if he could bring it to you as a sign of his respect."

"And what happened then, Carlos?"

"When we arrived at the water taxi, I turned to speak to the driver, then Cavallo hit me on the head with the bottle of cognac. When I awoke, the police were there, but Cavallo was gone. I'm sorry for my failure."

Benedetti tightened his jaw. "That settles it. The attack on Carlos was the act of a guilty man, without question. We will find Cavallo, and he will tell us what we need to know."

Gayle looked sideways at me, then shivered at the sinister tone of Benedetti's voice. Things didn't bode well for the missing bank manager.

Word went out. Find Angelo Cavallo and be rewarded. Hide Cavallo and beware of the consequences. Men remained stationed outside Cavallo's home and office on a twenty-four-hour basis in case he showed up.

Both Gayle and I were becoming impatient to return home, especially after Gayle held a tear-filled telephone conversation with her mother in New York. I finally decided that if the Don couldn't locate Cavallo within the next two weeks, we would have to go home without our reward.

Angelina and her new friend Pietro had just returned from a shopping trip to Venice. The young couple looked happy. Gayle marveled at how Angelina was blossoming into a vibrant, attractive young woman right before our eyes. They had just joined us for coffee when Pietro's cell phone rang.

He took the call, and his eyes widened. "Angelina, quick, this is urgent. Where is your father?"

I replied, "I think he's in the back gardens with Carlos. They wanted to check on some new plantings." Pietro excused himself and hurried off in search of the Don.

Within minutes, Pietro returned, accompanied by a grim-looking Carlos. He apologized to Angelina then said he had to leave immediately. We pressed him for details, but he refused to elaborate. They rushed out to the waiting car and quickly departed in a cloud of dust.

By this time, Don Benedetti had returned from the garden. He stopped at the door to his office and motioned for me to join him.

When Angelina and Gayle rose to accompany me to the meeting, Benedetti stopped them.

"Please, this discussion is for Mark only."

Inside the privacy of his lair, the Don asked me to be seated. He unwrapped a Monte Cristo cigar, paused to light it, and then said, "We have located the bastard, Angelo Cavallo. Pietro has a third cousin who owns a small travel agency in the little village of Ravello. The cousin reports that Cavallo has an appointment today to book a cruise to Gibraltar. The cretin was stupid enough to use his real name. I guess he didn't think we would cover even the smallest of towns."

"Wow, that's certainly good news, Don Benedetti. But why did you not include Gayle and Angelina in our meeting?"

"Because I want you to do me a favor," he responded. "Carlos will bring Cavallo here tonight, then we want to deal with this matter in our traditional way. I ask that you take Angelina and Gayle to Venice for a late meal. Keep them away from the villa, if possible. Please do not tell them about this situation. Tomorrow, I will explain everything to them."

I didn't ask what the "traditional way" entailed. I had a pretty good idea.

The ladies were quite excited when I told them I was taking them to a fancy dinner in Venice. However, not eager enough to quell the constant barrage of questions about Pietro's hasty departure and the mysterious meeting with The Don.

Finally, I put my foot down. "I promised the Don not to talk about it, and I won't."

We took the water taxi to Venice and walked the cobbled side streets for a few hours. Then, after an excellent multi-course meal at the Ristorante Rosa Rosso, I calculated it would be safe to start the return trip to the villa on Murano. The water taxi was virtually empty because of the lateness of the hour. However, the harbor still teemed with tourist-laden gondolas and numerous private vessels.

A gleaming white cruise ship ghosted past us on a late evening departure. The multitude of sparkling lights made it appear like a giant birthday cake floating out to the open sea. A car waited on the Murano docks to take us to the villa.

I wondered what carnage awaited us there.

• • • •

DON BENEDETTI'S SOLUTION

Benedetti warmly greeted us at the door, extending an invitation to join him in the office for a nightcap. Carlos was already seated, a warm glass of brandy in his hand. When he raised the glass to his lips, Gayle and I exchanged glances. The harsh crimson stains contrasting against the starched white of Carlos shirt cuffs gave mute evidence of the evening's activities.

With the drink served, Benedetti started. "This evening, Carlos and I had a discussion with Angelo Cavallo about the missing valuables. Before you ask, he is still alive, or at least he was when he arrived at the hospital."

Carlos chuckled. "Signore Cavallo may have some difficulty writing checks in the future, though."

Don Benedetti nodded. "Do you remember the story of the cleaning lady in Cortina, the cousin of Alba, our housemaid? She perfected the art of tiny thefts, taking only small amounts of money from guests at any one time. No one ever reported her because most people never really know the exact amount of money on their person. And, even if they do, there is a degree of uncertainty that prevents them from reporting the problem."

The Don stopped for a moment, placing an elaborately cut key on the desk in front of him. "It appears that Angelo Cavallo has been running his own version of 'tiny thefts' for many years."

He pointed to the key before continuing. "Cavallo spent a small fortune having this key made. It is a master key that will open every private deposit box at his branch. Periodically, he goes through several boxes at a time looking for cash. When he finds a box containing euros, he removes a few, leaving the bulk intact. He also looks for situations where a safety deposit box holder dies without relatives. In those cases, he removes the entire contents."

Angelina was spellbound. "But what does he do with all the things he steals, Papa?"

Her father snorted. "It seems Cavallo, too, believes that the best place to hide a stolen chicken is in a chicken coop. Evidently, three extra-large safety boxes are the sole property of signore Cavallo. We will all be going there tomorrow morning to see for ourselves."

Don Benedetti rose and said goodnight, but, as he was leaving, he left the group with a final thought.

"It matters little to me if Angelo Cavallo is a petty thief, taking advantage of his position as manager of the Banco San Paolo. He made his fatal mistake by not informing me immediately after becoming aware the lawyer, Amodeo, was renting a box to store the goods stolen from the villa. No one, and, I repeat, no one is permitted to steal from Don Benedetti."

We went to bed with those ominous words still ringing in our ears.

The following morning, we sat together enjoying a morning coffee at an outdoor café in the Piazza San Marco across from the Banco San Paolo. We were waiting for the Don and the others to arrive. Gayle looked pensive.

"I wonder if this will be our last trip to the Banco San Paolo, Mark?"

I was casually tossing crumbs from my bread roll to the flocks of hungry pigeons. "It will have to be, honey, because I have booked our flights back to New York. We leave tomorrow afternoon regardless of what happens here today."

"Oh, I'm so ready to go home," Gayle murmured.

I didn't answer because the moment of truth had arrived. "Okay, we should go now. I see Benedetti's limo coming."

The assistant manager, Durante, greeted us at the door. "I apologize again on behalf of the Banco San Paolo, Don Benedetti. I'm afraid our manager still hasn't returned. We have no idea where he is at this time."

"Don't worry about Cavallo. Is Roberto Farina, my evaluator, here?" The assistant manager nodded and escorted our group into the safety deposit box vault for the third time. Farina was sitting on a hard-backed chair, awaiting our arrival.

Benedetti glared at Gino Durante. "I have been informed that Cavallo has personal possession of three private boxes. Where are they?"

"With all due respect, Don Benedetti, I couldn't under any circumstances assist you with opening the boxes of signore Cavallo without his presence."

"I don't need your damned assistance," Benedetti growled. "Anyway, signore Angelo Cavallo has permitted us to open his boxes. In fact, he gave me his hand on it."

Carlos smirked at this last comment. The assistant manager nodded, then pointed at three boxes before hurrying back to the safety of his office.

The large boxes belonging to Cavallo were all located at floor level, marked #100, #200, and #300. Because Benedetti was having difficulty bending over, Angelina took the master key and inserted it in box #100. Gayle and I, along with Carlos, were holding our breath in anticipation.

Carlos lifted the interior container with some difficulty then placed it on the examining table. As Angelina cautiously lifted the lid, I dreaded to picture Benedetti's reaction if we ended up with another empty container.

My concern evaporated as we gazed down in amazement at the gleaming treasure that had ultimately cost the hermit, Antonio Fontana, his life.

Boxes #200 and #300 also gave up an overflowing accumulation of wealth stolen by Angelo Cavallo in small amounts from the other boxes over a long time. There were stacks of euro notes, US dollars, British pounds, gold coins, and even a thick sheaf of unmarked bearer bonds in large denominations.

Gayle was astounded by the collection of wealth. "What the heck is a bearer bond, Mark?"

"Actually, they are quite rare now. Normally a bond is made payable to a specific person or institution, but a 'bearer' bond can be cashed by anyone who presents it for payment—no questions asked."

The Don issued instructions. "Signore Farina, you will stay here with Carlos and prepare a complete inventory of the contents of these three boxes. I will expect your final evaluation report to be at my office by 9:00 a.m. tomorrow morning. Carlos, you will relock the boxes when you leave and bring the master key to me at the villa."

We left the vault, but Benedetti stopped briefly at the office of the assistant manager. Gino jumped to his feet, obviously petrified.

"Cavallo will not be returning to the Banco San Paolo," Benedetti grunted. "You, Gino Durante, are now promoted to the manager of this branch. Do not give me cause to regret my decision."

In the water taxi, my curiosity finally compelled me to ask. "I realize that Angelo Cavallo won't be returning to his job, but how could you promote Gino Durante on the spot?"

The Don smiled. "It's simple, Mark. I'm the major shareholder in the Banco San Paolo."

● ● ● ●

ARRIVEDERCI VENICE

Benedetti hosted a special but sad farewell dinner for us. Angelina and her friend Pietro were there, along with Carlos, his sister, and nephew Gino, who joined us at the long table. The animated conversation quickly switched back and forth from English to Italian. Finally, after multiple courses of delicious pasta, seafood, and roast boar, The Don clinked his glass and got up to make a speech.

"I would like to make a champagne toast to our honored guests. First, I salute signora Gunderson for her wisdom, her beauty, and her wonderful mentorship of my daughter Angelina. Next, I salute

Doctor Gunderson for his patience, his integrity, and the exceptional medical skills he has shown during his stay at the villa."

The Don stopped for a sip of his champagne. "Because of your presence here, we have avoided a blood feud with the Esposito family. Now, young Pietro is here at our table as a friend, not an enemy. While you were here as our guests, you saved Carlos's nephew from death by performing an emergency operation. You also repaired Carlos's head after his attack from the bastard, Cavallo."

Carlos joked. "My head is now better than before I was struck."

Benedetti smiled at his friend then continued. "I could go on and thank you for teaching us the English, for looking after the medical needs of the village and many other things. But most of all, I want to express my sincere and lasting thanks for bringing my Angelina out of the darkness and into the light."

Tears filled Gayle's eyes at the tribute. I sniffled a little, as well.

"One last thing. My daughter says I must apologize again for the joke I played by pretending our maid Alba under the black cloak was Angelina. It is a bad habit of mine to play the jokes. I will try hard to stop."

Everyone laughed while raising their champagne glasses in a return toast to The Don.

"Don Benedetti, our time here at the villa has been most interesting," I said, rising from my seat. "We come from different cultures, and although we may not see eye to eye on every issue, Gayle and I want to thank you for treating us with respect and making us feel like part of your family. Lastly, on behalf of the many injured children in the world, we thank you in advance for your contribution to the new children's medical charity."

Benedetti nodded. "Tomorrow morning, we will meet in my office and finalize the donation you mentioned. Then Carlos and Angelina will accompany you to Marco Polo airport for your flight home."

Everyone hugged, shook hands, and departed for the night.

◆ ◆ ◆ ◆

In the morning, we had just finished breakfast when we saw Roberto Farina, the evaluator, leaving Benedetti's office. Carlos indicated that the boss was ready to see us. We entered the office to see the Don sitting behind his desk with a formal look on his face. He motioned for us to take a seat.

"Signore Farina has finished his work. He has prepared a separate valuation for box #100, which contained the valuables originally stolen by Antonia Fontana from the villa on the night Angelina was born. These valuables are the property value I have pledged to you as a donation to your charity."

"Again, we thank you for the donation, Lorenzo."

"Farina has also given me a valuation for boxes #200 and #300, which contained the loot stolen by Angelo Cavallo from others over a long period. This amount will come in handy as we have had many unexpected expenses this past year."

Benedetti stopped when Alba arrived, delivering a tray of steaming hot coffee and morning rolls. He stopped to taste the coffee then continued. "I will now make out a check for the donation. Do you have a name for the charity yet?"

I looked at Gayle, and she nodded her assent. "Yes, we do. The name for the new charity is The Angelina Children's Medical Foundation."

Benedetti wiped a tear from the corner of his eye. "I wish to avoid any big show of emotion over this donation, so I am sealing the envelope. I want you to promise me that you will have a glass of champagne then open the envelope halfway across the Atlantic Ocean. Not one minute before."

We agreed to Lorenzo's request immediately.

The Don stood up, shook hands with me, then kissed Gayle on both cheeks. "I will go now to my room as I do not wish to see you leave. But as you go, remember you are now under the protection of the Benedetti family, anywhere in the world, forever."

Gayle started crying now and rushed to hug Benedetti before he left the room.

The ride to the airport was somber. We were both anxious to go home to see our friends and family. Still, we realized the people at the Benedetti Villa were now an integral part of our lives. Carlos drove carefully, intentionally keeping his focus on the road. In the back seat with Gayle, Angelina occasionally sobbed and lay her head on Gayle's shoulder.

I decided it would be a mistake to prolong our departure and the depths of sadness that both Carlos and Angelina felt.

"Gayle, say goodbye to Angelina and Carlos now," I said firmly. "We're going to fast track our way to the departure lounge and let them get on their way home."

Angelina was trying to be brave. "Signora Gayle, I will never forget you and Doctor Mark. You gave me my life back. I will be eternally grateful."

Carlos was unable to speak. He simply shook hands with me, kissed Gayle on both cheeks, turned, and left. Angelina waved and followed him out of the terminal.

• • • •

THE LAST LAUGH

As soon as we boarded the flight, we were treated like arriving royalty. It was apparent The Don had put out the word. To our great surprise, the crew on the giant Airbus 330 was the same crew that had served us on our original flight from New York almost a year ago.

I smiled at our attendant. "Maria, what a coincidence. It's so nice to see you again. Is Captain Victor Moretti also part of the crew?"

She indicated that not only was Captain Moretti at the controls, his co-pilot Gino, the man I had saved with the emergency procedure, was also aboard.

Maria said, "Captain Moretti would like to see you after we have reached our cruising altitude if you are available."

About an hour after takeoff, Maria returned to our seats and said Captain Moretti was ready for a visit. I left Gayle and went forward to the cockpit. Gino didn't remember me because he'd been unconscious as I'd worked on him. Both Gino and the captain thanked me again for my timely medical intervention.

"I told Gino he could only eat airline beef again if it has gone through a meat grinder at least twice," Moretti joked.

We all laughed, then I asked Captain Moretti if he could advise Maria when we were exactly halfway across the Atlantic. I shook hands again and returned to my seat.

A few hours later, Maria approached us, bearing a chilled bottle of champagne. "Doctor Gunderson, the captain said we are exactly halfway across the Atlantic. I have the champagne you asked for." She poured two large glasses and left.

I turned to Gayle with a smile. "Well, Mrs. Gunderson, it's time to open the envelope. But, before I do, I want you to write down how much you think the donation is."

Gayle remembered that when they opened box #100, it had been almost full. She wrote down one-hundred-twenty-five thousand on the envelope. I smiled and wrote down one hundred and seventy-five thousand. We clinked glasses before opening the envelope. My jaw dropped when I saw the amount.

The check said: *"PAYABLE TO THE ANGELINA CHILDREN'S MEDICAL FOUNDATION, the sum of One Dollar and Zero cents."* It was attached to a handwritten note. The note read:

"Don't ever forget. No one steals from Don Benedetti, no one!"

● ● ● ●

Gayle and I were crushed. All the plans for our new charity, up in smoke. We searched our minds for any possible reason Benedetti could have for betraying us but came up with none. I turned to Gayle and said, "I don't know about you, honey, but I'm going to get drunk."

I called Maria and ordered a double martini. Gayle did, too. We gulped them down and ordered another, then sat there in miserable silence.

I tried to recall any incident where we might have insulted the

Don. Other than lying to him about the hermit's treasure when we first met, I couldn't think of anything that would cause him to take such a drastic measure.

Gayle sat morosely staring out the window at the passing clouds. I racked my brain for anything to say to cheer her up, but I came up empty.

The captain announced that the plane was almost over Newfoundland and would land in about ninety minutes. As soon as the announcement ended, Maria approached our seat, carrying an elaborately wrapped package.

"Doctor Gunderson, we were instructed to give you this package, exactly ninety minutes before landing."

I looked at Gayle. After she shrugged, I opened the package to discover two smaller boxes and an envelope—one box marked for Gayle and one for me. Gayle opened hers first.

Gayle exhaled a long breath when she saw the contents. Her package contained a finely woven gold necklace adorned with a gold heart. Inside the heart was the flawless diamond that had been part of the stolen goods taken by the hermit.

I opened my package and was equally stunned. Inside I found an 18-carat gold Rolex watch. It was engraved: *TO MARK, WITH THANKS - LORENZO.*

Gayle took the envelope, and we slowly opened it together. Inside was a check payable to the Charity. Gayle started to cry when she saw the amount. It was made out to *THE ANGELINA CHILDREN'S MEDICAL FOUNDATION.*

The amount was eight million US dollars.

Another handwritten note accompanied the check.

Dear Mark and Gayle,
This check represents the total value of the contents of safety deposit boxes #100, #200, and # 300, minus the bearer bonds, which we kept for our account.

We decided it would be impossible to ever trace back the ownership of the goods stolen by the bastard, Cavallo. Instead, the best place for the value would be with your new Children's Charity.

Please forgive me for playing the bad joke again. I can't seem to help myself. I only hope Angelina doesn't find out; she would be angry with me!

Your friend,
Don Benedetti

Gayle began crying and didn't stop until our plane landed safely on the tarmac at Kennedy International Airport. We were finally home again, safe, sound, and happy after an experience we would never forget for the rest of our lives.

● ● ● ●

A HAPPY ENDING

I was in the process of placing a long-distance call to Murano, Italy. I wanted to talk directly to Benedetti. Finally, the call went through.

"Lorenzo, it's Mark. We both wanted to call to thank you again for the generous donation, although I must tell you Gayle is still mad at you for the joke you played."

"My friend, it's good to hear your voice again," Lorenzo boomed. "Tell Gayle I apologize for my bad joke. But tell me, how are your plans working out?"

"Well, we have run into a slight problem. We decided we could be operational faster if we offered to purchase the clinic we used to work for. Unfortunately, the owner, Donald Kingston, just laughed at us," I said. "We offered him four million dollars in cash, which is a fair price, but he said he wouldn't even take double. We have two real estate firms looking for possible sites, and, hopefully, they will come up with something soon."

Benedetti told us that Angelina was out with Pietro now, but he knew she wanted to talk to Gayle. "We will call you back tomorrow at 5:00 p.m. New York time. Goodbye for now."

Precisely at five the next day, the phone rang. It was Lorenzo. "How are you today, my friend?"

"I'm staggered. Just an hour ago, that cheapskate Kingston called and accepted our offer without any conditions. He even threw in a brand-new MRI machine that has been paid for but not delivered yet."

Benedetti chuckled. "That's excellent news, my friend."

I was suspicious. "Tell me something, Lorenzo, were you involved in Kingston's sudden change of heart?"

There was a short silence on the other end of the line before Lorenzo answered.

"It turns out this Donald Kingston is well known to my associates. It seems he has been instrumental over the years in helping certain people undergo cosmetic procedures to hide their true identities from the law."

I gulped involuntarily. "But how did you get Kingston to change his mind? He's a stubborn prick at the best of times."

That deep laugh again. "It was easy. We just made him an offer he couldn't refuse."

When I stopped laughing at the old Mafiosi cliché, I handed Gayle the phone to speak to Angelina. Her face lit up when Angelina came on the line. Gayle listened intently for several minutes, then said, "We wouldn't miss it for the world, Angelina."

After she hung up, she turned to me. "Angelia and Pietro are getting married next summer. We are both invited, and she wants me to be the matron of honor."

I laughed. "Honey, you might want to go on a small diet before buying your dress. I think all those pasta dinners at the villa are catching up with you."

Gayle stared at me. "Okay, smartass. You may be the world's best cosmetic reconstruction surgeon, but you certainly stink as a doctor."

I was puzzled. "What the hell are you talking about?"

"Well, it seems if a highly trained doctor can't tell the difference between pasta blubber and a baby bump, I can rest my case."

I was dumbfounded. I was delighted with the news, but I couldn't manage to get a word out, so I just kissed my wife twice, then three times more, with great enthusiasm. She smiled lovingly at me and then put my hand on her tummy to feel the movement myself.

After dinner, when Gayle went off to bed, I moved to my den and poured myself a small cognac nightcap. As I savored the fragrant liqueur, it reminded me of the many similar evenings I spent in the Don's office in front of the fireplace discussing the state of the world.

Even after my prolonged exposure to Don Benedetti, the man still remained an enigma to me. I recalled seeing him in moments of frightening rage and in moments of extreme happiness like the magical evening we experienced during the rare snowfall in Venice.

I'm not sure I was fully aware yet of the collective impact of my experiences in Benedetti's sphere of influence. I was looking forward to our return trip to Murano for Angelina's wedding. Still, my anticipation was dulled a little by a vague sense of apprehension.

Who knows what we might encounter when we return to the murky world of a man who lives his life on the edge? I knew from The Don's remarks that we would always be under his protection, but were we also profoundly in his debt.

Who knows what waits ahead, indeed?

ONCE UPON A GREEN

Want to know what hurts? The possibility of going bankrupt, that's what.

Sometimes it hits you fast like a runaway freight train. Other times it creeps up slowly, like a thief in the night. Regardless of how it arrives, it lingers over every decision you make. And it's hard not to take it personally. You end up blaming yourself for the failure until, finally, some obscure branch of authority arrives to tell you it's all over. Your dreams of building a business empire are dead.

It's becoming difficult to make any money in the sporting goods business these days. Competition from online giants and huge chain stores is cutting everyone's profit margins to ribbons. Still, I'm doing my best not to be a quitter.

Bolton Sporting Goods Inc., started by Grandpa George Bolton almost ninety years ago, has provided a decent living for the Bolton family for the better part of three generations. I'm determined to try almost anything to avoid being the family member that ends up closing the doors for good.

I listlessly pushed an untidy pile of unpaid supplier invoices across the scarred old desktop. I scratched my head with the stub of a pencil for the fifth time, trying to make sense of it all. Every month the gap between income and expenses was growing wider and not in a good way.

I just turned thirty-nine. Although it didn't bother me all that much, I have to admit I was starting to feel that Father Time had me in his sights. I might be a little overweight since I have one of those potbellies that seems determined to resist all efforts at slimming down. Numerous small things bothered me these days—things like needing glasses and getting up a bit slower from my chair.

Moving inventory around the store inevitably made me reach for painkillers the next day. My wife, Norma, didn't help with the situation either. Her constant nagging about the lack of money was becoming a real drag on my spirits. Maybe having a few kids would have helped shift Norma's focus away from my lack of success.

I wished now that we had tried harder to have a family, but the time had just passed with nothing to show for it.

• • • •

Outside the store, a gentle rain had been falling all day. Business volume was even slower than usual. Other than a few people wandering in to try the latest *PING* drivers and the odd customer looking for new grips, there wasn't much doing. I decided to fire up my computer and do a little surfing on the net.

I usually started by reviewing price comparisons with my largest competitors. Still, today, I found myself going through the golf improvement websites. When I typed in *Golf Improvement*, I was astounded to see references to over 384,000 websites.

I moved from website to website, sometimes breaking out into laughter at the more extreme gadgets and gizmos, all promising to lower the average golfer's score virtually overnight. There were swing trainers, wrist monitors, compression wraps, and no end of devices guaranteed to help keep your head down. I knew first hand that most of the stuff was total crap.

I chuckled when I saw an ad for the *BOOMERANG*. It was a unique golf club designed to provide resistance to the golf swing. It consisted of a conventional golf club handle with a flexible wand-like shaft.

At the end of the shaft, a heavy orange ball was attached to provide weight resistance. In theory, if a golfer swings this contraption several times in a row, he or she will get used to the heavyweight. Then, when the golfer switches back to a regular driver, the club would feel as light as a feather, thereby promoting a faster swing speed.

What a load of bullshit, I thought.

I stopped selling the training aid after Ted Corbin, one of my long-time customers, reported a bad experience. I recalled the day my customer had come into the store, fuming mad.

"Damn it, Bobby, this *BOOMERANG* thing you sold me isn't just a joke; it's pretty damned dangerous, too."

I scratched my head. "What are you talking about, Teddy? I haven't heard any other complaints."

"I was in my backyard, swinging the thing in a full arc, just like the instructions said when all hell broke loose," Teddy fumed. "Now, I admit I may have been swinging a little aggressively, but the blasted heavy ball broke loose from the end of the club. Damned thing took off like a rocket."

I tried not to laugh. "What happened to the weighted ball?"

Teddy looked sheepish. "The damned thing hit my next-door neighbor's deck chair so hard it tipped over. She fell headfirst, screaming, into her swimming pool."

I couldn't contain my laughter. "Teddy, I'm sorry for laughing, but it's funny. Seriously, though, is your neighbor okay?"

"After dumping Mrs. Peabody in the pool, the ball ricocheted off her clothesline. Just about killed two squirrels and a pigeon, too. I only hope she doesn't try to sue me for emotional distress."

When I stopped laughing, I assured Teddy he would receive a full refund. I offered to write a letter of apology to Mrs. Peabody as well. Then I wrote to the manufacturer that the training aid was total crap and asked for permission to return my inventory.

● ● ● ●

At the beginning of March, knowing the golf season would be in full swing soon, I decided to shut down the computer to do some work on my inventory numbers to get ready for our annual *Open Season* sales promotion. This year the sale had to be successful, or it really would be game over. I was rapidly running out of options.

Just as I was about to hit the off button on the computer, a strange advertisement flashed up on my screen. At first, I was annoyed. I was almost sure I had activated the software program that was supposed to prevent these unsolicited pop-up ads. Like most people, I didn't like this continuous invasion of my privacy.

These days, no matter what product website you looked at, you could count on being bombarded with targeted special offers for weeks on end. I put it down to the sophisticated artificial intelligence programs advertisers were using. It pissed me off.

The unwanted ad showing on my screen had most likely been triggered because I had visited some golf training products' websites. I was ready to push the delete button, but curiosity got the better of me. I decided to take a closer look at the advertisement. It was certainly intriguing.

ATTENTION ALL GOLFERS:

WANT TO HAVE A CHANCE AT WINNING ONE MILLION USA DOLLARS???
HAVE YOU ALWAYS WANTED TO BE A LOW HANDICAP GOLFER? ARE YOU TIRED OF TAKING
LESSON AFTER LESSON ONLY TO FIND YOUR "OLD SWING" RETURNING AFTER JUST A FEW
GAMES?
OUR PATENTED METHODOLOGY AND STATE OF THE ART EQUIPMENT CAN MAKE YOU A "SCRATCH" GOLFER – GUARANTEED.*
YOU'RE PROBABLY SCEPTICAL, SO WE'RE READY TO PROVE OUR WORDS!
IN THE NEXT 30 DAYS WE WILL BE SELECTING ONE GOLFER FROM YOUR AREA WHO CURRENTLY HAS A CERTIFIED HANDICAP OF BETWEEN 15 AND 20. WE WILL PROVIDE ALL EQUIPMENT AND TRAINING AT NO COST TO THE SELECTED GOLFER.
IF THE GOLFER WE SELECT BECOMES A CERTIFIED "SCRATCH" GOLFER WITHIN ONE YEAR FROM THE START*

OF THE CONTEST, WE WILL PAY HIM OR HER, A SPECIAL AWARD OF $1,000,000.00 (ONE MILLION US DOLLARS) TAX-FREE!
  (Certain Terms & Conditions may apply)

FOR INFORMATION ON THE MILLION DOLLAR "SCRATCH*" GOLFER CONTEST PLEASE CONTACT US AT:

<u>*SCRATCHGOLFERCONTEST.*</u>

NOTE: * USGA definition of a "SCRATCH" GOLFER is: "A player who can play to a Course Handicap of zero on <u>any</u> rated golf course."

ATTENTION: We will also be appointing exclusive distributors on a regional basis for our new line of equipment. If you have an interest in representing us, please contact us through the above website.

I shut off my computer and went home to bed. Even though I knew the ad was bullshit, I dreamt all night long of the enormous difference a prize of one million dollars would make in my miserable life.

• • • •

The next afternoon I finished unpacking the latest shipment of new leather golf bags. The goods had arrived on a C.O.D. (cash on demand) basis because this particular supplier would no longer extend credit terms. This was the beginning of a dangerous trend. If other suppliers started to ship on the same basis, Bolton Sporting Goods Inc. wouldn't have enough inventory to back the upcoming *Open Season* sales promotion.

I shrugged off the hint of depression spawned by my loss of credit terms and prepared to close up shop. Tonight was the one night of the week I looked forward to because it was Poker Night at the Uxbridge Golf & Country Club.

Poker, chicken wings, and beer were my all-time favorites, although they would never replace golf as my number one passion. My wife thought the country club was a waste of time and a luxury we couldn't afford. During the height of our last argument, I put my foot down.

"Norma, I don't give a hoot what the club costs. I work hard, and golf is my only outlet. The club is the last thing I'm willing to give up."

As usual, Norma retreated in a huff, then wouldn't talk to me for the rest of the week.

It was a chilly, springtime evening when I drove up through the Uxbridge Golf & Country Club entrance. Although I was a popular member, I always felt self-conscious parking my red nine-year-old Hyundai Sonata next to the long line of luxury vehicles that usually seemed to be in residence at the club. As one of the less wealthy members, I tried to overcome my feelings of not belonging by entering as many club events as possible.

As usual, the weekly poker game table was set up by the fireplace in the men's lounge. The gathered men greeted me with the familiar chorus of friendly insults.

"Oh my god, Bolton has arrived. He's back for more, boys. Hide your chicken wings and count your money."

I laughed, then shook hands all around before taking my regular seat at the table. Without being asked, the waiter dropped a large draft beer in front of me.

After the dealer shuffled the cards, the conversation shifted to the club's opening tournament scheduled for April 15th. The match was open to all club members, with players grouped into flights of players with similar handicaps.

"Are you entering this year, Bobby?" Wilbur Leyland asked. Wilbur was the owner of a successful auto dealership in town.

I hesitated. "I'm not sure, guys. It depends on which flight they decide to put me in."

"Don't worry," Wilbur laughed. "With a handicap of nineteen, you won't have to worry about being put in with any of the really good players."

I laughed too and grabbed another chicken wing from the basket.

When the players took a break from the game, I told them about the unusual advertisement that had popped up on my computer.

I shrugged. "For all I know, it could be more bullshit, but it certainly looked genuine."

"Wow, a million-dollar prize," Fred Singer said. "Unfortunately, our handicaps are way too high to even think of applying, but why don't you try and enter the contest?"

"Believe it or not, I already have," I said with a grin.

• • • •

THE ABADDON GOLF CORPORATION

So far this week, three more shipments had arrived C.O.D., significantly increasing my concern about the viability of the business. I was in the process of fitting a new fiberglass shaft onto a damaged driver while simultaneously thinking about my shrinking options when the phone rang, breaking my train of thought.

A low female voice asked if I was Mr. Robert Bolton. I assumed it was just another one of those pesky telemarketers. Before she could start her speech, I told her I wasn't interested.

The woman ignored my protest. "Please hold for our president, Mr. Jules Abaddon. He's calling regarding your entry into our golf contest."

At first, the call mystified me. Then I remembered my online application to the golfing contest several weeks back. I waited patiently until a man picked up the phone on the other end. He had a deep voice tinged with a slight middle east accent.

"Mr. Bolton, my name is Jules Abaddon. I'm calling you personally to give you some good news. You are now officially on our shortlist of candidates for the *Million Dollar* golfing contest my company, Abaddon Golf, is sponsoring."

For a few moments, I wondered if it was Fred Singer or one of the other guys from the golf club pulling my leg. I decided to play along with the joke.

"That's great, Mr. Abaddon, is there anything I need to know in advance before I get my million bucks?"

Abaddon chuckled. "Let's not get ahead of ourselves. We have an extensive review process to undergo before we make our final decision. However, I can tell you that so far, you are the only contest entrant that could also become a possible Regional Distributor for our new products. That combination stands you in excellent stead."

"I've been in the sporting goods business for quite a while," I said. "But I have to say I've never heard of Abaddon equipment."

"Precisely, Mr. Bolton. We make fabulous, exclusive equipment, but our brand is unknown. That's why we're willing to invest a million dollars in the contest."

"Why don't you send me a few samples, and I'll decide if I have any interest in being a regional distributor or not."

"You sound skeptical, Mr. Bolton, so I'm going to send our Director of Marketing, Nicholas Stanton, to talk to you personally. He will contact you soon."

As I put the phone down, I thought, *although I wouldn't put it past those guys at the club to try to pull something, this phone call sounded legit.*

● ● ● ●

The next day, a black van pulled up and parked outside the store. I watched with interest as the front door opened. Several seconds passed before a well-dressed man exited the van. A flaming crimson red pocket hanky adorned his light gray, pinstriped suit. He wore his long silver hair swept back from his forehead.

The man had deeply hooded eyes, sunken in a gaunt weathered face. He moved slowly toward the doors as if suffering from some internal pain. I thought his highly polished shoes were a little too pointy-toed for current fashion.

"I'm Nicholas Stanton, Director of Marketing for the Abaddon Golf Equipment Corporation, but, please, call me Nick." Stanton had a deep hypnotic voice, totally out of character for his lean body mass.

After we shook hands, I started to ask some questions, but Nick immediately intervened. "Sorry, Bobby, no details until I finish the interview process. You'll have all the answers soon enough."

I shook my head. "I'm not sure I want to take part in an interview. Why can't you just leave me a sample of your equipment, then I'll let you know if I'm interested in carrying the line?"

"My mistake. I should have clarified the situation." Nick retorted. "This interview is not about being our regional distributor. It's to determine if you qualify to be the lucky participant in our million-dollar contest."

"Oh, that's a different story. Fire away."

Stanton asked me in-depth questions on a wide variety of subjects, including my golf handicap, political orientation, marriage, religion, health, and my general mental state. Each time I responded, Nick made copious notes on his portable computer.

The interview took more than an hour to complete. When Stanton finished, he pushed the send button and sat back.

"My boss doesn't like to waste time. We should hear back from him shortly after he reviews your interview and contest application."

"Can I offer you a coffee, Nick?"

"Thanks, but I'll take a pass. While we're waiting for Mr. Abaddon's decision, let me outline the strategy we'll be following, providing, of course, you're the one selected as the lucky contest candidate."

"Of course," I said, still convinced this was a scam of some type.

"Our primary goal will be to make you the poster boy for Abaddon golf clubs. The challenge will be to turn you from a nineteen handicap to a scratch golfer in twelve months, using our special equipment and training techniques. If we're successful, every golfer in America will be beating a path to our door."

I listened to Nick's spiel with a degree of skepticism. Starting from a high handicap at my age and physical condition, the goal of being a scratch golfer was almost impossible. Even some of the best well-known golf professionals struggled to keep that level of play year after year.

I was starting to wonder if this whole thing was just a waste of time. The valuable time I could be spending on finding a solution to the real problems I was facing with the business.

Stanton continued talking, "Don't forget, Bobby, if we do this together successfully, you'll get a million bucks. And our company will catapult into the lead as one of the top suppliers of golf equipment in the world."

Nick explained that the upcoming million-dollar scratch golfer contest was structured as a highly publicized, suspense campaign. A favorite marketing strategy of Mr. Abaddon himself.

I asked, "What do you mean by a suspense campaign?"

Nick laughed. "First of all, we'll create an artificial shortage by not offering any of our new equipment until after the contest ends. Then, only very select golfers will be allowed to use the clubs under highly regulated conditions. We are going to position our equipment as the most prestigious, exclusive, sought-after golf clubs on the planet."

"You make it sound easy, Nick, but there's a ton of competition out there. Lots of guys are making good gear for sale these days."

Nick nodded. "That's a large part of our mystique. You can't just buy a set of Abaddon golf clubs outright. To get our clubs, a golfer has to go through an extensive review and approval process. If they pass, they will be permitted to lease a set under the terms and conditions of a strict legal contract."

I shook my head. "You've got to be kidding, Nick. None of the golfers I know would ever go for that arrangement."

Nick was just about to respond when his computer indicated an incoming message. He read the contents and smiled.

"Mr. Abaddon has given your application his personal approval. It looks like you're our million-dollar contestant, Bobby. Congratulations."

Although I was still skeptical, I tried to look happy, but I thought *I'd give up my million-dollar contest spot in a minute for five thousand cash in hand.*

Nick told me a custom fitting of the new equipment would be arranged over the next few days.

Spinning My Wheels

I watched as Nick left the store and returned to the black van. I couldn't help feeling the whole thing was some kind of a joke.

I guess I'll find out soon enough.

• • • •

Over dinner that night, I tried to explain the events of the day to my wife. I knew I would get a difficult reception.

"I know it's a pipe dream, Norma, but just think what a difference it would make in our lives if I could win a million bucks."

"Bobby, I've watched your golf game for years," Norma said scornfully. "Let's face it, you're just a duffer. You'll always be a duffer. You have about as much chance of becoming a scratch golfer as a snowball in Hell."

She got up and walked to the stove. "Also, Mr. Golf Professional, what exactly happens to our income if you stop working at the store for twelve months, and you don't win the contest?"

I had to admit Norma made a good point. I changed the subject to avoid any more bickering.

After a sleepless night, I decided I couldn't take a chance on going a whole year with no income. When I arrived at the store the following day, I called Nick to give him the news.

"Good morning, Nick. This won't take long. I'm afraid I'll have to decline the offer to be the contestant."

Dead silence for a moment, then. "May I ask why you're turning down the chance of winning a million dollars?"

"As much as I love golf and would give just about anything to become a scratch player, I can't take a chance of ending up broke if I don't win the contest. So, thanks anyway, Nick, but no can do."

"Don't be so hasty, Bobby. This is a once-in-a-lifetime opportunity. Let me talk to the boss and get back to you."

Two hours later, Nick called back with a response. "Mr. Abaddon will personally guarantee you will earn at least as much as you would have if you had stayed on at the store, even if you don't win the contest."

On that basis, I figured I couldn't lose on the deal. "Okay, Nick, you can count me in, but I want to see it in writing."

• • • •

A CUSTOM FITTING

After Nick delivered a signed letter from Jules Abaddon personally guaranteeing the minimum income deal, events started happening fast. The following day, the black van arrived at the store again, but three guys I assumed were technicians piled out this time.

I wasn't the slightest bit ready for the events that unfolded that day. But now that I think back, everything about the process was surreal.

The men all wore stark black uniforms with *ABADDON GOLF* printed in large red letters across the back. After unloading a large assortment of unrecognizable electronic equipment, the technicians wasted no time. Before I knew what was happening, they started using the devices to measure me from the top of my head to the bottom of my feet.

The men were surly, only grunting non-committal responses to my questions. I also thought they had a strange, unsettling odor about them.

Stanton finally showed up and took charge. "Let me explain our approach, Bobby. It's a three-part program."

"Three parts?" I said, surprised.

"Yes. The first part is an intensive physical training approach, with emphasis on core strengthening. The second part is a program package of golf techniques and psychological training. Third, and most important, is the specialized custom mating of our equipment to the individual golfer."

I was overwhelmed. There was so much stuff to remember. I had no idea the entire training process would be so intensive. I just wanted to hit golf balls.

The three technicians made me lie flat on a specialized table they had set up earlier in the back storage room. They connected me to numerous electrical leads, each one providing detailed measurements of my body mass.

"We'll take all this data back to our shop for the design of your custom-fitted clubs," Nick said. "The equipment should be ready in a week or so."

After they packed up and departed, it started to dawn on me that the contest might be the real thing. If nothing else came out of it, I was bound to at least be a better golfer. I could hardly wait now to get my first look at the new revolutionary Abaddon clubs

● ● ● ●

As my mysterious training program intensified, a buzz of excitement arose around the strange events taking place at *Bolton Sporting Goods*. Even Norma got involved by volunteering to run the store in my absence. Usually, she refused to set foot on the premises.

Various specialists arrived and departed every day: weight training, swing coaching, detailed studies of course management, all taking place in a blur. Wilbur, Fred, and Teddy, my playing buddies, kept dropping into the store. They were all eager to see my progress. I lost at least twenty pounds and had twice my normal flexibility.

Each time the guys showed up, Nick or one of his helpers politely but firmly told them the store's back rooms were off-limits for the duration of the contest.

Then came the hypnosis sessions. At first, I was reluctant to take part because I thought hypnosis was more bullshit. Still, I had to admit, I found the intense sessions quite relaxing. But, for some unknown reason, I often felt disturbed when I came back to reality. It was almost as if the hypnotist was nudging me in a direction that wasn't quite palatable with my core values.

After a session, I could never recall the exact words used during the hypnosis. Still, they always seemed to be quite persuasive. I shrugged off my misgivings because today was the day everyone was waiting for. My custom-produced Abaddon clubs were due any minute for the final adjustments. Nick gave me a pre-fitting lecture.

"Bobby, today is the most important part of our patented exclusive process to turn you into a scratch golfer."

I shook my head. "I'm not sure I understand."

"This is the final step," Nick said softly. "This is where we bond a player to his clubs. The player and the club will truly become one."

I thought it was all a bit of marketing hyperbole, but I nodded politely anyway.

When the clubs finally arrived, Nick took over, slowly unwrapping the clubs one at a time, with great fanfare. I had to admit they were hot-looking golf clubs: jet black shafts and club heads with the Abaddon logo outlined in crimson red. The grips were a striking crimson red as well.

After the clubs were all unpacked, I expected to do some trial swings. Instead, the technicians had me stretch out on their special table. After a period that seemed forever, I was finally wired up to all the electrical leads for the second time.

I tried to relieve the tension by cracking a joke. "I feel like I'm getting ready for my annual prostate exam. Should I at least take my pants off?"

No one smiled. The technicians were too focused on the flashing instruments.

Nick started with the driver. "Hold the driver with your right hand. Now, this is very important. Close your eyes and visualize hitting the longest drive of your life."

After I did the visualization as instructed, I peeked through my half-closed eyes. I was stunned to see the driver's grip momentarily turn bright fluorescent green before reverting to its usual crimson red.

Nick slowly repeated the process one at a time with the rest of the set. In each case, he had me visualize the best shot I had ever made with each of the respective clubs. Also, in each case, when I recalled a great shot, the grip flashed green momentarily.

Nick was finally satisfied. "Bobby, this is extremely important. This set of clubs are now exclusively mated to you. Every time you select a club, the grip will flash green to confirm you are the rightful holder."

"You're kidding, right?"

"Nope. If anyone else picks up a club, the grips will remain red. This is why no one is allowed to buy our clubs outright. Our clubs are only available by signing a lease agreement that stipulates that Abaddon Golf Corporation has the sole rights to ownership."

"Forever?"

"Yes. When a player's lease agreement ends, the clubs must come back to the company. We can then reprogram the grips for the next holder."

I half-listened to Nick, but what I really wanted to do was get out on the course and try out the equipment. So far this season, I had managed only eight games using my old gear. Still, at least with my conditioning program, my handicap had dropped from nineteen to sixteen.

"When can I try the new clubs out on the course," I asked?"

"Next week," Nick smiled, "in the opening tournament at the Uxbridge Golf & Country Club."

• • • •

THE CLUB CHAMPIONSHIP

I stood on the first tee, looking nervous because I was nervous. Up to this point, despite my protests, I hadn't been allowed to practice with the new clubs.

A big crowd had gathered at the tee to watch the match. I estimated that almost the entire club membership had shown up to cheer for their favorite players.

As the designated million-dollar contestant, I was wearing a complete golf outfit provided by the Abaddon Golf Corporation. The ensemble consisted of a black hat, shirt, and pants, all bearing the small *ABADDON* crimson logo. Norma had taken my picture, telling me that at least I looked like a golf pro, even if I was still a duffer. Actually, I did look pretty good.

The first hole was a challenging 425-yard par four with a green surrounded by deep sand bunkers. A finger of the lake cut the fairway in half at the 225-yard mark. The temperature was cool, with the wind blowing directly into the face of the golfers. Usually, I would lay up to avoid going into the water on my drive.

I took the driver out of my bag. Although my hands were sweating, I did feel a faint tingling as the grip momentarily flashed fluorescent green. The club felt like it was a living part of me when I took my first practice swing.

I could feel the impact of my core strengthening exercises when I executed a flawless picture-perfect, relaxed, full swing. My driver felt almost weightless, seemingly alive to my touch. My gleaming white golf ball soared high into a cloudless sky. It hung there for a few moments, looking like it would never return to earth.

A gasp went up from the crowd when the ball sailed serenely across the water hazard finally came to rest almost three hundred yards from the tee. I stared in amazement. Usually, on a perfect day with a tailwind, I might occasionally hit the two-hundred-yard mark.

My golfing buddies, Wilbur, Fred, and Teddy, cheered me on as I prepared for my shot into the green. At 125 yards into the wind, I would usually use a nine iron or maybe even an eight iron. But when I went to take a club from the bag, I noticed the grip on my pitching wedge had turned a slightly deeper red than the others. I selected the wedge on a hunch and hit a high soft shot, landing about thirty-five feet from the pin.

Before the match, Nick had presented me with a unique custom-made putter as a gift from Mr. Abaddon himself. I almost laughed when I first saw it. The club looked like an antique. The shaft was some exotic hardwood, crowned with one of the crimson red grips. I thought I had seen almost every make of putter, including the new ones that resembled a miniature spaceship, but this one took the cake.

The putter head was hand-carved out of some hard, ivory-like substance. It was almost oval except for a slot that intruded into the head about halfway. I took the putter from my bag, again feeling a tingle as the grip flashed fluorescent green before returning to its regular crimson color.

Jack Layton, my opponent, was only five feet from the cup. Jack could par the hole with a four if he sunk it. I walked around the green, examining the roll from several angles. I finally stood over the ball and, with shaking hands, stroked my new putter toward the hole. The ball traveled smoothly, catching the break in the green at precisely the right time. It hovered monetarily before dropping with a clunk for a one-under-par birdie.

After Layton sunk his putt, we moved to the next hole with me in the lead by one. Layton didn't have a chance. I went on to win hole after hole, finishing with a seven-over-par seventy-nine for the Club Championship. Even Norma was impressed. I was too, up until now, my lowest game was an 85.

● ● ● ●

A BINDING CONTRACT

The following day Stanton came into the store smiling. "Congratulations on behalf of *ABADDON GOLF*. Great tournament."

"Nick, it was all the clubs. I've never played like that in my life."

Nick just smiled and said, "Mr. Abaddon wants me to talk to you about becoming a master distributor of our equipment after the contest ends."

"What do I have to do as a regional distributor?"

"First of all, you'll have your choice of geographic territories. The only area not available right now is the Washington D.C. location. We've already assigned that area to a politician who is an avid golfer and owns quite a few golf courses."

We spent the rest of the morning reviewing the distribution details. Then, Nick reminded me that I had not yet signed my lease agreement for the exclusive use of my custom-fitted clubs.

"I just haven't had time to go over it with my lawyer. Maybe another day or two?"

"Sorry, Bobby. Mr. Abaddon was upset that you used the clubs in the tournament without the agreement in place. That broke one of his main rules. We need a signed copy today."

"Should I call my lawyer to see if he can come over to the store?"

"That's not necessary," Nick said as he turned the agreement to the signature page before handing it to me for signing. "Don't worry. It's just a standard lease with an additional provision granting us sole rights to the use and ownership of the clubs."

Nick handed me a gold-plated pen for signing and waited. I had some reservations about signing something without my lawyer's review. Still, I loved the clubs and was beginning to feel I might even have a slim chance of winning the million-dollar prize.

"Go ahead and sign, Bobby. What have you got to lose?" Nick urged.

I shrugged and pushed the button on the pen to open the point. The button had a rough edge and made a tiny prick in my finger. As I signed the document, a small drop of my blood fell on the white paper.

Embarrassed, I said, "Sorry, let me get some tissue paper and try and get this off."

"No problem, my friend. I'll just tell Mr. Abaddon you loved our deal so much that you signed in blood."

The three ill-smelling technicians who were watching the signing with interest all chuckled at Nick's comment. I'm not sure why, but I shivered at that moment. I wish now I had waited for my lawyer's opinion.

• • • •

"BOOM BOOM" BOLTON

The next few months went by in a whirlwind of activity. Abaddon Golf signed me up for every local, regional, and state tournament available. And, I kept piling up the wins, causing my handicap to drop like a rock. The news media were going mad. The excitement of a potential million-dollar prize, coupled with my advanced age, created a massive following on Facebook as well as all the other social media.

One reporter headlined his story: *"BOOM BOOM BOLTON WINS AGAIN."*

The catchy nickname soon caught on. Norma reported that sales at the store were booming too. There was even talk of a new line of golf clothing featuring the stylized *"BBB"* logo.

That night at dinner, I talked to Norma about my reluctance to sign the Abaddon legal agreement.

"Why, Bobby?"

"I don't really know," I said. "When Nick pushed me into signing, he handed me his pen. It had a rough spot that cut my finger. After a drop of my blood fell on the contract, those weird technicians laughed. The whole thing just felt wrong somehow."

"I thought of something else, too," Norma added. "We don't know much about this company at all. What if they don't have the money to pay you if you win the contest? Maybe they're counting on getting the benefits of all the free publicity and then reneging on the deal."

I hardly slept that night, worrying about the issue Norma had raised. I decided to call Nick first thing in the morning to express my concerns about the ability of Abaddon to deliver the prize if I won the contest.

I was just about to call Nick when my old golfing partner, Teddy Corbin, dropped in for a visit.

"Hi, Bobby, great tournament last week. You're killing these guys."

"Thanks," I said. "I can't quite explain my new game. It must be improvements in the equipment."

Teddy looked around, then lowered his voice. "I see that creepy guy from Abaddon isn't here. How about letting me see these fantastic clubs up close?"

I hesitated, but Teddy kept pleading with me. "Okay, but just a fast look."

We cautiously proceeded into the back room, where the new

clubs were held under tight security. I had been told numerous times not to allow others to examine my set, supposedly because the technology was patented.

Teddy was delighted. "Christ, buddy, these clubs look terrific."

Before I could warn him to look but not touch, Teddy grabbed my driver by the crimson red grip. He took a massive practice swing. Instantly, a flash of electricity surged from the handle. Teddy shuddered and fell on the floor in a dead faint.

I tried not to panic. I called 911, then attempted to give Teddy artificial respiration. The ambulance was just pulling away when Nick showed up.

Stanton was furious when I told him about Teddy.

"You've been told numerous times," Nick ranted. "This set of clubs is specifically bonded to you alone. If a caddy simply handles the clubs, there's no problem. But your agreement states, in no uncertain terms, that you should never allow anyone else to swing or try to play with your clubs."

Again, I wished now that I had read the agreement for myself.

I took the offensive. "Now that you're here, we have another problem to solve. How do I know that *ABADDON GOLF* has the resources to pay out the million-dollar prize? I'm fed up with all this crap. I'm backing out right now if you don't give me some assurances that the money will be there if I win the contest."

Nick glared at me for a moment, anger flashing across his hooded eyes. He turned his back and sent a text message to his boss. After ten minutes of frozen silence between us, Nick got a phone call.

He listened intently, then with a smirk said, "Mr. Abaddon has made arrangements with Price Waterhouse to hold the prize money in escrow. Price Waterhouse will make the sole determination if you have filled the contest requirements. On certification, they will release one million dollars directly into your bank account."

I couldn't think of any more reasons for not proceeding with the contest, so I said nothing.

Nick went on. "I came here to tell you about something far more important than the health of your wimpy friend or to reassure you about the damned prize money."

"I'm listening," I said, still smarting from the lecture.

"We just got word that your entry is approved. You are now a contestant in the USA Mid-Amateur competition."

I had only vaguely heard of the competition. "Why is this tournament such a big deal?"

"You really are a dolt. Everyone knows about this tournament. Just think what it means. The winner gets an automatic invitation to participate in one of the most prestigious tournaments in the world."

"Which tournament is that?"

Nick grinned. "The world-famous Masters Tournament at the prestigious Augusta National Golf Club."

"Oh, shit!"

SUSPICIONS ARISE

If I thought the previous training schedule was demanding, I was sadly mistaken. The new program was infinitely more difficult. Morning to night, seven days a week, the drills continued. Pitching, putting, and sand bunker shots galore.

I could understand the reasons for the regular routines, but some of the exercises were really weird. Particularly the sessions where I had to lie perfectly still on the special table attached to the instruments, while picture after picture of the Master's golf course layout flashed on a screen. Contour maps for every green too. After a few weeks, I found that I could play a complete round of the Augusta Golf Club in my head.

Meanwhile, the publicity machine was working in overdrive to the point that not a day passed without some form of a Bobby *"BoomBoom"* Bolton story appearing on the sports pages

Public interest reached an all-time high when I was declared the winner of the USA Mid-Amateur tournament after a tightly contested match. The win entitled me to receive a coveted invitation to the Masters.

The night after the amateur tournament, Norma woke at 3:00 a.m. to discover my side of the bed empty. She cautiously went downstairs to my den and found me staring at the fireplace with a half-full glass of dark rum in my hand.

"What's wrong, hon? Can't you sleep?"

I gave her a sleepy smile. "I don't know, Norma, but something's fishy about this whole contest idea. I'm starting to wonder if somehow I've gotten involved with organized crime or even the mafia itself."

"Why would you even think that?" she asked her tone one of surprise.

"I'm not sure. Too many coincidences for me. First of all, my business slows down. Then I start getting my goods shipped C.O.D. Then I get this big chance to win a million dollars. Maybe this is some form of money laundering."

"I'm not sure I understand, Bobby."

"Well, if the plan works the way they want it to, they launder a million bucks by making it a golf prize. And with all the publicity, they sell millions of dollars in golf clubs and equipment. The process creates an ongoing source of legitimate funds."

"What are you going to do, hon?"

"For now, I'm just going to concentrate on our trip to Augusta and the Masters tournament. When I get back, I'm going to hire a lawyer just in case we need one in a hurry."

Norma nodded. "You know, I've always felt there was something sinister about Nick. Maybe you're right."

"I hope not. Let's keep our fingers crossed."

• • • •

A DREAM COMES TRUE

Finally, the big day arrived. As we slowly drove up the magnolia-covered driveway to Augusta National Golf Club's entrance, it almost felt like a religious experience. One of my lifetime goals had always been to attend a Masters tournament in person instead of watching it on television with my buddies.

Never in my wildest dreams did I imagine that I would attend as a qualified player instead of as a patron.

I was traveling with Vic Nobel, the head pro at the Uxbridge Golf & Country Club. Vic had volunteered to act as my caddy for the tournament. Wilbur, Fred, and Teddy were driving to Augusta with Norma later to cheer me on.

Shortly after we arrived at Augusta, a problem arose. Because I was using unknown golf equipment, the tournament officials insisted they examine the clubs to ensure they conformed to all PGA specifications.

"What the hell is going on?" I called Stanton in a panic. "The tournament people want to see me tomorrow morning with a full set of Abaddon clubs. Haven't you guys had your clubs pre-approved by the PGA?"

"Don't worry," Nick said softly. "I'll handle this in the morning. You concentrate on your practice rounds and leave the details to me."

Practice rounds came next. The difficulty of the course and the complexities of the greens staggered me. I walked each fairway with Vic Nobel, my caddy, making detailed notes about the terrain and potential trouble spots.

When we arrived at the practice area for putting, I saw Nick Stanton huddled with a group of five PGA officials. An entire bag of Abaddon clubs lay on the grass beside the group.

I was puzzled because none of the officials seemed to be too interested in actually examining the clubs. They were standing in a loose circle around Nick, seemingly spellbound with whatever message he was delivering. When Nick finished talking, the five men nodded in unison and walked away. Nick joined me on the putting green with a grin on his face.

"Are the clubs approved, Nick? And what the hell did you say to the officials? They walked away from the meeting looking like zombies."

"The clubs are now approved for play, Bobby. Don't ask for any details." Nick strolled away without looking back.

I knew it was a stupid thought, but for a brief moment, I wondered if Nick had somehow hypnotized the officials.

• • • •

Earlier by the clubhouse, a solitary man had taken a great interest in the meeting between Nick and the PGA officials. The man was a plump, elderly fellow wearing wire-rimmed glasses and a bright purple golf hat. The purple hat looked oddly out of place since the old gentleman was wearing a three-piece dark blue business suit.

The man approached me just as I was retrieving the Abaddon clubs from the spot where Nick left them after meeting with the officials.

"Nice golf clubs, young fellow. Do you mind if I try one?"

"I'm sorry, sir, but these are new clubs manufactured by the Abaddon Golf Corporation. The clubs are not on the market yet. Until they are, the company has a stringent policy restricting the use of the clubs by anyone except for authorized individuals."

The man's ears perked up at this information, but he just smiled and walked away. I couldn't help noticing that although the man was quite elderly, his skin didn't appear to have a single wrinkle.

Strange dude, I thought.

The night before the big match, I took Norma, Vic Nobel, Wilbur, Fred, and Teddy to dinner. Everyone was excited about my impending battle against some of golf's greatest players. The food was great, and the wine was, too. Everyone had a few glasses except Vic and me. We had both sworn off alcohol until the match was over.

At the end of the meal, Norma raised her glass and proposed a toast. "To my husband, Bobby "Boom Boom" Bolton. I still can't believe you're here as a contestant in the Masters, but I want you to know I'm proud of you, win, lose or draw."

I went to bed that night tired but afraid I wouldn't get much sleep. I was happy that the whole experience brought Norma and me closer again. However, I still had a nagging feeling that something was inherently wrong with what was about to happen tomorrow.

THE MASTERS-OPENING DAY

Each of the eighteen unique holes at the legendary Augusta National Golf Course has a name along with its designated number. On the match's opening day, I was standing on the tee for *TEA OLIVE*, the first hole. *TEA OLIVE* was a 455-yard, par-four dog-leg with a tricky green.

The weather was superb for golf, with bright sunshine gently bathing the numerous red azalea flower beds. Although I was mesmerized by the course's stunning beauty, I was also trying every yoga technique I could think of to calm my nerves.

Norma and the guys were standing in the crowd. Nick was also there hovering around in the background. When the announcer introduced Bobby Bolton as the USA mid-amateur champion, the public gave me a nice round of applause.

"You can do this, Bobby," Vic said as he handed me my driver.

I took a deep breath and tried to ignore the massive crowd. Then with a textbook swing sent my opening drive 343 yards down the middle of the fairway. I looked over and saw Nick with a smile of satisfaction on his face.

I shot par on the first three holes and was starting to feel much more confident. The fourth hole, *FLOWERING CRAB APPLE*, was a challenging 240-yard par three. When Vic began to hand me a four iron, I noticed Nick standing in the crowd, slowly shaking his head.

Sure enough, when I looked at the bag, I saw that the grip on my five iron was a deeper shade of red than the other clubs.

"Give me the five iron," I said.

"Are you sure it's enough club, Bobby?"

I nodded, took the club, and executed a smooth full swing. I didn't realize what had happened until the crowd started to chant *"BOOM BOOM, BOOM BOOM"* over and over again.

I was in the cup for a hole-in-one—the first hole-in-one of my life.

● ● ● ●

The following two days passed almost dream-like for me. I had been plodding through intermittent rainfall for most of the final day and didn't quite realize what had happened until Vic grabbed my arm. We were on the 18th green.

"Bobby, if you sink this putt, you'll be tied for first place."

"Christ, I wish you hadn't told me," I said nervously

I took my time and looked at the put from all directions. It was an uphill 20-footer with a sharp break at the end. Using my unique Abaddon putter, I slowly lined up my putt, then sent the ball spiraling into the center of the cup. Vic jumped up and down, pounding my back with his fist.

There were only three groups still to come in. A relatively unknown player, Thor Ericsson, from the Doral Golf Club in Miami, playing in the final group, had been in sole possession of first place until I sunk my putt for the tie.

After I entered my score with the official scorekeeper, I joined Norma and my golfing buddies in the spectator area behind the 18th green. We watched the last group approaching the green through the rainfall, which was slowly increasing in volume. The group included Thor Ericsson, the co-leader, and two well-known players who were both trailing badly.

Vic said, "Ericsson had a bad drive. He needs to make his putt to remain in a tie with you. If he misses it, you win the Masters. If he sinks it, then it will just be you against him in a sudden-death playoff."

I hadn't seen Thor Ericsson up close until this point in the tournament. I took a long, hard look at the powerfully built, handsome young man walking with a confident stride to the green. Thor's caddy handed him a putter with the handle wrapped in a towel as protection from the rain.

As I watched intently, I was staggered to see a faint fluorescent green flash glow from under the towel when Thor Ericsson grasped the grip of his putter.

A roar rose from the crowd when Thor Ericsson sunk his tricky putt, ensuring a first-place tie with me. The patrons scattered when the rain started to fall in buckets. The soaking wet tournament officials huddled together under umbrellas to determine a course of action. They finally announced that because of weather conditions, the sudden death 18th hole playoff would take place the next day at 10:00 a.m.

A DEVIL OF A DEAL

I sat in my hotel room, trying to make sense of it all as I watched the tournament's delayed telecast. Most of the camera action was on Thor Ericsson because of his leading position. Sure enough, every time Thor's caddy handed him a club, the grip was wrapped in a towel. Despite the covering, I was sure I saw a faint fluorescent green flash each time Thor took the club.

I knew Nick Stanton was staying at a nearby hotel, so I phoned him.

"What the hell is going on, Nick?' I demanded. "Thor Ericsson is using the same equipment as me. You guys assured me I was the only player with Abaddon clubs. No equipment was supposed to be on the market until after the contest. Can you explain this?"

"I think you must be mistaken," Nick said smoothly. "Why don't I come over to your hotel? We can have dinner and talk things through."

I hung up and brooded. I wished now I had taken some time to investigate the Abaddon Corporation more thoroughly. While I waited for Nick, I took out my notebook computer and punched in the word *ABADDON*.

Most of the references concerned the Abaddon Golf Corporation and the million-dollar contest. Still, as I scrolled through the search, I stumbled upon an obscure definition of the word Abaddon.

I almost fell off my seat when the Google search showed that *ABADDON* was the Hebrew word for *Devil* or *Satan*.

I was nervous before. Now I was deathly afraid.

Being tied up with Abaddon was turning out to be a situation far worse than being mixed up with the mafia or organized crime.

The pieces started falling into place. How could I have missed it?

That awful rotten egg smell surrounding the three technicians had to be sulfur. The weird carved ivory head on the putter given to me by Mr. Abaddon had a slot in the middle. Could it be an actual animal's cloven hoof?

I looked at the computer again. *Oh no*, I thought.

The purpose of the contest was supposedly to turn me into a *scratch* golfer. According to the computer, *Old Scratch* was just another name for Satan. Now I was becoming more frightened with each new piece of the puzzle. I'm not religious or superstitious, but my instincts told me I was in trouble.

I found my briefcase and rummaged through it, frantically looking for a copy of the signed agreement. As I quickly scanned the document, my heart took a sickening plunge when I got to the details on page ten.

Nick Stanton had assured me verbally that the contract only covered Abaddon Golf Corporations' sole rights to the ownership of the clubs.

But the printed version read: *ABADDON RETAINS THE EXCLUSIVE SOUL RIGHTS TO ALL EQUIPMENT AND USERS.*

I was stunned. If I was reading this document correctly, Abaddon, or Lucifer, or Satan or the Devil, now owned control of my soul. All because I had allowed myself to be electronically bonded to the clubs.

I had to find a way out and find it fast. As I read the balance of the contract, I discovered a possible loophole in the fine print.

When Nick showed up at the hotel for the meeting, he had the three foul-smelling technicians with him.

"You bastard. I'm out of here right now, Nick. I read the contract. In my opinion, you guys broke it by also giving Abaddon clubs to Thor Ericsson to golf against me. The clubs were supposed to be exclusive to me. That's a deal-breaker."

To my astonishment, Nick didn't even try to deny any of the accusations. He lit a cigar then made himself comfortable on my couch.

"You're naïve, my friend, if you think you could have gotten this far without a little help from your new friends. Do you actually think an old, overweight duffer like you could have achieved any of this entirely on his own?"

I didn't answer because deep inside, I knew he was correct.

Nick continued in his patronizing way. "As far as Thor Ericsson goes, Mr. Abaddon just wanted to cover his bets by having two players. He wants a Masters win and a green jacket for Abaddon Golf at any cost. It's my job to make sure he gets what he wants."

I needed to get out of the room to think. I grabbed my briefcase and computer then headed for the door.

"Going someplace, Bobby?" Nick asked with a wicked laugh. "You signed our contract in blood, as I recall. There's no going back now. You don't seem to understand that when you bonded with the clubs, it was with both body and soul, forever."

"Nick, I promise you that you'll regret it if you don't let me out of this crooked deal without delay."

"Oh? What are you going to do about it?" Nick smirked.

"I'll hold a press conference with the media. When I give the details and blow the whistle, it will be game over for you and your boss. The only way to stop me is if you kill me before I meet the press."

"This is way beyond my pay grade," Nick said. "I'll call the boss and let him decide."

● ● ● ●

Although Nick talked to the boss from inside the bathroom, I heard the loud, heated discussion. Nick returned, wiping the sweat from his brow with his crimson pocket hanky.

"For some reason, the chief seems to think this is all my fault. He's extremely unhappy, and he's taking it out on me."

I was fuming, too. "Frankly, as far as I'm concerned, Abaddon can stick his pitchfork up your ass. Did you tell him I'm going to the newspaper and television reporters?"

Nick frowned. "That was the news that set him off. He doesn't like publicity, but he also doesn't like to lose, ever. It appears you have one chance and one chance only to keep your soul."

"What chance?"

"The only way he will tear up the contract is if you can manage to win the Masters tournament entirely on your own."

I gulped. "Can I still use the clubs?"

"Nope. No help from us and no use of Abaddon golf equipment. He also said to tell you if you renege or talk to any reporters, you, your lovely wife, your caddy, and your golfing buddies won't leave the golf course alive."

Nick stomped out of the room. The evil-smelling technicians, after glaring at me, left too. The stench of sulfur still hung in the air.

After Nick departed, I donned my raincoat and went searching for Norma. I had to make sure she was safe. I dreaded the thought of having to explain the ramifications of the Abaddon contract to her. I took the elevator to the main floor, and, as I started across the lobby, I saw the strange man who had asked about trying the Abaddon clubs.

The man was still wearing the three-piece suit, wire-rimmed glasses, and a bright purple golf hat, even though he was sitting indoors in the lobby. He smiled when he saw me approaching.

"Good luck tomorrow, Mr. Bolton, or should I call you, Boom Boom?" The man laughed.

"You can, or you can just call me Bobby," I said. "Everybody else does."

The man stuck out his hand. "Gabriel is my name, but you can call me Gabe."

"Okay, Gabe, I apologize for not letting you try the Abaddon clubs. But as I explained earlier, the company has a strict policy regarding the use of their clubs by anyone other than the designated player."

Gabe gave that enigmatic smile again. "I'm sure they do. Abaddon always seems to work in mysterious ways."

I was puzzled by his response, but I didn't push it. "As it turns out, I should have let you try the clubs anyway. As of this morning, I'm no longer playing for Abaddon Golf."

"That's interesting, Boom Boom, but won't it be difficult switching equipment just before the sudden death playoff?"

"It will be challenging, but all I can do is go out there and give it my best."

Gabe shook hands again. His grip was warm and comforting. "That's the right attitude, Bobby. And don't worry, you may have a little more support than you've been counting on."

As Gabe walked away, I couldn't help wondering how a guy that old could have such a smooth and unwrinkled face. Another mystery.

• • • •

SUDDEN DEATH

The rain had stopped by the morning, but the winds were gusting from all directions. Low dark clouds hung menacingly over the course. I was worried about equipment until I found out that my buddy had brought his clubs in the car, hoping for a game on the road.

"Teddy, I don't have time to explain, but I need to borrow your clubs."

Teddy shrugged, but he gave me the car keys without comment. Vic, my caddy, was mystified at the switch in equipment as he helped me struggle with the clubs to the first tee. Teddy's clubs were Taylor Made M2s. Good quality but nowhere near the feel of the Abaddon set.

Thousands of patrons crowded the course, excited about the upcoming duel between the two relatively unknown golfers.

I stood on the tee at HOLLY, the 18th hole, and my heart sank. The hole was a massive 465-yard-long par four. I didn't have a chance. I barely heard the official explaining the rules for the playoff.

"Ladies and gentlemen, this will be a sudden death competition. The first player to win a hole wins the match. In the event of a tie, we will replay hole eighteen again."

I won the toss and was first to tee off. The crowd clapped and chanted, *"BOOM BOOM,"* until the officials called for silence. I sent up a silent prayer then gave it my best swing. The ball arced high and came to a gentle stop in the middle of the fairway some 225 yards out—a worthwhile effort in my old game but useless in this arena of mega hitters.

The crowd was silent, wondering if I had mishit my drive. Thor Ericsson adjusted his stance to help avoid hitting the deep bunker lying 335 yards out on the fairway's left side.

I hung my head in dismay. I was on my own trying to defeat a young professional golfer who had the full backing and support of the unholy Abaddon gang. Thor smacked a massive drive right down the center of the fairway.

I couldn't watch, so I turned and faced the crowd. Norma and the guys smiled their encouragement. The three technicians were bunched right behind my wife, glaring out at me. But then I also saw Gabe, his kind old face positively radiating goodwill under the purple hat. He was sitting on a folding chair with a clear view of the action.

The old man saw he had caught my attention. He nodded with a smile then gave me a pronounced wink. Then I heard the crowd moan. I turned and saw that Thor's excellent drive had been caught in the shifting wind and was heading directly for the sand bunker.

I smiled and thought to myself, *After seeing that shot, maybe I'm not on my own out here after all.*

I hit first. I still had a long 245 yards to the pin. I took a full swing with my three wood and sent a great shot about 185 yards in the general direction of the green. Thor Ericsson tried a rescue club from the deep sand bunker. It was well struck but just caught the lip of the steep front bank before dropping back into the sand.

The crowd moaned again. This time the young golfer chose a more lofted club. I was watching and again saw the distinct fluorescent green flash when Thor took the grip. Thor hit an incredible long shot toward the green, but it struck the flag stick when the ball landed, then veered sharply right into a grove of trees. Thor had now taken three shots. I had taken two.

I had a good lie about 65 yards to the hole. Vic handed me a wedge and moved in close enough to whisper.

"Take a deep breath, Bobby. Even if you don't take this match, you're still a winner to everyone who knows you."

I thanked him then took the shot. My adrenaline must have been working overtime. My approach shot flew high and true but landed on the extreme back of the green and rolled off down a small hill into some heavier grass. The crowd moaned again.

Thor pulled off a miracle by maneuvering his shot through the trees and landing some four feet from the pin. Thor was now sitting at four strokes with an easy putt for a five, one over par. I was laying three in some very long grass. The best I could hope for was to land close enough with this shot to ensure the next putt for a tie.

I decided it was safer to do a short bump and run shot using my eight iron. I was just about to take the club from Vic when I noticed Gabe looking over toward the green, slowly shaking his head. I went back to the bag and took my lob wedge instead. The old man nodded and flashed that giant wink again.

Vic was petrified at my club choice. Being an instructor himself, Vic was aware that a lob wedge is a tough club to use. The golfer must take a full swing, even though the distance to travel is short. The slightest mishit can send the ball sculling far across the green.

"Are you sure that's the club you want?" Vic pleaded.

I wasn't at all sure, but I looked again at old Gabe. His innocent face showed a confident smile while he continued to nod his head. I made my choice.

"It's all or nothing at this stage, Vic. Thor will get his putt for sure. I need to be close enough to get my ball in with one putt for a tie."

I knew if I miss-hit the shot, the match would be over. I gulped, kept my head down, and took a full soft swing. I purposely tried to hit down at the back of my ball.

The great Phil Mickelson couldn't have done any better. My shot arced high into the air then landed softly three feet past the pin. I was elated, but then I saw my ball had incredible backspin. The crowd held its collective breath as the ball slowly rolled backward, hesitated momentarily, then fell directly into the cup, giving me a par four.

Thor was beaten.

The crowd roared the *BOOM BOOM* chant. Norma and the guys rushed out onto the green and covered me in giant hugs.

After giving a quick interview to the television crew, I hurried over to the official scorer's cabin with my scorecard. Out of the corner of my eye, over near a grove of trees, I spotted old Purple Hat Gabe amid a heated discussion with Nick Stanton, Thor Ericsson, and the three technicians.

I couldn't hear the words, but I could tell from the look on the other's faces that Gabe was winning the argument. Gabe kept pointing to the sky and then pointing at the ground, shaking his head while he did. Finally, Nick fled for the parking lot, followed by his minions.

Gabe raised his purple hat and arms in a victory salute, smiled, and then just seemed to disappear into the crowd.

I couldn't help thinking, *Today, I know I played against the Devil, but somehow, I don't think I played him on my own.*

• • • •

CELEBRATION DINNER

At the victory dinner that night, Norma and I were joined by Vic, Teddy, Wilbur, and Fred. I was still wearing my Masters green jacket. After a few glasses of wine, I told the group the whole story of Abaddon and about my confrontation with Nick Stanton, Abaddon's enforcer. They were enthralled when I described how purple hat Gabe seemed to intervene on my behalf.

"The old guy always seemed to be there every time I had to make a critical shot," I said. "He always called me Boom Boom. He seemed to get a kick out of it."

I didn't think it appropriate to tell them about Abaddon's threat to kill everyone if I had reneged on the deal.

"Do you think it's all over now?" Norma asked.

"I certainly hope so. I have a feeling Gabe represents a force that's substantially stronger than anything Abaddon can muster."

Spinning My Wheels

My caddy was on his third martini, celebrating the win. He rose unsteadily and proposed a toast, almost making it rhyme.

"Here's to Heaven, and here's to Hell, you didn't need either of them, Bobby, because you played so damned well."

The golf club manager capped off the evening when he announced our group meal compliments of the club to celebrate my win. He also had warm cognac snifters delivered to the table.

The following day all of us bleary-eyed travelers packed up our gear then began the long trip home from Augusta, Georgia. It was an experience that none of us would ever forget.

After we returned home, we found a registered letter from Price Waterhouse. The contents included a check for the one-million-dollar prize along with a signed release from the Abaddon Golf organization. Obviously, old Gabe had put the fear of God into his opponents.

I felt guilty about the money. I wasn't sure how much of the competition I had won without outside influences. Norma and I talked it over. Because of the win's unusual circumstances, we decided to donate all of the money to The First Tee Charity to support young golfers. I had a feeling Gabe would approve.

I was a happy golfer. I was sure the intensive training I experienced would lower my handicap at the club to the low single digits. My sporting goods business was booming because of all the publicity generated by the Masters and the million-dollar contest.

We were even considering the possibility of adopting a little one. I hoped a new child might be the beginning of the fourth generation of the *BOLTON SPORTING GOODS* enterprise. All was well in the Bolton family.

I went to bed that night a happy man. I had won the Masters, my business was saved, my marriage had improved, and my golf game couldn't be better.

I even wore my green jacket to bed.

● ● ● ●

A GOLFER'S DREAM

"Wake up, Bobby. For God's sake, you'll be late for opening the store. This is the first day of your annual *Open Season* sales promotion."

I struggled to open my eyes. I couldn't remember ever having fallen into such a deep sleep at any time in my life.

I shook my head to clear it. "Don't be silly, Norma. A green jacket Master's winner doesn't need to hold sales events. Customers are flocking to the store in droves. We may have to open another location or two."

Norma laughed. "What the hell have you been smoking, buster? Or more to the point, what the hell have you been drinking? You stumbled in from your poker night at the club, dropped on the bed then thrashed away all night long. Babbling and jerking your arms. I hardly slept a wink."

I sat up intending to show Norma my coveted green jacket, but, to my intense dismay, I saw that I was clad in my striped flannel pajamas. The same ones I wore every night.

"What the hell is going on?" I demanded. "Where's my green jacket? I won the Master's even if I had to beat the Devil to do it."

Now my wife was laughing so hard, she could hardly speak. "You're something else, Bobby. That must have been a world record dream, is all I can say. Now, get your ass moving. The store won't open itself."

I stumbled downstairs like a zombie. After a bowl of cold cereal, I jumped into my old car then headed for Bolton Sporting Goods. During the drive, I kept struggling to understand what had happened.

It can't have been a dream, I thought. *Every part of it seems so real.*

As soon as I reached my desk, I picked up the phone. Vic Nobel, the head pro at the Uxbridge Golf & Country Club, had acted as my caddie at the Masters. Surely, if anyone could, Vic would confirm my story. He answered on the first ring.

"Pro shop, Vic Nobel speaking."

"Hi Victor, it's Bobby Bolton."

"Oh, hi, Bobby. I bet you're looking forward to the season opener."

"Season opener?" I asked. "We've already had the club championship. I won it."

The club pro chuckled. "That will be the day. You're always good for a laugh, Bobby, boy. Now, what can I do for you?"

I gulped. "This may seem like an unusual question, Vic, but have you ever been to the Masters?"

"No, but I'd sure like to go someday. Providing you pay for the tickets, of course."

"Sorry, I have to go. I have a customer," I lied as I hung up the phone.

Dejected, I turned to my computer. Despite searching for an hour, I could find no mention of Abaddon Golf or their advertisement for the million-dollar contest.

I finally had to accept that all the wonderful things that happened to me were only figments of my imagination coming to life in a vivid dream. But remembering how terrific it felt to be a winner, I went on a significant weight loss and core strengthening program. Whenever I didn't have a customer to serve, I practiced on the indoor range at the back of the shop.

Fortunately, my annual *Open Season* sales promotion was a big success. Proceeds from the sale, coupled with a timely small business loan, looked like it would buy me enough time to ward off the threat of bankruptcy.

As our weather improved, the club finally announced opening day. I made a reservation to play the first game of the season with Teddy, Wilbur, and Fred, my usual playing partners. We had a regular beer bet on the line.

I lost the coin toss, so I had to tee off first. The first hole had wintered well, but it was still a difficult 425-yard par four with a green surrounded by deep sand bunkers. A finger of the lake cut the fairway in half at the 225-yard mark.

I placed a new ball on the tee, then stared out at the hole. During my Abaddon dream, Nick had trained me to see each shot before I hit. I decided to try the same technique.

I was about to start my backswing when Fred whispered, "Watch this miffed shot, boys."

Rather than tell him off, I smiled, then reimagined the shot. I pretended I was on the first hole of the Masters, then took a full relaxed swing with maximum follow-through. I heard the gasps from behind me when my ball soared high and long, coming to rest on the far side of the lake.

"Crap," Wilbur exclaimed. "You hit that sucker close to 300 yards."

"It's all in the training, boys," I said with a grin.

After the others teed off, we walked the soft fairway together, thoroughly enjoying the great weather and the enjoyment of good friends being together. When we finally reached my ball on the other side of the lake, we guessed my shot to be close to 315 yards.

I had my head down, concentrating on my next shot, so I didn't hear one of the new greenskeeper's carts when it rolled to a stop on the far side of the bunker. But I'm positive I heard the man's departing words quite clearly.

"Nice drive, Boom Boom. Worthy of the Masters."

I looked up just as the cart entered a grove of trees. I couldn't see the man's face, but I did catch a glimpse of something I'll never forget.

The bright purple golf hat perched on his head.

NEVER IN TIME

EDEN, MAINE
JUNE 1ST, 1856

A loud cheer arose from the crowd waiting patiently onshore as the ship finally emerged, ghost-like, from the early morning fog to round Point Cowan under full sail. With all flags fluttering, the schooner *Le Griffon* made a magnificent sight. She headed into the wind before setting a course for the main dock at the center of Eden's beautiful natural harbor.

None of the inhabitants of this sleepy port on that day in 1856 could have realized that some sixty years in the future, their little town of Eden would be renamed Bar Harbor and become famous, worldwide, as a flourishing tourist destination.

Nor did they know Eden would soon be the center of a mysterious event that would leave an otherwise decent man in danger of death on the gallows.

Antoine Landry stood on Eden's central wooden wharf with his granddaughter, 'Never Landry, at his side on this fine early summer day. The old man's hands trembled with excitement. The prize he had waited for was almost in sight.

"Take it easy, Poppy," 'Never whispered. "You'll have it soon enough."

Antoine, a man in his late 60s, was partially bent from arthritis but still actively involved in his business. He had gained a durable reputation as one of New England's finest clockmakers. Most of the better homes in the area showcased at least one of his hand-built grandfather clocks, or Tall Clocks, as they were known to most people.

Le Griffon had set sail from the Port of Le Havre, France, seventy-two days before carrying an assorted cargo of goods destined for the settlers of New England. Buried deep in her hull was the treasure Antoine had been waiting for. It was an antique Tall Clock, unlike any the new world had ever seen before.

Legend stated the clock had been custom-built for Catherine the Great of Imperial Russia in 1756 by Anatoly Federoff, a master craftsman. Legend also implied that the unfortunate Anatoly was put to death upon completing his masterpiece to ensure he could never build a duplicate. Catherine was said to have personally ordered Federoff's execution.

Many people believed Anatoly's widow had placed a curse on his clock in response to his undeserved demise. Legend said the curse would bring bad luck and haunt future owners for all time.

Over the years, this cursed antique was referred to throughout Europe simply as *The Empress* clock. Several original features made *The Empress* unique. At almost ten feet in height, it towered over lesser clocks that averaged six feet or less. It was double the standard width of other clocks as well. However, the most striking feature was the exquisite, hand-carved, miniature likeness of Catherine the Great that crowned the Tall Clock's top.

Originally, the miniature statue and surrounding area had been coated in delicately formed sheets of 18-carat gold. Unfortunately, due to the years of turmoil in Russia, the clock had fallen on hard times. The expensive gold had been replaced with copper sheathing. To this day, the sheets of gold had never been recovered.

'Never Landry turned to her grandfather. "Poppy, I know you're excited about getting your hands on this old clock, but what on earth are you going to do with it?"

"You might think I am an old fool," Antoine said. "But my dream is to build New England's finest clock museum. I'm going to use all the skills at my disposal to restore *The Empress* to her former glory before I install her as the centerpiece of my new Landry Museum of Time."

Although 'Never nodded her head, her full attention had strayed from Antoine's story. She was now focused on *Le Griffon* as the ship drew nearer to the dock. In particular, her gaze focused on the handsome young sea captain standing at the helm.

From his place at the wheel, Captain Andre Picard could see 'Never standing beside her grandfather. He was struck again to realize that she was one of the most beautiful creatures he had ever seen. Standing on the dock with the sunlight reflecting off her golden hair, she seemed almost dreamlike. Her willowy figure radiated a healthy glow.

He could hardly wait to see her again.

Andre had met 'Never when *Le Griffon* had visited the Port of Eden the previous year. Her grandfather had arranged a luncheon to discuss the possible transport by ship of *The Empress* clock from France. Andre had managed to take a seat next to 'Never at the table for the discussions.

After their first introduction, Andre had asked, "'Never is such an unusual name. May I ask the origin?"

'Never colored slightly before replying. "My father came originally from France, but my mother is from Wales. My actual Welsh name is Enever, but everyone drops the letter 'e,' so now I'm known as 'Never."

"Well," Picard said with a smile. "I will never forget meeting you, 'Never."

'Never thought she had heard every possible joke about her name, but this was the first time she couldn't think of a suitable response. Blushing brightly, she excused herself from the table and went to help with the lunch preparations.

Andre completed his discussions with Antoine Landry, and they struck a deal. The antique clock would be shipped aboard *Le Griffon* on her next trip back to Eden from France.

• • • •

THE LEGEND

With *Le Griffon* safely secured at the dock, preparations commenced for unloading. It was a slow process since the various pieces of cargo had to be sorted into different piles, depending on their final destination.

Still waiting on the pier, Antoine Landry was beside himself with impatience. "Surely, Captain Picard, you can unload *The Empress* clock before everything else?"

Andre took his eyes away from 'Never for a moment. "We wanted to keep your clock as safe as possible, Antoine. That's why we packed it at the bottom of the hold. Late afternoon tomorrow is the best we can hope to do. However, I will take personal responsibility for delivering it safely to your residence."

"If you can do that by tomorrow, Captain, I will appreciate it greatly. As a reward, after delivery, you can join us for a fine meal, accompanied by all you can drink of one of my best vintages."

Andre beamed at the invitation as it meant he would see 'Never again.

The next afternoon, 'Never eagerly awaited the arrival of both Captain Picard and the infamous clock. She lounged in the shade of the wide front porch sipping on some cool lemonade with her younger sister, Sara. 'Never had just turned eighteen on her last birthday. Sara, her only sister, was twelve.

'Never was Sara's idol. The younger girl worshipped her older sister, hanging on every word she said. They had been discussing the new arrival. Sara pestered, 'Never for details on the famous clock.

"Please 'Never, tell me again about the legend of the curse on *The Empress*."

"There seem to be many different stories about the curse. The cruelest legend says that Catherine the Great, the Empress of Imperial Russia, ordered the craftsman Anatoly Federoff to sign a blood pledge. He had to promise he would never build another Tall Clock for anyone else."

Sara winced. "You mean the clockmaker had to sign the pledge with his own blood?"

"Yes, and when he refused to sign the pledge, she had him locked inside *The Empress* clock until he starved to death."

"Oh, how cruel!"

'Never paused dramatically before continuing. "The legend

also says when they finally opened the clock door expecting to find Anatoly's body, nothing was there."

Sara made a face. "Oh, that's awful!"

"Don't get too upset, Sara. It's only a story."

● ● ● ●

'Never failed to tell Sara that an entirely different legend went on to say, on certain nights at the stroke of midnight, the ghost of Anatoly would sometimes emerge from the clock. She didn't want to scare Sara because of a myth.

Finally, the girls could see a heavily laden cart making its way slowly up the winding road from the harbor to the Landry Estate. An entire team of horses, laboring under the heavy load, struggled for breath as they plodded up the hill.

The Empress clock had been wrapped securely in several layers of thick canvas. The clock seemed immense to the watching bystanders as the workmen slowly unloaded it from the cart. After an hour of futile attempts at delivery, the four burly seamen gave up.

"Captain Picard, we've tried every angle, but this thing is just too big to fit through the front door of the main house. What do you want us to do now?"

Antoine intervened. "Andre, I think the only thing we can do for now is to move it to the gazebo in the back garden. If we leave the canvas wrapping in place, it will keep the clock protected from the weather. The gazebo has a good overhanging roof as well."

After Picard gave the appropriate orders, the seamen, with the estate staff's help, managed to move the heavy clock to the outdoor gazebo. Antoine was anxious about the safety of his prized possession.

"Please position it upright in the exact center of the gazebo," Antoine pleaded. "That should help to keep it protected in case it rains."

The tired workman did as requested and managed to move the heavy clock to the gazebo's protection. Antoine thanked each of them profusely before the crew members returned to the ship to complete the unloading process.

After seeing his crew off, Captain Picard stayed behind for his promised culinary reward. 'Never was looking forward to spending some time with the young captain again. It was evident from the looks they traded that the feeling was mutual.

The dinner and fine wine were everything Antoine had promised. After weeks at sea, Andre Picard appreciated the several seafood courses, accompanied by steaming platters of fresh garden vegetables.

The conversation over dinner was lively, too, with Andre bringing them up to date on the latest happenings in Europe. In turn, Antoine described in detail his plans for the new Landry Museum of Time.

Sara joined in on the conversation. "Do you think you can successfully restore that old clock, Poppy?"

"It will be a lot of hard work," Antoine said, after giving the matter some thought. "But as far as I know, all the mechanical parts are in working order. I will only have to concentrate our efforts on restoring the finished exterior. Unfortunately, I won't be able to fully restore *The Empress* to her glory days."

"A quitter? That doesn't sound like you, Poppy." 'Never said with a smile.

"You have to understand, ladies. Originally, in Russia, Anatoly Federoff covered the top of the clock in delicately formed sheets of 18-carat gold. It was so long ago no one seems to know exactly where the gold ended up."

"Sounds expensive," Picard ventured.

"It is costly," Antoine laughed. "I don't seem to have a lot of spare gold lying around here, so I guess we'll just have to leave the plain old copper top in place."

With a yawn, Antoine rose from the table. "I hope you will all excuse me. My arthritis is bad tonight, so I am going to turn in early. You two girls can keep the captain entertained for a little while, but don't stay up too long. Captain Picard is a busy man. I'm sure he has plenty of work to do aboard ship."

After the grandfather limped off to his bed, Sara, in an attempt to keep Andre's attention, asked 'Never to tell him of The Empress clock and the curse. The reference to a curse piqued the captain's attention.

"Please, tell me more," Andre implored.

'Never dutifully repeated the highlights of how the clock was built. When she mentioned the murder of the artisan Federoff and his body's subsequent disappearance from the clock, Andre's face darkened.

"Mon Dieu! If I had heard this story before I left France, I would never have taken that cursed timepiece aboard my ship."

"My goodness," 'Never exclaimed. "Are you that superstitious?"

"I'm not, but my sailors are a very superstitious lot. Life at sea is always dangerous, with the next threat only a storm or hidden reef away. If the men were aware we were carrying something with a curse hanging over it, the clock would probably be now laying on the ocean floor."

Sara giggled. "I wouldn't have wanted to be in the room on the day you told Poppy his prize possession was food for the fishes."

Everyone laughed, then Andre said, "Seriously, I would very much love to see this mysterious clock without its canvas covering before I return to France."

"I'm sure Poppy would love to show the clock unwrapped," 'Never said with a smile. "After all, it's his pride and joy. He talks of nothing else these days."

Perhaps it was the wine, or it could have just been his desire to spend more time with 'Never that prompted Andre to make a suggestion.

"I have to go back and check on my ship, but perhaps I could return later tonight. We could remove the canvas from *The Empress* together and have a good look. If it turns out to be close to midnight, we might even see the ghost."

'Never was intrigued with the idea and secretly thrilled at the thought of spending more time with the handsome sea captain. However, concern over Poppy's reaction to such a meeting caused her to shy away from the idea.

"Andre, I don't think it would be proper for me to meet you at the gazebo after dark. I'm sure my grandfather would disapprove."

Picard persisted. "Look 'Never, we won't be alone. Sara can join us as a chaperone, and I promise you I only have the most honorable of intentions."

Sara piped in. "Oh, please, please, 'Never. We should do it. I'm sure it will be the most exciting adventure ever. Poppy won't mind if we all go."

Despite her misgivings, 'Never agreed to meet Andre at the gazebo on his return from the ship, although she wasn't quite sure if her grandfather would approve. Fortunately, Poppy was a sound sleeper. Perhaps he would never know.

Just before 11:00 pm, 'Never slowly and quietly climbed the stairs to Sara's bedroom. She didn't want to take a chance of waking her grandfather. She knocked gently on Sara's door. There was no answer, so she entered. Sara was completely covered up and appeared to be in a deep sleep.

Despite several attempts to arouse her, Sara just mumbled that she wasn't getting out of bed to see some old ghosts. Although Sara could be stubborn, 'Never thought her little sister might also be a little too frightened to take part in the adventure.

Now, 'Never was in a quandary. With no way to get a message to the ship, Andre was sure to arrive at the gazebo as planned.

I'll just meet with Andre at the gazebo and tell him the plan isn't possible without Sara attending as the chaperone, 'Never thought.

By 11:30, the evening had turned dark. The gloom was pummeled with periodic gusts of wind and heavy rain. 'Never borrowed one of Poppy's old black raincoats to protect the long white party dress she had worn for dinner. She felt excited at meeting Andre but wished it was taking place under better circumstances.

'Never moved cautiously across the soaking wet grass, then froze when a bolt of lightning lit up the night sky. A rolling blast of thunder closely followed the arcing flash. Illumination from the lightning outlined the dark form of the sizable canvas-wrapped clock standing alone in the center of the gazebo.

In 'Never's heated imagination, the shrouded figure looked eerily like some ancient Egyptian mummy standing like a dark, eternal, and silent sentinel over some long-dead Pharaoh's tomb.

In her frightened state, 'Never started to turn back. She halted her progress on hearing a familiar voice from the darkness.

"It's okay. 'Never, I'm over here," Andre said reassuringly.

As 'Never climbed the stairs to the gazebo, she saw that Andre had already started to remove the canvas wrapping. When she questioned his actions, he responded that he thought she wouldn't come because of the storm.

"I only came to tell you Sara wouldn't wake up. I'll have to leave now as it's not proper for me to be here without her. My grandfather would be most upset."

"Please stay," Andre grinned. "It won't hurt to remain just long enough to see the unwrapped clock. You know you want to."

'Never couldn't resist the grin, and her curiosity was piqued. She said she would stay, but only for a few minutes.

Andre went back to work. When the canvas finally fell to the floor, the young couple stared at *The Empress*, mouths open in astonishment. The antique clock towered over them both. The exterior wood showed Federoff's true artistic ability. It was painstakingly carved to offer a detailed representation of some of the most famous French battles, with a miniature statue of Catherine the Great resting on the copper roof of the clock.

Despite the incredible workmanship, the clock seemed to radiate a dark aura. Perhaps a legacy of the curse that had hung over it for so many long years.

To break the uncomfortable silence, 'Never pointed at a sizeable semi-rusted metal key hanging from a cord attached to the door handle.

"Let's see if this thing works," Andre whispered.

"No, I think we should go. I really do."

"Just another minute," Andre pleaded, as he inserted the key into an elaborately engraved keyhole then began to wind up the old mechanism.

Almost immediately, the sounds of time ticking by emanated from somewhere deep inside the clock. Andre checked his pocket watch, then set the clock hands at precisely five minutes to midnight.

Although 'Never's hands shook, she could sense Captain Picard was trembling with excitement, too. She wasn't sure if it was the closeness of her presence or a fear of the so-called curse that was affecting him.

After a jarring bolt of lightning flashed across the sky, accompanied by the booming sounds of thunder, Andre jumped. On seeing his reaction, 'Never couldn't resist making a remark.

"So, our brave ship's captain can handle storms at sea and schools of hungry sharks but is perhaps frightened of a little ghost?"

Andre flushed. "Are you telling me this whole thing isn't scaring you, too, 'Never?"

"I'm from one of the famous Landry clans," 'Never boasted. "We Landry's don't scare easily. I'm much braver than you, Andre, and I can prove it."

Andre enjoyed her bravado. "And just how do you propose to prove that, young lady?"

'Never thought quickly. "I'll let you lock me inside the clock until midnight, as long as you promise to rescue me right after."

"If this is a bet, we need to first determine the stakes."

"What are you proposing, Captain?" 'Never asked cautiously.

"If you stay in the clock until one minute after midnight, I'll take you and Sara for a cruise of the harbor and lunch aboard my ship."

"And if I leave the clock before midnight?"

Andre grinned again. "I will claim my reward. A kiss for saving the fair maiden from the horrors of the clock."

'Never's face flushed, but she wasn't going to back down. "You had better start planning the lunch then, Captain Picard, because I am going to win this bet."

Andre was sure 'Never would easily panic and call him for help as soon as the clock door closed. As this would give him a chance to play the hero and claim his reward, he quickly agreed.

"Make sure to cover your ears when the clock strikes midnight. I suspect it will become quite loud in there."

• • • •

At one minute to midnight, Andre opened the double doors to the clock. 'Never tried to exude a calm appearance, but she was apprehensive. For a moment, she almost backed out. Then, after taking a deep breath, she removed her raincoat and stepped timidly inside the clock.

When the door first closed, 'Never almost screamed. The interior of the clock was dark, with an almost overpowering musty smell. She could hear the grinding of the mechanical wheels ticking down the remaining time to midnight. 'Never regretted having taken the bet.

Andre stood by the clock, waiting for 'Never to call out for him to release her. He was growing increasingly anxious as the seconds passed. He still felt convinced she wouldn't last until midnight. His concentration on the clock made him unaware of the growing, threatening situation occurring behind him.

Low, ominous dark clouds were forming in the sky above as the rainstorm's violence intensified outside the gazebo. Intermittent flashes of lightning were gradually closing in on the pavilion. The accompanying burst of thunder was deafening,

Then, precisely at the exact moment of that mysterious special time known as midnight, a vicious lightning bolt struck the giant oak tree standing immediately adjacent to the gazebo.

As a massive electrical discharge traveled through the heavy tree, the lightning arced through the air and struck the gazebo because of the tree's close proximity.

The first gong of midnight had just resonated from the clock when the lightning charge flashed through the gazebo, striking the copper roof of *The Empress*. The final destination for the lightning was not a matter of chance, with copper being one of the best conductors of electricity known to science.

The instant release of so much pent-up energy blew Andre entirely off his feet. *The Empress* clock, despite its bulk, was lifted off the floor then propelled halfway down the stairs of the gazebo. It ended up lying on its side in the driving rain.

An eerie stillness pervaded the darkness.

After several minutes, Andre rose unsteadily to his feet. He was severely shaken, but nothing seemed broken. His first thought was of 'Never. She must need medical help immediately. He rushed to the fallen clock, but, unfortunately, it had landed with the door side flat against the ground.

He tried desperately to move the clock to a position that would allow him to open the door, but the immense weight was too much for one man. In a panic, he screamed a message hoping 'Never could hear him through the thick walls of the clock.

"Hang on, 'Never, I'll go get help."

Andre ran to the main house screaming for help. His desperate cries woke up the estate staff as well as Antoine Landry. Everyone rushed back to the gazebo and, in concert, managed to roll the clock over, exposing the door.

Since several minutes had passed since the lightning strike, the ominous silence from within the clock did not bode well. Sara clutched her grandfather's shaking hand as Andre fearfully approached the clock.

The workers stood in silence. No one in the crowd believed the young woman could have survived the full fury of a direct lightning strike. Prepared for the worst outcome, Poppy held his breath as Andre pried the door open.

Mental images of a twisted, charred body suddenly ceased when it became glaringly apparent that The Empress clock's interior was completely empty.

The body of 'Never Landry had vanished.

The estate staff, along with some hastily recruited locals, searched the surrounding areas until dawn. No trace of 'Never could be found despite the painstaking search. Antoine joined in the effort until his strength gave out, then he retreated to a tree-shaded picnic table with Sara at his side. He was there when Andre came in to report.

"I am devastated, Antoine. We can't find a trace. I swear to you she was inside that clock when the lightning struck. With the clock on its side, there was absolutely no way she could have gotten out."

Poppy glared at the captain, his distrust of the man clearly showing on his lined face. He sat in silence for a moment, gathering his thoughts before addressing Picard.

"I don't know what has happened here, Andre. Your absurd story is hard to believe. I only know 'Never was alive when I went to bed. I left her with you. I trusted you, and now my darling girl is gone."

After Antoine wiped a tear from his eye, he hugged Sara then turned away from Andre to give instructions to his estate manager.

"Silas, send a messenger to town for the constable. Tell him there is an emergency at the Landry Estate. Tell him my granddaughter 'Never is missing. You can also tell him that I suspect foul play."

Sara took her grandfather by the hand to assist him in walking back to the main house, but he stopped to issue another instruction.

"And Silas, when you return from the town, I want you to have this cursed clock moved into the back of the barn. I never want to see it again for the rest of my life."

No one would listen to him when Andre swore the scent of 'Never's perfume still lingered in the air when he had opened the clock door.

● ● ● ●

ONE HUNDRED AND SIXTY-FOUR YEARS LATER
BAR HARBOR, MAINE - JUNE 1ST, 2020

"Going once, going twice, going three times," brayed the rotund auctioneer as he slammed his hammer down to end the bidding. "Sold to the gentleman in the checked shirt for the bargain price of $375.00."

Tom Nicholson was just as pleased as he could be. After attending the annual Bar Harbor Charity Auction, he was sure he had just grabbed the best bargain of the day. Tom was an amateur antique clock collector on the weekends and a first-class computer technician during the rest of the week.

The small fortune made trading a variety of digital currencies, including Bitcoin, allowed Tom to easily afford his unusual hobby.

Because Tom could fix almost anything, he was looking forward to restoring the old grandfather clock to its former glory. Before the bidding, potential buyers were always allowed to make a close inspection of items of interest.

When Tom had performed his pre-sale inspection, he could tell that all of the mechanical parts seemed to be in place, although the clock was old. He arranged for FedEx special services to pick up the clock and deliver it to his loft apartment the next day.

The delivery crew hoisted the giant clock into the place Tom had cleared for it in his bedroom. The move had taken hours of effort. When the team stopped to take a breath, the heavyset driver groaned.

"That sure is one heavy beast. I should have asked for danger pay. My back is still screaming at me to stop."

After making sure to give the workmen a good tip, Tom stood back, admiring his new possession from all angles. The clock was filthy and showed clear signs of having been exposed to fire. The copper top, in particular, revealed it had suffered significant trauma of some unknown origin. One side of the timepiece showed a clear indentation from a single blow with an ax. Fortunately, the gash hadn't penetrated the interior.

Tom was especially intrigued by the hand-carved figure of a woman perched on the battered copper top. He assumed the woman was some historical figure.

Tom was a bachelor in his late twenties. He had lots of female friends, but, so far, none he wanted to make a permanent part of his life. Although he wasn't a handsome man by current standards, his rugged features and straightforward manner appealed to many of the women he met.

He owned his computer repair depot business with no outstanding debt. Because of his excellent reputation, he always had more repeat work than he could handle. Although he enjoyed his computer work, Tom enjoyed his hobby collection of antique timepieces even more. He was entranced with the study of time in all its forms. His library contained numerous books on the subject of time travel.

Over the years, Tom had developed an unusual theory. He was utterly obsessed with the concept of 'disappearing' time.

He hadn't told many people about his conclusions, partly because he was sure they would laugh at him. Particularly since, so far, he couldn't manage to come up with any concrete form of proof.

In essence, Tom's theory revolved around the belief that each day, a tiny sliver of time just totally vanished from existence. Tom was convinced the missing time took place during the final minute of each day. He planned to electronically capture that lost moment and store it for future use.

Recently he had connected his latest and most powerful computer into a series of test clocks. An analysis of their soundwaves showed a microscopic time loss discrepancy between the first chime of midnight and the last.

The time loss was so tiny as to be almost non-existent, but Tom was convinced it was real. He was determined to find a way to replicate it. As a personal joke, he had a unique nickname for the missing time phenomena.

In that instant, when today was not quite yesterday, but still not yet tomorrow, Tom thought.

He called it *'TomTime.'*

He worked for an entire week on the old grandfather clock, cleaning the exterior as best he could and applying a special lubricant to the mechanical workings. Then, tired after putting in a full day at the shop, Tom watched television for a few minutes before deciding to head off to bed early.

Tom wound the antique clock for the first time, then set it to match his stopwatch. He wanted to check in the morning to see how accurately the old antique was keeping time. He pulled the covers over his head and fell into a sound sleep. A few hours later, when the huge clock struck the first note of midnight, the sound caused him to sit bolt upright in bed.

At first, he thought he was dreaming, then he thought he might be losing his mind. He rubbed his eyes to clear them from sleep, but the wispy figure remained floating in the air beside the grandfather clock.

Tom found himself staring in disbelief at the faint figure of a stunningly beautiful young lady.

She wore a long translucent white gown and appeared to be staring silently at him. Tom tried to speak, but no words would come from his parched throat. He tentatively reached out a hand toward her but could feel nothing of substance.

When the last chime of midnight rang out, the young woman started to disappear back into the clock, but not before she silently mouthed two distinct words:

"HELP ME!"

Tom stumbled from his bed and raced to the clock. He threw the doors open, then stared in disbelief at the empty interior. He retreated to the sanctuary of his bed, trying to make sense of what had happened.

I'm a scientist, Tom told himself. *I'll simply repeat the experiment to see if I get the same result.*

Tom dutifully wound up the clock each night, then attempted to stay awake until the midnight hour. Each time, the result was eerily the same. The newly acquired antique grandfather clock would strike the first chime of the twelve ominous tones of midnight. Then, the apparition would appear, standing silently beside the timepiece. She was breathtakingly beautiful, dressed in the same long flowing white gown. Despite her translucent appearance, in a dreamlike way, she seemed almost natural.

The visions always ended the same way. When the last chime of the midnight hour sounded, she retreated into the depths of the antique clock. He could not hear, touch, or smell her, but he could most definitely make out the outline of her lovely lips as she silently mouthed her plea. It was the same plea every night. Only two words, but they broke his heart.

"HELP ME!"

By the fifth night, Tom found himself eagerly awaiting the mysterious woman's appearance. He had run his computer non-stop for five days attempting to replicate and store a significant quantity of *TomTime*.

Tonight, he was going to hook an electrical feed from his main computer to the copper top of the clock. If the woman appeared, Tom would release the accumulated *TomTime* to see if he could communicate with her directly.

Sure enough, at the first stroke of midnight, she appeared on schedule. Tom threw the override switch on his computer and waited. The results were astounding. The previous ghostly form now took on the shape of a beautiful human figure. A figure that was now reaching out a hand toward him.

Tom trembled as he took her soft, warm hand. "Who are you? Why are you here?"

The twelfth chime of midnight was beginning when the girl formed her answer. She spoke so softly Tom could barely hear.

"My name is 'Never. I'm lost somewhere in time. Please help me!"

As she retreated into the grandfather clock, her haunting words lingered in his ears. Tom couldn't forget the magic of her touch. Tom was basically a decent man. After some thought, he reached a decision. Somehow, someway, despite the cost in money and time, he was determined to help the woman who was lost in the vast reaches of time.

After many mind-crushing experiments, Tom discovered by boosting the power input to his computer bank, he could substantially increase the amount of *TomTime* he was replicating.

Gradually he started banking *TomTime* with the goal of accumulating enough to free 'Never for more than a few seconds. When he calculated he had sufficient, he connected his computer to the copper top then waited for midnight to arrive.

At the sound of the first gong, Tom threw the switch. After a brief electric arc, 'Never's shadowy shape began to appear. As she slowly materialized into her human form, Tom started a series of questions. Knowing her time was limited, Tom spoke fast.

"Tell me as quickly as you can how you came to be stranded in time and space."

'Never gave Tom an outline of the legend of *The Empress* clock and the terrifying events of the night she first entered the clock.

"You say lightning struck the copper clock sometime between the first chime of midnight and the last?"

"Yes, Andre was…"

'Never stopped talking as a wave of horror crossed her face. "Dear God," she exclaimed. "Andre will surely be in terrible trouble. My grandfather, Antoine Landry, will be seeking revenge."

"Is Andre your brother?"

"No. He's the captain of the *Le Griffon*. He delivered *The Empress* clock from France."

Despite knowing it was totally irrational, Tom felt the tormenting pangs of jealousy on hearing about Andre.

"Can you help me, Tom? I'm so worried about my grandfather Antoine, my sister, Sara, and Captain Picard as well."

"I'll see what I can discover about the night of your disappearance," Tom replied. "And I'm working on a plan to try to free you for good."

As the last gong of midnight sounded, 'Never began her retreat back into the clock. Tom held her hand until it faded away. After her departure, Tom checked his stopwatch. He was astounded to find that, although his time-piece showed he was with 'Never for almost an hour, the actual time that passed on the grandfather clock was merely a minute.

Tom, weary from overwork, took himself off to bed. As he lay there in the darkness, he thought of 'Never. Something about her was getting to his inner core. His last thought before falling asleep brought a smile to his face.

How could I possibly be falling in love with a woman who is at least 150 years older than me? But I am.

The following morning, Tom did an extensive computer search of the year 1856. He was looking specifically for any historical records of the period dating back to when Bar Harbor was still named Eden, Maine. Not anticipating much success, he was surprised and elated to see that a local historical society had scanned many old, local Eden newspaper pages into a library data bank.

It took some work, but eventually, Tom came across the story of the disappearance of 'Never Landry. A chill traveled slowly up his backbone when he read the following account:

THE EDEN DAILY REPORTER   Final Edition July 1st, 1856

The courthouse erupted in applause today when French National Captain Andre Picard was sentenced to death by hanging for the murder of a local citizen, Miss 'Never Landry. Although Miss Landry's body has not yet been recovered, Judge Lester Wright ruled there was more than enough circumstantial evidence to justify his ruling.

The stress of the Picard trial caused Miss Landry's grandfather, Antoine Landry, to suffer a minor heart attack. The family is hopeful of a full recovery.

The date for the execution is set for August 15th, 1856, at 9:00 am.

• • • •

Tom captured a screenshot on his computer, then printed out a copy of the newspaper story. He didn't relish the thought of having to show it to 'Never.

Tom alternated between working on a solution for 'Never while also completing some critical repair work for long-term valuable customers for the rest of the week. He kept his computer bank running around the clock to generate more *TomTime* for 'Never's next appearance.

When he calculated he had accumulated enough *TomTime* to free 'Never for more than an hour, he set up the equipment again and waited for midnight. After 'Never materialized, she threw her arms around Tom. Other than holding hands, it was the first actual physical contact between them.

"I'm so happy to see you, Tom. Have you discovered anything?"

"Yes," Tom replied grimly. "The news is not good. You had better read it for yourself."

'Never took the printed copy, scanned it quickly, then her delicately formed face crumpled in dismay.

"Oh no!" she wailed. "Poppy has had a heart attack, and they're going to hang poor Andre Picard for something he didn't do. It's not fair."

When 'Never's tears began to fall, Tom took her in his arms to comfort her. Even though he knew she could disappear in a wisp, at the moment, she was more than real. Tom tried to reassure her that a solution was possible.

"I can't promise anything, 'Never, other than to tell you I will do my very best. I have some ideas I'm working on, so keep your fingers crossed."

Tom continued to hold her in his arms for a few moments. Then, in an attempt to take her mind off her troubles, he asked 'Never to tell him more about her alternate existence inside the clock. His scientific side craved an answer to the riddle of a person being lost in time.

"I wish I could see what you see," Tom said. "Can you tell me what it's like traveling through time and space?"

"It's so hard to describe," 'Never replied. "It's like a whole different world exists once you pass through the clock. I've seen many others also wandering through time, as well. Once, I'm sure I saw

Anatoly Federoff, the Russian craftsman who built *The Empress* clock for Catherine the Great. I wanted to cry when I saw him because the man looked so sad."

"He's the man she sentenced to death?"

"Yes. When Federoff wouldn't pledge to never make a clock for anyone else, she decreed he be locked inside The *Empress* until he died."

Tom was fascinated. "Can you communicate with the others? Can you touch them?"

"It's so difficult to explain. You can see other travelers, but they don't have a solid substance. You can communicate with gestures, but not with words."

"When you go back through the clock, do you remember being here?" Tom asked. "Do you remember me after the clock finishes striking midnight?"

'Never flashed her wistful smile. "I will never forget you, Tom, never."

"And I won't let you forget me even if you wanted to."

As the last chime of midnight approached, 'Never would soon have to depart. Tom kissed her gently, told her to have faith, and then he let her go. She had parting words as she started to dissolve into a mist.

"This is so unfair for Captain Andre, Tom. He's about to be hanged for something he didn't do. I must find a way to get back to Eden before the execution happens. Can you help me return to Eden before August 15th?"

Even though Picard was a rival, Tom realized he had little choice. He said, "I promise to do everything I can to save him."

● ● ● ●

After 'Never's departure, a thought suddenly struck Tom. Something that had not occurred before. *What if we're trying to save a man who has already been hung?*

Tom raced to his computer. He had previously stopped his search of the old newspaper clippings on finding the article dated July 1st, 1856. He frantically scrolled ahead, then stopped dead when he reached the newspaper account for the day after the scheduled execution of Andre Picard.

THE EDEN DAILY REPORTER Final Edition August 16th, 1856

A grim crowd gathered earlier today as the earthly remains of Antoine Landry were laid to rest at Harborview Cemetery.

The famous clockmaker collapsed and died yesterday after witnessing the hanging of French national Andre Picard for the murder of Landry's granddaughter earlier this year.

As befits a convicted murderer, Judge Lester Wright ordered Picard to be buried in an unmarked pauper's grave.

Antoine Landry's surviving granddaughter, Sara, gave a statement to the press on behalf of the family.

Miss Landry said, "Justice has been served."

• • • •

Tom realized immediately that he was faced with a time paradox. The events of the past had already occurred. The only solution was to somehow intervene back in time before they *took* place.

In a nutshell, if he couldn't get 'Never back to Eden before 9:00 am on August 15th, 1856, the execution would take place. The question remained - how to do it?

Tom was proud of his discovery of *TomTime*. It solved the question of what happened to the tiny slice of time that disappeared each day during that fleeting instant, just before today becomes tomorrow, but is not yet yesterday.

The problem was, despite generating *TomTime* as fast as possible, the immense amount required to break 'Never free would require months of computer time. Another solution would have to be found without delay.

With only a few days remaining before the date of Andre's execution on August 15th, 1856, Tom resorted to a theory he had been considering. Basically, Tom believed the lightning strike had created a massive surge of *TomTime* trapping 'Never in a vacuum in time.

As he worked desperately at his computer creating power models, Tom pondered over the undeniable fact that he was deeply in love with 'Never. The irony was, if he found a solution to Andre's death sentence, it would mean sending 'Never back in time and out of his life forever.

Despite his misgivings, Tom eventually decided on a possible solution. He planned to purchase ten high-powered portable generators and wire them in a series before connecting them to the copper top of The Empress.

From there, the plan was simple. At the stroke of midnight on August 14th, the computers' combined power and the generators' output would recreate the same massive surge of *TomTime* experienced when 'Never originally disappeared.

Although it was a gamble, with a high degree of risk involved, Tom felt it was the only chance of ever getting 'Never back to Eden in time to halt the execution.

The following evening at midnight, when 'Never appeared, Tom filled her in on the basics of his plan. She listened quietly as he talked.

"Is it dangerous, Tom?"

Tom shrugged. "I have to be honest. The answer is I really don't know. In theory, you should end up back where you started. The reality is you might end up in some other time and place or possibly remain trapped in time."

'Never remained silent for a time, then she leaned forward to take Tom's hand. He waited for her response.

"I'll have to try. I'll never forgive myself if an innocent man dies because of me."

For a moment, Tom considered revealing that Picard had already been hung. He discarded the idea as being unworthy of someone who cared for her as much as he did.

"How will you know if the experiment works?" 'Never asked quietly.

"A historical group keeps archived copies of your town's local newspaper. It's called the EDEN DAILY REPORTER. You can send me a message if you arrive safely."

"Will you be able to send messages to me in return?" 'Never asked hopefully.

"Unfortunately, not," Tom said sadly. "It doesn't work that way. I can receive a message from you because an archived copy of your newspaper written in 1856 still exists in 2020. If I left a message for you in today's paper, you would never see it because it wouldn't exist in 1856.

'Never looked so crestfallen at this disclosure that Tom took her in his arms to comfort her. Tom could tell from her sobs, the reality was starting to set in. They both knew if the experiment was successful, they would be separated by a vast gulf of time and destined to never cross paths again.

When the last chime marking the passing of midnight took place, 'Never reluctantly broke away from their warm embrace to retreat into *The Empress* clock. Tom would not see her again until the night of August 14th, when the attempt to return her home would take place.

After 'Never's departure, Tom was struck by an intense sadness. What irony to finally find the woman of his dreams only to be the person who would throw the switch that would send her out of his life forever. In a tragic but romantic gesture, Tom decided to change his name for the disappearing time syndrome from *TomTime* to *NeverTime*.

Tom stiffened his resolve, then returned to working on the problem. He ran all the computers, full tilt, replicating as much *NeverTime* as he could. While the computers ran untended, Tom wired up the newly purchased high-powered portable generators. When that work was completed, he ran a thick electric cable from the generators to the copper top of *The Empress* clock.

Finally, it was time. By 11:30 August 14th, Tom was totally exhausted, physically and mentally, from the relentless workload. As he waited for 'Never to appear at midnight, doubts about the wisdom of his plan started to creep into his tired brain.

It would be so easy to keep her near me, he thought. *All I would have to do is tell her the plan can't work. I know 'Never has deep feelings for me. It wouldn't be the perfect solution, but I'm sure 'Never would forgive me eventually. We might be happy together, sharing brief moments in time as often as I could bring her back.*

For a moment, Tom seriously considered not going through with the plan. But he knew if he backed down now, it would be selfish and unfair to 'Never and her family, not to mention Captain Picard's dire situation.

'Never would bear the pain of causing an innocent man's death for the rest of her life. Tom also knew himself well enough to know he would never be happy carrying the corrosive guilt for his actions.

Tom was still struggling with the dilemma when the first chimes of midnight struck and 'Never appeared. From the sad look on her face, Tom instinctively knew she had come to the same realization he had. The fleeting wonderful time they shared would end forever when the switch was thrown.

'Never glided into Tom's arms and kissed him with an abandoned passion. Then she stepped back and looked directly into his eyes.

"I don't want to leave you," 'Never whispered. "And my heart tells me you don't want to leave me either. I love you deeply, and I'll never forget you, but…"

"You don't have to say it, sweetheart. I've already come to the same conclusion. We'll never find peace unless we do the right thing."

'Never nodded, unable to speak.

Tom hesitated. "Before we proceed, I have to remind you that we are dealing with the unknown vagaries of time and space. From my calculations, I believe you will break out of your time trap and end up in Eden on August 15th, 1856. But the reality is you could end up anywhere at any time."

"I trust you, Tom. I know in my heart this will all end the way it should."

Tom nodded. "Then it's time for you to go. Kiss me goodbye, then walk straight back to the clock. Open the door and go inside. Don't look back."

'Never kissed Tom with an intensity of lovers parting for the last time. Then she slowly moved to the clock without looking back. She knew Tom gave her that instruction so she wouldn't see the tears streaming down his face. It was okay with 'Never because she didn't want Tom to see the flood of her tears as well.

When 'Never was safely inside the clock, Tom moved to the control panel. His hand hesitated over the power switches for the combined computer/generators. Then, he took a deep breath and threw the switch, just as the last chime of midnight commenced.

A giant arc of stored electrical power flowed through the wiring to the copper top of The Empress clock. A cloud of sparks encircled the little carved figure of Catherine the Great then a bright, warm glow filled the room. When the light subsided, Tom rushed to the clock to throw open the doors.

The Empress clock was empty. And 'Never Landry was somewhere in time.

• • • •

Tom waited in torment for the next few days. He couldn't eat or sleep, worrying about 'Never's fate. Finally, he summoned his nerve and went online to the historical website for Eden, Maine. Anxiously, he scrolled through page after page of old newspaper clippings. Finally, he found the one he was looking for.

THE EDEN DAILY REPORTER   Final Edition AUGUST 16th, 1856

The planned execution of French national Captain Henry Picard was abruptly canceled yesterday morning after Miss 'Never Landry was found, dazed and confused but unharmed, wandering on the grounds of the Landry Estate.

Readers may recall that Captain Andre Picard was under a death sentence by hanging for the presumed murder of Miss Landry.

Although Miss Landry was unable to deliver a credible account of her missing time, she was able to convince Judge Lester Wright that Captain Picard played no part in her disappearance.

The only comment from Miss Landry involving her trauma was to send a message of thanks to an unnamed individual who provided invaluable assistance in her return

Miss Landry was delighted to be reunited with her grandfather, Antoine Landry, and younger sister, Sara.

Captain Picard has returned to his ship Le Griffon and will be sailing on the morning tide for France.

••••

Tom immediately checked to see if the edition of the newspaper announcing the hanging of Picard and the death of 'Never's grandfather still existed. That issue had disappeared from the historical records.

EDEN MAINE SEPTEMBER 1ST, 1856

Antoine Landry walked painfully out onto the wide front porch, scratching his head. 'Never and her sister were chatting and drinking cool lemonade. He looked at his two granddaughters with fondness. He was happy beyond belief that 'Never had returned unharmed, but he was still troubled.

"Why won't you tell us where you were, 'Never?" he asked.

"I can't, Poppy. The story is too strange. No one would believe me."

"Go ahead and try me," Poppy coaxed. "You might be surprised. I've seen more than my fair share of strange things happening in my lifetime."

"I'll only tell you this much," 'Never said quietly. "It was all because of The Empress clock. There's something unnatural about it. Maybe it is cursed, after all. When the lighting hit at midnight, it sent me out into the mists of time. I was a prisoner against my will."

"In the mists of time?" Poppy said, trying to keep an open mind. "Then how did you manage to find your way home?"

"I'm not ready to talk about yet. The memories are still too painful. Maybe later."

Antoine stood up. His face was cast in stone. He limped off in the direction of the barn, picking up an ax from the woodpile on his way. His angry voice carried back to the girls.

"That does it," Antoine roared. "It's time to deal with that cursed clock once and for all."

Horrified at the ramifications of what her grandfather intended to do, 'Never raced after Poppy catching up with him just as he was about to deliver the first blow.

"Stop, Poppy!" she screamed. "You don't realize what you're doing."

"Yes, I do," Poppy panted. "I'm going to destroy The Empress before she can do any more harm."

Before 'Never could respond, Antoine swung the heavy ax against the side of the clock. The ax head bounced off the rigid wood surface, but not before leaving a gash. 'Never grabbed her grandfather's arm before he could strike again.

"Poppy, if you love me, you'll drop the ax right now. All I can tell you is, if The Empress is destroyed, I'll instantly vanish into time again. But this time, I won't be able to return."

Antoine stared at his granddaughter for a long moment, then dropped the ax. As he turned to leave the barn, he said, "I do love you, 'Never, and I trust you. But before long, you must promise to tell me the whole story. I'll be ready to listen when you're ready to talk."

Over the next few weeks, 'Never spent as much time as she could manage to catch up with her younger sister, Sara. One morning while they were doing the breakfast dishes, Sara asked a question that had been on her mind.

"Do you miss Andre Picard?" Sara gushed. "He was such a handsome man."

"Captain Picard was a charming man. I'm happy he escaped the gallows, but the truth is, Sara, I met…"

'Never's words were interrupted by a loud knocking from the back door. Poppy being close to the door, said he would answer it. He returned moments later with a perplexed look on his face.

● ● ● ●

"You have a visitor, 'Never. There's a young man at the back door. He says he knows you and just stopped for a visit. He looks like a traveler, maybe from England or somewhere because he certainly wears different clothes."

It can't be, it's not possible, 'Never thought, as she raced through the house, then out onto the back lawn. She caught up with Tom just as he arrived at the gazebo.

"My God, it is you," 'Never breathed. "I thought I would never see you again. How did you do it?"

When Tom finished covering her face with kisses, he took a deep breath then answered her question.

"After you left, I felt like my life was over. I couldn't live with the thought I would never see your lovely face again, so I went back to work. I was about to abandon all hope, then I got a breakthrough. I finally cracked the problem of creating and storing *NeverTime* in abundance."

"What does that mean, now?"

"Well, it will allow us to get married, for starters. If you'll have me, of course."

"Of course, I'll have you. But how on earth would it work?"

"With a little more tinkering, I believe I'll be able to go to any time and any place whenever I want. We could be married in Eden, then have our honeymoon in Hawaii. Celebrate Christmas in Paris and Easter in London. The best part of all is The Empress is big enough for two."

"I love the idea of traveling through time with you, Tom, but I hate the old clock. It's evil and haunted."

Tom laughed. "No, the clock is just the opposite. It's now a portal in time, and I have some great ideas of how we can use it for the good of everyone."

"I'm not sure how I'll ever be able to explain this to my grandfather. Poppy was so angry he was about to destroy The *Empress* with an ax. I stopped him just in time."

"Why don't you and I talk to your grandfather and Sara together?" Tom said. "From what you tell me, he and I are both rabid clock lovers. I'm sure he'll be fascinated with the technology involved."

'Never nodded. "That could work particularly if Poppy knows we're going to use the technology for good reasons."

"I've given this a lot of thought. Traveling through time can be very destructive if the utmost care isn't taken. For example, if your grandfather had destroyed The Empress, we would never have met.

"And I would still be wandering through the mists of time," 'Never added.

"The key is to be always aware that the slightest change can have significant implications for the future. Having said that, I firmly believe there will be opportunities to correct some historical wrongs. Take poor Anatoly Federoff, for example. Imagine Catherine the Great locking him in time forever just for not submitting to her demand to never build another clock for anyone else."

"Yes, I remember seeing Federoff as I drifted through the mists of time. The poor man looked so miserable."

"After we talk to your grandfather, I have to return to my time. I still have plenty of work to do before we start our new lives together."

"But how will you return?" 'Never asked, with a worried frown. "The Empress clock s in your bedroom back in Bar Harbor."

"Science can solve anything," Tom said with a grin. "I installed a homing device in the clock. All I have to do is press this button, and I'm on my way back."

'Never stared at the small black device, Tom held in his hand.

"Oh God, what would happen if you lost it?"

"It would be a disaster," Tom laughed. "That's why I'm carrying five spares, not including the one I buried near your gazebo."

"'Never, where are you?" came a call from the main house.

"That will be Poppy, Tom. We better go and have that meeting with him before you head home."

"Before we go, I want to tell you something I'm sure of," Tom said softly.

"Please do,"

"I know our love will always stand the test of time."

"I never doubted that for a minute," 'Never replied.

'Never kissed Tom, then took his hand, and they strolled together to their meeting with Poppy and Sara.

And then on to the timeless world of wonders that awaited them.

EPILOGUE

December 24th, 1757

It was bitterly cold on the back streets of Saint Petersburg, Russia, with snow falling in large flakes. A lone figure trudged painfully along the old cobblestone streets, making his way through the darkening night. He was still not entirely sure how the mysterious stranger had found him.

The man stopped at a modest dwelling and knocked gently. He waited patiently while examining the large black wreath of mourning attached to the door. The shabby wreath showed unmistakable signs of aging.

The door cautiously opened. A scream rang out then Mrs. Anatoly Federoff collapsed slowly, in a joyous faint, onto the cold stone floor. The shock of seeing her long-lost husband standing in the doorway, his hands clutching a treasure trove of delicately formed 18-carat gold sheets, was more than her frail old body could endure.

Anatoly was finally home. He was dazed and confused, not really sure of what had happened to him after his welcome rescue from the eternal mists of time by the unknown young man.

It had hurt his artistic feelings to strip the top of The Empress clock of its golden treasure, but he felt the sheets of gold a fair price for all he had endured at the cruel hands of Catherine the Great.

After a long-needed rest, Anatoly planned to leave Russia with his wife to take up a studio in a small village in Austria. He would use the stolen gold to finance the manufacture of several duplicates of The Empress clock.

Anatoly went to sleep that night smiling as he dreamt his dreams of revenge.

YESTERDAY'S GIANT

DAVENPORT, CALIFORNIA

Ralph Ogden stood on the rustic porch of his downtown office, watching a seemingly never-ending stream of heavily laden trucks parade down the main street. The trucks groaned from the weight of large cut sections of a giant redwood tree. The vehicles were destined for the processing yard at the Green Mountain Sawmill.

Ogden turned to his foreman, Rusty Knox. "So that's the famous Yesterday's Giant. I never thought I would see the day we would get our hands on her."

"Me neither," Knox said. "We got the damned tree down just a few minutes before those bloody environmentalists showed up with their court order. There was hell to pay. Screaming and crying like mad, but it was too late, we just kept cutting."

"Crazy hippies," Ogden snorted. "These people don't seem to realize that we all got to make a living. If it weren't for this sawmill, this place would be an abandoned ghost town."

"Why the hell would anyone want to give a tree a name?" Rusty asked.

"Shit, those tree huggers got names for almost all the old redwoods protected inside the National Park. I've heard names like Hyperion, Helios Icarus, Del Norte Titan, and more. Lucky for us, the Giant was outside the safety of the park's boundaries."

"Yeah," Rusty laughed. "Outside the boundaries by all of 36 feet. That's what pissed the hippies off."

"Okay, get back to work. I'm tired, so I'm heading for home."

Ogden, a heavy-set man in his late forties, lived alone except for his three-year-old son, Cory. Although Ralph was the wealthiest man in town, he tended to spend far too many evenings sitting alone by the fireside brooding over glory days past. A full glass of smooth single malt Scotch usually kept him company.

Although his health was poor, there was nothing terminal as far as he knew. Still, much of his brooding time these recent days centered on thoughts of his mortality. He had other things to think about, as well.

His son Cory was being raised by his attractive young housekeeper, Lily Carson, a local woman. Ogden often brooded over her, too—in fact, far too often.

The morning after the truck delivery, Ralph did the rounds at his sawmill. The smell of freshly sawn redwood drifting lightly on the morning air was like perfume to his nose. The mill was running at total capacity now because of a backlog of orders. He was hoping the kiln-dried lumber from Yesterday's Giant would fill all of the backorders and replenish their raw material inventories as well.

One of his newer employees, Johnny Hunter, approached him slowly. He held his cap in his hand as a gesture of respect.

"Morning, Mr. Ogden," Hunter said. "That's one right big redwood they brought in yesterday. You can tell from here that those boards are going to be beautiful, for sure."

Ralph only nodded, barely listening as the young man continued. "As you know, sir, Lily Carson and I are getting married next month. I was hoping to get some of the best-grained wood pieces from Yesterday's Giant for a special project."

Ralph was highly envious of the younger man. Secretly he had been hoping that Lily might eventually warm up to his advances. Now she was going to marry this fool and spoil it all.

"I'm going to surprise Lily and build her our wedding bed as a present. It will please her no end to be sleeping on the wood of a two-thousand-year-old tree."

Although Johnny worked as a lumberjack, he was noted locally for his skill as a fine cabinet maker.

Ralph's first inclination was to say no, but his warm feelings for Lily overcame his jealousy of the young man.

"It's okay with me," Ogden grunted. "But you'll have to set it up with Rusty. Tell him I said you're to get double the employee discount as a wedding present to Lily from Cory and me."

Johnny struggled to hold back his astonishment. Usually, Ralph Ogden was not noted for his generosity. Johnny had half expected to be charged a premium for the unique top-quality lumber. He thanked his boss and hurried off to find the foreman.

The conversation with Johnny triggered thoughts in Ralph's mind. An intriguing idea about building something unique. Something that would allow a person to become part of the immense age and almost immortality of Yesterday's Giant.

That night, staring into his drink by the fireplace, he fleshed out the germ of an idea. In the morning, he decided to go ahead with his project.

He worked at his desk for a few hours then, right after lunch, Ralph strolled along the main street and stopped in front of the McNulty Funeral Home. He paused in contemplation for a few moments, then entered. The proprietor, Horace McNulty, sat behind his antique rolltop desk reading the morning newspaper.

"Howdy, Ralph. What brings you to my establishment on this lovely day?"

Ralph wiped the dust off one of the cracked leather chairs then sat down. McNulty waited expectantly to hear what the town's richest man had in mind.

"I want to make some confidential arrangements," Ralph began. "But, before I do, I want to warn you I'm not in the mood for any wisecracks."

Horace was smart enough to shut up and listen.

"Have you heard about Yesterday's Giant?"

The funeral director nodded. Everybody in town knew about the cutting of the two-thousand-year-old redwood tree. Horace personally thought it was a tragedy. So, did most of the others.

"I'm going to send over some of the best kiln-dried planks from that tree," Ogden said quietly. "I want you to have a custom-made casket fashioned out of that specific wood. When it's finished and polished to a high gloss, I want a brass plaque fastened to the lid."

"What do you want the plaque to say, Ralph?"

Ralph lowered his head as if he couldn't quite make up his mind. Finally, he responded, "I want the brass plaque to read: *ON THIS DAY, TWO OF YESTERDAY'S GIANTS ARE RETURNING TO THE EARTH FROM WHICH THEY CAME.*"

Horace, trying not to smile, made a careful note of this unusual request then asked, "Ralph, it could be years before you ever need the casket. What do you want me to do with it in the interim?"

Ralph told the funeral director to send an annual bill for the storage of the coffin. He then headed back to the office, comfortable in his decision to ultimately rest for eternity in the gentle embrace of a two-thousand-year-old giant.

• • • •

JOHNNY HUNTER

A few months later, Johnny Hunter backed up his old truck to the sawmill entrance where foreman Rusty Knox stood waiting.

"I don't know why the old man is giving you the pick of the best redwood, Johnny, but orders are orders."

Johnny just grinned and began making his selection. He took enough lumber to build the wedding bed and then began to load extra boards.

Rusty intervened. "How big is this damned bed anyway?"

Johnny reddened. "I have a feeling we might need a smaller crib alongside the wedding bed before too long." Rusty made a lewd remark and sent Johnny on his way.

With the wedding only a few weeks away, Lily continued her work as the housekeeper at Ogden's residence. Although she adored his son, Cory, she was beginning to have grave misgivings about his father. Several times recently, she had noticed him staring at her, although he quickly turned away when she spotted him.

She decided it was all in her imagination. She concentrated all her attention on Cory. He was a curly-headed, good-natured child with an angelic smile. Lily was hopeful that she would be blessed with a young one as wonderful as Cory one day.

Ralph watched his housekeeper and son laughing together as they played. He tried to suppress the forbidden thought that kept slowly creeping into his mind. Lily Carson would make a wonderful wife and mother for the Ogden household if it just weren't for that yahoo she planned to marry.

Doctor Norman Porter listened closely to Ralph's erratic heartbeat. He put the stethoscope away then motioned for his patient to join him in the office.

"Ralph, I don't know what to say. Despite all my warnings, you continue to drink and smoke like there's no tomorrow. Well, let me tell you, there is a tomorrow, and if you keep this up, it won't be a bright one."

Ralph snorted. "You're just an old lady, Doc. Nothing wrong with me that a few days on a beach wouldn't cure."

Doc Porter gave up and pressed Ralph for more details on the cutting of Yesterday's Giant. "You know, Ralph, there are a lot of unhappy people in this county regarding your decision to cut down that magnificent specimen. In a few more days, the state would have extended the National Park's protection boundaries. Why the heck did you do it?"

"I'm a logger, Doc. I am now, and I always will be. To me, a tree is just a tree. My job is to cut them down, provide jobs for people, and wood for future homes. There isn't any mystery about it. It's just wood."

Doc Porter just shook his head. As far as he was concerned, Ralph Ogden was an insensitive lout.

Some of the people who were unhappy initially about Ralph's decision were still unhappy and pledged to do something about it. Rumors started circulating in town that the Green Mountain Sawmill folks were thinking of hiring a helicopter to search the inaccessible back canyons for more ancient trees like Yesterday's Giant. Several of the hippies from out of town decided to mount a picket line at the mill.

Ralph was furious. "Blast it, Rusty. You got to get rid of these bums. Although we're a non-union operation, at least six customers today alone can't take delivery because of their unionized truck drivers."

The foreman was a resourceful guy. He knew Ralph wouldn't rest while the picket lines stayed in place. One of the significant hazards around a sawmill was fire. The mill was old but had state-of-the-art fire suppression systems installed in all the cutting and timber storage areas. However, there were several smaller areas not covered by the existing equipment.

Ralph's solution had been to purchase a mobile four-wheeled, miniature fire engine consisting of a 500-gallon tank and power hoses. Rusty simply moved the vehicle to the front entrance of the sawmill. Every time a picketer showed up, he or she received a continuous unwanted shower. After a week of water torture, the picket line broke, but Ralph Ogden didn't make any new friends.

A few days after the picket line ended, Ralph decided to check up on his secret project. He called the funeral home director for an update.

"Glad you called, Ralph. The brass plaque just arrived this morning, and the boys are fixing it to the casket as we speak. If you give us an hour or so, you can come over and take a look."

For some reason or another, although it was a magnificent piece of work, Ralph was afraid to look directly at the coffin. Maybe it reinforced his feelings of mortality or something. He broke out of his morbid thoughts when McNulty kept babbling.

"If it's okay with you, Ralph, I'd like to put this baby on display in our showroom. It sure is a beauty. Might even help me drum up some business."

Ralph was livid. "Horace, you stupid asshole. I told you this was a highly confidential matter. If you show the casket, my private property, without permission, I'll run you out of town."

The chastened funeral director quickly assured Ralph the redwood casket would remain in covered storage until the day of need.

● ● ● ●

THE WEDDING BED

At Saint Oliver Episcopal Church, for the Hunter wedding, Ralph had sat quietly in a back pew with his foreman, Rusty Knox. He watched the proceedings in silent despair. Lily Carson looked like an angel, dressed in an all-white, full-length shimmering gown. As far as Ralph's gaze went, Johnny Hunter wasn't even there. Ralph's young son, Cory, had been pressed into duty as the ring bearer. Everyone thought the boy looked adorable in his miniature tuxedo.

The trouble started at the reception when the bar opened for business. Ralph quickly downed two double shots of Black Label whiskey before retiring to a dark corner of the hall. When Rusty approached him to say the reception line was starting, Ralph refused to get up. Every time a waiter or waitress came with an appetizer, he sent them to the bar for a refill instead.

During the speeches, Ralph sat muttering regrets to himself. Several of the townspeople approached to say hello but backed off quickly when they saw the black look on Ogden's face. Finally, the disc jockey started to play music. As was customary, Johnny led Lily to the center of the floor for the traditional first dance. Lily's favorite song was playing.

The music had no sooner ended for the first dance when Ralph lurched out to the center of the room to demand the next dance. The bride's father had been standing by waiting for this honor, but no one wanted to confront Ralph. Johnny tried to intervene, but Lily stopped him.

"It's okay, Johnny. It's just one dance. I'll reserve the next one for my dad."

When the DJ started to play a slow waltz, Ralph took Lily in his arms for the first time. Although she tried to keep some distance between them, Ralph held her in a firm embrace. His breath, reeking of whiskey, was almost overpowering. Goaded by the soft feel of Lily's breasts against his chest, Ralph tightened his hold.

It was all too much for Lily—she just wanted to escape. She was wearing her best stiletto high heels. The length of her dress mostly covered them, so few people noticed when she jammed her heel down on Ralph's unsuspecting shoe. He bent over in agony, releasing his hold on her.

She quickly apologized for standing on his foot. "Oh, I'm so sorry, Mr. Ogden. How clumsy of me. Johnny, will you help Mr. Ogden back to his seat?"

Johnny had no idea what had taken place. He helped Ralph hobble back to his seat in the corner. Although Johnny was oblivious to Lily's defensive move, Rusty Knox was not. He hurriedly escorted Ralph to his car, then drove him home before he could do any more damage to his already bad reputation.

After the reception, Johnny carried his new bride across the threshold of the small log cabin he called home.

"Close your eyes, honey. I have a surprise for you."

When Lily opened her eyes, she was amazed. The beautiful queen-sized wedding bed, even in the dim light of the cabin, was stunning. The richly grained redwood headboard threw off a warm, inviting glow.

"Lily, I built this bed with my own hands from the best planks of the Yesterday's Giant redwood tree. The foundation of this bed is from wood over two thousand years old. I hope our families will still be sleeping on it two thousand years in the future."

"This is a wonderful present," Lily sobbed. "I can't thank you enough. You really are a talented man. I know this bed will be passed on for many generations. It's truly a gift from your heart, and I do appreciate it."

Johnny knew that the gift would move Lily. Her rough upbringing had saddled her with a great sense of insecurity. Johnny hoped he could bring some peace and stability into her life.

My married life is progressing just fine, Lily thought. *I just wish that work wasn't so nerve-racking these days.*

Although little Cory was still a delight, his father's actions were becoming downright creepy. It almost seemed that her boss was holding a grudge. He went out of his way to find small things to complain about. He was also back to staring at her whenever he thought she wasn't looking. She resolved to talk about it with Johnny at the first opportunity.

A few weeks later, Johnny arrived home early with a big smile on his face. He told Lily the company had chartered a helicopter for a trip into the backwoods area in search of another unprotected giant redwood. Ralph Ogden wanted him to go on the overnight trip with Rusty, the foreman.

Lily was surprised. "When did this happen, hon?"

"I'm not sure. The old man called me into the office this afternoon and told me to pack my gear. I'm supposed to head out with Rusty at two o'clock tomorrow afternoon. We should be back by the next night in time for dinner."

When Lily expressed her concern about staying alone in the cabin, Johnny laughed. "Don't worry, hon, the bears are too full of berries this time of year to worry about a skinny little thing like you. Come to bed, and I'll give you something to really worry about."

Lily went to bed, but she didn't go to sleep right away.

The next day, Johnny came home from work at noon in time to pack his bag and have a bite to eat before heading out on his overnight trip. Little Cory was spending the day with his aunt, so Lily could take the day off to help Johnny prepare. She felt a vague sense of unease but still managed to smile brightly at her husband as she kissed him goodbye. She spent the rest of the day catching up on laundry and cleaning the cupboards.

Lily found it depressing, sitting by herself eating a hastily prepared dinner for one. She read for an hour or so, then decided to go to bed. Lily had just finished brushing her teeth and putting on her frilly pink nightdress when a knock sounded on the cabin door. She hastily grabbed a dressing gown and slowly approached the entrance.

"Who is it?" she asked in a whisper.

"It's okay, Lily, it's just me, Ralph Ogden."

Worried, she asked, "Is Cory all right, sir?"

When Ralph replied, his voice slurred. "He's fine, Lily. I just want to talk to you about something important."

Lily was uncertain about what to do. Ogden was her boss and Johnny's employer, too. She didn't want to offend him, but she was frightened. The knocking persisted, so she hesitantly opened the door. Ralph Ogden pushed into the room carrying two glasses and a bottle of champagne. He seemed inebriated already. Frightened, Lily drew the housecoat tightly around her.

"Lily, I think you are wonderful," Ralph slurred. "You shud be with me, a man of substance 'stead of that junior boy scout you married."

Lily tried to talk some sense into the drunken man without success. Finally, she said, "You have to leave, Mr. Ogden. Johnny will be furious when he comes back and finds out you were here."

Ralph stared at her with a glazed look. "Don't you mean *if* he comes back?"

The rest of the ordeal was a nightmare for Lily. Ogden refused to leave until he had seen the famous wedding bed that Johnny had built by hand. Lily reasoned that he might leave peacefully if she agreed to his demand. On the way to the bedroom, she slipped a small kitchen knife into the pocket of her nightdress, just in case.

The sight of the bed seemed to inflame the drunken man. He lost all sense of reason. Despite the numerous minor cuts that Lily inflicted on him, it was easy for the older burly man to overpower the slight young woman. Her anguished cries for help went unheard in the isolation of the backwoods cabin. In the early hours of the morning, Ralph Ogden, still bleeding, abandoned the house.

He left Lily alone, in tears, on her hand-crafted redwood wedding bed.

● ● ● ●

THE ACCIDENT

The screeching sound of an ambulance speeding by the cabin on the way from the local airport to the little hospital down the hill aroused Lily from her troubled sleep. She ached all over from the previous night's attack. She decided not to wait for Johnny's return before reporting the rape to Sheriff Don Anderson.

She was determined to see Ralph Ogden behind bars by nightfall. She picked up the phone and dialed 911. The sheriff answered on the first ring.

"Sheriff Anderson, it's Lily Hunter, I want to report—"

"Lily, thank God. I was heading up to your cabin. The hospital just called. Johnny has been badly injured in an accident. He is in surgery."

Lily started to cry. "How bad is it, Sheriff?"

"I don't know, Lily. I'm sending up a car for you right now. I'll meet you at the hospital, and we'll get the whole story."

The beeping sounds of hospital equipment, coupled with the eerie green glow of dim night lights, made the private room seem even more frightening. Lily stood with Sheriff Anderson, staring down at the unconscious form of the man she loved. Even in the dim light, it was impossible not to focus on the emptiness in the bed where Johnny's right leg should have rested.

"Do you know what happened, Sheriff?"

Don Anderson was a kindly man. He put his arm around Lily's shoulders. "The early reports state that Johnny had scaled a large tree to make measurements of its height when his safety harness failed. There will be a complete investigation, of course."

Sheriff Anderson felt sorry for the young couple. It was evident that even with rehabilitation, Johnny would never earn a living as a logger again.

"Do you know if Johnny has any insurance, Lily?"

She shook her head. "No. We couldn't afford insurance. I don't know what we'll do now. I don't even know how we will cover this hospital stay, never mind the operation itself."

The sheriff arranged for his deputy to take Lily back home. When Lily felt the full impact of the day's events, she sat on her bed and cried. Her mind reeled with all of the tragic happenings of the last twenty-four hours. Although her first concern was for her husband's well-being, her second concern was her planned revenge on Ralph Ogden for his unspeakable attack.

Sitting on the unmade bed, Lily noticed some blood stains and unmistakable signs of other bodily fluids still on the bed sheet. She had cut her attacker. Lily was positive the bloodstains would prove that Ogden was the culprit. After some time, she calmed down and began to ponder all the uncertainties that she and Johnny faced for the rest of their lives. A bleak future with no insurance and little income.

Sometimes, you have to forget your values and do the right thing, Lily thought. She gradually worked her way through all the possible solutions to their dilemma. When Lily finally reached a bitter and fateful decision about their future lives, she was troubled but resolved.

She moved slowly to the kitchen and retrieved a sharp pair of scissors and the morning newspaper. She used the scissors to cut out a one-foot square piece of the bedsheet. After Lily placed the stained bedsheet beside the morning newspaper, she took a photograph with her smartphone. The digital image clearly showed the incriminating stains, alongside the date on the paper.

Lily had her ammunition. Now she prayed she was mentally and emotionally strong enough to carry out the most challenging part of her plan.

Although it was early afternoon, Ogden was still at home, wandering from room to room in his pajamas. He had a massive hangover and a paralyzing sense of guilt. Ralph wasn't everyone's favorite man, but, deep down, he was not truly a bad person. He blamed his behavior at Lily's cabin on a combination of alcohol, loneliness, frustration, and a warped fascination with Lily herself.

But he knew in his heart no excuse could ever justify the wrong he had done to a sweet young woman. Although Ralph anticipated his arrest at any moment, he resolved not to try and defend his actions in any way. The loud knocking on the front door did not come as a surprise, but it did increase the shooting pains in his head.

To his astonishment, he opened the door to find Lily Hunter glaring at him. There were no policemen in sight.

"Lily, I'm so sorry for—"

"Shut up, Ralph, and sit your fat ass down. There's nothing you can say to make the situation better, so I will do all the talking."

Ralph was astounded. The Lily he knew as his housekeeper was a mild-mannered, almost timid, soft-spoken woman. She had ever talked this way to him in the past.

"You are guilty of two major crimes, you jerk. The attack on me last night plus the so-called accidental fall of my husband."

"What accident?" Ralph asked, obviously bewildered. "I know nothing about an accident."

Skeptical of his claims, she continued. "Johnny has lost his right leg and will never be able to work as a logger again. Sheriff Anderson is investigating the accident to determine if criminal charges are justified."

"Have you told the sheriff about last night, Lily?" Ralph asked with a quiver in his voice.

"No, Ralph. I've decided on a very different course of action," Lily said with contempt dripping from her voice. "You're a big man in this town, so you probably think you won't be brought to trial or, at worst, get off with a hand slap."

Ralph tried to intervene, but Lily continued. "If you think that, you're very wrong. I have definite proof of the attack and undeniable proof that it was you. No judge would dare let you off in light of the evidence."

She showed Ralph the picture of the stained sheet and newspaper.

"Now, this is the way it's going to be, now and forever. First, you will never again refer to me as Lily. From now on, I will always be Mrs.

Hunter to you. Second, Johnny will remain on your payroll at full rates for the rest of his life. Third, I will remain on the payroll as your housekeeper, but I will never set foot in this house again."

"But what about, Cory?" Ogden whined.

"You will drop Cory off at my cabin every morning, then pick him up every evening. You will never enter our cabin again for any reason. And last, you will cover any medical expenses Johnny needs for his treatment and rehabilitation. I really don't care what happens to you, Ralph, but I do care about Johnny and your son, Cory. I wouldn't want the boy to grow up knowing his father is a rapist pig."

Ralph hung his head in shame and unconditionally agreed to her terms.

After Lily left, Ralph sat down and cried like a baby. He was so ashamed of his whole approach to life and particularly his vile treatment of Lily. Ogden made a solemn vow to change his ways. He pledged to spend the rest of his life atoning for his sins.

Several weeks later, the unmistakable sounds of morning sickness echoed through the little cabin. A situation Lily was dealing with on her own. Johnny remained in the hospital but was expected to be released soon. Lily delayed as long as she could but finally phoned and made an appointment to see Doc Porter the following Friday.

Lily waited anxiously for Doctor Porter to finish his pelvic examination. "Go and dress, Lily. I'll see you in my office when you're ready."

The doctor was reviewing his notes when Lily sat down. Norman Porter was a competent, compassionate man, and he was aware that the Hunter family was anything but wealthy.

"Lily, I know what I'm about to tell you will come as a shock, but I hope one day you will see it as a blessing. It was a little early for the ultrasound, but there is no question. You'll soon be the mother of twins."

Doctor Porter laughed at the shocked look on Lily's face.

First, the rape, then Johnny's accident, and now this. Somehow, we will find a way to get through this whole mess, she thought.

"You're probably wondering how you are going to break the news to Johnny. That's only normal, Lily. Most women are nervous about breaking the news about twins to the baby's father, or the fathers, for that matter."

Lily quickly pounced on Doctor Porter's use of the plural. "What do you mean, *fathers*?"

"Well, it's actually not that common, but there are numerous cases of twins being born to different men. They are always fraternal twins rather than identical babies. But don't concern yourself, Lily. That's certainly not the situation here."

Lily didn't join in the doctor's laughter. Her heart sank, then she hung her head and looked at the floor.

Lily hurried home in a panic. She dropped her purse as she entered the house and went immediately to Johnny's computer. She looked up, '*twins by different fathers,*' on Google. Doctor Porter was right. They even had a medical term *superfecundation* for the condition. Deep in her heart, fear was growing stronger by the minute that Ralph could be the father of one or even both of the twins.

She hurried to the hospital to tell Johnny about her concerns. She couldn't keep him in the dark. He would have to hear the truth about Ralph's nocturnal visit and the possible consequences. When she entered the hospital room, she found Johnny sitting up. A huge smile broke out when he saw her coming through the door.

"Hey babe, I got great news today. They are letting me out of this dump tomorrow, and I'm scheduled for a fitting of my bionic leg next Tuesday."

Lily tried to smile. "That's wonderful, Johnny, but I have something I have to tell you."

Johnny nodded and told her to go ahead with her news. As she looked down at her husband, his gaunt face told the story of the suffering he had undergone. Would it be fair to burden him with more trouble when he was already traumatized by losing his leg and livelihood?

She summoned up her internal strength and smiled, "Johnny Hunter, you're about to become a father. It's time for you to get out of bed and come home. I need you to start building a crib. I hope you have plenty of that special lumber because we're going to need two cribs instead of one."

• • • •

WHO'S YOUR DADDY?

On a rainy night in April, Lily brought two new lives into the world in Room 326 at the tiny Davenport General Hospital. The first to be born was 5lbs 2 oz, David Hunter. He was followed seven minutes later by his baby sister 4lbs 5oz, Tammy. Doctor Porter assured the anxious parents that both children were in perfect shape, with all attachments in their proper places.

Lily looked worriedly at the little wrinkled faces. Still, it was impossible to discern any differences in their appearance at this early stage. The babies soon went home to the warmth and comfort of their identical new, hand-made redwood cribs. Lily cried when she first saw them lying together, side by side.

Johnny assumed she was crying tears of joy. He was wrong. As time passed by, Lily became more and more obsessed with the question of the baby's paternal legacy. She drove to the nearest town and secretly purchased two of the new do-it-yourself DNA testing kits. Each kit contained two small test tubes and a set of instructions.

Lily followed the instructions to the letter. First, she took a swab from baby David and placed it in the tube, followed by a sample of Johnny's hair in a second test tube. When the first test was complete, Lily repeated the sequence with a sample from baby Tammy and a hair sample from Johnny. She marked the labels on the two tubes with Johnny's hair sample, FATHER. She left the tubes with samples from David and Tammy unmarked.

Lily was struggling with a dilemma. She desperately needed to know if one or more of the twins resulted from the attack by Ralph Ogden. On the other hand, if Ralph was the father of only one of the twins, Lily didn't want to know which one. She knew in her heart that, despite her best efforts, she could never feel the same about that particular child.

She finally arrived at a solution. Lily took all of the test samples into the bathroom then turned off the lights. She placed the identical tubes in a brown paper bag then gently mixed them up. When she turned the lights back on, Lily honestly had no idea of which tube sample was David's and which sample was Tammy's. She marked the labels BABY "A" and BABY "B" and mailed them off to the lab. She prayed that she wasn't making a big mistake.

While waiting for the response from the lab, Lily had a surprise visitor. Johnny was at the hospital for rehabilitation when the Davenport County police car pulled up in front of the cabin. Sheriff Anderson entered and immediately complimented her on the twins. Lily wondered what triggered his visit. She wished now she had told him about Ralph's attack, but she knew in her heart it was too late.

After accepting a cup of coffee, the sheriff got to the point. "Lily, I know you have some doubts about Johnny's accident, but I have to tell you there was no evidence found of any foul play. The forensics team has determined that the cause of Johnny's safety harness failure was metal fatigue. Plain and simple."

Lily thanked the sheriff and felt somewhat relieved. Ralph Ogden would always be a villain in her mind, but at least he wasn't responsible for Johnny's tragedy.

Life continued on a relatively smooth path for the young couple and the twins, except for Lily's frustration whenever Johnny talked about his boss.

"It's hard to believe, honey. Who would have guessed that old coot had a hidden heart of gold. Imagine paying me disability wages and continuing to pay your full salary as a housekeeper for just babysitting."

Lily had to bite her tongue to keep from blurting out the truth.

Finally, just before Christmas, Lily received her response from the DNA lab. Because Johnny was outside exercising his new artificial limb, she was safe to read the contents in private. With shaking hands, she slit the envelope open and withdrew the printed test results.

The falling tears from her eyes partially blotted the report as she read: TEST RESULT ONE: CONFIRMS POSITIVE PATERNITY OF FATHER SAMPLE TO BABY "B." TEST RESULT TWO: CONFIRMS NEGATIVE PATERNITY OF FATHER SAMPLE TO BABY "A."

Lily looked closely at the two smiling twins in their cribs before burning the test results in the fireplace. There was no doubt. The babies had different fathers, and there was no way of knowing the identity of each.

Lily made a sobbing retreat to the solitude of her bedroom. She tried to pull herself together. She knew from the internet search that some women faced the same challenges of bringing up twins with different fathers. She would just have to buck up and make it work somehow.

And so, she did.

• • • •

TWENTY YEARS LATER

Despite his earlier reputation, Ogden lived up to his agreement with Lily. He dropped Cory off at the cabin every morning then picked him up every night, always addressing Lily with respect as Mrs. Hunter. The payroll checks for both Johnny and Lily arrived every month like clockwork. They even increased over time to allow for inflation.

People all over town were constantly remarking on the positive changes in Ralph's life. He had stopped drinking and became a fervent supporter of the local chapter of Alcoholics Anonymous. He joined every charity in town, offering hours of personal time in addition to money. He coached the local kid's baseball team and sat on the hospital building fund committee as chairman. He even committed the Green Mountain Sawmill Company to support the environmentalist movement against the cutting of old-growth redwood timber.

Ralph was particularly proud of the way his only son Cory had grown up. Over the years, Lily had done a fine job of raising him. Cory even looked at Lily as a substitute mother. Ralph was excited because Cory was due home today. Cory had been attending an exclusive boarding school in England, rarely making it home over the past four years.

Ralph drove to the San Francisco Airport in a daze, thinking about the return of his son and the things they would do together. He was hoping to talk Cory into taking the helm at the company. It seemed like ages as he paced back and forth, anxiously awaiting Cory's arrival.

His heart filled with pride when he saw his boy walking through the exit gates. At twenty-three years of age, Cory made quite an appearance. He was over six feet tall, slimly built with fair curly hair and a brilliant smile. They hugged, and then the two had an animated conversation all the way back to Davenport.

After dinner that evening, Cory said, "I think I'll run up and say a quick hello to Mom Hunter. I haven't seen any of the Hunter family for ages."

Ralph handed over the car keys, telling Cory to drive safely and have a good time. When Cory showed up at the door unannounced, he created a shock wave of excitement in the Hunter family. Johnny shook his hand and pounded him on the back. David did the same. Lily hugged him, but Cory was staring intently over Lily's shoulder.

His total attention centered on Tammy. She had been away on a school trip the last time he was in town, so he hadn't seen her since she was a skinny little teenager.

Now she was a bombshell. At almost twenty, Tammy was most definitely all woman. Her beautiful, creamy complexion was highlighted by her long curly fair hair. Her eyes were extraordinary in their color and depth. She was a stunning creature, and her radiating self-confidence showed that she knew it.

She came over to Cory with a half-smile, gently extending her hand in greeting. It took all of Cory's restraint to keep from planting a full kiss on her smiling lips.

David, like most of the young men in town, worked at the sawmill.

He had known Cory all his life and took great delight in filling him in on all the latest town gossip.

"The biggest shock around this burg, Cory, is the unexpected change in your old man. He's gone from being hated to becoming the most popular guy in town. Nobody knows what happened to make him change, and, frankly, no one cares. The results tell the story."

With Cory back in Davenport for good, the visits increased, and gradually, Cory and Tammy started to get closer. It was inevitable at some point that he would begin a serious courtship. But that threw Lily into a panic. Tammy was either Cory's half-sister, or she was not. David was either Cory's half-brother, or he was not.

Lily's head spun with all the potential problems on the horizon. She decided to do the unthinkable.

Ralph was stunned when Lily showed up unannounced at his house. He hadn't exchanged more than a simple greeting with her in over twenty years. She was clearly in a panic when she entered the house. Ralph poured her a glass of cold water and insisted she sit down.

"Tell me what's gone wrong, Mrs. Hunter."

Lily started crying. "I have confirmed DNA test results. Either David is your son or Tammy is your daughter. But I don't know which one is true." She explained how she had purposely not identified the DNA samples.

Ralph shook his head in disbelief until Lily explained the concept of superfecundation, twins by different fathers. The news shook Ralph.

"What can I do, Lily? This is all my fault."

Lily was firm in her resolve. "Somehow, you have to persuade Cory to stop seeing Tammy as a potential life partner. There is at least a fifty-percent chance she could be his sister."

Ralph promised to do everything in his power to help.

That night in bed, Ralph reflected on the monstrous circumstances his one moment of madness had caused so many innocent people. Despite his good works and other efforts at redemption,

Ralph could not forgive himself. The guilt for raping Lily still gnawed at him every day, without fail.

But despite the guilt, he did feel a slight pang of perverse pleasure in the thought that he had another secret son or daughter. He resolved to talk to Cory as soon as he returned from his fishing trip to Canada. In the meantime, Ralph decided he needed to speak to his lawyer.

The following morning, Ralph headed over to the legal offices of *Underwood & Scully* for his 10:00 a.m. appointment. Dennis Underwood, the senior partner, poured two cups of coffee before asking Ralph what he wanted to discuss.

"Denny, I think I need a new will, and I need it fast."

Underwood jokingly said, "I don't want to turn away any business, my friend, but as far as I know, your current will is perfectly adequate."

Ralph asked for assurances that any discussion would be kept strictly confidential. When the lawyer nodded, Ralph began to tell him the whole story, holding nothing back. Underwood stared at Ralph for a moment.

"Yes, you certainly do need a new will. We can do the changes right now so you can sign it in front of our witnesses."

Ralph went to bed that night, confident he was doing the right thing. Cory was due back from his fishing trip the next day. Ralph was determined to sit him down and tell him the whole sordid story. He was sure the act of telling Cory the truth might finally rid him of the overwhelming sense of guilt. He just hoped his son would forgive him.

Unfortunately, Ralph never had the opportunity to find out. Sometime in the night, Doctor Porter's dire predictions came true, and Ralph died from a massive heart attack. He was all alone when Cory found him cold and still in the morning.

Word spread like wildfire through the town. Ralph Ogden, leading citizen and benefactor, was gone.

● ● ● ●

THE CASKET

Virtually the whole town showed up for the funeral. Because Ralph had kept up the storage payments to the McNulty Funeral Home for the past twenty years, Horace McNulty had kept up his end of the deal. The highly polished redwood coffin positioned at the head of the church reflected a warm red glow from the multitude of candles.

The Reverend Peter Wilson was effusive in his praise for the deceased. "Many of you newer folks in town may not know the story behind the brass plaque on this casket, but truer words were never written."

The reverend then proceeded to tell the story about the harvesting of Yesterday's Giant and how the special two-thousand-year-old wood was used in the construction of the coffin.

"Mr. Ralph Ogden was a true friend to many in need over the years," the reverend continued. "He was also a faithful member of this congregation. He will be sorely missed by us all. May God bless his soul."

One by one, the town folks shuffled to the front of the church to pay their respects. When Lily, at last, stood in front of the closed casket, she slowly read the shiny brass plaque for the first time:

"ON THIS DAY, TWO OF YESTERDAY'S GIANTS ARE RETURNING TO THE EARTH FROM WHICH THEY CAME."

Lily searched her heart to try and determine how she truly felt about the dead man. She silently addressed her remarks to the man within the casket.

"Ralph Ogden, you were a pygmy twenty years ago. Still, I honestly feel you might now have attained the giant status you have been desperately seeking. You raised a fine young man in Cory, and you are the natural father of one of my beloved children. Without you, one of them would not have been born. I forgive you, Ralph. May you rest in peace."

Tears dropped slowly from her eyes as Lily placed a single white rose on the redwood casket and left the church. She never looked back.

Lily could tell from the increasingly warm attention Cory was paying Tammy that Ralph had never had the opportunity to persuade Cory to abandon the budding romance. She was deep in thought when the phone rang.

"Hello, Mrs. Hunter?" a deep male voice said.

"Yes, this is Lily Hunter. What can I do for you?"

"My name is Dennis Underwood. I was Ralph Ogden's lawyer."

"What does this have to do with me?"

"Mr. Ogden's will contains some provisions that could affect your family. Could you and your family meet with me tomorrow? It's important."

Lily lie awake half that night worrying about the contents of Ralph's will and what it could possibly mean to the family.

At 3:00 p.m. sharp, Lily, Johnny, David, and Tammy arrived at the law offices of Underwood & Scully. Dennis Underwood greeted them at the door and escorted them into his private office. The only other person in attendance was Cory Ogden.

Tammy whispered to Cory as he was hugging her, "What on earth is this all about, Cory?"

He just shrugged. "I'm as in the dark as you are. I have no idea what my Dad said in his will."

As soon as they were all seated, the lawyer proceeded to explain the mystery.

"Mr. Ogden's will is fairly straightforward. He left his entire estate to his son, Cory Ogden. However, he recently added a codicil that could have a major impact on the estate. I have made individual copies of the codicil for you to read."

Tammy asked, "I'm sorry, Mr. Underwood, but what is a codicil?"

Underwood quickly explained that a codicil was a legally binding amendment to an existing will. He then handed out copies for them to examine. The codicil read as follows:

This is a Codicil to the Last Will and Testament of Ralph Frederick Ogden of Davenport, California.

"I, Ralph Frederick Ogden, attest that I am of sound mind and under no duress as I make the following declaration and modifications to my will.

It has recently come to my attention that I may have fathered a child out of wedlock, in addition to my beloved son Cory. The child could be the issue of a violent and non consensual, brief encounter I instigated against an unwilling person, Mrs. Lily Hunter, many years ago.

It is of paramount importance to me that all concerned fully realize that Mrs. Hunter was in no way responsible for the criminal events that occurred. The blame and shame are solely mine to bear.

As of this codicil, the exact identity of my possible child is unknown. It could be Miss Tammy Hunter or, equally possible, it could be Mr. David Hunter. Only an official DNA test can answer the question.

I humbly request that the Hunter family agree to appropriate DNA testing under the supervision of Doctor Norman Porter. I have deposited samples of my DNA with my lawyer to facilitate the testing process.

If Doctor Porter confirms that one of the Hunter twins is my legal issue through DNA testing, I then direct that my entire estate is divided equally between my son Cory and my newly confirmed child.

Signed: Ralph Frederick Ogden

● ● ● ●

When the reading was complete, there was complete silence in the room. Then pandemonium broke out. Everyone tried to speak at the same time. Cory had great difficulty in meeting Tammy's gaze. Johnny just stared at his wife in painful disbelief.

Lawyer Underwood shouted over the din, "I know this must all come as a great shock. My advice is to go home and talk things out before you decide on your next steps. I realize there are many factors for you to consider, but I must advise you of the extent of Mr. Ogden's estate. The auditor's current estimate of the value of the Green Mountain Sawmill Corporation and the extensive land holdings is approximately fifty million dollars after estate taxes. This estimate could be revised upward as Mr. Ogden's stock portfolio is still being valued."

The shocked silence in the room spoke for itself.

After a few days of reflection, Lily asked her family if they were ready to talk. She knew the current situation would begin to fester if it wasn't aired.

"Mom," David said, "it's only fair to have Cory join us. Nothing in this mess is his fault. He should be part of any discussions."

Tammy and Johnny both agreed, so Lily picked up the phone and asked Cory to join them for dinner. It was a somber group that gathered around the table that night. Everyone had inner thoughts about the situation, but they were looking forward to clearing the air.

Lily started. "I'm certainly not proud of the decision I made that evening so many years ago. My only defense was the situation Johnny and I was facing without hope of insurance or any income. I made a deal with Ralph Ogden, and we both lived up to it."

Tammy moved across to embrace her mom. "I'm sure we all agree that you did the best you could under the circumstances. As far as we're concerned, you're the best mother that ever lived."

Lily tried not to cry. "Regardless of what may happen next, I am proud of my family today. I love all of you with all my heart, and nothing that might arise from DNA tests will ever change the way I feel."

"I'm one-hundred percent in agreement with your mother," Johnny added. "I will always be your father in my head as well as in my heart."

By now, everyone at the table could no longer hold back their tears.

Lily then addressed her remarks to Cory. After caring for him since his birth, she knew he was of a far different nature than his father.

"Although I wasn't your birth mother, Cory, I've always considered you to be one of my own. I want you to know that, in the end, I finally forgave your father for the attack. I hope the rest of this family will, too."

The question of DNA testing remained. They discussed the pros and cons openly, including the vast wealth residing in the estate.

Lily finally settled it. "Regardless of the estate considerations, we need to do this simply for the sake of Cory and Tammy's future together. If Cory is Tammy's half-brother, they need to know. If they ever want a family of their own, they need to know their blood status."

The combined family voted, and the recommendation for specific DNA testing was a unanimous yes.

Several weeks later, the Hunter family, along with Cory, met at the offices of Underwood & Scully. This time, Doctor Norman Porter joined them for the meeting. The doctor was holding the results of the DNA test.

"Are you satisfied with the veracity of the tests?" the lawyer asked Doc Porter.

"Yes. I'm willing to swear an affidavit to that effect, if necessary."

"You might as well open the envelope, Doctor. I'm sure some of the folks here are dying to hear the results."

Because the old doctor was rarely the center of attention anymore, he made the most out of his moment in the spotlight. With everyone hanging on his next words, he fumbled with the envelope before finally withdrawing the laboratory test results.

In the ensuing silence, Cory held up crossed fingers to Tammy and mouthed the words, *I will always love you no matter what.*

As the entire combined family held hands in a show of solidarity, Doctor Porter read out the DNA results in a low and solemn voice.

First, dead silence, then someone in the room screamed out loud.

And another person fainted.

• • • •

TWO YEARS LATER

It was New Year's Eve at the bustling Hunter household. A large turkey slowly roasted in the oven, filling the room with succulent aromas. As Lily waited patiently for the others to join her at the table, she looked fondly at the picture of her two sons standing in front of their newly renamed business.

In the photo, the old sign showing Green Mountain Sawmills Corporation had been replaced with a new sign showing Ogden & Hunter Sawmills Inc. The young men were both beaming in the picture.

Tammy finally made her way slowly up to the laden table. At eight months pregnant, she wasn't moving too fast these days. She returned from examining the redwood wedding bed and redwood cribs that Lily had promised for her new family.

Lily and Johnny exchanged affectionate glances as they watched the evident warmth of the family, laughing and joking with each other. After several glasses of wine, Cory stood and said he would like to make a toast.

"I must be the luckiest man on the planet," Cory said softly, with his wine glass raised. "When I married into this family, I inherited a real blood brother instead of an ordinary brother-in-law. I married a beautiful woman and inherited a new mother instead of a mother-in-law. Although my real father has passed away, I inherited a man I am proud to call my father in his place."

Everyone clapped in appreciation of Cory's heartfelt words. Tammy beamed at her husband, still thanking God that Cory hadn't ended up as her blood relative.

Lily paused, all the old memories flooding back to her. Despite her earlier assertions, she still harbored a residual smoldering resentment against Ralph because of that fateful night so many years ago. Then Lily looked at her son, David, who she loved as only a mother can. She realized that he wouldn't exist if not for Ralph Ogden. That realization made her heart lighten, and she determined to put the past behind her, once and for all.

Lily rose and raised her glass in the direction of the night sky. "I'd like to make a somewhat unusual toast, in honor of Cory and David."

"Go ahead, Lily," Johnny urged.

"Here's to you, Yesterday's Giant," Lily said softly. "Your two sons are a genuine tribute to your memory. May you forever rest in peace."

Everyone at the table joined in the toast, then returned to the festivities, ready to face the challenges of a New Year together as one.

DOLPHINS AT SUNSET

I sat alone in the empty staff lunchroom, hunched over my book. With only five minutes left in my afternoon coffee break, I didn't want to waste a moment. I had been forced to leave Laurel Run High School before my graduation for financial reasons. To better myself, I was slowly and methodically trying to work my way through a selection of literary classics.

At my current rate of reading, I had a lot of catching up to do.

I checked my watch, then headed up the stairs to the salon. As I made my way, a quotation from today's reading still lingered in my mind. It was a famous quotation by Henry David Thoreau. I thought the words were the saddest thing I had ever read.

"Most men lead lives of quiet desperation and go to the grave with the song still in them."

I almost made it back to my workstation unnoticed, then I heard the sarcastic voice of my boss, Donna Williams.

"Nice of you to show up, Rhonda."

"Sorry," I murmured. "I was studying and lost track of time."

Donna, as befitting the manager of the Shears to Share Salon, didn't take kindly to empty workstations, especially when customers were waiting. I checked my watch. Just three hours to go until the time of day arrived that I hated the most—when my safe refuge at work closed and I had to go home.

I swept the area around my chair, dealt with three squirming kids in a row, then the door to the salon opened, and my last customer of the day entered. The old fellow walked haltingly, leaning for support on the aluminum walker that was his constant companion. A portable miniature oxygen tank was strapped tightly to his sunken chest.

Old Bert Medley was a retired coal miner. Like many of his breed, he suffered greatly from the devastating effects of black lung disease, the penalty for his many years of labor in the poorly ventilated coal pits.

I greeted the old man with a cheerful hug before helping him into the chair. He was one of my favorites.

"What will it be today, Bert?"

"Just make me look young again, Rhonda," Bert said, then coughed with a rasping, wet, disturbing sound.

"I'm a hairstylist, not a bloody miracle worker," I said with a laugh.

With Bert's thinning hair, I could easily finish up in less than five minutes, but I knew Bert never thought he got his money's worth unless he was in the chair for at least a half-hour or more.

I didn't mind because Bert was a great storyteller. He always had a tale or two about the raging coal fires burning deep below many coal towns. According to Bert, most people were unaware that the fires continued to rage below their feet.

"You know, Rhonda, most folks don't realize how bad these underground coal fires can be. Lots of them are still burning all over the States. We had one right here in Laurel Run that started back in 1915 and didn't get put out until 1973."

"That's way before my time," I said.

"Then how about this?" Bert wheezed. "Down the road in Centralia, a huge fire has been burning for forty-seven years right under the town. They say at its peak, when someone died, you could take them to the cemetery for a traditional burial and a cremation all at the same time. Two for the price of one."

I laughed, even though I had heard the tale many times over.

"Bert," I said, "you guys are extinct as the dodo birds. Coal is dead and clean energy is the wave of the future."

We continued our good-natured argument until Donna came and announced it was closing time for the salon.

Shit, I thought, *I have to go home to the asshole.*

● ● ● ●

Outside the shop, a constant drizzle from dark leaden skies made our bleak coal town of Laurel Run look even more forlorn than usual. I was forced to walk home because our old pick-up was still being held hostage at Ernie's garage awaiting payment for repairs.

As I walked, I took stock of myself. *Thirty-two years old, always depressed, fat, and my feet hurt. I was born in this hell hole, and I'll probably die here, too.*

If I were truthful, I would have to say I wasn't really heavy, just a little on the pudgy side. Other than a few care lines on my face, people have said I'm quite an attractive woman. I knew I could slim down if I'd resist joining my useless husband, Joe Turner, in his constant diet of pizza, chicken wings, and beer.

I turned into the walkway, almost tripping over the broken cement, trying not to be overly depressed at the sight of home. Our two-story clapboard bungalow was severely in need of a paint job. The front lawn was a joke.

Anything I tried to plant on my own immediately died from the toxic buildup in the soil from the many years of surrounding mining activities. The original red shingle roof showed numerous black tar patches, eerily similar to the decayed teeth on a vagrant.

I didn't need my key because the door was unlocked. As I entered, the familiar pungent odor of cheap cigars and stale beer washed over me in waves. I also didn't need to see the half dozen empty beer cans or overflowing ashtrays to tell me the story. I'd seen it plenty of times before.

Joe lay on the sagging old brown couch in a drunken stupor again, his drooling mouth wide open. His high-volume snores partially drowned out the television in the background. The set was still mindlessly tuned to a rerun of last week's football final. The congealed surface of a half-eaten cheese pizza crawled with hungry houseflies.

I stared down in disgust at my husband of fifteen years. The bottom three buttons on his soiled plaid shirt had finally surrendered to the strain of his ample stomach. I watched in morbid fascination as his round white belly rose and fell through the opening in his shirt.

Joe's skin was as pale as a dead, bloated fish. Course, curly black hair covered the pockmarked surface of his stomach.

Joe's heavy breathing movement caused the hairs to move in unison like tiny black dancing worms. I took a picture of sleeping beauty with my cell phone, then laughed hysterically before breaking into tears.

How the hell did I ever find myself living with a slob like this? I thought.

My marriage, if I was honest with myself, was a mistake from day one. Joe wasn't a particularly smart guy or even that good-looking, but he was tenacious. He had pursued me with a single-minded determination despite my lack of interest. He finally got me to say yes while I was still mending from a painfully broken relationship with my first true love.

To this day, I'm still not sure why I ever agreed to the marriage. I was only seventeen at the time of our wedding, far too young for a lifetime commitment.

I had to face facts. Joe was a loser. Every setback in life was always someone else's fault. After losing his pipefitting job at the mines almost four years ago for drinking on the job, I'd been the primary breadwinner for us both. The few part-time jobs Joe managed to hold down barely paid for his daily beer allotment.

To be fair, things hadn't been too bad with our marriage in the early years. The downhill slide had started when Joe conveniently remembered, long after the wedding, to tell me that he was unable to father any children because of an old football injury. My dreams of having a family of my own disappeared on that day.

I took one last look at my drunken spouse, shook my head, then retreated to the kitchen. Joe still hadn't replaced the three burned-out ceiling bulbs, so I sat on my own in the dim light, eating a boiled egg and a whole wheat bagel leftover from breakfast.

When the meal was over, I picked up the latest copy of the World Traveler magazine and started to leaf through the pages. As usual, because I had never traveled much, I was mesmerized by the exotic locales featured in the full-color pages.

I held my breath when I reached a four-page spread on the

enchanting Greek Islands. Every page highlighted a different island, but they all had one thing in common. In each picture, two dolphins soared gracefully out of an azure sea in a gentle rainbow arc before plunging back into the depths of the Mediterranean.

My favorite photograph was the last one of the four. It showed two dolphins flying from the water's surface in tandem against a glorious full-color sunset. It was entitled, *Dolphins at Sunset*. The picture moved something inside me. I pledged to myself, *Before I die, I'll find a way to see dolphins at sunset for myself.*

I left my husband snoring on the couch, then headed off to bed. As I turned the light off, the words of Thoreau's quotation came flooding back.

"Most men lead lives of quiet desperation and go to the grave with the song still in them."

I tried to hold back my tears, but I failed miserably. I'm stuck in a dead-end job, living with a man I detest. One thought kept persisting in my mind.

How cruel would it be to reach the end of my life with a song still in me?

Outside, the rain continued to fall. I heard it beating on our dilapidated roof and wondered if it would ever end.

THE HUSBAND:

Joe Turner was pissed off, and he showed it. The only things packed into the dented old aluminum motorboat with any care were the two cases of Three Star ale. The fishing rods, bait, and life jackets barely survived the loading process.

Joe's fishing buddy frowned. "What the hell's wrong with you?"

"Same old crap, Toby," Joe bitched. "The old lady is on my back non-stop these days. I'm fed up with all the bullshit. Most days, I can hardly wait for her to go to work so I can get some peace."

They pushed the boat away from the dock with Joe at the helm. During the thirty-minute ride out to their favorite fishing spot, Toby took a close look at his long-time friend. He didn't like what he saw.

Joe's features were bloated, his stomach much more pronounced, his clothing dirty, and, frankly, Toby thought, *He looks like a homeless bum.*

Joe tossed the anchor over the side while Toby baited the rods. They were fishing for black bass, a local favorite. For years, Toby and Joe had a pact that, so far, had never been broken. The deal was: *No Fish-No Beer.*

Under the terms of the agreement, each fisherman couldn't open a beer until he caught a fish. The rivalry to be the first to open a brew was quite intense. On a few trips, Toby and Joe had each come close to being the only one without a beer, but one or the other always managed to snag at least a small one.

"Got one!" Toby yelled as he boated a nice three-pounder.

The fish was still flopping on the bottom of the boat when Toby cracked the twist top of his first cold ale. He made an exaggerated point of waving the beer in front of Joe's face. Joe swore at him and made an obscene gesture.

If Joe was pissed off before, he was doubly so when Toby proceeded to boat the next three fish, each one accompanied by another cold beer. Toby couldn't resist goading his friend.

"Maybe your foul mood is traveling down your fishing line and scaring them off," Toby said with a laugh.

With only an hour of fishing left, Joe had still not boated a fish. His black mood had slowly intensified over the afternoon. When Toby hooked yet another one, Joe lost control, threw his fishing rod in the water, then grabbed two cans of beer. He sat in the bow, glaring at Toby, almost daring him to comment.

One after another, Joe quickly downed the remaining cans of beer. Toby watched in dismay. Finally, when the alcohol hit, Joe started to talk.

"That's it for me, Toby. When we get home, I'm going to give Rhonda an ultimatum."

"What kind of ultimatum?"

"To get off my back or get the hell out."

Toby tried to talk some sense into Joe, even going as far as to point out that Joe's drinking and lack of a job would make any woman unhappy. Joe wasn't listening to any advice, so Toby pulled the anchor and headed for the dock. He thought Joe's behavior lately showed he was in serious need of professional help.

● ● ● ●

THE CONTEST:

Despite my day starting off with a vicious argument with Joe about his drinking, I didn't give a shit. I was just anxious to get to work for a change because today was the day of the big announcement we had been waiting for.

The company I worked for had over two hundred salon franchises in North America. The corporate office had recently announced a chain-wide contest for the title of Stylist of the Year. Each franchise was allowed to submit one pictorial entry depicting their best original individual hair treatment.

Donna had encouraged me to enter the contest. I hadn't wanted to do it, but she persisted. She said it would enhance our shop's reputation, so I had reluctantly agreed. My official contest entry ended up being a striking portrait of Casandra Norton. Cassy was a promising young local artist and one of the few close friends I had in town.

For the contest, I had carefully teased Casandra's hair into a high-feathered crest. The highlights were skillfully blended into a pleasing color combination of steel gray and cobalt blue. The final product was an intriguing blend of premature aging and youth. I submitted the entry with the simple title of *CASSY*.

The grand prize was still a mystery, but the rumor mill said it would be something terrific. I hoped it was something like a new car. With our pick-up constantly needing repairs, we were getting desperate for wheels.

Mid-afternoon, Cassy dropped into the salon. She parked her wet umbrella in the corner before giving me a big hug.

"I couldn't wait any longer," she said. "The suspense is killing me. Do you think we have any chance of winning?"

"Who knows?" I shrugged. "I haven't got a clue if we're even in the running, but at least we gave it a good try. Besides, you're okay. You at least got a free hairdo out of it."

We were about to break for coffee when a UPS delivery van stopped in front of the salon. The heavy-set driver slowly emerged from the vehicle. He was wearing one of those bright yellow rain slickers as he approached the salon doors.

The guy appeared to be having trouble identifying the address. For a moment, it looked like he was returning to his truck, but then he stuck his head through the door. He peered down at the sodden label. Everyone in the salon stopped talking and stared at him.

"Is there a Mrs. Rhonda Turner here?" he asked. "I have a special delivery for her."

I couldn't speak. I was too nervous to answer. I've never won anything in my life. In fact, most of my life has been riddled with bad luck. A mining accident that claimed my father's life scarred my early years in Laurel Run. My mother did the best she could to care for me on her own, but it was always a constant struggle to make ends meet.

I had tried to help by working at several part-time jobs in addition to going to school. Still, when my mother developed a terminal illness, it was the last straw. I was forced to leave school just months before graduation. I know it's not rational, but I still blame my father for dying.

Now, I held a special delivery envelope that could be the first big thing that had ever happened to me. I wanted desperately to wait and open it in the privacy of home, but the salon crowd wouldn't let me.

"If you don't open it right now," Cassy threatened, "we'll have to do it for you."

I sat in one of the empty styling chairs so I wouldn't faint. My hands trembled. I felt beads of sweat running down my back. I looked at Casandra. She nodded, so I opened the envelope. The regular customers crowded around, anxious to hear the results.

Special Delivery
PERSONAL & CONFIDENTIAL

Dear Mrs. Turner,

We are pleased to announce that your entry is the winner of our "STYLIST OF THE YEAR" competition. Everyone here at our head office loved your presentation. With your permission, we would like to feature it in all of our seasonal advertising programs.

Now for the good news! As the first-place winner, you will receive an all-expense-paid luxury vacation aboard a 365-foot Windjammer sailing vessel, the Star Galaxy, for her 30-day repositioning cruise from New York to Istanbul, Turkey. The Star Galaxy will make multiple stops, including Tenerife, London, the Amalfi Coast, and the Greek Islands.

It is important to note that your prize only covers trip expenses for one person. You are free to invite a spouse or friend to accompany you, providing they are responsible for their own costs. Full details about the trip are on the way to you under separate cover.

Because we had so many wonderful contest entries to choose from, our panel decided to award a second-place prize as well. Ms. Gina Morton from our Seattle franchise will also be aboard the Star Galaxy for the trip. Hopefully, you will get the opportunity to meet her on the ship.

Again, congratulations from all of us.

Peter Thompson,
Vice President, Marketing

The balance of the day went by in a daze. Clients flooded in to congratulate me on my win. Even Donna, a normally tough old bird, broke down in tears in a rare show of emotion. The turmoil went on for such a long time we gave up trying to do hair treatments. Donna closed the shop and gave everyone the rest of the day off, with pay.

I trudged home through the falling rain, my mind spinning from an overload of conflicting thoughts. As I approached the house, I saw the dilapidated red pickup was back in the driveway. I wondered what Joe did to free the truck from Ernie's Garage.

It was still early in the afternoon. I knew Joe probably wouldn't be passed out yet but would have had enough alcohol to be in a combative mood. I could almost see his violently adverse reaction to my news about winning the fabulous trip.

I entered the house, ready for the confrontation. I steeled my resolve because I was one-hundred percent sure of three things. One, I was going on the trip because I desperately needed it. Two, Joe Turner would not be going with me under any circumstances. Lastly, I was determined I was never going to go to my grave with a song still buried inside me.

NICHOLAS:

The popular meeting spot called BUZZ! was crowded as usual for a Friday night in New York. Patrons from all walks of life were engaged in the regular weekend mating ritual, which was now frantically taking place at the bar.

"Hey Nicky," said Denny Lee. "Check out the beautiful redhead at the end of the bar. She looks perfect for you."

Nick looked over at the glamorous woman smiling at him, then shrugged. He turned back to his friends.

"How many times do I have to tell you guys. I have no interest in New York women. Too hard, too brittle, and way too mercenary for me."

The third member of the trio, Jack Youngman, laughed. "I think you're just terrified of what your old Greek momma would say if you brought someone like that bombshell home with you to Naxos."

Nick said ruefully, "There just might be some truth in that. I can see her face now."

"Are you sure you have to go to Naxos?" Denny asked.

"Yep. Since my dad died last year, my mother has been trying to run the inn on her own. My sister called to let me know mom was having a tough time."

"What's it like on Naxos?" Jack asked

"Naxos is the best of the Greek islands," Nick replied. "It's like heaven on earth. Long sandy beaches, misty mountains rising from an azure sea, flowers in abundance, gentle breezes always blowing. But most of all, it's the people. Full of life, singing and dancing at the drop of a hat and always welcoming to strangers."

"How about the inn?" Denny asked.

"The Blue Shutters Inn has been in our family for generations. It's perched on a hillside overlooking the town of Chora and the harbor. I love the place."

"Christ, Nicky," Jack grunted, "it's hard to believe you can go from developing advanced artificial intelligence programs to cooking overdone octopus for American tourists."

"It's even harder to understand how he's making a fortune from that stupid app he developed as a joke," Denny added.

Strictly out of boredom, Nick had developed a smartphone application called *PETS NO GO*. The app was designed to keep track of household pets' fertility cycles to help ensure a pet wouldn't get loose at a time that could produce unwanted offspring.

At first, only a few pet owners downloaded the new app. Customers like Parisian ladies wanting to ensure their poodle, Fifi remained celibate. Then, to everyone's amazement, the program came to the attention of farmers all over the world. It appeared that the software turned out to be extremely useful in keeping track of the breeding cycles of their livestock.

Internet revenues last month for the program exceeded one-hundred-thousand dollars for the first time with no sign of slowing down. This newfound revenue stream convinced Nick that he could give up his high-paying New York position and return home to help manage the inn.

Denny pointed to several ladies now staring at their table with interest. "This is why we like to bring you here, Nick. You're irresistible."

Nicky was embarrassed at being used as bait, but what his friends said was true. Nick Alexandros was an attractive man. Long and lean, dark black wavy hair, plus a killer smile to round out the package. Nick was in his early thirties, and because of his fanatical exercise regime, he looked like he could run a marathon at the drop of a hat. Although he had an easy-going manner, Nick was a dependable guy in a clutch.

Finally, it was time to wind up the evening, but Nick refused to leave until his good friends had both sworn an oath to come to visit him on the Greek island of Naxos.

"I better get home and pack guys," Nick said with regret. "I'm on the early flight to London in the morning."

"We're going to miss you, buddy," Jack said. "See you on Naxos. Make sure to have a bottle of that shitty Greek wine ready for us."

• • • •

THE STAR GALAXY:

I stood at the railing of the ship, waving a sad farewell to my friends. Casandra and old Bert Medley had driven down from Laurel Run to see me off.

Earlier, Bert had presented me with a bouquet of slightly wilted flowers. The sight of the old man standing there with his oxygen tank brought tears to my eyes. I was fond of the old coal miner and wondered if I would ever see him again.

"Bon Voyage, Rhonda, don't forget to send us a postcard," Bert yelled from the dock.

"I won't forget, you old coot," I said with a laugh. "And don't you dare have your hair cut by anyone else before I get back."

I stayed at the rail until the ship pulled slowly away from the wharf. When my friends were no longer in sight, I took a look at my fellow travelers. Everyone appeared to be well-dressed. The women, in particular, were decked out in their finest.

I felt out of place. I was wearing my second-best dress. My first choice for my new holiday going away outfit was a classic little black dress. It was my first real extravagance. Cassy accompanied me when I made my purchase from Lou's Clothing Emporium in Laurel Run. According to Cassy, the dress looked great on me. I thought so, too.

Unfortunately, my pretty new dress had fallen victim to one of Joe's 'middle of the night' drunken rages. I moved into the spare bedroom after a series of arguments with Joe about the trip. He was adamant that I wasn't to go, and I was equally determined that I would. The stalemate ended up in frigid silence.

The night before leaving, I hung my new outfit on the back of the kitchen door to have it free of creases, ready to go for an early departure. When I woke in the morning, I found my outfit ruined. It was soaking wet, reeking of beer, and lying crumpled on the kitchen floor.

Joe's note said, *"Gone fishing. Have a nice time, bitch. Don't hurry back!"*

If Joe hadn't left the house already, I'm sure I would have removed his testicles with a kitchen knife. I put on one of the dresses I usually wore to work then left for the bus terminal. I boarded my bus crying and didn't stop until I got off in New York.

Once we had cleared the harbor, the ship's intercom announced a welcome aboard cocktail party. I made my way to the elegantly decorated Galaxy Room, where fine French champagne was flowing like water. Waiters in evening wear continually circled the room with tray after tray of delicious snacks.

After a few drinks, feeling slightly out of place, I made my way down to cabin A-249. I used my key to open the door, then came to a screeching halt at the sight of a strange woman clad only in a bra and panties.

"Oh, my God," I exclaimed. "I'm so sorry. There must be a mistake. I thought this was my cabin."

"If you're Rhonda Turner, there's no mistake," the stranger said with a grin. "I'm Gina Morton, the second-place contest winner from Seattle."

"I don't understand…"

"I do," Gina said. "The cheap bastards booked us into a double cabin to save a few lousy bucks."

"So, what do we do now?"

"What can we do? Let's open the complimentary champagne and get pissed."

I laughed. Gina looked like a fun companion for the voyage. We opened the bubbly then started sharing experiences about work. I took an instant liking to Gina. She was outgoing, warm, and hilarious, although a bit on the raunchy side.

Our cabin was a little on the small side for two but luxuriously furnished with fine towels, expensive bedding, and the very best cosmetic products. We chatted easily while preparing for bed. I finished first, then climbed into my bunk. I was a moderate drinker at home, so I felt the effects of far more alcohol than I would typically consume. The wine loosened my tongue.

"Are you married, Gina?"

"Nope, been there, done that. No interest in repeating a disaster. How about you?"

"I guess legally I'm married, but, after last night, I'm not sure anymore."

"What happened last night?"

Usually, I wouldn't have confided in someone I just met, but the alcohol and my pain combined to open the floodgates. I told Gina about Joe's drunken rages, our soul-destroying living conditions, the hopelessness of Laurel Run, and finally about my ruined going away dress.

"Christ," Gina exclaimed. "I thought my ex was a stinker, but this guy sounds even worse. I hope you can find a way out before he ruins the rest of your life."

"You're right there, Gina, my new friend. Joe Turner is a bastard extraordinaire."

"That's a big word."

"I've been studying the classics. Good night. I'm drunk, and I need to sleep."

"Are you into girls, Rhonda?"

"What?" I panicked until I heard the muffled laughter.

"Don't get excited," Gina snorted. "I'm just kidding. See you in the morning. We've got a whole ship to explore."

Unfortunately, Gina had to explore the ship on her own. Shortly after midnight, the *Star Galaxy* sailed into a violent Atlantic storm, one of the worst in many years, according to the crew.

Never having been to sea before, I was so seasick I couldn't even get out of my bunk without assistance. Gina, fortunately, was not inflicted by the turbulence. She took care of me, making sure I at least had a bowl of chicken broth each day.

"My God, Gina," I croaked while retching into a bucket. "I never knew it was possible to feel so sick. Is this bloody storm almost over?"

"The captain says we're on course to be in port early tomorrow morning, and from then on, the weather looks much better. Now try and get some more of this broth down. It will help."

After a full day at the dock in Tenerife, I felt almost human. Gina helped me prepare for some fresh air out on the deck. When I passed the full-length cabin mirror, I was astonished. I had lost almost twelve pounds from my forced dieting. It seemed my youthful figure had returned. I made a silent vow to keep it that way.

From Tenerife to London, the *Star Galaxy* made smooth sailing. I was starting to enjoy the bracing sea air, and the ship's gentle motion as the vessel rose to meet the oncoming waves. My sea sickness vanished as quickly as it had started.

Feeling renewed, I took advantage of the crew's yoga and exercise programs, and gradually my depression faded. I felt like a new woman.

As the days passed, I steadily increased the frequency of my speed walking trips around the open main deck. Although my weight was down, I still filled out my emerald green jogging suit in all the right places. I started to notice that a growing number of male passengers were giving me more than just a passing glance. And not just passengers, crew members, too. One, in particular, was becoming a pest.

"Gina, I'm having a real problem with the purser, Ricardo Sanchez. He keeps asking me to join him for a drink. I told him three times that I'm married."

"Did that work?"

"No, he just laughed and said at sea, no one is married."

"Well, he may have a point. Sea air does tend to make one horny."

"I'm serious, Gina. Look at this invitation. Someone slid it under the door early this morning. He wants me to join him for a private dinner in his cabin tonight. What should I do?"

"What does he look like?"

"Fairly handsome, in a greasy, disturbing way."

"I have plenty of experience dealing with oversexed males," Gina said. "I think I've got a great idea, kiddo. Leave it to me."

"Okay, but wouldn't it be better if I just tell him to bugger off?"

"Nope. Trust me. My idea will be a hell of a lot more enjoyable."

• • • •

THE PERVERT:

Promptly at 7:00 p.m., I knocked on the door of the purser's cabin. As instructed by Gina, I wore the lowest cut sweater top I owned, along with my tightest dress and plenty of makeup. I felt like a streetwalker getting ready to report to her pimp. I hoped Gina knew what she was doing because I felt nervous.

Ricardo opened the door. He was a tall, wiry man with a pencil-thin mustache. He wore tight black pants, a ruffled white shirt, and reeked of strong cologne. When his eyes zeroed in on my low-cut sweater, I felt like turning around and running for cover.

Sanchez took me by the hand, then ushered me into his cabin. His free hand hovered perilously close to my backside, but just as he started to close the door, Gina ran from her hiding place in the hall. When she followed us in, Ricardo looked startled at the unexpected intrusion.

"Oh, I'm so sorry to be late, Mr. Sanchez," Gina mumbled. "I couldn't get that damned hair dryer to work properly. I hope I didn't keep anyone waiting."

I checked out the room while trying not to laugh at the purser's expression. In the center of the spacious cabin, a table for two waited with candles already lit. The small table gleamed with sparkling silverware and multiple wine glasses. A silver bucket of iced champagne stood waiting while soft romantic music played in the background.

Before Sanchez could react, Gina quickly pulled out one of the two seats for me and then sat in the other. Ricardo looked startled at being left without a seat.

"Oh, isn't this nice," Gina said. "Imagine being served an exclusive dinner by the purser himself. I must compliment the captain for the treat."

"Yes, it's going to be an interesting evening," I responded.

We could tell Ricardo was in a quandary. After all, we were paying passengers, and he couldn't afford to give us any reason to report him to the captain. We didn't know it at the time, but Sanchez was already on thin ice because of several previous misunderstandings with female passengers.

"I wasn't aware that I would have the pleasure of two lovely ladies tonight," Sanchez grumbled.

"Surely, you didn't think that Mrs. Rhonda Turner would attend a private dinner with a man, unattended by her chaperone?" Gina said accusingly.

"Chaperone?"

"Yes, you may not be aware that Mrs. Turner is here representing our company, Shears to Share. Our president will not allow any circumstance to occur that could reflect badly on our organization. In fact, he's appointed me to be her chaperone for the entire company-sponsored trip. Everywhere she goes, I go too."

Sanchez was crestfallen. "Everywhere?"

"Yes, everywhere."

"Oh."

After that, we totally ignored Sanchez, talking between ourselves. At the same time, he served a sumptuous meal delivered by a room service porter. Finally, we finished and departed, leaving Ricardo with a table full of dirty dishes. He looked most disappointed at the outcome of the evening. I knew it was cheesy, but I purposely wiggled my butt on the way out.

"Did you see Ricardo's face when he saw you hanging out the front of your sweater? I thought his eyes would bug out of his face. He's probably still got a big fat 'you know what' in his pants."

"Gina, you really are disgusting," I said, trying not to laugh.

She grinned. "I told you it would be fun."

A NEW ARRIVAL:

After arriving from New York, Nicholas spent several days touring all the historical spots in London and the surrounding areas. But, after hearing his mother's voice on the phone, he was anxious to get home to the island of Naxos. He stopped in at the travel agency located in his hotel lobby.

"I need to get a flight to Naxos, Greece. What do you have available?"

"I'm really sorry, Mr. Alexandros, but there isn't a direct flight from London to Naxos this time of year. The best we can do is to get you on a flight to Athens. From there, you can board the Blue Line ferry to Naxos."

Nick was about to tell her to book the flight to Athens when he noticed a brochure advertising last-minute specials for a Windjammer cruise to Istanbul, Turkey. He asked the woman if the ship stopped anywhere in the Greek Islands.

She made a phone call, and her face lit up. "Great news, Mr. Alexandros, the last stop for the *Star Galaxy* before ending her cruise at Istanbul is the island of Naxos. I can get you a nice first-class cabin at a discount if you book right away."

Nick booked a cabin for the 10:00 a.m. sailing the next day, blissfully unaware that his random decision would change his life forever.

Although I didn't know it at the time, Nick's decision to take the Star Galaxy changed my life too. In many more ways than I could have ever imagined. To celebrate the sailing from London to Gibraltar, Gina and I received an invitation to be seated at Captain Rolf Hoffman's table for a gala dinner.

Armed with our engraved invitation, Gina and I set off to the Neptune dining room. I was excited about the prospects of meeting the captain, while Gina seemed to take it all in her stride.

"He's probably an overstuffed bore who will try to grope you under the table every time he gets a chance," Gina said knowingly.

Contrary to my shipmate's negative outlook, Captain Rolf Hoffman was the epitome of a world-class gentleman. Hoffman stood as we approached his table. He was a tall, wiry, attractive man with a full head of steel gray, wavy hair, and a charming smile. Two other men were sitting at the table set for five.

"Good evening, Mrs. Turner and Miss Morton," Hoffman said, with a light European accent.

Although Gina and I returned the greeting, I thought she might have held the captain's handshake a little longer than was necessary.

May I introduce your fellow passengers?" Hoffman said. "The gentleman on my right is Mr. Nicholas Alexandros from New York, and across the table is Mr. Gregory Fairchild from Vancouver, Canada."

We shook hands before taking our seats around the most elegantly laid-out table I had ever seen. Multiple crystal wine glasses sparkled with the reflection of the flickering candles. Fresh flowers in vibrant colors contrasted wonderfully against the starched white table coverings. A string quartet played soft dinner music in the background.

At first, I was petrified. There was such an abundance of silverware that I had no idea what to use first. I took my cue from Nick Alexandros, who seemed very much at home with the surroundings. We started with Caesar salad, followed by Scottish smoked salmon, Chateaubriand of rare roast beef, and Tiramisu for dessert.

None of the gourmet items, or anything remotely resembling them, had ever graced the table of Scotty's Diner in Laurel Run. I tried them all and loved them.

Gina and I enjoyed the evening. Captain Hoffman's easy going manner made it easy to relax. Both Greg and Nick entertained us with hilarious stories of life in New York and Vancouver. I didn't talk much, but I didn't have to. Whenever there was a lull in the conversation, Gina jumped in, usually with something quite controversial.

When we noticed the captain glancing at his watch, I signaled to Gina that we should leave so the captain could get back to running the ship. Greg and Nick both rose to shake hands as we departed. They seemed disappointed we were going.

"Spoilsport," Gina scolded as we exited the Neptune dining room.

"What?"

"We're sitting with the three most eligible hunks aboard the ship, and you can't wait to get back to our cabin."

"I'm tired," I lied. "My seasickness might be coming back."

"Bullshit," Gina snorted. "You're not seasick. You're just suffering from that Hawaiian disorder."

"What Hawaiian disorder?" I asked hesitantly.

"Lackanookie."

Gina was still laughing at her own wit when we reached the cabin. I washed up quickly, then climbed into my bunk. Gina soon followed. She read for a few minutes, then turned out her bedside lamp. As it turned out, she wasn't ready for sleep.

"Okay. Which one do you want? The lawyer, the innkeeper, or the sea captain? I'll let you take the first choice."

"What?" I sputtered.

"Christ, Rhonda. Weren't you listening to those guys talk?"

"I was too busy eating. That beef was better than any I've ever tasted."

"Greg is a lawyer. He just sold his practice in Vancouver, so he's taking a break. Nick is some kind of computer geek. He's going to some island in Greece to help run his family's inn. Rolf divorced his wife last year. He's hoping to move up to a bigger ship."

"That's nice," I said sleepily.

"Quit stalling, which one?"

"I don't want any of them, Gina. I'm off men, period. Living with Joe Turner ensured that."

"So, you are into girls after all?"

"I give up, go to sleep before…"

My unspoken threat was interrupted by a gentle rapping on the door. I pulled the covers over my head and made Gina answer the summons. She quickly threw a robe over her filmy nightgown.

"Who is it?" Gina asked.

"Greg Fairchild," came a muffled voice through the cabin door. "Sorry to bother you. I was hoping you might still be awake."

I heard Gina open the door. "Of course, we're awake. What did you have in mind? Dancing? A swim in the pool? A nightcap on the back deck?"

Greg laughed. "Nothing that exciting, I'm afraid. Nick and I are renting a car for a tour of Gibraltar tomorrow. We thought we might have lunch off the ship. You're most welcome to join us if you like."

Before I could say a word, Gina jumped in. "You bet we would. What time and where?"

"How about the bottom of the gangplank at nine?"

"Sounds great. We'll be there," Gina replied. She closed the door then jumped back in bed.

"You shouldn't make commitments on my behalf," I groused.

"Sorry, you're going to have a good time on this trip even if it kills me," Gina chortled. "Goodnight, sweet dreams. Oh, and I've decided, I'm choosing Greg."

"You can have all three of them and the purser, as far as I'm concerned."

All I got in response was more muffled laughter.

• • • •

GIBRALTAR:

"That's the coast of Africa, a mere eight miles away," Roberto, our guide, said as he pointed across the wind-swept straights.

I stood on the observation platform, looking out at the Mediterranean Sea. The winds were churning the wave tops to a foaming white. It looked like whipped cream dotted at random on the rolling crests of the deep blue water. I drank in the beauty of it all.

The outline of that mysterious dark continent visible through the drifting clouds triggered my imagination. I was miles away in thought.

I wonder what it would feel like to swim across the sea and explore the hidden secrets of that lush land instead of going home to the misery of Laurel Run?

"A penny for your thoughts, Rhonda?"

"I'm sorry, Nick, I don't usually share my thoughts with strangers. Besides, I'm sure you would laugh at them."

"Try me."

"Okay. I was daydreaming that I was a mermaid preparing to swim across the straits to Africa."

Nick grinned. "I don't know how good a swimmer you are, but I think you have a much better chance of having a gourmet lunch than paddling across to Africa. Come and join us. Lunch is all laid out."

The ship's catering manager had provided us with a sumptuous picnic lunch of fancy sandwiches, smoked salmon, chilled shrimp, and a large bottle of dry Chablis. Gina unpacked then placed everything on one of the larger picnic tables. She also invited Roberto to join us for the meal.

The food had barely touched the table when we found ourselves surrounded by a motley assortment of gibbering monkeys.

"Don't feed them, folks," Roberto cautioned. "If you do, the damned pests won't give us a minute's peace."

One monkey landed on Greg's shoulder then started happily licking his ear. Greg jumped up to escape the beast, spilling his wine over the front of his pants in the process.

"Oh, crap," Greg yelled. "Where did the damned things come from?"

"Relax, they won't hurt you," our guide assured us. "The monkeys are the famous Gibraltar apes. There are about three hundred of them still living. The apes have been here for a long time, even before the British took possession of the Rock. The story says that if the apes ever abandoned Gibraltar, the British troops would leave as well."

Gina checked her watch. "This has been great, guys, but we better get moving. The ship's due to sail for Malta at 4:00 p.m. sharp."

Just as we reached the ship, Nick kidded Greg. "You must have been terrified when that beast attacked you."

"What makes you think that?"

Nick pointed. "It still looks like you pissed your pants."

We were still laughing when Greg covered his front with Gina's jacket and hobbled up the gangway. I wasn't going to admit it to my shipmate, but I was pleased I had gone on the excursion.

MALTA:

Determined not to put my old blubber back on, I talked Gina into doing multiple exercise laps with me around the main deck. The weather was superb, giving us a magical sunny day with a constant cooling light breeze. The Star Galaxy crested easily on gently rolling waves. At the same time, seabirds circled the ship in search of food, occasionally landing for a rest on the azure sea.

""Wow, take a peek," Gina panted. "Our Greek friend is quite a hunk."

Despite myself, I took a sideways glance. Nick lay stretched out on a deck chair, enjoying some sun. His metallic white bathing suit stood out in stark contrast to his olive complexion. There wasn't an ounce of fat on his lean torso.

To my embarrassment, Nick caught me staring. He waved us over, then rose to retrieve two empty deck chairs. He set them up next to his.

"Can I interest you ladies in a pre-lunch cocktail?"

"Sorry," I said. "We haven't finished our exercise rounds."

"Yes, we have," Gina interjected. "I'm always ready for a libation any hour of the day or night, Nick, but where's Greg?"

Nick laughed. "Greg's taking in a lecture on the history of Malta. I'll be listening to non-stop historical details for the rest of the day."

We spent a relaxing hour sipping chilled white wine while listening spellbound as Nick enthused over the many delights waiting for us on the island of Naxos.

"Do you think I'll see any dolphins on this trip?"

"Absolutely," Nick said warmly. "Once we near the Greek islands, you'll see plenty of dolphins. I always get a charge when they follow my boat when I go out fishing. They're good luck, you know."

"I didn't realize that. I just think dolphins are magical from the pictures I've seen."

"Perhaps we should go to lunch now, ladies," Nick said after checking his watch. We're due to dock in the next hour or so. I better go below. I can't wait to take my wet bathing suit off."

Gina standing behind Nick, started rolling her eyes and licking her lips in an exaggerated pantomime after Nick mentioned removing his bathing suit. I tried not to laugh at her antics, but it was difficult.

Nick invited us to share a table for lunch, and before long, Greg joined us. I could tell from Gina's beaming smile she was happy to see him. He looked pleased to see her as well. When the men asked us to join them for the Malta tour, it seemed like a natural thing to do.

Our time in Malta was short but interesting. Greg had a folder full of notes from the shore briefing on the main sights of Valletta. He filled us in on the pertinent details as we walked the cobblestone side streets.

"According to the lecturer," Greg said, "the Knights of Malta initially started to build on this site in 1566. Those vast fortifications atop the rocky heights kept the island secure until Napoleon seized Valletta in 1798."

We stayed on the move for most of the afternoon, traveling from one famous site to another. Greg, as a history buff, was in his element. He wanted to keep going, but I needed to return to the ship.

"I'm enjoying the tour, guys, but I have to get back to the ship a little early today."

"Why?" Gina asked.

"Sorry, I'm not at liberty to say."

"I hope you're not meeting up with that pervert purser again."

"You'll find out in good time. Now, stop being so nosey. I have to run."

RHONDA'S DEBUT:

I hadn't mentioned a word to Gina. Still, earlier, Julie Layton, the manager of the onboard boutique, the *Nautical Lady*, had approached me when I was window shopping.

"I hope you don't mind," Julie said after introducing herself. "I couldn't help noticing you have the perfect figure for some of our new dresses."

"Thanks," I said. "It's amazing what a bout of seasickness and hours of forced exercise can accomplish."

Julie laughed. "On every trip, we host a special cocktail party and fashion shows the day we leave from Malta. Would you consider being one of the models for the show?"

Although I was intrigued, I declined. "I have no modeling experience at all. I'd probably trip and fall on the stage."

Julie was persistent. She finally convinced me to give it a try. I reluctantly agreed as long as she promised to keep my involvement secret.

"A secret? Why?"

"I want to surprise my roommate. She thinks I'm dull and boring."

Julie gave me an appraising glance. "I don't think you'll be boring in the dress I have in mind. In fact, I think you'll dazzle the crowd."

When Gina arrived at the cabin, I told her I was interested in attending the cocktail/party fashion show. I invited her to join me.

"Nope, I'm going for a pre-dinner drink with Greg."

"Oh crap," I said. "Invite Greg as well if you have to."

"How about Nick?"

I sighed. "Go ahead, but you'll have to show up early to get good seats. I've got something to do, so I'll meet you there at 5:30."

After Gina departed, I reflected on why I had hesitated when she asked if Nick could be included. Although I wouldn't admit it to Gina, I did find Nick attractive. During our shore excursions and meals together, he was always attentive, courteous, and fun to be with. Down deep, I hoped Gina could convince the two men to attend the show.

I didn't realize there would be a logistics problem until Julie advised me in the dressing room that I was scheduled to go on last.

"I can't do that," I complained. "I have three friends invited. If I don't show up, they'll be gone long before the end of the show. I'm sorry, but it looks like I'll have to pull out."

Julie was an old hand at organizing fashion shows. She was particularly adept at dealing with the last-minute problems of amateur models.

"No problem," she said soothingly. "Your dress, shoes, and accessories are all ready to go. We have eight models in total. When number six makes her entrance, tell your friends you're going to the washroom and head back here. We'll have you ready in time for your debut."

I headed for the auditorium, arriving just as Gina entered from the alternate door. She smiled and waved.

"Do we need two seats or four?"

"Who knows? I extended the invitation. When Greg asked if it was a lingerie show, I hit him with my purse," Gina laughed. "When last seen, they were having a glass of wine on the back deck. But, let's hold four front row seats, just in case."

Greg and Nicky showed up just as chilled Margaritas were being served to the guests. Although Gina and I had been sitting side by side, she quickly moved to make room for Nick to sit beside me with Greg beside her. I gave Gina the evil eye treatment, but she just ignored me.

"Thinking of buying a dress, Rhonda?" Nick asked with a smile.

"I might if I see the right one."

Contrary to my expectations, Nick and Greg, instead of being bored, took a genuine interest in the show. With each showing, they voted on whether the outfit would better suit Gina or me. The lively, good-natured betting almost made me miss the arrival of model number six.

"Excuse me," I said, "I have to go to the ladies' room."

Nick stood and held my chair. I decided if I ever met his mother, I'd give her a medal for raising a son with good manners. I bypassed the washroom, then headed straight for the dressing room. Julie was standing by, ready to get me prepared in a rush.

Seeing her holding my dress suddenly made the fact that I was about to parade around on public display frighteningly real. I had a panic attack.

"I don't think I can do this, Julie," I said shakily. "I'm so nervous. I might be sick."

"Take two or three deep breaths, hon, and listen to me. You're a beautiful woman with a gorgeous dress to show off. The crowd is friendly and very receptive. Just relax, hold your shoulders back and show them what you've got. I'll introduce you, then, when the music starts, the curtains will open. Just stand there smiling for a moment, then circle the room."

"Okay, but be ready to pick me up if I faint."

Julie and her assistant finished dressing me then she winked at me before heading through the curtains. When the curtains opened, I got a brief glimpse of Nick and the others. They looked concerned. I could hear Julie at the microphone.

"On behalf of the *Nautical Lady Boutique,* I'd like to introduce our top design of the evening. It will be the final showing. As an extra treat, we were able to entice a lovely young lady to model this stunning creation. Ladies and Gentlemen, we give you for her world modeling debut, Ms. Rhonda Turner!"

I didn't realize that Julie had substituted the usual theme music for the soundtrack from 'Pretty Woman' only for my performance. My face flushed when I heard the song, but it was too late. The house lights dimmed, the curtain rolled back, then three spotlights flooded the stage.

I heard a gasp when I stepped into the light. Julie and her assistants had done an excellent job getting me ready. My long ash-blonde hair was swept up and fastened with a diamond tiara. The tiara sparkled in the beams of the spotlight.

The gown Julie chose was a long, form-fitting aquamarine silk masterpiece. The dress shimmered in the spotlight, shifting into different subtle shades of color as I turned and began to slowly circle the room. My confidence level soared on hearing the tremendous rounds of applause. By the time I reached Gina and the others, I had my shoulders back, and I was smiling a smile that would have made Julia Roberts proud.

As Nick rose to his feet, the others followed, and soon the entire room was honoring me with a standing ovation. Gina grinned from ear to ear, but Greg and Nick looked like stunned schoolboys. The crowd's applause kept me onstage while the ship's photographer took shot after shot of me blowing kisses to the group.

When the curtains closed, Julie hugged and thanked me for making the fashion show a success.

"I'm telling you, Rhonda, you made a real splash out there. In fact, you did such a good job I'm going to break one of my own rules."

"You're giving me a discount on the tiara?" I joked.

"Not a chance. But I'm letting you keep the entire outfit, including the tiara, until morning. You can wear it at the Fashion Show Ball tonight. You look stunning in it, and it will be great publicity for the boutique too."

"Thanks, Julie. I'm delighted you convinced me to do it. It was quite exciting."

"Well, if you thought that was exciting, I have something to tell you that might make you even more intrigued."

So, she did tell me something, and she was right. I was intrigued.

• • • •

NOTHING TO LOSE:

When I left Julie and rejoined the others in the cocktail lounge, they all started talking simultaneously.

"I knew there was another woman hidden inside you," Gina laughed. "And, wow, was I ever right on the money."

"I'm still waiting for the Victoria's Secret segment," Greg said with an exaggerated leer.

"Better get used to waiting then. That was the end of my modeling career."

Nick took my hand. "You were wonderful out there, Rhonda. We're all proud of you. Now, how about some champagne to celebrate?"

After the champagne, we moved to the Neptune room for an elegant gourmet dinner, then to a private ballroom for some dancing.

I hadn't danced in years, but tonight I didn't miss a turn. I danced with the captain, Greg, and twice with Nick. I even took a spin on the floor with Gina, but when I saw Ricardo, the purser heading my way, I made a hasty exit for the washroom.

While washing up, I thought about the dancing. While both Captain Hoffman and Greg were good dancers, Nick was exceptional. When I had complimented him, he reminded me he was from Naxos.

"You know us Greeks," Nick had grinned. "We're always dancing and smashing dishes."

By the time I returned from the washroom, the band leader had announced the last dance of the evening. Gina quickly grasped Greg's hand then headed for the floor. That left Nick and I looking at each other.

"Can you stand one more?" Nick asked.

"Do I have to bring some dishes from the table?"

Nick laughed then took me in his arms for the last dance. The music was slow and romantic as we moved in close unison around the dancefloor. I felt warm and comfortable in Nick's embrace, but I was also upset with myself. Despite my reluctance, I found myself increasingly attracted to my dance partner.

When the music ended, Gina said, "Greg and I are staying for the midnight cold seafood buffet. It's supposed to be fabulous. How about you guys?"

Nick looked over at me, a question in his eyes. "I think I'm going to do a few turns around the deck before bed. Are you interested in joining me, Rhonda?"

Gina's wicked wit kicked in. "Do you realize you just asked Rhonda if she was interested in joining you in bed, Nick?"

"Of course, I meant joining me for the walk," Nick stammered.

I noticed Nick's handsome face had colored, so I rescued him by agreeing to go for a few rounds of the deck.

Out on the open deck, the atmosphere was magical. The ship's running lights danced on the full-rigged sails while silver strands of moonlight glistened off the breaking wave tops. Despite the beauty of the scene surrounding us, I couldn't shake the memory of home. I also had a new troubling situation to mull over.

"Is something bothering you?" Nick asked after we had walked in silence for a prolonged time.

"I'm not sure what to do, Nick. The boutique manager told me after the show that the president of Magic Models Inc. is onboard. Supposedly, he loved my modeling in the show. The man insists on meeting me to talk about a career opportunity in New York. Julie has booked an appointment for me with him at 9:00 a.m. tomorrow."

"What are you going to do?"

"Well, Julie made the appointment without even asking if I was interested. Maybe I'll cancel the meeting. Besides, New York is a world away from Laurel Run."

We stopped at the stern railing to watch the moonbeams dance of the gurgling wake. My mention of home spurred Nick to ask a question.

"If you don't mind me asking, why didn't your husband come on this trip with you?"

I remained silent for a moment, trying to frame an appropriate response. Then I decided to be blunt.

"He's not here because I didn't want him here," I said flatly. "Our situation at home is…"

"Oh, there you are," Gina interrupted. "Greg and I thought we might join you for one last turn around the deck before calling it a night."

Nick and I joined them, but I could tell from the look on Nick's face our earlier conversation wasn't over. At the end of our walk, Gina and I strolled back to the cabin. She took my hand and squeezed it.

"I don't know if it was your modeling or your walk with Nick, but you're much different than the girl I met when we boarded."

"Oh? In what way?"

"You're far more animated. You laugh more, and those faint worry lines on your forehead aren't nearly as noticeable."

"Thanks," I said sarcastically. "However, the worry lines are about to come back. I have a new situation to deal with."

"Tell me more," Gina urged. "Is this a problem of a sexual nature by any chance?"

"No," I scoffed. "I've been propositioned…"

"Then it is sexual," Gina interrupted. "Is it dreamboat Nicky?"

"Someone wants to see me about a possible career. The president of a New York modeling agency wants to meet me in the morning. What do you think I should do, Gina? You know more about this stuff than I do."

That bastard of a husband must be grinding her into dust. I can't imagine how she lives with him, Gina thought. *This could be the catalyst that gets this poor woman out of her downward cycle.*

Out loud, she said, "Go for it, Rhonda, what have you got to lose?"

● ● ● ●

AN INTRIGUING OFFER:

"I'm Don Morland, Rhonda. It's nice to meet you. Would you like some coffee?

"Yes, thank you. Black is fine."

While Morland organized the coffee, I took a close look at my host. Moreland was a short, pudgy man, probably in his mid-fifties. My overall impression was that I was dealing with a no-nonsense successful man.

"Before we start, I want you to look at something," Moreland said as he handed me a large brown envelope. "I had the poor ship's photographer work all night to get these ready for this morning."

I opened the envelope then removed about two dozen large color photographs, all taken at the fashion show. The photos were only of me. In all modesty, I had to admit, the pictures were stunning.

"Now, before you respond, let me tell you what I see in these photos. I see something badly needed in the New York fashion scene. A sense of genuine freshness and natural enthusiasm. Unfortunately, our industry is full of plastic people. Even our youngest models these days project a certain brittleness. In my opinion, and I do know this business, you would be an instant success."

"What are you suggesting, Mr. Moreland?"

"Please call me, Don."

"Okay, Don, it is."

"I want you to come to New York on a one-year contract. If we're both happy at the end of the year, we can extend it for another term. I have a draft of our contract here for you to review. I'll put it in the envelope with the pictures. I believe you'll be pleased with the proposal. The terms are far more generous than we would normally offer a new model."

"What's the catch? Why so sudden, and why would I get such a generous offer?"

"There is no catch. I act fast because that's my nature. I can afford to take chances, but I'm not often wrong. My gut tells me you'll be on the cover of some of the top magazines before the year is out."

I was stunned. "I need some time to think this over."

"Of course, that's understandable. But I'll need your answer before the end of the cruise."

We shook hands. I took the envelope then departed, still reeling over the totally unexpected offer. I found Greg, Gina, and Nick having a pre-lunch drink on the back deck.

"How did you make out with the guy?" Gina asked.

"I like him, Gina. He seems like someone you can trust."

"What's in the envelope?" Greg asked.

"Don gave me a draft of a proposed contract," I said. "I haven't even looked at it yet."

"Do you want me to give it a fast read? I'm still a lawyer even though I'm out of my jurisdiction."

"That would be great, thank you." As I opened the envelope to hand the draft contract to Greg, Nick spotted the photographs.

"Can I have a quick look at those?"

I was slightly embarrassed, but I passed them over. Gina crowded over next to Nick to take a look as well.

"Oh my God, these shots are gorgeous," Gina said. "Can I get a copy of one to show my friends at home?"

Greg finished his review of the proposed contract. "I wish I'd become a model instead of a lawyer. If you don't take this deal, I will. I can go over the details with you later if you like. In summary, you get a great salary, a one-year lease on a downtown apartment with domestic staff, and a car and driver thrown in as well."

Nick wasn't even listening to the details. He was still staring at the photographs. I got a strange feeling that he wanted a copy of them but was afraid to ask.

When we went in for lunch, Gina told us she wanted to go back to the cabin to get her purse and freshen up. I said I would hold a seat for her. Down in the cabin, she combed her hair, refreshed her makeup, and was about to leave the cabin when she heard a knock at the door.

"Sorry, Madame. The ship's communication officer asked me to deliver this with an apology. This telegram arrived before the ship departed from New York but somehow got delayed."

Gina took the white envelope from the deckhand. It was not

sealed, but it was marked for Mrs. Rhonda Turner. Gina couldn't resist taking a quick peek. The telegram from Laurel Run was brief.

TELEGRAM
TO MRS. JOE TURNER, COME HOME IMMEDIATELY, YOU ARE FORGIVEN.......JOE

What an absolute prick that guy must be. Rhonda doesn't need to see this crap. She deserves to enjoy the trip. Gina thought as she flushed the offending message down the toilet.

• • • •

AMALFI DREAMING:

The air around the outdoor waterfront patio was pungent with the scent of aromatic, tree-ripened lemons. The four of us were sharing a chilled bottle of locally made, highly potent, Limoncello.

"Ah, the nectar of the gods," Nick said as he took his first sip.

After a private boat tour of the majestic Blue Grotto at the Isle of Capri, we had just returned from exploring the ancient hillside town of Sorrento. The panoramic view of the harbor, with the *Star Galaxy* riding at anchor, brought tears of joy to my eyes.

"Are you having a good time?" Gina asked.

"This is like a dream come true for me," I whispered. "I never knew a world like this even existed."

As I spoke, I stole a sideways glance at Nick. He wore an unbuttoned white linen shirt, white beach pants, and sandals. The wind teased his glossy black hair as he leaned back, laughing at a story Greg was telling.

He's so different from Joe, I thought. *Nicky is such an easy-going, generous, and interesting man.*

Almost as if he had heard my thoughts, Nick turned and flashed his killer smile at me.

Oh God, I think I'm in deep trouble, I said to myself.

To break the spell, I took out my favorite picture. The magazine page that showed two dolphins flying from the water's surface in tandem against a glorious full-color sunset. I showed it to the others.

"When am I going to see my two dolphins at sunset, Nick?"

"Soon, maybe even tonight," he grinned. "We're getting close to the magic of the Greek Islands."

"I guess we should head back, guys," Greg said.

"I'm going to ask the waiter to take a picture of the four of us before we go," Nick said. "If he takes it from this vantage point, he'll get the ship in the background."

After the photo, I didn't want to go back to the ship. I loved the Amalfi coast, the winding highways, and picturesque towns hanging on cliff edges that stood in such stark contrast to the grubby coal town I called home.

Finally, we couldn't linger any longer, so we made our way back to the *Star Galaxy*. I had tears in my eyes when the anchor came aboard, and the ship departed. I felt like I was leaving a part of my heart behind.

● ● ● ●

The *Star Galaxy*, with all the sails set, was riding smoothly through moderate seas. Although we enjoyed the outdoor buffet lunch, there was a palpable air of sadness surrounding us like a dark blanket. The ship was due to drop anchor the following morning on the Greek island of Naxos. Nick would be disembarking while we remained on board for the final leg of the voyage to Istanbul.

On the bright side, Nick had made contact with his mother. He told us we were invited for lunch at the Blue Shutters Inn before departing from the island of Naxos.

"Cheer up, buddy," Greg said. "We still have the 'Spirit of Neptune' party tonight. We'll use it as our final celebration to see you off in style."

"I am going to miss you guys," Nick said softly. "I've only known you for a short time, but it seems like a lifetime."

Nick's comment was meant for all of us, but he looked directly at me as he spoke. I nodded, then turned away.

I didn't want Nick to see the tears in my eyes.

That night the gala Spirit of Neptune dinner was in full swing. Greg and Gina ordered two bottles of champagne for the table. Gina patted me on the back because she sensed how upset I was.

Greg tried to cheer everybody up. "Hey, take a look at the captain. He's got an evil look in his eye."

The dining room staff were dressed in a variety of sea-themed costumes for the special event. A shapely cocktail waitress, dressed as a mermaid, scampered around the dining room with Captain Rolf Hoffman in hot pursuit. He was playing the part of the sea god Neptune, complete with a three-pronged plastic trident.

"I hope Hoffman doesn't trip and stick that trident into her ass."

"Gina, that was crude but funny," Greg said with a laugh.

I noticed Nick was trying to read the elaborate menu by candlelight. He finally had to give up.

"It's an extensive menu," I said. "But I can try to read it to you if that will help."

"No problem. You guys go ahead and order. I'll just run down to my cabin to get my reading glasses. Be right back."

Felix, our attentive waiter, intervened. "Stay right here, sir. I'll run down and have them back to you before you're to order your food. I believe you're in Cabin B444?"

"Thanks, Felix. I appreciate the gesture. Cabin B444 is correct. Here's my pass card. The glasses should be on the nightstand by the bed."

We sipped on our wine until Nick's glasses appeared, then we ordered. As plate after plate of sumptuous seafood was delivered to our table, I couldn't help thinking about the contrast with home.

Joe is probably sitting on the old brown couch watching football reruns on television, eating pizza and chicken wings. Then he'll wash everything down with copious quantities of beer. Outside, it's probably still pouring rain.

I hadn't heard from Joe since the big fight and my departure for the trip, and, on reflection, it didn't bother me a bit. At that time, I was blissfully unaware of the telegram Gina had intercepted earlier.

"Wow, that was a lot of food," Nick said with a grin. "I think I'll walk around the
deck a few times to see if I can work off some of the calories. Anybody care to join me?"

Greg and Gina took a pass because they both wanted to go to the lounge to hear the Naxos travelogue presentation. Secretly, I felt a little guilty because I was hoping they would decline so I could walk with Nick on my own.

"I could use a walk, too, Nick. That meal was enough food for a week."

When Gina and Greg departed, Nick grinned. "I was hoping they would say no. I have something special in mind for you."

"Should I go and borrow the captain's trident for my defense?"

"Nope. Just give me your hand."

Mystified, I let Nick take my hand to lead me out to the stern of the ship. The setting sun cast a warm red and gold reflection on both the low-lying wispy clouds and the shimmering surface of the water. We stood at the rail, drinking in the scene. I enjoyed the feel of Nick's smooth hand in mine.

Then, without warning, a school of dolphins broke through the surface of the crimson waters only a few feet from the ship's stern. They raced in pairs alongside, leaping in graceful high arcs, before plunging back into the sunset-washed surf. I could see the silver and blue of the dolphin's backs in contrast to their milky white undersides.

The spectacular show went on for several minutes before the school broke off their pursuit of the *Star Galaxy*. The dolphins turned in unison toward the blazing sunset, dancing across the surface of the water toward that magic spot where the distant sky kissed the sea.

I was beside myself with excitement. "Oh, I can't believe it, Nick. They were even more beautiful than I dreamed."

Nick laughed. "As we get closer to the Greek Islands, you'll see more and more wonderful sights like this. I must admit I've seen many dolphins, but they are quite spectacular when they jump at sunset."

"Did you know they would be putting on a show like this? Is that why you asked if I wanted to go for a walk?"

"I knew one of your greatest desires was to see dolphins jumping at sunset," Nick admitted. "I was fairly sure in these waters we would have their company."

"Well, thank you for making one of my dreams come true. I'll never forget my first sighting of those beautiful creatures. They are magical."

So are you, Nick thought.

After a few more trips around the open deck, Nick spotted two empty full-length lounge chairs at the ship's bow. We settled in comfortably on the thickly padded deck chairs, then Nick asked if I wanted a drink.

I didn't really need any more alcohol. But to prolong Nick's last night on board, I said yes.

When a waiter passed by, Nick ordered a bottle of chilled Limoncello with two glasses. He poured a drink for both of us. When we clinked glasses in a toast, I noticed Nick observing my eyes.

"We've spent quite a bit of time together but usually always in a group. You've heard a lot about me and my background in New York and on Naxos, but I know very little about you."

"Oh, I'm not a very interesting person," I murmured. "This trip is probably the only fun and excitement I'll ever have in my life, but I'm doing okay."

"That's not the vibes I'm getting," Nick said softly. "Sometimes, when you think no one is watching and you're in an unguarded moment, I sense a deep underlying sadness in you. I'm a good listener if you want to talk."

At first, I was reluctant to talk, but when I started, the floodgates burst. I told Nick about my dead-end job, my friend Casandra, the hopeless despair of a town based on coal, my ruined garden, old Bert Medley and his oxygen tank, the constant rain, my beer-stained going away outfit, and finally about my husband, Joe, and the wreckage of our marriage.

When I finished, I was breathless and crying. Nick had a tear in his eye too. He wasn't sure what to say, so he held me in a close and comforting hug. We stayed like that for several minutes, enjoying the warmth of kindred spirits.

"I better get back to my cabin before Gina sends out a search party," I said reluctantly as I broke away from Nick's embrace.

When Nick reached out to shake my hand, my resolve momentarily broke. I moved his hand aside then leaned in to give him a long, lingering kiss. Although I caught him off guard, Nick responded with a passion matching my own.

I broke free and then fled in my cabin's direction, leaving Nick standing alone on the deck. I couldn't stop my tears at the unfairness of life.

Gina didn't stir when I lay down, fully clothed on my bunk with my head spinning.

I felt like a fairy princess sailing over an enchanting sea on a magical sailing ship. The dolphins at sunset had seemed like an omen, beckoning me to explore new horizons. But now that I had finally met my handsome prince, I was still destined to return home to the bedside of a frog.

After an hour, I knew sleep would be impossible. I decided to see if another stroll around the deck would help. After getting up quietly and stealing out of the cabin, I did five slow laps around the ship, repeatedly thinking about Henry David Thoreau's famous quotation.

"Most men lead lives of quiet desperation and go to the grave with the song still in them."

When I arrived at the ship's stern, I slowly climbed the few stairs to the navigation deck. It was time for me to decide my future.

■ ■ ■ ■

A BIG DECISION:

I stood alone by the railing of the bridge, looking down at the glistening water passing below. Other passengers moved casually by, but they didn't intrude on my personal space. It was almost as if they could sense my desperate struggle with the turmoil raging within me.

It was a beautiful spring evening, a full moon bathing everything in a warm, inviting glow. A night made for happiness, not for despair.

Finally, I stood erect, looked around with determination, and made my decision. The die was cast, no turning back. Regardless of where I ended up, I knew after the life-changing impact of the trip I would never be going back to my old life in Laurel Run. There was no Joe Turner in my future.

I slowly removed the wedding band from my finger and held it in the palm of my hand. A single tear rolled gently down my cheek.

After a deep breath, I threw the ring in a high arc from the bridge. A stray moonbeam briefly illuminated the cheap, silver-plated circle, as the symbol of my broken vow made a final lazy descent into the dark waters below.

I stared at the ocean for a few more minutes then returned to my cabin. Although my hand was on the door handle, I hesitated for more than a minute. Then, almost in a dream-like state, I turned and walked down the corridor to the other end of the ship. One part of my brain told me to turn back, but my heart wouldn't listen.

I paused timidly before knocking. I hoped Nick wouldn't be asleep. Then, the door to Cabin B444 slowly opened, and Nicky stared at me. He took my hand without a spoken word, then led me inside. The door closed softly behind me.

I stood there trembling in silence as Nick slowly undressed me. After he removed his robe, we embraced. I still remember the thrill I felt when my bare breasts first made contact with the warmth of his chest. I followed him willingly to his bed.

My intimate experience with Nick that night was the stuff of dreams. I didn't know how or when our affair would end, but I didn't care—finally, I was living in the moment. My song would never go to the grave unsung.

As I lay entwined with Nick two decks below, the magnificent *Star*

Galaxy sailed on in solitude through moonlit seas, oblivious to the problems of the mere mortals aboard.

A safe harbor waited for her and the sleeping passengers ahead on the enchanting island of Naxos.

• • • •

THE BLUE SHUTTERS INN:

The following morning Nick and I joined the other passengers on deck to watch the ship approach the picturesque harbor of Chora, the central town on the island of Naxos. Small multi-colored fishing boats dotted the spacious harbor at random.

Faint strains of happy music from the waterside cafés drifted across the placid water as we drew closer to the main pier. A variety of octopus, drying slowly in the bright sunshine, hung from the railings of the old timber docks. The scent of morning flowers wafted across the water, bathing the ship with fragrant odors.

I smiled up at Nick, squeezing his hand. "You were right. This is paradise on earth."

"And the best is yet to come," Nick whispered as he kissed my ear.

I didn't hear Gina and Greg arrive, but it was soon clear the new intimacy between Nick, and I hadn't gone unnoticed. Gina had a slight smile playing at the corners of her mouth.

"You must have been up and out early this morning, Rhonda. I didn't even hear you leave the cabin."

When I felt myself blushing, I mumbled something about going out for some early morning exercise.

"Well, your 'exercise' must have done you some good, hon," Gina grinned. "You look positively radiant this morning. Nick does too."

Nick began blushing as well. It was clear to both of us that Greg was trying desperately not to laugh at the guilty expressions on our faces.

Nick quickly changed the subject. "Usually, I'd walk up the hill to the inn, but today we're going to take a taxi. We can walk back later this afternoon when you have to be back on board."

• • • •

After the ship was safely secured to the main dock, a brightly painted, heavily battered taxi pulled up to a screeching stop in front of the gangplank. The driver, a large, heavyset man with a full bushy beard, jumped out, ran to Nick, then smothered him in a huge bear hug.

"Stop Georgios, my ribs are cracking," Nick groaned.

Georgios gave a booming laugh then continued his massive bear hugs until we had all been welcomed to Naxos, Georgios style. After loading Nick's luggage, we started up the steep hill to the inn.

"We hear you big lucky in New York, Nicholas," Georgios said in mangled English. "But no people say you also get the beautiful new wife, too."

Nick had to fall back on his rusty Greek to convince Georgios that he wasn't bringing home a new bride.

"Too bad," Georgios shrugged. "Looks like a good one for making the children."

When the Blue Shutters Inn came into view, I instantly fell in love with the place.

The whitewashed walls, outlined by brilliant blue shutters, were tastefully draped in crimson bougainvillea vines. The inn, nestled comfortably on the hillside, looked as if it had been there for centuries. Each balcony faced toward the sea, providing a magnificent view of the picturesque town and the entire harbor.

An apron-clad, attractive older woman waited for us at the entrance. She had tears in her eyes but a brilliant smile on her face as she rushed forward to welcome her only son's return to his birthplace.

I was nervous about meeting her. I needn't have worried as she turned out to be warm and gracious. She hugged each one of us in turn, then escorted us into the cool interior.

After the introductions, Alexia insisted we join her for a midday meal in the inn's dining room. I couldn't believe my eyes when I saw the abundance of colorful, fragrant dishes laid out family-style on the large table.

Nick tried to explain some of the dishes to me with a translation. "Here we have kalamarakia (deep-fried squid), some dolmadakia (stuffed grapevine leaves), horiatiki (country-style salad), and gemista (stuffed peppers)."

"Please stop," Greg said. "I'm starving. I want to eat."

Alexia laughed, too, but she was closely observing Nick's manner towards me. I could see she sensed a bond between us. No doubt Alexia had always pictured her son returning to Naxos and marrying a nice local Greek girl.

Still, she gave no indication she was unhappy with what she saw. On the contrary, her treatment of me couldn't have been warmer.

The chilled ouzo continued to flow through the afternoon until, finally, Nick reluctantly said, "I guess all good things must come to an end. We better get back to the ship, or Captain Hoffman will sail without you."

Alexia bid us a fond farewell. She had tears in her eyes when she hugged me for an extra minute, then she whispered in my ear, "I am so happy we met, Rhonda. I do hope we will see you again sometime soon. Remember, you will always be welcome here at the Blue Shutters Inn."

I couldn't stop my tears. Even though I had only known Alexia for a few hours, I felt like I was leaving my own mother behind. I was still sobbing as I thanked her and said goodbye.

We walked in silence back down the hill to the waiting ship. No one could think of anything to say. Fortunately, the gangplank was almost about to be retrieved, leaving little time for long farewells. Nick shook Greg's hand warmly then hugged Gina before imploring them both to keep in touch.

When the other two started their climb up the gangplank, Nick took me in his arms and whispered, "I wish we had met in a different place and time, Rhonda. I will never, ever forget you."

"And I will never forget you," I said softly. "You changed my life forever."

"Have I changed it enough for you to stay here on Naxos with me?"

I took Nick's hand before answering. "My God, I'm tempted. You'll never know how much, but I can't."

"Why?" Nick implored.

"The timing," I said quietly. "I've only discovered what it means to be alive. After all those years in a coal town, I have a chance to go to New York for an exciting modeling career. I'd never forgive myself if I don't at least give it a try."

"You deserve it, Rhonda. I won't come between you and a dream. But, remember, there will always be a place for you on Naxos—and in my heart."

I couldn't speak. I intensified our hug, then I turned and hurried up the gangplank and down into the solitude of my cabin.

Nick remained on the dock watching the departing *Star Galaxy* until she was hull down on the horizon. Then, with deep regret, he trudged back up the hill to the inn.

Alexia was watching from her balcony as Nicky made the lonely voyage home. A single thought crossed her mind as she watched him walk with his head down.

I know my son will always regret ever letting that one leave.

● ● ● ●

UNEXPECTED NEWS:

The final leg of the voyage from Naxos to Istanbul was anticlimactic. With Nick no longer part of our group, everything seemed flat. Greg and Gina did their best to keep my spirits up. I appreciated the efforts, but my mind was in continuous turmoil. I went up on deck and gravitated to the same deck chairs I had shared with Nick.

I usually didn't drink alone, but now I decided to order a glass of Limoncello in memory of the erotic night I had spent with Nick in his cabin. I lay back on the lounger, closed my eyes, and began to analyze my situation.

I have three potential paths to the future. If I make the right choice, my life could be fantastic, and my song might finally be free. If I make the wrong choice, I'll pay for it for the rest of my days.

If I choose to go back to Laurel Run and Joe, my life will be a living hell again, but at least I will be able to live with my conscience.

If I choose to take the Magic Models lifetime opportunity in New York, I'll never have to worry about money, but will I be living with regrets for the rest of my life?

If I choose to make my way back to Naxos, I'm sure I'll find a warm reception, but can I live in a small town in a foreign country for the rest of my life?

Sometimes the fickle finger of fate intervenes in each person's life when least expected. Fate intervened that day, and I didn't have to decide which path to follow after all.

"Mrs. Turner?" the deck steward asked. "Captain Hoffman needs to see you in his office. He asked if you would kindly come as soon as possible."

I was mystified. I had no idea why the captain would want to see me. I followed the steward to the captain's office. I found him sitting behind a small metal desk covered with charts. Pictures of his family adorned the paneled walls behind him. He had a somber look on his face.

"Please be seated, Mrs. Turner. I'm afraid I have some disturbing news for you. We've just received a communication from our head office regarding your husband. They received a phone call from a Mrs. Donna Williams in Laurel Run, Pennsylvania. She was trying to reach you."

"Do you know why she was calling me?"

"I'm afraid I do. I regret to inform you that Joseph Turner and two friends were involved in a hunting accident. The two friends had minor injuries, but your husband was gravely injured. He's now in serious condition in the Laurel Run Community Hospital."

"Do you know what happened, Captain?" I asked, my voice cracking.

"No one appears to know for sure, but the officers investigating the incident reported that excess alcohol was a contributing factor."

"Thank you, Captain. I'm in a bit of shock. I'm not sure what to do next."

"We assumed you would want to get home as soon as possible, so we have you booked on a flight from Istanbul at 3:00 p.m. today. I'm very sorry to be the bearer of bad news."

We shook hands, and I left in a daze to begin packing for the trip home. Within a few hours of hearing about Joe, I had said my goodbyes to Gina and Greg then sat on my USA-bound plane, thinking about my future.

NEW LIFE FOR OLD:

On the long taxi ride to the hospital from the regional airport, I was reminded of how depressing the surroundings were. Abandoned pit heads, shabby structures, wet mud, and dirt everywhere I looked. I entered the small hospital with trepidation, inquiring at the reception desk for Joe Turner's room.

"Are you family?"

"I'm his wife."

After being escorted up to the hospital's critical care area, I found the room with Joe's name tag. An elderly doctor was finishing his examination when I cautiously entered the room. Joe lay on the bed motionless, hooked up to several humming machines.

"How is he, Doctor?"

The old man just shook his head. "I'm afraid his condition has deteriorated rapidly over the last forty-eight hours."

"What treatment is he getting?"

"Just sedation, I'm afraid. Your husband is now on total life support. He's officially brain dead, meaning he can't survive without mechanical assistance."

"What now?" I asked although I suspected the answer.

The doctor shrugged. "Our records show that you're his wife, so it's up to you to decide between continuing life support or not."

I moved over to the bedside to stare down at my wreck of a husband. I wasn't sure I had ever really loved Joe, but I felt saddened by his current circumstances. I thought back to our early days and the gradual deterioration of our marriage. All the arguments, fights, and petty actions came flooding back. I remembered how much I was looking forward to wearing my new going away outfit only to find it soaking in Joe's beer.

It didn't take me long to decide. "Go ahead and pull the plug," I said quietly. "You have my consent."

I signed the necessary forms, then left the room without shedding a tear and never looked back.

After returning home from the hospital, I stood in my living room staring at the wreckage of Joe's final days. The pile of empty pizza boxes, beer cans, and wrappings from frozen dinners made it challenging to navigate the rooms. The three kitchen light bulbs still hadn't been replaced.

I felt no regrets about Joe, although I wasn't sure if giving my consent to end Joe's life was an act of mercy or one of petty revenge. I felt only a profound sense of relief. I cleared a spot by the telephone and made two calls. The first was to Laurel Run Realty, where I advised them to list the house for sale. My second call was to Don Moreland at Magic Models Inc.

"Hi, Don, this is Rhonda Turner. We met on the *Star Galaxy*. Is the job in New York still available?"

I heard a very enthusiastic, "When can you start, Rhonda?"

"Tomorrow."

● ● ● ●

NEW YORK:

Magic Models delivered on everything they had promised. I had my own nicely furnished apartment with domestic staff along with a car and driver. I was living the dream, but still, something was missing. My hectic schedule made it almost impossible to feel lonely, although I occasionally felt a little blue. I was having one of those lonely days on a rainy Sunday when the phone rang.

"Hi, kiddo, long time no see."

"Gina! How are you? I've missed you so much. Where are you?"

"I'm here in the Big Apple, hon. My long-lost relatives decided to have a once-in-a-lifetime family reunion, so I flew in from Seattle."

"Where are you staying?"

"At some fleabag hotel, the Belmont on the west side."

"Pack your stuff right now. I'm sending Kenny, my driver, to pick you up. You're staying with me until you have to go home."

"Is Kenny cute?"

"Christ, Gina. You never change."

All three hundred pounds of Kenny survived the ride with Gina, and soon we were reminiscing over a bottle of wine. I was in the middle of telling her about the sad ending with Joe being on life support when Gina stopped me.

"I have to tell you something. I still feel guilty about it, but I think I did the right thing. I opened a telegram that was meant to be delivered to you before the ship sailed from New York, but it got delayed. It showed up when we were on the Amalfi coast."

I was puzzled. "A telegram for me? What did it say?"

"It was short but definitely not sweet. It was from your husband. It said, 'Come home immediately, I forgive you. Joe.' It wasn't signed with any love or kisses."

"Why didn't you give it to me, Gina?"

"Honey, I sensed that, for the first time in your life, you were really enjoying yourself. It concerned me that the telegram might upset you and ruin your holiday. I hope I did the right thing. Besides, I thought the telegram was insulting. You hadn't done anything to be forgiven for."

"You know what? This will sound terrible, but I'm happy you didn't let me see that telegram. I know you're not supposed to speak ill of the dead, but my husband was a real asshole."

"Rhonda, you shock me," Gina laughed.

The wine bottle was almost empty, so I opened another, which we had along with a plate of sandwiches my cook had prepared earlier.

"It's so good to see you again, Gina. I often think about the great times we had on the *Star Galaxy* with Greg and Nick. By the way, do you ever hear from Greg?"

"As a matter of fact, because he lives in Vancouver and I'm in Seattle, I see Greg quite often. I spent a weekend with him at his place last month."

"Did you have a good time?"

"Greg may be a lawyer, but I can tell you some of the stuff he showed me in bed never came out of any law books."

"Gina, you never change. You're still disgusting."

"Don't tell me you never think about Nicky that way?" Gina chided.

"Honestly, I think about Nicky and Naxos often. Meeting him changed my life."

"Have you talked to him since leaving?"

"No, I came to the conclusion it would only hurt both of us."

"You know what they say, honey?"

"What?"

"No pain-no gain."

"Let's change the subject, or I'm going to bed. Why don't I tell you about my life as a glamorous model in high demand by all the top fashion magazines."

"Please do. Maybe I'll give modeling a shot too."

The following morning Kenny brought the car around. It was time for Gina to leave for her reunion. I had enjoyed seeing Gina and the warm memories it rekindled.

"I'll try and come to Seattle soon, Gina. My contract is almost up, then I need to decide what my next step will be."

"Whatever you decide will be the right choice, kiddo. I'm sure of that."

I was still sniffling over Gina's departure when the phone rang. It was the owner of the modeling agency. With the first year of my contract nearing an end, Don was bugging me almost every day about the deal's renewal.

"Look, Rhonda," Don's voice boomed through the phone, "everything I told you has worked out great. You're in constant demand. All the clients love you. Two more years, and you can retire at the very top of the business."

"Thanks for everything you've done for me, Don. I'm just not sure I want to spend the rest of my life doing this stuff and living here in New York. But I promise to give it some real thought. I'll let you know as soon as I can."

I enjoyed the modeling assignments, but the rest of my life in New York was not very satisfying. I had been on multiple dates, but I found the men either shallow or too full of self-importance. I often daydreamed I was back aboard the *Star Galaxy* under full sail, watching my magic dolphins at sunset.

After moping around for a few more weeks, thinking about Gina's conversations, I called Moreland.

"I still don't know what to do," I confessed. "I don't want to make any mistakes because this is an important decision for me. We don't have any pressing photo shoots for the next few weeks, so I'm going to take a holiday break to try to come to a final decision about my future. Is that okay with you?"

"No, it's not okay, but I know better than to argue with a woman when I know I'll lose. Take your holiday, you deserve it. Then get back here. We need you."

I put down the phone, thought for a minute, and then picked it up again. *I need a memorable vacation, and I know just the perfect place for it.*

I smiled and dialed the number.

• • • •

FINAL CHAPTER:

I only came to Naxos for a week's vacation, but I stayed for a lifetime.

When my taxi pulled up to the entrance of the inn, and I saw Nick waiting on the steps with a bouquet of fresh flowers, flashing his devilish grin, I knew I would never go home. From the look in Nick's eyes, I knew he felt the same way, too.

"I knew in my heart that you would come back to Naxos to see your magical dolphins at sunset,"

I kissed Nick then said, "I didn't come for Naxos or the dolphins. I came for you."

After spending some time renewing our relationship and over numerous discussions with Alexia, we set a wedding date. Nick called his old friends Denny Lee and Jack Youngman in New York and invited them to the wedding. I phoned my friend Casandra along with Gina and Greg and extended an invitation to them as well.

When everyone accepted with enthusiasm, Alexia set aside a block of the best rooms for our wedding guests.

The day before our wedding, Nick asked us to join him on the main balcony. It was another glorious day with the brilliant sun shining brightly on the harbor and the azure seas.

"This is lovely," I said. "But what are we doing out here?"

"Patience, everyone," Nick said with a mysterious smile. "I believe something magical is about to happen."

"You're going to conjure up a large bottle of Limoncello?" Denny Lee quipped.

"For Christ's sake, Denny, you just got out of bed," his buddy said.

"Take a good look at the Mediterranean Sea, my friends," Nick grinned. "Tell me if you can spot anything special."

Because I have excellent vision, I spotted it first. Minute by minute, the outline of a beautiful Windjammer under full sail started rising from the horizon.

"Oh, Nick, it can't be! Is that the *Star Galaxy*?"

"It is," Nick said as he kissed me. "It took all of my Greek charms to manage it, but we'll be getting married aboard her tomorrow."

Because of Nick, we had the perfect fairytale wedding. On the day of the ceremony, the weather couldn't have been better. Alexia and I were dressed, ready to depart for the ship when we heard the wild tooting of a car horn announcing Georgios' arrival.

His ancient battered taxi had been entirely covered with an abundance of fresh, colorful island flowers. Georgios, dressed to the nines in an old-fashioned tuxedo, bowed when he saw us. He opened the taxi's back door to allow three pretty young girls to emerge. Each child carried a wicker basket of fresh flower petals.

I started to laugh. Alexia did too. "What's happening, Nick? Is this our limo to the ship?"

Nick grinned. "Nope. Just wait and see."

Within minutes the lawn in front of the Blue Shutters Inn had been transformed into an unforgettable spectacle. A dozen local musicians all strumming their eight-stringed bouzoukis, showed up, then quickly formed a line behind the beautifully decorated taxi.

After Georgios arranged the flower girls in front of the taxi, he took Alexa by the arm and escorted her to the passenger seat beside him.

"Are we supposed to get in the back seat?" I asked.

"Nope. This is a wedding parade. We walk."

With that, Nick took my hand and led me to a position directly behind the musicians. Once we were in place, our guests formed a long line behind us. With a toot of his horn, Georgios signaled the start of the procession. The musicians started up, then the flower girls began to sing and scatter flower petals as we proceeded to make our way slowly down the hill to the harbor.

Attracted by the music and the singing, neighbors abandoned their front steps along the way to join in the procession. The combination of sights and sounds will stay with me until the end of my days. A vivid red blossom from the flower girl's efforts caught up in the gentle breeze and landed on Nick's chest. It looked as if he was wearing his heart for all to see.

And perhaps he was. I know I was that day in enchanted Naxos.

● ● ● ●

Captain Hoffman welcomed us aboard with a special cocktail party for the wedding group and the ship's officers. A string quartet played soft music in the background while waiters circulated with champagne cocktails.

Gina looked casually around the private room before asking, "Captain, I don't see your purser, Ricardo Sanchez. Is he still with the shipping line?"

"No, I'm afraid he's in a hospital in Rome suffering from a broken arm and several ribs."

"Oh, no! What happened to him?"

"We're not too sure. The crew found Sanchez at the bottom of the upper deck stairs. He says he slipped and fell, but rumors circulated that he might have become a little too familiar with one of our lady passengers traveling with her husband. He won't be coming back to this ship."

Gina started to laugh but stopped when I pinched her arm.

The captain took the *Star Galaxy* out beyond the seven-mile limit to establish his authority as a registered sea captain duly authorized to conduct marriages at sea. To be on the safe side, a local priest from Naxos was aboard to also officiate in the ceremony. The captain stood on the bridge in a crisp white uniform with Nick and I standing before him. The priest wore his usual black attire.

Afterward, Gina said I had looked radiant and blissfully happy. I was wearing Alexia's carefully restored ivory lace wedding dress. In a navy-blue blazer with brass buttons, white cotton pants, and an open-necked white linen shirt, Nick looked like a young boy going on his first date.

When the captain pronounced us man and wife, the crowd broke out in cheers. The passengers aboard were delighted at being invited to participate in an authentic Greek wedding. Most of the other local guests from Naxos proclaimed it the best wedding ever.

After the ceremony, Nick took me for a walk to the ship's stern just as the sun was setting. The rest of the guests discreetly left us alone. As before, the sun painted the gently rolling waves with a mixture of gold and crimson red, and, on cue, my dolphins did their part, soaring up and down in the ship's foaming wake.

"I don't know how the hell you keep doing that on-demand, Mr. Alexandros."

"It's straightforward, Mrs. Alexandros. I just pay them."

We left the dolphins cavorting in the azure sea and returned to join our friends. I truly believed this was the happiest moment of my life.

The party went on for hours until Captain Hoffman navigated the *Star Galaxy* safely back to port under a twinkling starlit sky. The passengers and guests lined up in two rows to shower us with rice from the galley before my husband and I departed hand in hand to start our new life together.

Georgios was standing by, ready to drive us up the hill to the enchanting Blue Shutters Inn. I could hardly wait for the honeymoon to start.

• • • •

HOW TIME FLIES BY:

Nick and I were sitting on the balcony admiring the Christmas lights shimmering on the harbor and the streets of the little town nestled below the hill. Inside, the inn was filled with guests sitting by the crackling fireplace, enjoying their Christmas cheer. Sumptuous aromas wafted out of the kitchen, a harbinger of the feast still to come.

"Here's to you, Rhonda," Nick said as he raised his glass to me. "You've made the last twenty-five years of my life a wonderful experience. I'm so happy I met you when I did."

I raised my glass in return, but first, I glanced into the dining room where our three teenage offspring worked busily, setting tables for the Christmas dinner.

Then with a bursting heart and tears in my eyes, I answered Nick's toast in fluent Greek.

"And here's to you, my love. You've done many wonderful things for me over the years, and I appreciate them all. I'll never forget how you managed to arrange my first magical sighting of the dolphins at sunset."

"That was part of my grand plan to seduce you," Nick grinned.

"As I recall, I was the brazen hussy who showed up at your cabin door, so who seduced who?"

"If you hadn't shown up as you did, I was ready to go to your room to drag you from your bed."

I laughed. "Gina would have applauded, I'm sure."

When the dinner bell chimed from inside, Nick rose to go in, but I stopped him. This wonderful man had watched me leave his side, then waited patiently until I finally realized my true destiny. I needed to say one last thing.

"I want you to know that I've never had a single moment of regret since I joined you at the Blue Shutters Inn," I said softly. "And, above all, I want to thank you for sharing your life with me and for making sure I'll never go to my grave with a song still left deep inside me."

Nick took me by the hand, kissed me gently, and we went inside to join in the ancient celebration of Christmas with the family I loved so deeply.

We lived the rest of our lives together in harmony, on our magical island of Naxos.

FORTESQUE

Some days it doesn't pay to answer the phone.

Unfortunately for me, this was one of those days. Instead of ignoring the shrill ring as my instincts demanded, I put aside my watercolor brush and picked up. As soon as I heard the cultured voice on the other end, I knew trouble was brewing.

"Hello George," the Honorable Justice Joseph M. Carter drawled. "I've got a new assignment for you."

"Christ, Joe, give me a break. I haven't recovered from the last one."

The judge ignored me. "Ever heard of the Grenville family?"

"The food empire one?"

"Yes. After the parents died in an automobile accident, their son Fortesque inherited the estate. That was two years ago when he was thirteen. The kid's been a ward of the court since then.

"So why are you bothering me?"

"The woman we appointed as a guardian has just resigned. Says the kid is unmanageable. Even the household butler resigned. I know you have a lot of time on your hands these days, and, as ex-military, you know how to be tough when you have to."

"Wait a minute, Joe, is this conversation heading where I think it is?"

Justice Carter laughed. "Yes, I'm officially appointing you to the position of the court-appointed guardian for young Mr. Fortesque Grenville."

"Can't you find another sucker?"

"No. You're the sucker I want. You're stuck with it."

Even though the judge was a golfing friend that I'd known since we went to school together, I knew he wouldn't budge if his mind was made up.

"Okay," I said wearily. "Send me the file, but keep searching for someone else to take over for me."

I tried to hang up before Joe could, but he beat me again. While I waited for the file, I did a Google search on the Grenville family.

It seems Fortesque had inherited the family name of Grenville from his mother's side. It was an illustrious name dating back to the Norman conquest of 1066 in England. In addition to the prestigious family name, Fortesque had also inherited the accumulated wealth of generations after both parents died due to a car accident with a New York City bus.

After the bus driver was found to be inebriated, the court awarded significant financial damages to the parents' estate. This generous settlement was the icing on an already rich cake. I didn't arrive at a sum of his assets, but, on the surface, the kid was filthy rich.

When the kid's official file arrived, it didn't take me long to see I was going to have my hands full. In addition to numerous close encounters with the law, it appeared that everyone who knew Fortesque had a low opinion of him. The descriptive words most used in the big pile of staff complaints were: incredibly spoiled, petulant, irritating, useless, vain, puffed up, and entirely unlikeable little jerk.

I could hardly wait to meet him.

On my first day on the job, I arrived at the beautiful penthouse apartment on 5th Avenue where Fortesque lived alone, surrounded by his opulent possessions. He also had a country home in the Hamptons, covering more than fifty acres. Swimming pools, stables, and a helicopter pad for his frequent travels were just a few of the pleasures available to him

Our first meeting did not go well. The young jerk, eating breakfast in bed, was in the middle of one of his tantrums. He was screaming at one of the unfortunate staff members who was fervently wishing she had never left her home in Honduras.

"You, stupid bitch," Fortesque screamed. "How many times do I have to tell you? I don't want any of the red ones."

The boy finished his tirade by firing his uneaten cereal bowl in the maid's general direction. The bowl didn't break, but a handwoven carpet worth half my life savings took the brunt of a deluge of milk and Crispy Circles.

He saw me standing in the doorway, and I guess he mistakenly assumed I was the new replacement butler. He pointed an accusing finger in my direction.

"You there, don't just stand around looking like a dummy," Fortesque demanded. "Get rid of this incompetent person immediately. I don't want to see her ugly face again."

I stifled my first urge, which was to yank Fortesque out of his plush bed, then drag him out to the proverbial woodshed for a well-deserved thrashing. But, in a flash of brilliance, I conjured up an alternate approach. One that might better serve my longer-term needs.

I bowed and went along with the butler subterfuge. "Of course, Master Grenville, I'll deal with the problem immediately."

"Do it, then get your scrawny ass back here on the double," Fortesque snarled. "I've got some errands for you to do."

I kept my cool and escorted the shaking maid away from the dining room. As soon as we were out of hearing range, I asked her name.

"Maria," she replied with her head down.

"Well, Maria. My name is George Collins. Can you take me somewhere for a cup of coffee and a chat?"

"Si, in the staff kitchen."

While Maria busied herself brewing the coffee, I reflected on my hastily chosen strategy. In my role as a court-appointed guardian, I usually worked from home. However, if I could put up with the bullshit of becoming the estate butler for a few days, I would be living in the Grenville residence full-time.

This would allow me to make a much better assessment of the situation. Being away from home for a few days wasn't a problem. I'd been living on my own since my wife, Jennie, passed away two years ago. I had taken early retirement from the marine corps to care for her while she recovered from a series of operations.

I didn't relish exposing myself to the kid's tantrums for even a few days. Still, I had to admit, with my silver hair, slim build, and military bearing, I could probably pass as a butler quite well.

I had to coax Maria to sit with me. Her reluctance told me she believed having coffee with the butler was above her station.

"Tell me, Maria, is Master Grenville always this bad?"

"Oh, no, senor," Maria exclaimed. "Some days, he's much worse."

Great, I thought. *I'm taking on Atilla the Hun as a project.*

"Tell me what happened today? What caused master Grenville's rage?"

Maria shrugged. "El Jefe found a red circle in his bowl of Crispy Circles."

"So?" I asked.

"It is forbidden to give El Jefe his favorite breakfast unless the box has been hand-sorted first to remove any of the red circles. I missed one." She paused with her eyes downcast. "Does this mean I've lost my job?"

"It's probably safer for you to leave," I said gently. "I'll make sure you receive an outstanding severance payment and an excellent reference."

We chatted for a while, then I left Maria feeling better about her future prospects. I think she considered herself lucky, considering that several staff members had been fired without notice this month alone.

Fortesque was easy to locate. All I had to do was follow the screams. By this time, Grenville Jr. was out of bed, creating havoc with the staff. His current victim appeared to be the chauffeur, Eric Williams.

"Bring the limo to the front door," Fortesque yelled. "I want to go shopping for a new drone before my noon meeting with my investment manager. And make sure the damned car is clean this time, you idiot!"

Having thrown his breakfast at Maria, Fortesque was now quite hungry. He stormed into the kitchen, demanding that Lucy, the day cook, stop everything and cook him bacon and eggs. He finally stopped shouting when he noticed me standing in the doorway.

"I gather you're the new butler," Fortesque sneered. "Don't you know you're supposed to stand at attention when I enter a room?"

My first instinct was to stand and belt him one. Instead, I apologized. "I'm dreadfully sorry, Master Fortesque, it won't happen again."

I decided to take a few more days of observing before sitting down with the jerk to set him straight. I had a good chance of success since Fortesque obviously didn't know that I was now his court-appointed guardian.

Fortesque ordered Lucy to have the bacon and eggs sent to his room. Then, he stormed out of the kitchen without a backward glance. Lucy cowered by the stove, trembling in her haste to prepare the meal.

"Are you okay, Lucy?" I asked gently.

She sniffed. "Sure. At least the little bastard didn't throw anything at me today."

● ● ● ●

MORNINGSIDE INVESTMENTS

I waited in the circular driveway as Eric pulled the limo up to the front door. He introduced himself, then we chatted while waiting for Fortesque to make an appearance.

As part of my obligations as guardian, I wanted a first-hand look at his investment manager. Safeguarding assets for wards of the court was one of my prime responsibilities. Many a family fortune had been squandered by irresponsible behaviors. I wanted to make sure it didn't happen on my watch.

Eric spotted the boy first and hurried to open the rear door. Fortesque climbed into the backseat without a glance. I opened the front door and sat beside the driver.

"Where the hell do you think you're going?" Fortesque demanded.

"Forgive me, Master Fortesque, for taking such a liberty. In my previous employment, I became somewhat of an expert on aerial drones. I thought I might be of some help with your purchase."

My answer appeared to mollify the little squirt. Fortesque ignored me while barking orders directly to Eric.

"Macy's first, then the offices of Morningside Investments and make it snappy."

We drove in silence for a few minutes, then I snuck a sideways peek at the driver. I could tell Eric was unhappy. He wrestled with something before speaking.

"Master Fortesque, when the estate hired me, I was promised a raise after a six-month trial. I've been waiting for over two years. I was hoping to get my increase before I get married next month."

"As far as I'm concerned," Fortesque sneered, "you're overpaid for the crummy job you do. I could probably hire a monkey to do a better job for half the price."

"But, sir..."

Fortesque cut him off. "I told you my decision. If you don't like it, you can leave. Now shut up, I'm trying to think."

Eric glanced at me with anger in his eyes. Nothing else was said until the silver limo pulled up at the entrance to Macy's Department store. As Fortesque climbed out, an old, one-armed beggar shambled up with his hand extended,

"Spare some change, sir?" the bum pleaded.

The beggar had seen better days. The old guy smelled foul. His clothing was badly stained and patched. The cigarette butt he was puffing looked like it had been rescued from a gutter. He was probably its second or third owner.

Why don't you get a job?" Fortesque grunted as he wrinkled up his nose. "If you saved your money, instead of wasting it on smokes and booze, you might have amounted to something."

Fortesque spat in the man's outstretched hand to add to his insult, then nonchalantly strolled into the store. Eric looked at me with disgust at Fortesque's actions.

I handed a Kleenex and five bucks to the poor bum then hurried after Eric's cheapskate employer.

After spending almost an hour haggling with the store clerks over the price of a new MX-490 Aerial Surveillance Drone, we returned to the car, then headed for the offices of Morningside Investments. This firm had handled all of the Grenville family's financial matters since the death of Fortesque's parents.

"You're not invited," Fortesque snarled as I attempted to follow him into the building.

"Sometimes, sir," I scrambled, "in these important meetings, it helps to have an assistant take notes, in case there's a future disagreement."

I could see that Grenville Jr. was puffed up at the idea of having a private secretary. He didn't say no, so I tagged along.

The elegantly furnished offices of Morningside Investments gave a subtle impression of a safe haven for the stewardship of old money. Winston Brownley, the investment manager, was a middle-aged, portly fellow with slicked-back hair, wearing silver wire-rimmed glasses. His dark blue pinstripe suit was well cut and expensive.

"Oh, Master Grenville," Brownley oozed as he rushed forward to greet Fortesque with his hands outstretched. "What a pleasure it is to see you again."

"Forget the horseshit, Brownley," Fortesque growled while ignoring the handshake. "Just tell me how my investment portfolios are doing."

For the remainder of the afternoon, Brownley produced chart after chart, showing the impressive compounded investment gains accrued on the Grenville stock portfolios. I'm no investment genius, but even to me, it seemed strange that none of the charts showed any sign of a downturn.

When I started to take notes, I could see Brownley was getting uncomfortable. He quickly suggested we take a break for a light lunch in the boardroom.

"Should we send something to eat or drink down to your driver?" Brownley asked.

"Stop worrying about the god damned hired help," Fortesque warned. "You better start spending more time concentrating on my stuff. These investment returns are just barely okay. Jack them up, or I'll find myself a new advisor."

Brownley looked troubled when the meeting ended. I made a note to myself to do some background checking on both the manager and his firm as soon as I had a chance. Back at the penthouse, Fortesque issued a new set of orders.

"Start preparing for a two-week stay at my Hampton Estate," Fortesque growled. "We leave tomorrow morning. Make sure my drone isn't broken, or I'll take it from your pay."

Eric turned away, so I couldn't tell for sure what he was mumbling. But it certainly sounded like "little asshole."

My sentiments, exactly.

● ● ● ●

The fifty-acre Grenville estate was gorgeous. Rolling hills and lush green meadows were home to a small herd of spectacular thoroughbred horses. The main house was huge, as were the Olympic-sized pool and tennis courts.

I was sure I might like it here - if I could drown Fortesque in the fishing pond.

I had hoped the kid would be better away from the city, but my hopes were dashed when he unleashed the terror of his new toy drone. The shrill whining of the drone's engines was bothering the highly-strung thoroughbred horses. The herd kept moving nervously around the corral, looking for some escape from the noise.

Being easily bored, Fortesque decided it might be fun to try to stampede the herd. He started flying the drone directly at the horses, pulling up only at the last second. Terrified, the tortured animals were driven to galloping around in a frenzy, lathered up, drooling saliva from their gaping mouths.

Tony Hasbro, the stable manager, was an animal lover. He couldn't stand seeing his beloved horses mistreated like this. He rushed out to the paddock, screaming as he ran.

"Stop that god-damned drone immediately, or I'll get my shotgun and shoot it down."

Fortesque laughed at the threat. "Hasbro, if you know what's good for you, you'll forget my drone and go back to shoveling horse shit in the stables, where you belong."

The boy and the older man glared at each other for a few moments. Then, reluctantly, Hasbro dropped his gaze and turned slowly back to the stables. He desperately needed his job. He had seen too many Grenville employees shown the door for minor offenses.

As he walked past me with his head down, I could hear Tony muttering. His voice was low, but the message was clear.

"One day, you little arrogant jerk, you might find out what life is really like on the poor side of town."

That evening, things turned even worse. I was summoned to the kitchen by Maurice, the head chef. Maurice had been recruited from Paris by Fortesque's parents, at great expense, to join the estate staff. I found him in the middle of a meltdown.

"What's the problem, chef?" I asked.

"The barbarian in the dining room. I am at my wit's end. I have offered my best dishes, yet he refuses them all. Look for yourself," Maurice wailed as he threw me a copy of tonight's printed menu.

The menu was equal to that of the best dining spot in New York. Juicy Baron of Beef, Cold poached Lobster, Grilled Dover Sole, and stuffed Pork Tenderloin. All the choices looked delicious to me.

"I'll see what I can do, Maurice," I promised before heading to the dining room.

Fortesque sat alone, as he usually did, at the end of the long and elegantly arranged table. He sat with his head down, unaware I had entered until I coughed discreetly.

"What the hell do you want?" he growled.

"Master Grenville, the chef is anxious to proceed with your meal. Have you had a chance to make your selection?"

"I don't want any of his fancy pants crap," Fortesque moaned. "Bring me a peanut butter and banana sandwich and make it snappy,"

By the time I hit the kitchen, Maurice was already packing his knives for departure on the next plane to Paris. Despite my pleading, he left in a huff leaving me with little choice but to make the sandwich as requested.

I decided it was getting close to the time that Mr. Grenville Jr. and I had our little heart-to-heart chat.

The following morning, I found Fortesque at the poolside, suspiciously examining his bowl of Crispy Circles in case a red one had somehow slipped through the kitchen staff's inspection. As usual, he ignored my presence.

That changed in a hurry when I plunked myself down on a deck chair beside him. I enjoyed the look of astonishment on his face. A face that was now rapidly turning beet red with rage.

"How dare you" he demanded indignantly. "Get out of here immediately."

"Shut up, you little shit," I barked. "It's time for you to listen. And listen to me with your undivided attention."

Fortesque sat in stunned silence, his beet-red face now rapidly changing to a shade of pasty grey.

"I'm George Collins. I'm not your butler. I'm your court-appointed guardian. And right now, I'm the only thing standing between you and reform school."

"What the hell did I do?" Fortesque asked defensively.

I explained Judge Carter's concern that Fortesque's actions were becoming uncontrolled, possibly leading to serious legal consequences. I then went through the items one at a time: the ill-treatment of his staff, the drone attack on the horses, his inhumane treatment of the beggar, his miserly treatment of suppliers, and so on.

Fortesque sat there with a face carved out of stone, not speaking, just staring at the swimming pool. He finally turned to me and spoke. His words came as quite a shock; they were the last thing I expected.

"I'm an orphan, you know," he murmured. "No one gives a shit about me. They only care about my money."

I had no idea what the lad was like before the tragic death of his parents. I started to feel guilty that perhaps people around this boy were not considering the long-lasting effects of his parents' accident.

Fortesque gradually started to open up as we talked. It was clear that the shock of realizing he was totally on his own had caused the boy to develop a tough shell as a defense against further hurt.

I was just about to introduce the idea of counseling. The kid obviously needed help. I stopped talking when my cell phone rang. The call was from Judge Carter. I wasn't sure why he was trying to reach me.

But I never, for an instant, had the slightest inkling his message would trigger a chain of events that would totally upend young Fortesque's life forever.

"George, I don't have time to explain, but the proverbial shit has hit the fan," Judge Carter said quickly, with an edge to his voice. "You need to go to the Grenville family lawyer's office. It's urgent. Take the kid with you."

I put my phone down, wondering what had triggered the call. I looked at Fortesque to see he was back rummaging through his cereal bowl for red circles.

"Go to the house and change," I barked. "Put on a business suit, then meet me out front. I'll organize Eric and the car."

"Why would I do that?" Fortesque objected. "I'm going swimming when I finish my breakfast."

"If you don't hop to it. You'll be swimming with a sore arse," I threatened

After Fortesque took off for the house, I rang Eric to tell him we were heading for the family lawyer's office. Eric confirmed he knew the address from previous trips.

A short while later, we found ourselves sitting in the offices of Periwinkle, Johnson & Krakow, lawyers for the Grenville Estate. All three partners, looking solemn, attended the meeting in keeping with the seriousness of the situation.

At a nod from Frederick Periwinkle, the senior partner, Gordon Krakow, opened a folder, then addressed his remarks to Fortesque.

"I'm sorry to be the bearer of bad news," Krakow said somberly. "We were advised that Winston Brownley of Morningside Investments took his own life last night."

"So? There are a million money managers out there. I can replace him in minutes," Fortesque scoffed.

"That's not all, I'm afraid. Mr. Brownley left behind a detailed suicide note in the form of a confession. All twenty-five pages of it."

"Can we cut through the crap and just get to the bottom line?" Fortesque groaned. "I'm tired of this shit, and I want to go home."

"Shut up, Fortesque," I hissed. "This is serious. Let Mr. Krakow talk uninterrupted, or I'll send you to wait in the car."

Krakow nodded his thanks for my intervention, then, still bristling, he turned and unloaded on Fortesque with both barrels.

"You want the bottom line, son? Well, here it is. You don't have a home to go to. You're bankrupt. If the truth be known, you've probably been bankrupt for some months. Your money is gone."

Fortesque looked like he had been hit by an asteroid. "What do you mean, my money is gone?"

It took more than an hour for the whole sordid story to unfold, and when it did, the situation was dire. It turned out that Brownley had been milking the estate for years to feed a growing gambling addiction, even going back to before the parents' deaths.

Morningside Investments had discretionary powers, allowing them to make investment decisions on behalf of the estate without consultation. The firm also handled tax filings and bill payments as well.

Over the years, as Brownley sank deeper into debt, he began producing false statements showing positive results. After a series of disastrous long-shot investments to try to recoup the losses, Brownley had also arranged for mortgages to be placed on all the properties.

With checks bouncing and suppliers demanding to be paid, Brownley took the easy way out by jumping off his 24th-floor balcony.

When Krakow finished his disclosure, we all sat in stunned silence. I looked at Fortesque and, for the first time, saw him as he really was. A vulnerable, desperately scared young boy on his own.

"What happens now?" Fortesque asked with a frightened quiver in his voice.

Periwinkle replied, "The secured lenders have already taken action. I'm afraid that a Notice of Seizure has already arrived. All assets of the estate will have to be turned over to the bailiff within forty-eight hours.

"But what about me? Where will I live?"

"Because you're a minor, you're a ward of the court," Krakow said. "Judge Carter is working on trying to find a permanent placement for you. The process could take some time. In the interim, we have rented a room for you in Brooklyn for thirty days. Hopefully, the judge will have a solution before long."

I stood up. "Thanks, gentlemen. I'm going to take Fortesque home. If he only has forty-eight hours, he'll need to pack up. I'll work directly with Judge Carter for the next steps."

"Before you go," Krakow interrupted, "it's my sad duty to formally advise you, because of a conflict of interest, the firm can no longer represent you or the estate. Several rather large legal bills remain unpaid, making us one of your many creditors."

It suddenly dawned on me that I was a creditor, too. I had yet to receive a payment from the estate.

Fortesque said nothing when I joined him at the long table that evening. In fact, he had said little since our meeting with the lawyers.

Dinner that night consisted of cold left-overs on a bun, Maurice, the chef, having already departed for the airport. Our mood was somber. I was worried for the boy's future, but Fortesque was terrified.

I tried to comfort the now penniless Fortesque by offering him a place to stay until the judge found a solution. Still, curiously, he was having none of it. When I retired for the evening, I could hear Fortesque sobbing, alone in his bedroom.

The following morning, a convoy of sheriff's vehicles showed up at the estate to start the process of removing all assets from the house. Up in his bedroom, Fortesque packed a small bag of clothing under the direct supervision of one of the deputies.

The lawman was there to ensure Fortesque did not leave with anything belonging to the estate. They were having a heated discussion about the ownership of the new MX-490 Aerial Surveillance Drone when I arrived.

The deputy finally backed down when I stared directly at him and told him that I had purchased the drone with my funds as a birthday gift for the boy. I'm not sure he believed the story, but he didn't attempt to stop Fortesque when he packed the drone in his belongings.

I think it was the first time I heard the boy use the words, '*Thank you.*'

Surprisingly, despite his despicable treatment of them, the entire staff had lined up along the driveway to watch Fortesque depart the estate for the last time.

Old Tom Edwards, the gardener, was the longest-serving employee of the estate. He came forward and said in a quaking voice, "We don't have much money, son, but we didn't like the thought of you arriving in the city penniless. We hope this helps you get established."

When Tom handed over a crumpled brown paper bag containing a collection of small bills and loose change, Fortesque just hung his head. He didn't know how to respond to their generous gift.

The paper bag contained $574.80 in cash.

I was in a dilemma. I was no longer the estate manager, and my status as a guardian was in limbo. As a creditor, I wasn't even sure I could remain a guardian without also having a conflict of interest. I walked over to Fortesque to hug him. I could tell by the flinch that it had been a long time between hugs for the boy.

"I'm going to head back to the city to meet with Judge Carter," I said. "He's working to find you a permanent placement. Here's my cell phone number. Call me as soon as you can so I can tell you where to go."

We shook hands for the first time, then I put aside my reserve to give him another bear hug.

Despite trying to hold back, tears flowed down Fortesque's face as he waved goodbye to everyone from the limo.

As I watched Fortesque looking back at the receding mansion, I had a feeling the boy was feeling the first of many regrets over what might have been if he had been taught how to treat people as he should have.

●●●●

A DIFFERENT LIFE

A few hours later, the silver limo pulled up in front of an old brownstone apartment building in the lower Bronx area. The building had seen better days. The half-opened green bags of assorted garbage, carelessly littered on the broken sidewalks outside the building, did nothing to improve the picture.

"Here we are," Eric said as he stared at the surroundings. "Good luck, kid. I think you're going to need it."

"Thanks for the ride," Fortesque said quietly, then added, "I'm sorry for any problems I may have caused you."

Eric was stunned. It was the first time he had ever heard a kind word from his now ex-employer.

Fortesque watched Eric drive off, then made his way into the fleabag hotel. A miserable pimply-faced clerk sat behind a security screen. He handed Fortesque a rusty key.

"Room forty-six, kid. You've got it until the end of the month. If your new rent ain't paid by 5:00 p.m. on the last day, your room will be locked, and your stuff will be out on the street."

With no elevator available, Fortesque had to lug his heavy suitcase up four flights of worn stairs. The room was worse than he could have imagined. Peeling wallpaper, fading paint, and a dirty window were the highlights. The bed was small with a stained, skinny, straw-filled mattress. Fortesque fell on the mattress and cried himself to sleep.

The short-term accommodations for Fortesque had been arranged by the law firm of Periwinkle, Johnson & Krakow. When I found out later the kind of dump they had sent him to, I went ballistic. To this day, I don't know if it was an honest mistake by someone at the firm or an act of petty revenge for their unpaid legal bills.

The problem compounded itself as I waited in vain for a phone call from Fortesque, but nothing came. I found out later he had lost my business card and had no idea how to contact me or anyone else. For the next three weeks, the bewildered boy just wandered the streets, trying to fill his time until he could seek the dubious solace of his bed.

Fortesque had never paid any attention to money before, so he was alarmed how quickly his gift from the staff was evaporating. He checked the contents of the brown bag. There was barely enough to cover his rent when it came due in one more week.

On top of that, he was now starving. The boy, who had made a habit of turning down fabulous meals especially prepared by a French chef, now found himself searching for anything to eat.

The fresh aromas from a local fish and chip shop wafted out to the sidewalk, beckoning to him as would bait to a feeding seagull.

When Fortesque entered the enticing smelling shop, he noticed a sign in the dirty window, advertising for a delivery boy.

"What do you want, kid?" growled Larry McNab, the owner.

"I would like to apply for the delivery job, sir."

"You don't look like you've ever worked a day in your life."

"I'm a quick learner," Fortesque said defensively.

"All right, I'm shorthanded right now. I'll hire you on a trial basis. Seventy cents an hour if you have your own bike, fifty cents an hour if you use one of mine. Plus, you keep any tips."

"Okay," Fortesque said. "I'll take the job. I haven't had lunch today. Could I have some fish and chips?"

McNab motioned for Fortesque to take a booth in the back, then proceeded to fry up a plate of fresh-cut chips and two pieces of halibut.

After Fortesque gobbled down the piping hit dish, he smiled, then moved to deliver his first orders. McNab stopped him.

"Haven't you forgotten something?"

"What?"

"A buck and a half for the meal."

"You mean I have to pay for meals?" Fortesque asked incredulously.

"Sure. What the hell did you think this was? A soup kitchen?"

Fortesque dug into his dwindling funds, paid the bill, then departed in search of his delivery bicycle. He was halfway to the door when McNab stopped him.

"I got two golden rules, kid. Absolutely no free grub. You pay for anything you eat, and you get the ax if you show up late, even once. No exceptions."

• • • •

SCRUFF

For the next few days, everything worked out okay. The delivery routes were simple, and sometimes Fortesque even got a small tip or two. The trouble started when a hungry, mangy-looking mongrel dog started following him around on the deliveries. Despite yelling threats at the ragged animal, it just wouldn't go away.

Because Fortesque was lonely, he found himself looking forward to seeing the dog each day when he started work. It didn't seem to have an owner or a home. Fortesque decided to adopt the dog as a pet and companion. Because of his appearance, the name of Scruff seemed appropriate. Like most dogs, Scruff was always hungry.

It started quite innocently. Feeling sorry for the dog, Fortesque started carefully unsealing the odd package. Then he would take a chip or two to feed to Scruff before resealing the package. Despite himself, the smell of the hot, steaming fish and chips kept beckoning Fortesque. Before long, he was joining Scruff in devouring their stolen booty. The two probably would have escaped detection if they had stuck with just removing a few chips here and there. However, the delicately deep-fried halibut fish was their downfall.

Most of the delivery orders called for two or more pieces of fish. But quite a few orders started arriving at the customers' homes with fewer contents than when they left the shop.

Back at the store, McNab was perplexed. He was getting more and more calls from angry customers. One customer even said, "I ordered fish and *chips*, not fish and *chip*." He had more demands for refunds than he had ever experienced since opening the shop. Some of his best long-term customers had switched to his hated competitor.

Because McNab had four delivery boys, it took quite some time to discover that all of the complaints were coming from customers on Fortesque's route. Angry, McNab decided to put an end to the theft once and for all.

The next time Fortesque returned to the shop, McNab stopped cutting up a side of halibut then grabbed Fortesque by the throat.

"Open your mouth, you little crook," McNab growled.

Fortesque had no choice but to open his mouth. McNab took a deep whiff, smelled inside, then squeezed tighter.

"Just as I thought, I can smell the fish and chips on your breath. Probably on that mutt's breath, too."

McNab made the mistake of raising his hand to strike Fortesque. The aggressive action triggered Scruff's protective instinct. The dog darted forward and nipped McNab on the ankle.

The bite enraged McNab. He seized his wicked fish cutting knife. Then he started to charge toward the defenseless dog.

Horrified that Scruff would be killed, Fortesque stuck his foot out, causing McNab to fall heavily to the hard tile floor. When Fortesque heard the unmistakable sound of a bone snapping, he panicked.

"C'mon Scuff, we have to run," Fortesque screamed. Then the two fugitives fled from the shop in search of a safe hiding place.

The police found them in less than an hour.

● ● ● ●

BEFORE THE LAW:

"Am I going to reform school, Mr. Collins?"

"Not if Judge Carter and I can help it. Although the matter is serious. McNab is demanding jail time for you, and he wants the dog put down."

"It's not Scruff's fault. He thought McNab was going to hit me."

"And was he?"

"Yes. Then McNab went after the dog with a knife."

"Okay, you're scheduled to go before the Judge at 1:00 p.m. Tell me everything since you left the estate."

As I watched Fortesque's animated face as he talked about finding the dog and about having his first real job. It told me a lot about the positive changes this kid was experiencing over a very short period.

Just before 1:00 p.m., a guard arrived at the holding cell to escort Fortesque to the courtroom. No one stopped me when I followed along. I guess they just assumed I was his lawyer. When the judge appeared, my jaw dropped. I had thought Judge Carter would preclude himself, but there he was as large as life.

I knew from Joe's earlier comments that he was worried Fortesque could end up with a criminal record plus an extended stay in a juvenile delinquent facility if this case went to trial. I knew Joe well enough that he would do whatever he could to avoid that outcome.

Usually, my old friend wore his mismatched golf outfits when we were together, so I was quite impressed with his courtly demeanor as he sat on the bench in his full-length black robes.

Judge Carter called the prosecutor over for a conference. The prosecutor was well aware that the boy had committed some foolish acts, but he didn't think the kid was a criminal.

"This isn't much of a criminal case, Fred. Any chance the shop owner will drop the charges if the boy makes some financial compensation?"

"No, Your Honor. We've made several approaches, but the guy insists on making an example of the defendant."

Judge Carter looked over at me and shook his head. He knew that McNab was sitting in the back of the courtroom, a white bandage prominently displayed on his wrist. Justice must at least appear to have been served. He called on Fortesque to stand.

Judge Carter looked sternly down at Fortesque. "Young man, I could start proceedings that would end up sending you to a regular juvenile detention center. However, because of extenuating circumstances, I am going to try something different with you. I am sending you to Revision House, on probation.

Joe had told me about the new experimental facility called Revision House. It was a state-sponsored shelter that focussed on special programs designed to keep kids out of jail. Under the terms of his sentence, Fortesque would be released on his eighteenth birthday, providing he kept his nose clean.

Judge Carter asked for progress reports to be sent to him every six months for review. He released Fortesque to my immediate care, providing I made sure he was at Revision House by noon the next day. I watched McNab's face as the sentence was handed down. I'm not sure he understood what was happening, but he seemed satisfied with the outcome.

I drove Fortesque to his old rooming house to pick up his stuff. We arrived just in the nick of time because the desk clerk was depositing all of his belongings on the sidewalk for non-payment of rent. In this neighborhood, the MX-490 Drone and the other items would disappear in minutes.

Because I wasn't sure what the future had in store for Fortesque, I took him out for a big steak dinner. We talked for hours about many things before he broached the question that was bothering him most.

"What's going to happen to Scruff? He's my only friend in the world."

We hashed it around for a while, then I said, "We'll stop at the pound and take him with us to Revision House. All they can say is no." Fortesque thought that was a good idea, but I phoned Joe Carter later, just in case.

• • • •

REVISION HOUSE

Revision House was located on the outskirts of New York City. The building, although old, was in good repair. It had once been the local high school for the area. Significant modifications had been made to the school, adding cooking and sleeping arrangements for the hundred students/inmates as well as a baseball field and a small swimming pool. The grounds were immaculate.

As we drove up, we could see some of the occupants working on the gardens. They appeared to be laboring without the presence of guards.

My first impression of David Ralston, the director of Revision House, was favorable. I knew from Judge Carter the director was respected because of his no-nonsense but fair approach to each situation.

"Welcome to Revision House, Fortesque," Ralston said as he extended his hand. "We don't normally accommodate animals, but Judge Carter called and specifically asked if we could make an exception in your case. He felt having the dog would be beneficial in your rehabilitation. So, as long as he behaves himself, Scruff is welcome here, too."

I handed Fortesque over to David Ralston, wished him well, then headed back home. My job was finished for the moment, and I only hoped, for Fortesque's sake, the program was as effective as Judge Joe Carter said it was.

Back at Revision House, Fortesque was in the middle of a tour of the facilities with the director. When they reached the gymnasium, they bumped into several kids playing basketball. Ralston introduced the newcomer to the other students.

"Guys, this is Fortesque Grenville and his dog Scruff. I want you to make them feel at home here at Revision House."

As soon as Ralston was gone, a tall, lanky kid with several tattoos on his muscular arms walked up, stared at Fortesque, and said, "What the hell kind of sissy name is Fortesque?"

Fortesque responded by punching the tall kid in the nose.

A few minutes later, the two boys stood defiantly in front of the director's desk. Ralston shook his head. The new boy was not off to a good start.

"What happened, Toby?" Ralston asked quietly.

"Why don't you ask fancy pants here? He started it."

"It seems this jerk doesn't like my name," Fortesque responded.

Ralston grinned. "You know, Fortesque, Toby might have a point. Your moniker might be a little rich for Revision House. I have an idea for a new name for you."

"A new name?"

"Yes, from now on, we're going to call you, Que."

● ● ● ●

From that day on, things began to improve for young Fortesque. Fortesque didn't have a friend in his previous life, but now he seemed to have an abundance. After the fight with Toby Kelly, they soon bonded and became best friends. He also added Gillian Walker and

Norman Pence to his list of buddies. Norman was a young mathematical genius, while Gillian was a deep thinker. She could add thoughtful input on almost any topic that arose.

Fortesque found that he enjoyed being at Revision House. The daily routine provided him with a much-needed sense of accomplishment. The curriculum subjects were an exciting blend of theory and practicality. As an example, French lessons might follow a practical class on woodworking. The cooking classes became Que's favorite. He was almost a near-genius in chemistry class.

● ● ● ●

One day I received a call from Joe Carter. Other than a few golf games, I hadn't seen him since the court appearance.

"It's almost time for the six-month progress report on Fortesque Grenville, George. When you were his guardian, you developed a good rapport with the boy. How about taking a run-up to Revision House for a first-hand look?"

I didn't have much on my schedule, so I readily agreed. Besides, I did want to see young Fortesque again.

When I arrived at Revision House, the place was in turmoil. I found Fortesque in the lunchroom with some friends, and he filled me in on the situation. It seems that the state budget director had just informed Director Ralston that the school's budget for the coming year was going to be cut by almost one-half.

I excused myself and went to find David Ralston. He was in his office, feverishly working on a spreadsheet.

"What's happened, David?"

"Oh, hi, George. I didn't know you were coming. You sure picked an interesting day for a visit. It looks like our funding will be cut in half soon. It seems the new administration feels the benefits of rehabilitation don't warrant the expense. The mandate for the cuts is coming straight from the top. We have two choices—shut the place down or find other sources of funding."

I went back to the gym and sat down with Fortesque and his friends again. They were worried because rumors were spreading like wildfire.

"If Revision House closes, will we go to a regular reform school?" Fortesque asked.

"I don't know, guys," I said. "But when I was in the marines, we had a saying. 'When the going gets tough, the tough get going.' It seems to me that you have to decide if you're going to be a part of the problem or a part of the solution."

It seems my pep talk fell on fertile ground. With the director's blessing, Fortesque formed an advisory group/think tank charged with the task of developing funding ideas for Revision House. The group concluded it would be almost impossible to create one single plan to solve the funding crisis. They agreed that the most promising approach would be to introduce a multitude of small, revenue-producing ventures, all at the same time.

One by one, students and staff members came forward with fund-raising ideas. Some ideas were promising, while others would never see the light of day. Toby Kelly thought a charity car wash might work. At the same time, Gillian Walker felt they could use the school kitchen to develop a *'meals on wheels'* delivery service for nearby residents.

Norman believed they could set up a small office and do tax returns for clients. Other ideas ranged from providing student labor for lawn and garden services to house painting and garage cleaning. One kid even suggested giving paid swimming lessons in the school pool. The idea that caused the most laughter was the one that suggested Scruff could be rented out as a guard dog.

Fortesque nervously pitched his idea in person to the director. He had given it some deep thought.

"We get a lot of traffic in front of the school. I want to open a hamburger stand at lunchtime, and maybe even after school hours. Everyone loves a good hamburger. If the idea works, we could make a lot of money."

"Not a bad idea, Que. But remember, all projects have to be

self-funded from the start. There's no Revision House money available for any supplies that might be needed."

Norman Pence, the group's math genius, did some preliminary estimates. He thought they would need about $425.00 for initial supplies, plus building material for the hamburger stand

or Que's idea would never get off the ground.

The breakthrough idea came from Fortesque himself. It was a brilliant solution but simple to implement.

"We can use my MX-490 Drone to take aerial pictures of homes in the local neighborhood," Que proposed. "Then we'll have the students sell the photos, door to door, to the homeowners."

The plan worked great. The group had almost $3,500 in the kitty and a large backlog of orders after only two weeks of work.

The Grenville side of the family had produced a long line of successful business people over the years. Some of that inherited financial acumen started to surface in Fortesque. Because he was envisioning a growing business in the future, Fortesque decided to use some of the funds from the drone operations to form a legal entity known as Q-Enterprises Inc. The director was impressed with Fortesque's ambition and agreed to help with the legal applications.

Once he was set up as a real business, Fortesque went full speed ahead. He appointed his buddy, Toby Kelly, as Director of Drone Operations. Toby was instructed to put half of any drone earnings into the Revision House fund, then use the other half to buy additional drones. By the end of the second month, they had fifteen drones in operation.

Fortesque focussed his attention on developing the hamburger stand. He used a portion of drone revenues to buy materials for building the actual stand plus sufficient raw materials to get started. Gillian convinced Fortesque that the hamburgers should be cooked to order on the outdoor BBQ for extra flavor.

Although the weather was excellent and the stand looked great, opening day was a disaster. They only sold five hamburgers.

Director Ralston had been a marketing genius for a large consumer goods company before deciding on a complete career change as director of Revision House. He gave Fortesque some advice that the boy never forgot.

"Que, your business failed for one simple reason. You didn't attempt to make your product any different from all other zillion hamburgers on the market. Trust me, the key to success in business is finding a way to stand out from the crowd."

Fortesque was determined to discover something that would make his business unique. The Revision House kitchen was rapidly transformed into a food laboratory. With Gillian's help, Que experimented with as many variations of the hamburger patty as they could imagine. They often tested their new creations on Scruff, but the dog either turned his nose up or spit most of them out.

At his wit's end, Fortesque decided a new approach was required. He started at the chemistry lab, where he entered the topic FLAVOR on the school computer. He read about flavorants, substances that can alter the flavors of natural food products like meat or vegetables. He was interrupted by Ronnie Lee, a young Chinese boy. Like Que, Ronnie was a chemistry whiz.

"What are you looking at, Que?"

"I'm trying to find out if there's some easy way to flavor hamburger patties by using a highly condensed form of natural ingredients."

Finding a solution was a challenge that Ronnie couldn't resist. He wanted to help with the project and quickly became Q-Enterprises' first paid employee. For the next sixty days, they worked together almost non-stop, distilling and condensing various flavors until they finally had a breakthrough.

The final product was similar in shape and size to kid's candies that come in a range of colors, coated with a hard sugar surface. The pair managed to synthesize three distinct flavor combinations: *Bacon & Cheddar, Mushroom & Bacon, Brie Cheese & Onion.*

The pair tinkered with the coating until they reached the perfect combination. The final version did not require refrigeration. It would be inserted by hand into the center of a burger patty. The hard layer dissolved at the correct temperature for a properly cooked burger. The resulting flavor was intense, and, most importantly, it was inexpensive to produce.

"All we need now is a name and maybe one additional unique flavor," Fortesque remarked to his assistant.

After a few hours looking at possible names, they decided to call the new invention FlavorBalls. Still, no ideas for an additional flavor surfaced.

Shortly after the invention of FlavorBalls, Fortesque was preparing his favorite lunch of a peanut butter and banana sandwich. Gillian had gone to her room for another notepad. While she was away, Fortesque decided to play a joke on her. He put a blob of creamy peanut butter and half of a banana in the food processor. When the mixture was thin enough, he loaded a flavor injector with the concoction, then squirted it deep inside two of the raw hamburger patties, waiting on the counter.

Gillian found him gently sautéing the burgers in a non-stick pan on the stove. He had added some finely diced cooking onions to the pot as well.

"Sit down, Gillian. I have a real treat for you and one for Scruff as well."

Fortesque served Gillian her burger before placing the other one on the floor for the dog. He prepared for a laugh at the expected reaction from Gillian when she got the first taste of his peanut butter and banana burger. He was astounded at what happened.

"My gosh, Que," Gillian gushed. "This burger is fantastic. I'm not sure what the secret ingredient is, but this one tastes like a winner to me."

Fortesque was stunned. He looked down and saw that Scruff had devoured his burger as well. Scruff was actually sitting up, begging for more. He had expected Gillian to laugh at his joke, but she loved it, and so did the dog.

Que couldn't wait to tell Ronnie that a fourth and final unique flavor had been discovered entirely by accident. Ronnie quickly synthesized the ingredients, and a new Flavorball was born.

The new lineup now consisted of, *Bacon & Cheddar, Mushroom & Bacon, Brie Cheese & Onion, and Peanut Butter & Banana.*

Gillian designed an entirely fresh, square bun to complement the flavored burgers. It had a brown, whole wheat bottom, coupled with a white flour and sesame seeds top. Everyone who tried the new burgers gave them a rave review. After several group discussions, they decided to name the latest product, The Q-Burger.

Within a few weeks of the new burger introduction, business was booming. Word spread in the neighborhood. Soon they had long lineups at the stand. Passing cars, stopping or slowing, created mini-traffic jams. Even with most of the staff and student body at work, they couldn't keep up with the demand. The new slogan on the stand read, *Q-Burger- Quality ingredients - Quickly served.*

When news of Fortesque's success reached the city, I got a call from Judge Carter suggesting we both take a trip to Revision House to see for ourselves. We drove up together, chatting about Joe's new golf clubs.

When we arrived at the school, we could hardly make our way into the parking lot because of the crowds at the Q-Burger stand. Fortesque was too busy to talk to us, so we settled for a chat with David Ralston.

"I'm telling you, Judge, I was in marketing for years, and I've never seen anything like it. If this keeps up, the school's budget deficit will be covered in no time."

Joe Carter's legal mind kicked into gear. "If this thing is as successful as you think it will be, Dave, I'm worried someone will take advantage of the boy. We should help him get some patent and trademark protection as soon as possible."

"That's a great idea, Judge, but don't be worried about anybody taking advantage of Fortesque Grenville. The kid's as sharp as a tack. He has also got the people and organizational skills of someone three times his age."

David Ralston's assessment proved to be accurate. When Joe and I sat down with Fortesque, we could hardly believe the changes in the young man. In addition to his mature manner, he was filling out physically as well. He talked to us as friends and equals.

"Judge, I have to thank you for sending me here. My time here has probably been the most positive experience of my life. I've learned a lot, and, hopefully, I can give back to the school and society as well."

Joe was beaming. His decision to send Fortesque to Revision House was working out better than anyone could imagine.

"Tell me, son, do you think the Q-Burger concept is something franchisable?"

• • • •

"On the subject of franchising," Ralston interjected, "I'm certain Fortesque is onto something big. The problem with most franchises is the high up-front costs. I've been helping Que develop an approach we call Franchise Lite."

"How does it work?" I asked.

"The Q-Burger approach will be to find existing outlets that can benefit from a simple rebranding," Ralston replied. "The owner won't be forced to pour a small fortune into building things like fancy arches and so on."

Que added, "With our simple décor and menu package, any owner can have a whole new look almost overnight. And at a cost that won't break the budget."

"If I were still Fortesque's guardian, my first question would be, how does the boy benefit?"

"Don't worry, George, everything would flow through Fortesque's company, Q-Enterprises. The brilliance of the plan is that Fortesque controls the profit flow through the exclusive production and distribution of the FlavorBalls."

Judge Carter asked Que if he was still operating the drone business and working on the franchise idea too.

"Although the drone business is doing quite well, I believe the burger division has more future potential. I think we have over one hundred drones in operation now, and, under Toby's direction, it's expanding. We're even experimenting with drone deliveries of Q-Burgers."

The judge looked thoughtful. "You've been here almost three years, Fortesque. The terms of your probation call for your release on your eighteenth birthday next year. But, in light of your terrific progress, I'm prepared to petition for an early release as a reward for your efforts on behalf of the school."

We were both surprised when Que shook his head. "Thanks, Judge, but I would just as soon stay here. There's lots more for me to accomplish, and Director Ralston just gave me the green light for a new course I've been developing for the other students. It's called Business Building-101."

• • • •

Q-ENTERPRISES INC

True to his word, Judge Carter arranged for Fortesque's company, Q-Enterprises Inc, to successfully apply for patent and trademark protections. I managed to get up to the school to see Fortesque as often as possible. Still, I always departed with the impression that the young man was light years ahead of me, on all fronts.

Ralston used his marketing background to help Fortesque develop a franchise package. Before long, Q-Burgers were popping up at multiple locations across the state. The chain grew in popularity with teenagers who referred to the experience as meeting at the 'Q.'

The drone division under Toby's direction was still growing. As a reward for his efforts, Fortesque spun the drone operations into a separate company and made Toby a fifty-percent partner.

Over the next few years, the growth rate of Q-Enterprises was quite incredible. Time Magazine and even the elite Barron's business publication came to Revision House to do photos and interviews with Fortesque and his associates. Venture capitalists started approaching Fortesque about taking his organization public. He turned them all down.

Although Que kept a close association with Revision House and David Ralston over the years, he finally felt it was time to move on. With some legal help from the judge, he was able to repurchase the old Grenville penthouse on 5th Avenue.

When he returned to his old apartment, it triggered many memories, some good, but many were primarily bad. Fortesque cringed when he recalled what a jerk he had been when he last lived in the penthouse.

We kept in touch on occasion, so I wasn't shocked when Fortesque phoned me on his thirty-third birthday. What surprised me was the suggestion he made after we finished catching up.

"I'm not sure if you know that Q-Enterprises went international last year," Que said. "I'm heading to Paris for our first opening there, and I'd like to have you and the judge join me as my guests."

"Que. I'm not sure about the judge, but you can count me in for sure."

Judge Carter enthusiastically accepted the invitation, and that's how we ended up on the beautiful new Global Explorer Company jet, flying across the Atlantic on the way to Paris. Toby Kelly, now the president of Drones Unlimited, was aboard, and Norman Pence, the math genius. Norman was now the group finance director. Gillian Walker had blossomed into a beautiful, graceful young lady. Her job was as the director of human resources for the group of companies.

We were having a glass of wine, laughing over some of the stories about Fortesque in his earlier days. After we talked about the great fish and chips theft, I finally asked Fortesque what had become of Scruff.

"He was a great little dog and a great friend to me when I needed one," Que said sadly. "In the end, he just passed away from old age."

Gillian laughed, "Come on, Fortesque, everybody knows the dog never recovered from eating all the experimental burgers you fed him."

Everyone, including Que, laughed at this, but it was easy to see he truly missed his old companion.

Fortesque stood and put his arms around Gillian. Although it was not public knowledge yet, people on the inside were aware that Gillian and Fortesque were dating regularly. She smiled at him, and the mutual affection between them was good to see.

The opening of the Q-Burger franchise #762 in central Paris was a first-class event. The mayor and his staff showed up in full formal wear for the cutting of the ribbon. Que made a terrific speech about how business could lead to better relationships between countries and people both.

Afterward, we stood on the roof of the café, sipping champagne. Down below, we could see the first crowds lining up for several blocks down the boulevard. I mentioned to Fortesque that it appeared franchise 762 was going to make some local business people wealthy.

Que grinned. "I think you have already met the new owner. I located my old head chef, Maurice Gagnon, the man in charge of the kitchens at the Hampton's Estate. I talked Maurice into giving it a go. If he ever gets over his fright of peanut butter, I think he'll become a rich man."

We spent a few more delightful days in Paris before finally boarding the gleaming company jet for the trip home. Most of the others had retired to the sleeping cabin when Que asked the Judge and me to stay and join him for a nightcap.

It was a beautifully clear and still night for flying. Looking out over the horizon, we could see all the way down to the ocean surface, sparkling from reflected moonbeams.

Joe and I had a glass of cognac while Que sat quietly, sipping on a glass of red wine. He seemed in a pensive mood, so I said, "What's on your mind, kiddo? The opening went well, but you seem troubled."

"I've been spending a lot of time reflecting on time before I went to the Revision House. It's difficult for me remembering what a little shit I was. I know now that I hurt many people. I feel ashamed."

"Well, on the other hand, Que, you have certainly turned your life around," I said with a smile.

"I still have some fences to mend," Que said softly. "That's why I asked you to join me on this trip. Although I enjoy your company, I have to admit that I have a secret plan I want to implement. To make it happen, I need your help."

Que told us what he wanted us to do.

● ● ● ●

THE SECRET PLAN

Because Que's secret plan was quite involved, the judge and I had to hire additional resources to assist us in doing our part. However, the 4th of July was finally set for the big event. Engraved invitations were sent out by courier. Each message included the appropriate first-class transportation voucher for a round trip for the individual guest to travel to the event and then back home again.

Most of the guests were highly surprised at receiving the invitation. They were even more astonished by the location of the event. It was being held at the old Grenville Estate in the Hamptons.

The 4th of July dawned bright and clear, not too hot but with a light breeze keeping everything fresh and clean. The event was supposed to start at 3:00 p.m., but people had been drifting in for the past few hours. Some arrived by taxi, some by chartered bus, one man even came on horseback.

Waiters circulated through the waiting crowds offering a selection of fancy sandwiches accompanied by a wide variety of alcohol and non-alcoholic cold drinks. A small musical group played soft background tunes. Even though everybody seemed to be enjoying the event, most of the guests were unsure what they were doing here.

Gillian Walker, Toby Kelly, and Norman Pence circulated among the crowd, wearing expensively cut, dark blue blazers with the corporate logo, Q-Enterprises, embroidered on the breast pocket.

People, assuming the three were part of the program, bombarded them with questions about the event. Everyone got the same answer: wait till 3:00 p.m.

Precisely at 3:00 p.m., the distinct sounds of a large helicopter approaching overhead echoed across the lawns. After gently touching down, Fortesque Grenville stepped out, wearing one of the corporate blazers.

The band started playing an old familiar song, *'Thanks for the Memories',* as Que made his way up to the waiting microphones. Murmurs of disbelief rose from the crowd when they sighted him.

The judge and I had ringside seats, sitting beside David Ralston from Revision House. The three of us had done an admirable job with our part of the program. By hiring private detectives, we had managed to locate the bulk of the old Grenville Estate employees as well as a list of special non-employee guests. I pointed out some of the special guests for the judge.

The first person I spotted was Maria, the victim of Que's cereal tantrums. Maria had traveled all the way from Honduras. Then I saw Eric, the chauffeur, Lucy the cook, Tony Hasbro, the animal trainer, Tom Edwards, the gardener. Plus, many more staffers whose names escaped me.

There were quite a few surprise guests as well. The three lawyers from Periwinkle, Johnson & Krakow attended along with McNab from the fish and chip shop, Maurice Gagnon, previous head chef and now a Q-Burger franchise owner. The judge laughed when I pointed out the one-armed panhandler that Que had spit at in front of Macy's.

"I don't know how the hell they found him," I said with a laugh, "but that's the same guy. I'm sure of it."

Somebody had helped clean up the vagrant because he looked almost respectable. The man was enjoying himself to the fullest with the abundance of free food and drink.

When Que tapped the microphone, the crowd fell into an unnatural silence. Almost every person at the event was still mystified as to the purpose of the gathering.

"My friends, welcome back to the new Grenville Estate. Because of numerous legal challenges, the estate ownership has been in limbo for many years. With the help of my friend and mentor, Judge Joseph M. Carter, I have recently managed to purchase the family estate back from the bankruptcy court."

"First of all, I want to apologize to all of the people I treated badly over the years. It hurts me to think of what a despicable young jerk I must have been."

Laughter and applause broke out from the crowd. Someone shouted, "You got it right there, brother."

His well-deserved remark embarrassed Que but he continued. "My new company, Q-Enterprises, has become a big success because of the efforts and support of many people. On July 5th, the company is going public, and its shares will begin to trade on the New York Stock Exchange."

The crowd clapped, assuming the announcement was the reason for the gathering, but Que wasn't finished.

"I want you all to share in my success," Que said sincerely, "as a small gesture of apology for my previous actions. And also, to many of you as a thank you for your generosity in making sure I didn't leave the estate that day penniless."

On cue, the three lawyers from Periwinkle, Johnson & Krakow came to the podium with a large brown carton. They then proceeded to call each person to the stage, where Que shook hands then handed each person a large white envelope.

Stunned faces broke out all through the crowd when the envelopes were opened. The contents revealed a share certificate for either 500 or 1000 shares of Q-Enterprises Inc. Minor participants like the panhandler received 500 while the ex-employees received the larger quantity.

The chauffeur had some stock market knowledge, so he Googled for information on the company going public.

"Wow," Eric screamed. "The IPO reference price per share was twenty-five dollars, but the brokers are saying first-day trading could break the fifty-dollar mark."

The news spread like wildfire. For most people, the gift would make a significant difference in their lives. Maria was first in line to hug Que. She whispered something in his ear that turned his face red. I found out later she had asked if he was eating any red cereal these days.

As the guests milled around, thanking Que and shaking hands, the noise level rose so high that it took Judge Carter more than a few minutes to get everyone's attention. He was standing at the microphone.

"Well, folks, this has been a great day for us all," Judge Carter said, "but I always think a great day should be one that finishes with a great surprise. Could I ask Miss Gillian Walker to come to the stand?"

Gillian looked to be completely surprised as she made her way up to the podium. Que joined her there, then he reached into the brown box.

"Gillian, the lawyers forgot to give you your envelope" Que grinned. "I beg you to accept it with my most sincere gratitude."

Gillian took the envelope then started to leave the stage. She wanted to open it in private, but the judge stopped her.

"This won't be much of a surprise if you don't share it with us, young lady."

Gillian was trapped. She knew Fortesque wanted her to be a shareholder. Still, she was afraid of the crowd's reaction if her share certificate was for a number more substantial than theirs. She opened the envelope with shaking hands.

When Gillian saw the contents, tears started rolling down her face. Her certificate wasn't for Q-Enterprises Inc. stock. Instead, it was an unsigned, valid Certificate of Marriage made out in the names of Gillian Walker and Fortesque Grenville.

"Never a dull moment, right, honey?" Que grinned as he embraced her in front of the crowd.

The judge waited for the crowd's applause to slow down before he continued with his unscripted remarks.

"In the practice of law, we were always taught to prepare for the unexpected. This young lady has just received a most unusual proposal of marriage from our good friend Fortesque," Judge Carter said.

"What if she says no?" yelled the vagrant.

The judge laughed. "In that case, we can all head for home. But, in the event, she says yes, I'm a duly sworn Justice of the Peace, and George Collins is standing by as a potential best man. We also have a marriage license, a fully stocked bar, caterers by the dozen, and a musical band ready to go. All we need is a bride."

With eyes sparkling, the potential bride did indeed say yes with great enthusiasm. Then Judge Carter did his part, I did mine, and so did all the guests. The perfect wedding party was a blast. It went on till the wee hours of the morning until, finally, the gleaming white corporate helicopter whisked the newlyweds off on their honeymoon.

Joe Carter and I stood on the lawn, still waving as the craft slowly disappeared into the night sky. I noticed the judge had a tear running from the corner of his eye. And, to tell the truth, I might have had one as well.

What a couple of old softies we were.

I stood there a little longer watching the helicopter's trail, thinking about Fortesque Grenville. Reveling in his fantastic voyage from the pinnacle of wealth to the bottom of the heap, then back to the top again. His fortitude and sheer determination to succeed had been inspiring.

Fortesque is still a young man but a young man with a burning ambition. With Gillian at his side, it wouldn't surprise me at all to see him enter politics with an eventual bid for the presidency of the U.S.A.

I can tell you one thing with absolute certainty, if Que ever did decide to run for the nation's highest office, he could count on two votes for sure.

Judge Carter's and mine.

A WORD FROM THE AUTHOR

I hope you enjoyed reading 'Spinning my Wheels.' I hope I can ask a favor without imposing on your goodwill. Reviews are becoming extremely important in the competitive world of book publishing.

I would appreciate it if you would take a moment to leave a review on Amazon or Goodreads. If you follow these links and go to the bottom of the page, it is a simple process, but one that is much appreciated!

Thanks,
Wes Snowden

WWW.amazon.com/author/wessnowden
www.goodreads.com/author/list/18371088.Wes_Snowden

ABOUT THE AUTHOR

After a successful career as an international business owner, Wes Snowden now spends his writing time between Toronto, Vancouver, and Scottsdale, Arizona.

As a relatively new author, Wes has written a broad range of books, all unique in their storyline.

Although his writings are enjoyable for all ages, the author enjoys writing kid's stories for grown-ups the best.

In addition to numerous shorter stories, Wes has written seven full-length adult novels- *White Swan Wishes, Zachary's Gold, One Last Move, The Leprechaun Wars, Firebug, On Distant Shores and Spinning my Wheels.*

TERMINAL- a two story collection will be published in the late summer of 2021.

Reviews and comments always appreciated at:

wessnowden98@gmail.com
www.amazon.com/author/wessnowden

Made in the USA
Columbia, SC
20 May 2021